Rescued by a Stranger

By Lizbeth Selvig

Rescued by a Stranger
The Rancher and the Rock Star

Rescued by a Stranger

LIZBETH SELVIG

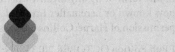

AVON IMPULSE

An Imprint of HarperCollins Publishers

Excerpt from *The Governess Club: Claire* copyright © 2013 by Heather Johnson.

Excerpt from *Ashes, Ashes, They All Fall Dead* copyright © 2013 by Lena Diaz.

Excerpt from *The Governess Club: Bonnie* copyright © 2013 by Heather Johnson.

EPub Edition OCTOBER 2013 ISBN: 9780062300362
Print Edition ISBN: 9780062300386

10 9 8 7 6 5 4 3 2

This book is dedicated to
*Jan Selvig, my amazing husband, and the best
friend, cheerleader, and book shill a girl could ever
ask for. Thanks for always understanding about
the voices in my head! Most of all, thanks for being
the role model for every one of my heroes.*

And to
*John Feuk, my dad and another perfect role model,
who was the first person ever to give this story a
written critique—and a five-star rating. Thank
you for a lifetime of praise and support, Papa.*

Acknowledgments

THANK YOU A million times over to my beautiful and talented critique partners, without whom I would have walked out on this story long before it was done. They won't let me quit OR leave crappy writing in my books. Nancy Holland, Ellen Lindseth, and Naomi Stone—you are magicians, incredible writers, and most of all the best friends.

Love and thanks to Maxine Mansfield and Morgan Q. O'Reilly, who read the original draft of this story and didn't tell me to quit writing, but did tell me how to make it "Olympic" quality and kept me honest right through to "The End." Same to Vicki Devine (for sending it to her friend LaVyrle) and Angela Bitzenhofer (for reading it and then nudging me to get off my bum and get it published).

Tons more gratitude and many hugs to my wonderful friend—and amazing author in her own right—Jennifer Bernard, who does the most thorough and insightful final read-throughs in the world.

I am forever grateful to my brilliant (and patient) agent, Elizabeth Winick Rubinstein, who knows what a story needs to make it shine, and to my super-savvy—and also brilliant—editor, Tessa Woodward, who knows what a story needs to make it perfect.

And, finally, the biggest thanks to my kids—Jennifer, Adam, and Jodi—for reading my reviews and always saying they're proud, and to my mom, Grace, who's been saying she's proud since my first minute on Earth.

Chapter One

THE DOG IN the middle of the road was all legs and mottled black patches. It stood still beside the yellow centerline, a good fifty feet away but too close to ignore, and Jill Carpenter eased off the accelerator of her Chevy Suburban.

"Get out of the way, sweetie," she murmured, switching her foot to the brake.

Because she'd worked at the only vet clinic in Kennison Falls since junior high school, she knew most of the dogs in the area. This one, however, was shabbily unfamiliar. And stubbornly unmoving. It stared at her with a mutt-in-the-headlights look that didn't bode well.

Finally, twenty feet from the unblinking animal, Jill blared her horn and stomped her brakes until the anti-lock system grabbed, and loose pebbles pinged the chassis like buckshot. At the very last moment the dog leaped—directly in front of her.

Accidents supposedly happened in slow motion, but

no leisurely parade of her life played before her eyes. The jerk of her steering wheel, her shriek, a blur of darting, raggedy fur, and the boulder of dread dropping into the pit of her stomach all happened in something under five nanoseconds.

Then her stomach dropped again as it followed the nose of her truck across the narrow county road and down a six-foot ditch. The Suburban gave a carnival-ride fishtail, its rear axle grinding in protest. Something warm spurted into her face, and she came to rest parallel to the road on the steep ditch bank, wedged in precarious place against a slender maple sapling.

For a moment, all she noticed was her own wheezing breath—her lungs forcing twice as much carbon dioxide out as they sucked oxygen in.

Had she missed the dog? She was sure she had. Please let her have missed the dog. Her heart pounded in concern until she peered out her windshield, shifted to see better, and the Suburban rocked. The dog's fate was forgotten in a gasp.

The world was sideways.

Something sticky ran down one cheek, and an old Counting Crows song filled the truck interior. The turn signal *ploink-ploink*ed to the music like a metronome. Through the windshield and up to her right she could see the edge of the road. To her left through her driver's window lay the bottom of the ditch three feet below. All she'd have to do was shift the wrong way, and she'd be roof down, hanging from her seat belt.

A flurry of sailor-approved words charged through

her mind, but her frantic heartbeat choked them off before they turned into sound—almost certainly a good thing, since the air stream caused by swearing would probably be enough to roll her. She pressed her lips together and tried to slow her respiration. Her shoulder, jammed against the door, ached slightly, her seat belt effectively throttled her, but as far as she could tell, she hadn't hit her head.

The Creature, her un-pet name for the vehicle she'd detested since buying it, growled as if angry its spinning back tire wasn't getting anywhere. "Crap!" Jill shot her arm forward, ignoring the pinch of her seat belt, and turned the key.

The truck rocked again, the Crows quit Counting, and the turn signal halted its irritating pinging. At last time stopped whizzing past like an old Super 8 movie, and her thoughts careened into each other with a little less force.

This was definitely going to wreck an already no-good, very bad day.

Sudden pounding startled her, rocking the SUV again. She swiveled her head to the passenger window and let loose a terrified scream. Pressed to the glass was a smoosh-nosed, flattened-featured face. Jill squeezed her eyes shut.

"Ma'am? Ma'am? Can you hear me?" The window-pane muffled the gargoyle's voice.

Slowly Jill forced her eyes open, and the face pulled back. Her panic dissipated as the nose unflattened, lengthening into straightness with perfect oval flares at its tip, and divided a strong, masculine face into two flawless halves. Inky, disheveled bangs fell across deep furrows in his forehead. For an instant Jill forgot her straits, and her mouth went dry. A brilliant sculptor somewhere was missing his masterwork.

"Can you get the window down?" he shouted, refocusing her attention on the phone in his hand. "I'm calling 911. Can you tell me where you're hurt?"

Intense navy-blue eyes pierced her for answers, her pulse accelerated, and embarrassed heat infused her face. "No!" she called. Shaking off her adrenaline-fueled hormones and forcing her brain to function, Jill turned her key once more to activate the accessory system and twisted to punch the window button, jostling The Creature. "No!" she gasped again, as the glass whirred into the door frame. "No calls. I'm fine."

"You are not fine, honey. Stay still now." His drawl was comforting and sing-songy—born of the South.

Truly confused, Jill watched him swipe the face of his phone. He might be the best-looking Samaritan between her predicament and the Iowa border, but although she *was* balanced pretty precariously, his intensity was a tick past overreactive.

"Honestly. All I need is to get out of this murderous truck without rolling it on top of me."

His eyes switched from worry to the kind of sympathy a person used when about to impart bad news. "I'm afraid your face and the front of your shirt tell a different story. You're in shock."

She peered down at herself. At first she gasped at the bright red splotches staining her white tank top. She touched her cheek and brought a red fingertip away. Strangled laughter replaced her shock. He reached for her and made the Suburban wobble.

"Don't lean!" She choked. "Seriously, don't! I'm not bleeding to death, I swear."

His eyes narrowed. "Are you bleeding not to death?"

"No." She stuck her red-coated finger into her mouth and, with the other hand, scooped up a half-dozen French fries caught between her hip and the door. She'd picked them up not ten minutes ago from the Loon Feather Café in town, and Effie had put three little paper cups of ketchup in the take-out tray. Eating fries while driving— another of her vices, along with owning too many horses, flightiness in all things, and swerving to avoid dumb dogs in the road. Gingerly she held up the flat, empty, red-checkered box. "It's only Type A Heinz," she said. "See? No 911 needed. Besides, this is rural Rice County, and it'd take the rescue guys twenty minutes to find me. Is the dog all right?"

"Dog?"

"The one I swerved to miss. You didn't see an injured dog?"

His indigo eyes performed a laser scan from her head to her toes. They settled on her face and softened. "It must have disappeared. I wasn't watching it since I was prayin' to all the angels while you barreled down this ditch."

"But it didn't get hit?"

"I'm pretty sure it didn't get hit," he repeated gently. "You really all right? The dog isn't exactly important at the moment. Nothing hurts? Did you black out?"

Jill let out a breath of relief. This morning, the docs at Southwater Vet Clinic had put down two families' beloved dogs and a young client's show horse. Knowing the stray in the road had survived didn't balance the scales, but it helped a little.

"I just didn't want the dog to be dead. Nothing hurts. I didn't black out. All I want is to get out of my homicidal truck."

"Homicidal?" He laughed and took a step back. "Are you blaming your poor stuck truck for this?"

"Poor truck?" Jill glanced around her seat to see how she dared start extricating herself. The first thing she did was unlatch the seat belt, and the pressure on her arm eased. "This is The Creature. She's a diva. Any other vehicle would *not* have kept going left after I cranked the wheel back to the right." She looked at the man. "She'd kill me outright, but who else would pour college loan money into her like I do?"

The right side of his upper lip, as perfectly sculpted as the rest of his features, lifted in an Elvis-y half grin—a cute-on-handsome action that made Jill's mouth go parched again.

"Sounds like we'd best get you out before Lizzie Borden the truck here changes her mind." His warm, humor-filled voice calmed with its hypnotic Southern cadence.

"I'd be very, very good with that," she replied.

"Let's try the door." He reached for the handle.

"No! Wait. Don't! Whenever I move the whole thing rocks. I—"

"Okay, it's okay." He held up his hands. "I'll look first and see how solid she's sitting."

He stepped away and walked slowly around the front of the Suburban. Jill took the time to regroup. She wasn't a wimp, dang it. This was stupid. The man already believed she was half baked. She needed to stop whining and simply crawl out. And she had to get the stupid truck out of this stupid ditch or she'd miss the most important riding lesson of her life. Maybe if she could see how to straighten her wheels she could just drive—

"She isn't hanging on by a lot, you're right." He returned to the window. "But you should be able to ease out this way. I'll open the door very carefully. Trust me."

Trust him? For all she knew he had a handgun in his pocket, a twelve-page rap sheet, and a mug shot at the post office. "Fine." She grimaced. "Just don't mug me until I'm fully out. One crisis at a time."

His slightly nasal laugh flowed between them, as musical as his voice. "Gotta love a woman who's funny in the face of adversity."

Funny? This merely kept her from weeping. In addition to causing expense for which there was no money, this accident was messing up two appointments she couldn't afford to miss.

"I'm not being funny." She wriggled out from behind the steering wheel. "On the other hand, if you murder me right here I'll have a great excuse for being late." She edged to the passenger side and glanced at her watch. "Make that very late."

"Lizzie here didn't murder you, and I'm not going to either."

He tugged on the door and it hit the slope, barely opening ten inches. Jill was small, but not that small.

"Great. Just awesome." She eyed the stranger dubiously.

"I'm afraid it's out the window for you." He shrugged.

"Well, this gets better and better." She simply wanted out, and she reached for the oversized tote she used as purse, clothing bag, and carry-all. "Would you toss this on the ground? I hope that stupid dog appreciates its life."

"It's on its knees thanking—"

"All the angels?" she teased.

"Yes, ma'am." The return of his Elvis grin sent a flutter through her belly. He hefted her striped, leather-handled bag and grunted. "Lord love a monkey, what have you got in here? Car parts?"

"Riding boots." She reached for the top of the window opening and suddenly heard what he'd said. "*What?*"

"Sorry, my granddaddy's saying. Gotta admit," he grunted, "didn't expect you to say boots."

"Only because you don't know me," she muttered.

"Let's go then. We can do getting-to-know-you once you're free."

The easiest way out was headfirst, since it caused the least amount of wiggling. But halfway out, with her torso flopped over the door frame and her knees hovering above the passenger seat, The Creature slowly swung its nose downward. She shrieked.

"Got you!" Strong hands caught her beneath the armpits.

The Creature spun left and spit her from the window.

The momentum squirted her out and propelled the stranger backward. One second Jill's shoe toes skimmed the window frame, the next she sprawled atop a very long, very hard male body. He grabbed her and held the back of her head expertly, as if people fell on him all the time and he knew precisely what to do.

"Sorry. Sorry. I'm okay. Are you okay?" Her words were muffled in his shoulder.

She should move.

He should move.

Instead, his chest rose and fell beneath her, and his breath warmed the top of her head. His fingers formed a firm brace at the base of her neck, and he lay like a stone beneath her. When she finally made the tiniest effort to roll away, his free hand planted itself on her hip.

"No," he commanded in a hoarse whisper.

No?

"Relax. Make sure you're all in one piece."

She certainly didn't know this guy well enough to relax in a reverse missionary position with him . . . but the pleasant musk of masculine perspiration prickled her nose and mingled with the redolent scent of his leather jacket. Her eyelids floated closed in spite of herself, and she went all but limp with relief. When he relaxed, too, however, she couldn't ignore his long, lean form beneath her or the intense pressure gathering low in her body. She tried to concentrate on the fact that nothing bad was happening while he held her—no accidents, no animals dying, no worry she was late for—

"Oh my gosh!" She jerked hard against his hold.

Immediately he released her, gave her shoulder a squeeze, and a mini explosion of sparks raced for every nerve ending in her body. She pushed onto her hands and stared into eyes as calm as a waveless lake.

"Hi," he said, his mouth only inches from hers. "I'm Chase Preston. Nice to meet you."

She rolled off him laughing and sat up on the incline. "Hi, back. I'm Jill Carpenter. How can I thank you for rescuing me?"

He waved dismissively. "You'd have figured out how to escape, Jill Carpenter, but glad I could help."

He sat up, too, and stuck out his hand, but Jill was almost afraid to take it. Her stomach dipped in anticipation at the sight of his long, clever-looking e knHe-HisHiTheThefingers and knuckles flanked by prominent tendons. At last, she let his grip engulf hers, as warm and comforting as his full-body hold had been. When he rocked to a stand he pulled her along, and her body rose with no more effort than surfacing from buoyant water.

She tried to smile—to thank him by holding their clasped hands a second longer, but after a final, slow squeeze, he let his fingers slide free.

"Now that you're safe, it's time to find you a way out of this ditch. Is there anyone you can call way out here in rural whatever county?"

Jill took her first good look at The Creature, and her heart sank. She'd harbored the ghostly hope that, once free, she'd see how to drive it from the ditch. It hadn't been a very strong hope, but now it was dashed beyond any stretch of imagination. The Creature's grille touched the bottom of the ditch, one rear tire had spun a bald patch into the grass, and the passenger side corner hovered six inches off the ground. It wasn't going anywhere under its own power. Anger at her predicament started a slow burn.

Jill grabbed the bag Chase had set on the hillside, the anger heating up as reality smacked her in the face. How was this fair? For once it had seemed her dream would have a fighting chance, but oh no. With short, angry stomps she marched up the steep slope, and when she reached the road after working up to full-fledged fury, she nearly crashed into a gleaming, silver and red motorcycle. She glimpsed the intricate Triumph logo on the gas tank and jumped back. Motorcycles were not her thing.

"So, who can you call?"

She stopped short of snapping at him, dropped her bag, and pressed her fingertips against her eyes to hide her frustration. "Dewey's Garage and Gas in town." She sighed.

"Can I take you there? Or call for you?"

"No. I have my phone, and you've helped too much already. Believe me, Dewey knows this truck. He won't be at all surprised he has to tow her out of a ditch."

"Then give him a call. I'll wait with you."

She started to object. Being rescued was far out of her realm of experience, but the man's presence had a calming, spell-like effect on her worry and her anger. She found Dewey's number and punched the call button. A familiar voice came answered. "Dewey Mitchell."

She explained her problem and waited for Dewey to calculate his ETA.

"I'm out delivering some fuel, and it'll take forty-five minutes or so to get back to the tow truck. Sorry I'm not closer."

Disappointment spread through her like chills. "I'll take you as soon as I can get you, Dewey. Thanks." She described where she was and hung up.

"He could be an hour." She tried desperately to hide her rekindled anger. Of all the days for disaster to hit . . . "All he said was he'll hurry."

She plopped to her seat in the grass beside the road. Her consultation with a brand-new riding student was supposed to start in five minutes, but the bigger issue was Colin Pitts-Matherson. The visiting coach of the U.S. Equestrian Eventing Team was not known for magnanimity. As a talent scout would for any sport, he'd asked for one chance to see her perform. He'd expect to see her ride. In forty-five minutes. With no sob-story excuse about a dog in the road. Her shot at an Olympic dream could well be resting in the ditch along with The Creature's hood ornament.

A mellow rustling of clothing distracted her, and something heavy draped across her shoulders, steeping the air in a scent she recognized as his, even after this short time. Chase squatted in front of her and drew the jacket securely around her body. She stared at him, mesmerized and annoyed in equal measure.

"What the heck?"

"You're shivering. I don't want to see you go into shock."

Chase now wore only a soft, heathery gray Henley, fitted to his broad pecs like superhero Lycra. A smear of ketchup marred the front, and she couldn't stop her fingers from brushing at it. The juxtaposition of fur-soft brushed cotton over the hard wall of muscle behind it made her quiver.

Oh brother.

She shoved at him with all her strength. He barely moved.

"For crying out loud!" She tried to fling the jacket off, but he held it firmly in place. "I'm missing two important appointments while I'm sitting here on my ass, and I can't get help for an hour. I'm not in shock. I'm majorly pissed off."

When she quit struggling, he released his hold on the jacket, grasped her chin gently, and studied her face.

"I'm sorry." His voice tightened. "First responder training from an old job. It's habit." He released her chin. An odd emptiness replaced his touch. "Let me take you to your appointment. You'll get there safely and on time. The truck's not going anywhere until it's towed."

"But I'm going six miles in the opposite direction of where you were going. I can call my boss to come get me."

"Heck, six miles? That's barely spittin' distance after what I've done the last two days."

A swirl of nervousness circled through her chest. She wouldn't climb aboard a motorcycle with someone she knew, much less a random stranger—despite the fact that he'd rescued her butt and had a phenomenal body. "That's very nice of you," she said. "You've gone above and beyond, but I'll give David a call."

"You sure? I can have you there in ten minutes."

Or he could have her splatted like a dead raccoon on the asphalt in thirty seconds.

"Oh, I'm pretty sure." She nodded emphatically.

A eureka-moment smile blossomed on his lips. "Hey. You aren't afraid of a little ol' motorcycle?"

Over her shoulder, she took in the Triumph with a serious eye. Its crimson gas tank and chrome fenders shone in the sunshine, and although she knew next to nothing about motorcycles—except that when someone wiped out at fifty miles per hour he wound up half mangled and in casts in the hospital, scaring his kids half to death—she could tell this one was not new.

"It's a good-looking machine," she allowed. "It's gotta be an older model?"

"Vintage is what the bike geeks call it. It's a '75 Bonneville. Belongs to my grandfather actually, his pride and joy. Would you believe he bought it in right here in Minnesota? When I decided to come this way, he thought the old girl should have a road trip home."

"Ooo-kay, there's not much of a story in *that* teaser." She lifted her eyes and got a wink.

"Hop on and I'll tell it to you."

"Now, that sounds like a bad biker boy's version of 'come see my etchings.'"

"I'll have to remember that." His laugh added to the warmth emanating from his jacket.

"How far *have* you come in two days?"

"From Memphis."

She let out a low, appreciative whistle. "How much farther are you going?"

"I'm not entirely sure. I'm heading for a town somewhere around here called Northfield."

"Oh, it's *close*. Maybe fifteen miles once you go through Kennison Falls."

His Elvis smile enchanted her as always. "That's very, very good news."

He stood and held out his hand to pull her to her feet. Jill brushed away a smudge of dust on her thigh. She wasn't wary by nature, and strangers weren't rare. Kennison Falls, Minnesota got enough through-traffic to keep the local merchants in good business. But leather-jacketed bikers with gorgeous, penetrating eyes were not the norm.

She wished she could control the sudden pounding of her pulse, but tangled as she was in his eyes, his accent, and her ridiculous fear, containing her heartbeat was a lost cause.

"My mama warned me about taking rides from strangers."

"I won't let the big, bad Triumph hurt you, you know."

She closed her eyes and took another deep breath. "This is nuts."

He peered at her. "You really are scared."

"Always was." She forced herself not to look embarrassed. "Even when my father had one."

He didn't tease or even comment. From the seat, he picked up a black, shiny-visored helmet and held it out to her. "You can wear this. It possesses the power to keep you safe. Put your arms into the jacket, too, that's more protection."

Twice, now, he'd promised to protect her. Something primitive finally calmed her nerves, if only slightly. With resignation she pulled the helmet over her head. It fit like a fishbowl and dimmed the light like three pairs of sunglasses.

Chase rapped on the hard shell while she snapped the chinstrap.

"Where's your bag of boots?" He chuckled.

She grabbed it from the grass, and he plopped it atop a small duffel, pushing them to the metal tail behind the seat and stretching a bungee cord around both bags. He flipped down the passenger foot pegs and swung his leg over the seat.

"Squeeze on," he said blithely, and she did. The padded seat cushioned her better than her best riding saddle did, but there was no life beneath her, no living thing to partner with. "Put your feet on the rests here over the pipes. Don't let them dangle—the metal gets good and hot. Hang on to me or hold that strap on the seat. And don't worry."

She flipped up the visor. "I ride horses not Hogs. You can reason with a horse. And they're smart enough to keep from doing stupid things because they don't want to die any more than I do." She snapped the visor back in place.

"Well, this isn't a Hog, it's a Triumph. And, honey, I'm smart enough to know I don't want to die either." He laughed and shifted one hip to bring a boot heel down on the kick-starter.

The bike answered with a grumpy rumble but didn't catch. He stomped again. The Bonneville sprang to life, vibrating beneath Jill like a purring lion. The pulsations went through her like electrical current.

"One more thing," he called, twisting over his shoulder. "Lean with me into the turns. It won't be your instinct but it'll be safer. Ready?"

She clutched the seat strap, and the motorcycle rolled forward a foot. Chase let out the clutch. With a slight jolt, and a tilt to the right, the bike roared onto the road.

They picked up speed like a launched rocket, and Jill swayed side to side, her wimpy grip on the leather seat strap not nearly secure enough to keep her stable. As they followed a curve to the left and the bike leaned, she held in a screech, squeezed her eyes shut, and threw her arms around Chase's waist. Immediately her torso quit swaying.

Don't crash. Don't crash. Don't crash. The mantra played through her mind until, finally, they'd been underway long enough that the silliness of her fear hit home. She opened her eyes and watched familiar sights flash past in an unfamiliar way. The wind whipped at Chase's jacket, but sheltered in its folds she felt no chill. Beneath her hands, Chase's stomach muscles contracted and flexed as he moved as one with the motorcycle. Hanging onto him was like pressing up against a safe, brick wall. It took a second for her to comprehend when his fingers pried gently at hers, wiggling and loosening her grip.

"Relax!" he called over his shoulder, the word barely audible as it whizzed past her helmeted ear with the wind.

She hadn't realized how tightly she'd been squeezing. With effort, she pulled her hands apart and let go, grasping for a hold on the leather again, but he caught one hand and tugged her arm forward, patting it when the hold was just right. A hard shiver rolled through her body and then, for the first time, Jill found the ability to relax as he'd commanded. Beneath her hold, he came to life, not a brick wall at all but a supple, tensile lifeline.

"Be ready to tell me where to turn," he shouted again. "I've got you. Trust me."

Chapter Two

THREE MILES PASSED before Chase's beautiful rescuee stopped fighting the motion of the bike. Once he'd adjusted her hold around his waist she hadn't let go, her arms tightening with every curve of the road, relaxing when the Triumph straightened. Now, her torso curved against his back, finally following his movements and holding him like she trusted his ability.

He didn't want to admit it, but the girl had power over him. It flowed from her touch and through his body from toes to wind-whipped hair. Every dark memory he ran from, all his demons, had fled the instant her metallic-tan Chevy had slipped down the ditch. Every good instinct he'd honed over the years had kicked in. She might be scared of the ride she was on, but her arms clamped around his hips and her fingers clasped over his belly felt like they held his entire world together.

Dangerous thinking. He hadn't come here to meet

anyone—especially not a girl likely a decade or more younger than he. All this minor hero stuff would only be okay if he remembered this was a rescue of *her*.

But, dang, she was great. Pretty as a daisy in the breeze. Tough and snappy even in trouble. And funny. Once upon a time he'd been funny, and she'd brought it out again. Along with a few other feelings that had been dormant for a very long time.

He couldn't afford such schoolboy hormonal surges, and yet what red-blooded American boy *with* hormones could have stopped a reaction to a beautiful girl falling on top of him out of the blue? A guy simply didn't get that lucky every day.

And her arms wrapped around him now felt good. As good as the wind tearing through his helmetless hair. It was hard to deny the breeze in his face was heavenly. He wore the helmet because he believed in it, and he'd given it to Jill because preaching such safety practices to patients and clients came automatically.

Patients. Clients.

Black thoughts reared their ugly heads slowly, like insidious little termites eating away at his temporary peace. Clara. Brody. Tiana. His breath hitched slightly. *Aw, shit. Tiana.*

Unexpectedly, the motorcycle hiccuped and jerked beneath them, banishing the specters before they could fully form. Jill's arms constricted and every bit of her newfound fluidity stiffened into ramrod alertness. When the bike coughed and popped a second time and then a third, she turned into a human vise grip.

"Hey, it's all right," he called over his shoulder, and rubbed her knuckles, which were so taut he could almost see their icy whiteness with his fingers.

Not that he knew for sure everything was all right. They weren't going to crash or die, but the Triumph had not been running well for the past three hundred miles. His fervent hope was that the last tank of gas was bad. His fervent fear was that gas had nothing to do with the problem.

The bike pulled its choking act three more times before it smoothed out for the last two miles. When Jill finally tugged on his shirt and pointed to a gravel road coming up on the right, her gesture was almost wildly insistent. The gravel spun beneath the bike as they left the pavement. Wild ditch grass gave way to a field of new corn, then one of stubbly alfalfa, and then to a series of well-maintained pastures surrounded by brown post and rail fences. They reminded him of the endless miles of famous dark fencing around Lexington.

They turned right again onto a wide, sweeping gravel driveway lined with handsome maples. A gold-and-white sign, elegant but tasteful, announced they'd reached Bridge Creek Stables. Twenty yards later, two neat white railings marked the sides of a picturesque bridge over a meandering stream. My, my. They had their own creek.

He passed more pastures and came to a pristine complex of buildings. A large, two-story house stood to the left, and across the football field–sized yard stood a white-and-green barn, an outdoor riding arena, and several other structures. Jill guided him past the barn's main double doors to a large parking area. Chase pulled up beside a van with its back end open and a handicap-accessible lift on the ground. When he turned off the bike and its sonorous rumble faded, Jill slumped against his back. He patted her hand and unclasped her fingers.

Easing from his seat, he unsnapped her chinstrap, pulled the heavy helmet off her head, and revealed a pair of molten brown eyes beneath a tangle of honey-gold hair. She scrambled off the bike as if she'd been stung.

"What were those death throes we rode through?" she demanded. "Your motorcycle wants me dead, too."

He laughed out loud. "I'm sorry. I think they were the result of a tank of bad gas. I am sure you were never going to die."

"Yeah? Here's what I think." She kissed her fingertips, squatted, and patted them firmly on the ground.

"You seriously didn't enjoy that, did you?"

She popped to her feet. "It *was* quicker than waiting for Dewey, so, don't get me wrong, I'm grateful. But I'll stick to my ponies, thanks."

Now that they stood beside each other with no angst and no problem solving required, her face relaxed into a sweet, impish oval, and her eyes lost their uncertainty. She stood a petite eight inches shorter than he, and her figure curved in very non-young-girlish places.

How old could she be? She was too mature and quick to be a teenager, although her features could pass for eighteen or nineteen. Early twenties? A little older? It didn't matter. He was far older and he wasn't here to window-shop the local women.

Nor did he have the right to find her as compelling, as pretty, as funny and mysterious as he did. Or to hold on with such a zing of pleasure to the memory of her arms clinging around his waist.

She pointed to her bag bungee-corded to the back of the bike. "If you'll unhook my bag o' bricks, I'll give you a very inadequate thank-you, and you can get on your way to Northfield. I've kind of messed up your day, since you had to stand in for my guardian angels who obviously took the day off."

A slice of pain dragged the smile from his face. "I ain't nobody's guardian angel, Miss Jill Carpenter."

He handed her the weighty, multicolored striped bag, and an unwelcome sense of melancholy settled over him at the knowledge he had to leave. She was safety and mystery all packaged into one spirited body—an unexpected oasis in a solitary journey he didn't really want to be taking.

I want you to go away for a while, Brody had said, five days ago. His brother, ever the clown, for once hadn't been joking. *You're no good to yourself, this community, or anyone else until you get over thinking you have to save the world.*

Save the world? No. He would have settled for saving one innocent, nine-year-old child.

"What the heck are *they* doing here?" Once again, Jill's voice stopped him from sinking into the quicksand of dark thoughts.

He followed her gaze to a forest-green panel truck crunching slowly past them toward a parking spot next to the barn. The side of the truck bore a white logo—a circle surrounding the outline of a house and tree, flanked by the words "Connery Construction Company." Chase's heart thumped faster in disbelief. What *were* they doing here? This would be too big a coincidence if he believed in coincidences.

"Why *they* as if they're the school outcasts?"

She scowled. "It sounds stupid, but that's kind of what they are. Connery Construction isn't exactly flavor of the month around here."

"Oh?" The words unsettled him.

"They're planning to build a gravel quarry right outside of town. It's a pretty unpopular project. A lot of people are boycotting them."

"Harsh." The unsettled feeling grew.

"It's a very local boycott. In truth, nothing we do is going to run them out of business," she said. "Connery is a very rich man, and Kennison Falls is a pretty tiny cog in their business. Even if we do have construction jobs up the wazoo waiting to get done since our storm last summer."

"Storm?"

"We had a class-three tornado come through here last August," she said. "If you go into town you'll see the aftermath. David, the owner here, lost a riding arena and the roof off of one barn and had some damage to his house. It's not like we don't need construction workers."

He shook his head. "This all sounds like typical small-town politics to me."

"It is. But it's big doings for people here. The quarry

will go in only a mile from the state park next to town. We were originally only an alternate site, but big money got involved and, well, sorry. Talking politics is rude and not ever interesting to outsiders."

She had no idea how wrong she was in his case. She didn't need to know Connery Construction was precisely the reason he'd come to Minnesota, but he wondered how she *would* react if she knew of his relationship with the very rich Duncan Connery.

"It's always wise to know the local goings-on." He scratched the back of his head, checking his surroundings more carefully, taking in the pristine stable yard, the tidy flower beds lining the side of the barn. The scent of wood shavings and horses gave the place working farm ambience in a wealthy estate sort of way. Bridge Creek Stables was no two-bit operation.

"Jill!"

A youthful man Chase's height but a few years younger appeared at the wide barn door. Tan riding breeches and a navy polo shirt emphasized an athletic lower body and a broad chest and arms. The sight of a guy in tight pants took Chase aback. Growing up on a tobacco farm outside Lexington had conditioned him to think of barn wear as sweaty jeans and smelly chambray. This man's tall black boots and body-hugging clothing would have been as ridiculous on a Preston family work crew as perfume on a pirate.

"David, sorry." Jill's voice dropped a notch on the apology. "I'm finally here. I'm very late, I'm afraid."

"Actually, not so awfully, love." His accent, broad and

British, took Chase by surprise. "Mrs. Barnes only just arrived with her daughters."

"Daught*ers*?" Jill asked. "The letter from the middle school principal said nothing about more than one."

"One of them isn't here to ride," he promised. "She's in a wheelchair."

Every nerve ending in Chase's body scrambled to full alert, but he pushed back. Hyperawareness always surfaced at the whiff of a medical problem, and he was here to squelch that awareness.

Here to *not* save the world.

Jill's brow creased. "They're in the office?"

"They're in the arena watching Da' ride. I said I'd fetch them when you arrived."

Jill's shoulders squared visibly, as if she was shoring up for an ordeal. "Give me five minutes?"

"Of course. You have time."

"Not really. I'm scheduled for three o'clock with your father and it's nearly two-thirty."

"Not to worry, love. He's plenty busy and quite content putting my horses to rights and showing me how poorly I've trained them. And in addition," the man—David—snickered, "we finally got your sister off her high horse, and she's taking a lesson. She'll go right before you. You don't need to rush."

Chase hadn't known Jill half an hour, but the evaporation of her smile was as transparent as cling wrap.

"Dee? Is riding with your father?" Her measured tone registered irritation.

David appeared not to notice. "I know. Miracles, 'eh?"

He peered more closely and pointed at Jill's red blotches for the first time. "Good Lord, what's happened?" He swung his gaze suspiciously toward Chase.

She shook herself loose from whatever had momentarily upset her. "I'm sorry. This is Chase Preston, he's my champion of the day. Chase, this is David Pitts-Matherson, Bridge Creek's owner."

"Champion, was it?" David asked, his handshake and quick, thorough assessment those of a very protective friend.

"Hardly. *She* saved the life of a dog by swerving her truck down a ditch." Chase released David's firm grip. "I just gave her a hand getting out."

"That's our Jill, isn't it? She would end up off the road over an animal. But you're all right? The Creature isn't damaged?" David asked.

Jill slipped off Chase's jacket, fully revealing the red Rorschach blob on her chest. "No. The only casualty was my order of fries. At first, Chase thought I'd been skewered." She folded the jacket, stroking the leather as if it were a mink. "But it's only ketchup. I'm going to grab a logo T-shirt from the office."

"Fine. I'll garnish your next paycheck."

She made a yeah-sure face and handed Chase his jacket. "I can't thank you enough, Chase Preston," she said.

"There's no need. Do you have a way back to your truck later?"

"Plenty of ways, I promise."

"All right." The heaviness at her imminent departure

rose within him again. She was a sexy package of chameleon emotions, changing in front of him. He wanted to know how many more colors she possessed.

Her delicate fingers slipped into his grip, and she gave a surprisingly strong squeeze. She let the warm handshake lock them together for extra-long seconds before sliding her hand free.

"If you happen back through KF some afternoon, stop in. I'm probably here."

"I'll remember."

She nodded and headed for the barn but turned before reaching the door. "Hey, David, you traitor," she called. "What's Connery doing here?"

David sighed. "I hoped you wouldn't notice that yet. We'll talk about it."

"Yup. We will." She forked her fingers and pointed to her eyes, then flipped her hand in the international I'm-watching-you gesture. David snorted.

She waved a last time and disappeared.

The intrigue was too strong to ignore. Chase knew he should get out of Dodge and away from Jill Carpenter five minutes ago, but instead he shrugged into his jacket. "Do you have a minute for a question that's none of my business?"

David folded his arms in front of him, his face neutral. "Yes, sure."

"Jill says the company is unpopular around here. I ask only because I'm supposed to meet with Duncan Connery tomorrow morning."

"I see." He rubbed at his chin and laughed a little humorlessly. "True enough, I'd be careful whom I tell that to around here."

"And yet . . ." Chase glanced at the truck.

"Sometimes you have to choose between appeasing an overbearing father and suffering the wrath of an entire community." The corner of his mouth gave a rueful uptick. "I've chosen the lesser of two evils."

"Overbearing fathers. We may have to swap stories sometime."

"Over a beer one day," David agreed. "I'm on my way to talk to the Connery bloke now. If *you've* got the time, come on along. Perhaps you'll get some insight."

"Really? I'd appreciate it, thanks."

"My father is a former Olympic equestrian for England, recently hired to coach the United States team. His facility in Virginia won't be ready until September. I have him here for three months."

"And that's . . . not a good thing?"

The high afternoon sun gleamed off the white metal barn and highlighted flowers along the foundation. In Chase's experience, barn sides had cobwebs and dirt spatters, not petunia beds. This place had to have a full-time barn washer and petunia weeder to look like this.

"Da's exacting and gets what he wants, but he's a huge draw. My riders are ecstatic to have him. In fact, Jill"—he inclined his head toward the barn—"is one reason he's here. She's got Olympic potential and Da' is eager to watch her. Not that I want to lose her to the U.S. Equestrian Team, but she's such a phenomenal rider I can't hold her back."

"She definitely has a spark to her."

"That she does. A very special spark." He stopped walking and faced Chase fully. "Thank you for helping her. She really was all right? I was flippant about the accident only because I've learned not to fuss over Jill."

"She was far more worried about the dog in the road and getting here than she was about going into the ditch."

David nodded. "All right, then, it does sound like she's fine. Thanks just the same. She's special to us."

"To you?" Chase raised one brow and started off again.

David laughed at the implied question. "She's one of my best friends, but that sort of fire never started. I doubt it's occurred to either of us to strike a match."

For some reason that made Chase exceedingly happy. And uneasy.

They neared the green Connery truck. Beside it, assessing the yard, stood a middle-aged man with gray-templed brown hair, a clipboard, and a green button-down shirt tucked into faded jeans.

"What are you building?" Chase asked.

"A riding arena. To replace the one we lost last summer in a tornado, of all things."

"I heard about it."

The worker from Connery introduced himself as Jeff Rigby and laid out a proposal and building schedule efficiently and clearly.

"We could start next week," Rigby said. "And we could finish in three weeks plus, depending on the finishing details."

"Quite impressive," David said.

"Can I ask how big the company is?" Chase asked. "You must have a decent workforce to field a crew this quickly."

"They'll have to dig me up four or five," Rigby said. "I think we have twenty-five full-time crew and a handful of part-timers." Rigby scratched the side of his mouth. "They'll be hiring more soon for a big project."

"So, you've had a look 'round the building site?" David asked, and Rigby nodded. "I think the plan sounds fine," David continued. "I think I'd like to seal the deal here and now. Will a handshake do, or have you papers to sign?"

Jeff Rigby held out his hand. "I'll report on the site, tell them there's nothing that'll require us to change the quote at this point. We'll write up a final work order and someone will call about a start date."

Chase liked the man's easy professionalism.

"Is that it for now, then?" David asked.

"I think so."

"I have to get some new clients sorted if you'll excuse me, you two feel free to look around." He held out his hand to Chase a last time. "Good luck. Thanks again for rescuing our Jill."

Chase's pulse tripped at the sound of her name. "I'm glad I was there to help."

"David?"

Chase spun in surprise at Jill's familiar voice, but she was nowhere in sight. The woman who did approach, however, sounded so similar he'd been fooled. This had to be Jill's sister, but other than their voices, they were as unalike as a house cat and a lioness.

"My, my, what have we here?" The leggy blonde sashayed toward their group of three in form-fitting riding breeches, boots shined to military perfection, and a polo shirt of vivid red. "A convention of romance cover models?" Her eyes lingered on Chase, and the tip of her tongue actually swept from one corner of her mouth to the other, as if she'd chosen her prey.

"Dee." David's voice held a friendly warning. "Haven't you got a lesson in about two minutes?"

"Yes. But, your dad sent me to find you before we start. He'd like you to do something about the spectators you put in the arena. He claims they're too distracting."

"Bloody hell," David replied dully. "He's been here two days. Perhaps I'll shoot him after all and get it over with."

Chase laughed. "The very reason I ran away from home years ago. To keep myself out of prison."

"My goodness," Dee practically purred and sidled closer. "Whatever is such a delightful accent doing this far north?"

"Ma'am," he greeted her. "Just passin' through."

"A pity you're in such a hurry." Her smile started in her lips and slowly lit her eyes into come-hither pools of hazel. "A North-South union might be kinda fun."

"I think we handled that merger pretty successfully a hundred and fifty years ago." He winked at her, and David snorted.

Dee pursed sultry lips. "If you do decide to stay for

a while, look me up. Dee Carpenter." She held out her hand. "Nice to meet you."

"Chase Preston. Likewise. Ma'am."

She turned in place and walked back toward the barn.

"That's our Dee," David said simply. "Have a care. She's exactly what she seems."

Chase watched her hips sway out of sight. "She seems like my signal to run for the hills."

"Good plan." David laughed again. "Good plan."

Chapter Three

It would have been much easier for Jill to focus if Chase Preston had simply gone on his drifter's way once he'd dropped her off. Instead, after she'd changed into breeches, boots, and a ketchup-free shirt, her heart gave a leap at the sight of the red and silver Triumph still standing where she'd gratefully climbed off it ten minutes before.

If she closed her eyes she could still feel the terror and exhilaration of their ride. She hadn't thought for a long time about the panic that had blindsided her fifteen years before when police had come to their door to say her father had been in the accident. In the end he'd been fine, after three surgeries and a six-month recuperation. Her father had taken her on many a ride before that, but then and there she'd vowed never to ride a motorcycle again.

How had some stranger, then, convinced her to climb on an ancient bike? One that had coughed and sputtered like it was hacking up a mechanical lung. He definitely possessed more than powers of persuasion. Something before she'd ever straddled the seat had convinced her he wouldn't let anything happen to her. And leaning with his long, strong body into the turns, feeling his reassuring hands on hers, had made her believe she could ride with him, even on a motorcycle, forever.

Asinine. He was mysterious as a phantom. The last thing her complicated life needed was a leather-clad mystery.

With effort, she spun her focus to the imminent meeting with her new student. She sat at the huge desk in Bridge Creek's office and reached into a drawer designated as hers. She pulled out the short-but-fateful letter printed from her personal e-mail. In the past two weeks she'd read the words twenty times and still knew little more than nothing about the letter's subject.

Dear Miss Carpenter,

In reference to our phone conversation of May 20, I'm writing to let you know how grateful I am for your support of our student, Rebecca Barnes. Mrs. Barnes informs me her daughter's first riding lesson has already been scheduled.

As we've discussed, Rebecca has been an exceptional student. We will continue working closely with the family to determine why she is suddenly failing. I truly hope her interest in horses and your success last year with another student, Cassie Johnson, will combine to create more success this summer.

> *Please feel free to contact me any time. Our*
> *school counselor and the district social worker are*
> *also available. I wish you a pleasant summer. Many*
> *thanks again for your help.*
>
> *Sincerely,*
> *Randall Knapp*
> *Principal, Cannon Falls Middle School*

Rebecca Barnes. How could such a sweetly named thirteen-year-old cause this big a stir? In conversations, Randall Knapp made her sound like a bomb ticking toward detonation.

Jill loved new riding students. They were like Christmas presents to be opened—full of potential and surprise. However, she'd never been expected to take on a disturbed teenager with the express expectation of turning her life around.

Hearing voices and footsteps in the short hall outside the door, Jill tucked the letter back in her drawer right before David appeared, gesturing for a woman and a sullen-faced teenager to enter the office ahead of him. He then guided a second teen over the threshold in a wheelchair.

"Jill, may I introduce Mrs. Anita Barnes and her daughters, Rebecca and Jamie."

Only he could pull off such a deadly proper announcement with total naturalness. Jill reached for Anita Barnes's hand, fascinated by the curious anachronism she presented. Not a single age line marred her face, but the rest of her looked like she'd fallen through a time tunnel and hit every decade for forty years. She'd poufed her mousy-brown hair into a bouffant bob that could have made a sixties stylist proud. Her burgundy-framed glasses were eighties owlish, and she wore tight, gold-colored capri pants under a flowered, sleeveless, button-down blouse from Jill-had-no-idea-when.

"It's nice to meet you, Mrs. Barnes. I'm Jill Carpenter."

"Jill. You're younger than I expected. Have you been teaching long?"

Jill set a smile in place. "Seven years."

"Jill's a wonderful instructor and a top-notch rider herself." David came to her aid. "Your daughter couldn't be in better hands."

"I'm glad to hear that."

Rebecca stood a full body length from anyone else, and Jill worked very hard not to judge on first impressions. The girl had obviously been practicing the art of looking older and wore her makeup fairly expertly applied, if far too dark. She was gymnast short, her sandy, cropped hair stood in stiff spikes with a swath of bright blue bangs, and her tight flared jeans matched her tight knit top. The jeans left her knees showing, the top left her midriff bare, but what killed the attempt at visual maturity were the cherub-round cheeks beneath the mix of Goth and garish colors.

"Hi, Rebecca."

The girl cast her eyes briefly over Jill and lifted her arm to a disinterested handshake.

Jill offered the same greeting to the younger girl in the wheelchair. "Hi, Jamie."

This sister couldn't have been a more clichéd opposite. From her elbow-length chestnut hair to her softly faded jeans and pink T-shirt, Jamie exuded sugar and spice like puppies oozed cute.

"This is so cool," she replied.

"I'm glad you think so. And I'm glad you could all come an extra day to get acquainted," Jill said. "How about if we take our tour, and you can ask all the questions you want?"

Rebecca shrugged, leaving Jill to accept it as an affirmative answer. "Our first lesson is still on for tomorrow, right?"

Anita Barnes nodded. "Rebecca's looking forward to it."

Jill stared at the girl, who absolutely could have fooled her.

"I'll be off, then," David said. "I look forward to seeing all of you around the stables. Look me up whenever you need anything." He gave a two-finger salute and left.

Five minutes into the tour of Bridge Creek's two impressive barns and arena, it was clear Rebecca's problem, whatever it was, had not been invented by the school psychiatrist. She was uncommunicative, sarcastic when she deigned to speak, and possessed an infinite array of shrugs she used much more frequently and eloquently than words.

"Have you ridden before, Rebecca?"

They stood right inside the arena, where the girls had already spent time, watching a lone rider circle the space. Jill could barely mask her awe over the expert calm and classic position of Colin Pitts-Matherson. Muffled hoof beats and the slip of leather against leather whispered like soft music. The loamy scent of sand, shavings, and wood filled her nostrils as she ogled the Michael Phelps of her sport.

"A couple of times." Rebecca searched the space with uninterested eyes.

"We both rode," Jamie added. "It was awesome. Becky was good."

"Rebecca has a knack for sports, doesn't she?" Anita smoothed Jamie's hair with a quick motion. "You've always been good at the crafty things. You girls have such different strengths."

Jill swore a shadow crossed Jamie's face, but the girl nodded.

"So, if you don't mind me asking," Jill said, "you haven't always been in the wheelchair?"

"A little over a year."

"Oh." For one instant Jill didn't know what to say. She studied Jamie, but any clouds in her eyes had vanished. "I'm impressed at how skilled and strong you are. We'll have to turn you into a groom."

"Really?" Jamie's hazel eyes lit with anticipatory sunlight.

"Sure." She sensed Anita tensing beside her like a mother bear. "It'll be good for the horses to learn about your chair. You can help get them used to something new."

"Awesome!"

Movement at the far end of the arena caught Jill's

eyes and another rider entered, leading a bright chestnut mare. She knew the pair well. Colin stopped his horse and greeted Dee with a crisp British "Good afternoon, Miss Carpenter." She cocked her hip and replied—perfect and perfectly confident, as always, around any human with testosterone.

"So." Jill spun her attention away from her sister and led her small group out of the arena. "What kind of riding would like to do, Rebecca?" A shrug. "Have you ever ridden in an English saddle?" A head shake. "Would you like to? Or do you want a big Western saddle with a horn? Either is fine. With an English saddle we'd work on some dressage—like we were just watching—and maybe jumping. In a Western saddle we'd do more balance work and get outside on some trails."

"If I have to do this I'd rather, like, jump."

They were the first words of interest, if it could be called that, the girl had uttered. Jill seized on them. "Good! That's exactly what I needed to know. Here's the deal then. We'll need to work a lesson or two on the flat. When I see how your balance is we'll go on. Sound fair?"

"Fair. Sure." Rebecca snorted.

"You'll need to make sure you wear riding breeches or riding jeans—and I mean not regular jeans. The inner seams will chafe. Your shoes need to cover your ankles and have at least a half-inch heel." Jill looked to Anita Barnes. They'd already been over this.

"She has them."

"Excellent. And a helmet?"

"A helmet?" The girl's lip curled up against nostrils

flared in disgust. At least the emotion was honest. A lot of girls balked at the helmet at first.

"Yup. Nonnegotiable. One fall is all it takes."

"We're getting one tonight," Anita assured her.

"Excellent."

"I think they look really cool, Becky," Jamie said. "Like you're a professional."

Jill rested a hand on Jamie's shoulder, and the girl looked up with an expression as opposite her sister's as could be imagined.

"You would."

"You know." The idea came to Jill from an unknown place. "It wouldn't hurt you to have a helmet either, Jamie. You'll be low and close to the horses' legs—safety first, right?"

"Oh, can I, Mom?" Jamie's hazel eyes begged.

"I don't know," Anita Barnes replied, a little curtly. "You aren't going to be here all that much. Don't you think you'd rather get the equipment for your own classes?"

"Sure, but . . ."

"What else are you doing?" Jill asked, honestly curious.

"Some things at Courage Center." Jamie gave her first shrug. "They have wheelchair basketball and stuff like that."

"Sounds fun."

"Yeah." She nodded, with only slightly more enthusiasm than her sister showed for the horses.

"You're welcome here anytime you can come."

After twenty-five more minutes, Jill had answered a

hundred Anita Barnes questions, found nothing to spark interest in one daughter, developed a soft spot for the other, and used up mental reserves she hadn't wanted to tap. Forget the fact that, after a morning of animal deaths at the clinic, she'd driven her truck into a ditch. Forget she'd risked her life on a motorcycle to get here. She had the student from apathy hell. Most kids at least *wanted* to take riding lessons. If Rebecca wasn't here under duress, Jill would eat her riding crop.

She invited Anita and the girls to look around on their own as long as they wished, hoping for the first time in all her years of teaching that a potential student would drop out before she started. Only when she caught the incredible sight of Chase's motorcycle, still standing where he'd left it, did she stop worrying about the next day's lesson with Rebecca.

What was he still doing here? Her heart worked itself into an erratic thumping as she searched for Chase on the way to fetch her horse. She scowled at the Connery van, also still in the drive. Annoyance was futile. David was allowed to hire whatever company he chose. This simply rubbed her the wrong way. Connery was about to build a facility that could mar Kennison Falls's beautiful, natural park forever, and Duncan Connery had shown he didn't care about repercussions. In her opinion, nobody in town should be giving him work until a whole lot of questions got answered.

She reined in her emotions. The lesson of her lifetime would start in fifteen minutes, and she was by gosh going to make up for her crappy morning, come handsome Triumph driver or traitorous boss.

DRAGON LIFTED HIS fine, black head as she approached him in the pasture and snorted when she put her hand in her pocket to pull out a peppermint. The wonder horse she'd found through a Thoroughbred rescue lipped it from her palm, ducked his head so she could put on his halter, and let her run a hand along his elegant neck. He hadn't been the most successful racehorse, but he could jump anything she put in front of him, and he had the potential to take her to the pinnacle of three-day eventing. If they proved themselves today, the journey could start. Colin Pitts-Matherson was a powerful enough man to help her. In many ways, she'd been dreaming about this lesson since she'd mounted her first horse at age seven.

Dragon's shod feet clopped along the cement aisle in the empty barn. The regular cadence of his hoof falls eased her nervous excitement until Chase Preston wriggled unbidden into her thoughts, throwing her brain off-balance. Like a blue-eyed Merlin, he'd pretty much cast some magic spell over her day. He'd be gone by the time her lesson was done, but remembering their microadventure—his long, hard body beneath her, his dexterous, sinewy hands cupping her . . .

Without warning, Dragon screamed. As if he'd been whipped, he lunged forward and his lead rope seared through Jill's fist. From the corner of her eye, she saw

Jamie Barnes in her wheelchair stopped at the arena doorway ten feet away. Jill turned to calm her spooked horse, and he reared, the knee of his powerful foreleg rising like the piston in a semi-truck. It met with her right shoulder in a sickening thud.

She crumpled. Dragon broke away, and someone, human this time, screeched. Through a haze of pain Jill heard her name, and a tall, wide body materialized beside her.

With a huge effort, she staggered to her feet and held her stomach tightly against a flash of nausea. "Jamie, it's all right," she called.

"You get down, right now," Chase commanded at the same moment.

She ignored him and made a successful lunge for Dragon's flailing lead rope. Automatically, she began a quiet litany, and thirty seconds after it had begun, Dragon's hissy fit was over. Jill grabbed a cross tie hanging from the wall and clipped it to his halter. Ignoring the stabbing pain in her shoulder, she attached the other cross tie and finally bent forward, gasping for breath.

A pair of strong, firm hands gripped her by the upper arms and all but pushed her to the wall. She let herself slide down a stall door and plop to the floor, mewling softly in pain when her butt hit the cement.

"Here's a blanket. Lie down."

At last she looked at him. Chase. He guided her to her back before she could protest, and despite her growing discomfort, a spark from his touch slid over her shoulders and spiraled down her spine. Startled by such powerful attraction, she pushed him away.

"Would you stop telling me to lie down? Someone's going to get the wrong idea."

His expression didn't ease despite her humor. "Don't tell me this time you aren't hurt. I saw how hard you got slammed." He took her arm, gently.

She shrugged him away. "It's only a bump. He saw Jamie's wheelchair and spooked. Is Jamie all right?" The Barnes family was no longer in sight.

"I don't care if he saw the Ghost of Christmas Past. You need to get that shoulder checked."

"I'm fine. Do you fuss like this all the time?"

His gorgeous face twisted with what looked like embarrassment, but he didn't back down when she fought to rise again. "I worry when I see accidents, and I've seen you have two today. Are you always this disaster prone? Stay down."

"No." She glared at him and pushed against the floor.

"Are you always this stubborn?"

"Yes. Give me a hand or get out of the way."

He helped her up and then raised his palms in surrender. "It looked like a lot more than a bump."

"It wasn't." She hesitated. "But thank you."

A quiet hiccup pulled her away from his mesmerizing eyes, and Anita Barnes appeared from behind the arena door.

"It's all right," Jill called. "He's settled down, you guys can come out."

"I don't think it's a good idea for us to bring the wheel-chair near that horse," Anita said. "I needed to be sure you're not hurt, but I think we'll go out through the arena."

"There's no need, Mrs. Barnes." Jill didn't know whether to appreciate the woman's concern or be annoyed at the slightly supercilious tone accompanying her that-horse comment. "He's tied now, and it would be good for him to see Jamie again. Like I told her earlier, she can help get him used to new things."

"I hardly feel that's safe."

"It's completely up to you, of course," Jill replied. "But I promise, Jamie doesn't have to come very close. She'll be in no danger."

"How about you?" Chase asked in her ear. "Will you be in no danger?"

"Less danger than you'll be in if I decide to punch you," she whispered. "Quit hovering."

He grinned.

Before Anita could protest further, Jamie rolled back into the aisle. This time Dragon did no more than snort, and Jill gave him a pat. "Hi, kiddo," she called. "I'm so sorry about that."

"I didn't mean to scare him."

Something strained in the girl's voice made Jill step toward her. Jamie's eyes brimmed with tears.

"Jamie, honey, you didn't do anything wrong. Good-ness, I told you to go anywhere you wanted. You didn't know I was here. You're fine, the horse is, too, silly boy, and so am I."

"Really?"

"Stop being such a baby, Jamie. She told you she's fine." Rebecca's sneer showed in her voice and her face, but underlying it all was a slight ashen tinge. What? The girl had worried about something?

"Everything's fine, I promise," Jill said. "I didn't mean to scare you either." She looked from the girls to Chase and back. He only raised his Elvis lip yet again.

"Come here, Rebecca. You can meet Dragon. Jamie, you can come, too, if your mom's okay with it."

"Jamie, I think you'd better stay here."

"Mo-om." Jamie rolled her chair slowly but defiantly forward. Rebecca stood still.

"C'mon," Jill insisted. "Rule number one around horses is that you have to get to know how they act and react. You don't want to let a little spook become a big fear. Dragon here is really pretty sensible most of the time. Come and find out."

It took long minutes, but both girls were finally close enough to pet Dragon, Rebecca with a desultory touch, Jamie as if she were stroking an ebony unicorn. Dragon, in turn, sniffed and snorted at the wheelchair, and once he discovered it wouldn't eat him, switched to nosing its occupant for treats.

Chase watched over the proceedings as if he believed steady, steely eyeballs would keep anything more from happening. Although Jill didn't know what he was still doing at the barn, his presence, overbearing as it was, comforted, and when the Barnes family finally left in a mishmash of thanks, shrugs, and apologies, Chase remained.

"You're great with those kids," he said, surprising her by not mentioning her arm.

"Not a big deal. I did what had to be done to keep them from freaking out around the horses tomorrow."

She rolled her shoulder, and it responded with a deep shot of pain.

"I saw that grimace."

"I've had worse." She rubbed the front of the shoulder tentatively and frowned. "If you work with animals, you get stepped on once in a while. Hang on, I have to get my tack." She headed down the aisle but looked over her shoulder. "What are you still doing here anyhow? Not that I don't appreciate the rescue. Again."

"I just finished talking with the guy from Connery Construction. Came in to say good-bye a last time, and all hell broke loose."

"If this is your idea of hell, you need a life."

He went strangely quiet. Her motorcycle man was fun and funny, and she'd forgive his overconcern as long as it ended soon, but his reactions to some things seemed odd. Off. She lifted her saddle off its rack. All the breezy thoughts disappeared on the heels of a hot, painful stab through her shoulder. She nearly dropped the saddle on its pommel.

"Shi—" She stopped herself.

She didn't want him to tell her to lie down again.

With effort she adjusted the saddle over her good arm and reached for her bridle, which hung at eye level. Her arm barely moved. Oh crap, what had she done? This couldn't happen now. With a deep breath, she straightened. Once she got on the horse she'd be fine. Being on a horse always made her fine.

Chase took one skeptical look at her when she returned. "You are not all right," he said.

"What are you, some sort of whacked-out reverse hypochondriac?" She sighed, and concern finally got the better of her. "I'm perfectly all right," she lied. "But for the sake of argument, do you know how to saddle a horse?"

Chapter Four

"YOUR TORSO IS caving in again. Keep it bloody well upright, and get those shoulders back."

Jill squeezed her eyes shut briefly, trying to do as
she'd been asked and stop flopping on Dragon's back
like a wrung-out dishrag. She'd had tough riding lessons
before. She welcomed them. But Colin Pitts-Matherson
was a drill sergeant's drill sergeant, and she was lucky to
be on her horse at all, much less upright.

Pain now radiated up into her skull, crashing into
nerve endings with every one of Dragon's canter strides—
three beats at a time, over and over. Only for two blessed
seconds of flight over each jump did the pain stop. Then
his front legs would drill into the arena footing, collaps-
ing Jill over his neck like a raw beginner.

Despite the painful red haze, she refused to complain.

"Don't let him pop that outside shoulder this time,"
he called. "Sit up, quit mucking with his mouth, and keep

your eyes up. David says you rarely miss your spot, but these are instructions I give a novice, Jill."

The criticism worked like a gauntlet slapped across her cheek. She sent her last reserves of energy to her legs and blocked out the fog of pain from her upper body. Two jumps left on a diagonal line through the arena—a huge oxer to a vertical fence. If she could have one small success on the day, this would be a good time to pull it out of her butt.

Like a miracle, her leg coordinated with her rein, Dragon swept around the corner turn in a collected, graceful bend and locked onto the oxer—two fence rails, one right behind the other. He surged off the ground, and Jill flew with him. This time when she landed she forced herself upright, made herself sit back, and gathered her big black horse. The next jump, a single vertical fence, was harder because she couldn't let Dragon spread out over it. He had to collect himself in just two strides. One . . . two . . .

"At last!" Colin cried from the end of the arena. "Now tell me, love, was that really so difficult? Well done."

Jill gathered her reins into one hand and wiped her cheeks free of relieved tears before he saw.

"I think that'll do." Colin strode toward her, reaching to pat Dragon on the neck.

"I'm sorry," Jill said quietly. "This was not a good ride for me today."

He nodded curtly. "I'd like to see you work on your posture and your hands. They were quite noisy."

"They were, and I will."

You didn't argue with or make excuses to someone of his stature. Like the tornado that had swept through town nine months earlier, she'd destroyed this lesson. Maybe her dream, too.

"Good then." Colin said nothing about another lesson and gave her boot top one pat. "Thank you for taking the time to work with me today. It's good to meet you."

"Thank *you*."

He walked away. As Jill crawled from the saddle, Colin stopped briefly beside David, watching from the arena door. She pressed her forehead against the flap of her saddle and choked back a sob.

"Jill?" David placed a hand on her shoulder, and she tensed. "What happened?"

A little bump from a horse. She'd had worse injuries. This should not have been a big deal. Dragon shuffled sideways and she straightened, running her stirrup iron up its leather. "I had the crappiest ride in years, that's what happened. I had a bad day."

"Rubbish. I watch you ride three times a week. Now, tell me what's wrong."

Without fanfare, Chase appeared. His narrowed, knowing blue eyes, added to David's badgering, took away any fight she had left. She spilled the stupid story with gritted teeth, and to her amazement, David broke into a smile.

"Thank God. For goodness' sake, are you daft? Why didn't you ask Da' to postpone?"

"I didn't think I needed to, honestly. Remember the

time I rode with a broken arm for six weeks? This was just a little bump. I thought."

David's lips twitched with humor and he shrugged apologetically at Chase. "Athletes. We all need our heads examined." He looked at Jill. "I get it. So tell him now."

"No. I screwed this up. I'll have to fix it. I'm not going to make an excuse after the fact. That's no way to start a relationship."

"I hate to say it, love, but neither was this."

"I know. But I'll sweet-talk him into one more try."

"Sweet-talk him. There's a laugh. Well, no tries for a week or more by the look of you."

"It'll be fine after I rest it." She didn't admit to the doubts forming in her mind. "I'll be good and cancel my two other students for tonight—unless you want them?"

"I can take the lessons. I'll take the Dragon, too."

"Don't be ridiculous. I'm not a whingeing child." She used David's favorite British phrase for students who complained. "He's my responsibility."

He held up his hands the same as Chase had. "All right. But then go home. You're no good to me injured." He spun on his booted heels, and got halfway to the door before calling back to her. "It wasn't that bad, you know."

She loved him to death. But, oh yes. It had been that bad.

"Why?" Chase spoke for the first time.

"Why what?"

She gathered Dragon's reins and led him forward.

"Why be so stubborn? It makes no sense to have kept

the injury from David's father. Why let him think you're a bad rider?"

"Look. I . . ."

How could she explain? Colin was her Olympic idol, someone she'd dreamed of riding with for years, and David had bragged her up. The last thing she'd wanted to do was come up with an excuse for postponing the first ride. As if she weren't confident of her ability. This had been her equivalent of the one big shot with a football or baseball scout. Colin had likely made up his mind about her already—and she'd have to scramble to get him to look twice.

"If this had happened during a show or, heaven forbid, Olympic trials," she continued, "I couldn't have used it as an excuse. I'd have had one of two choices—withdraw from the competition because I couldn't ride, or suck it up and finish. I sucked it up."

"So tell him after the fact. That's not an excuse to get out of anything."

"It's looking for absolution. 'Oh, Colin.'" She adopted a squeaky cartoon voice. "'I'm really such a good rider, but my horsey banged my shoulder and it hurts.'"

He sighed, long and low. "You have to be one of the most stubborn people I've ever met." The chastisement didn't reach his eyes. "And one of the toughest. For what it's worth, *I've* never seen anyone ride like that. I was damn impressed. Means nothing coming from a motorcycle driver, still . . ."

On the contrary, warmth spread from Jill's belly to her face, to her sore shoulder, to her fingertips. She had ridden with as much grace as spaghetti on a Brahman bull, but Chase had stayed and been impressed. It kind of made up for her letting Colin think she was crap.

CHASE WATCHED JILL struggle through the process of cooling her horse, wondering what possessed him to stay. It wasn't just her injury. There was the simple fact that she and Dragon were mesmerizing. Chase had grown up in the heart of Lexington horse country, and he knew pretty horseflesh when he saw it. Dragon, with his powerful black haunches and stark white burst of lightning on his forehead, would definitely come out tops on a most-beautiful list. But what truly kept Chase spellbound was the way Jill seemed one with the horse—on the ground as well as mounted.

And, for as short a time as he'd known her, his attraction was as stubborn as she was.

She let him help carry her saddle to the tack room, open the pasture gate for her to let the horse out, and close it again. He slipped into the little routine effortlessly.

"I can't thank you enough," she said, once Dragon had bucked off to find his pasture mates. "You really have earned about six Boy Scout badges today."

He laughed. "I am nobody's Boy Scout."

"You're good in a crisis."

He winced inwardly, but her smile spilled impishly into her eyes, banishing memories of home before they could take hold. He remembered the short meeting with her sister earlier. Jill's smile was everything Dee's had not been, inviting, fun, guileless.

"You are going to get that shoulder checked, right?"

Her sigh pushed through her smile, dimming it. "What I'm going to *do* is get my truck back. I'd rather leave it in the ditch, but since I'd be kinda screwed, that's not an option. After that, a hot shower will make it all better. I honestly think it'll be fine in the morning."

He opened his mouth but forced himself not to speak. She was not his to protect although he desperately wanted to protect her. And he was red-blooded enough to let an image of her in the shower distract him and linger in that part of his brain that would forever be a randy teenage boy.

"You know best how it feels," he conceded. "So, what can I do next?"

She halted and looked at him in confusion. "Next? I don't know why you're still here. You've helped so much, and you have places to go. There's not a thing I'd ask you to do."

"How are you getting to your truck?"

She started walking again. "Dee or David will take me."

What the heck? The only place he had to go tonight was a hotel. "I'd be happy to do it."

"What? Make me ride on that overgrown chainsaw again?" Her brown eyes shone.

"Listen, Miss Jumps Tall, Hard Objects on a Thousand-Pound Animal, your supposed fear of motorcycles doesn't fly with me anymore. That harebrained horse ride was way more likely to splatter you on the ground than my motorcycle is."

At the mention of the harebrained ride, she looked for

the briefest second as if she might cry. Then the tiniest quirk at the corner of her mouth showed the shake-it-off spirit he was coming to recognize.

"You think a bicycle-on-'roids with a rocket engine strapped to it is safer than my horse? What the heck, then, I might as well live dangerously. I'd be more coordinated jumping your broken motorcycle than I was jumping the horse anyway."

"Hey, it's not broken. I told you—bad gas. But, if you let me take you, I'll have your town's expert mechanic have a look at the bike. To prove it."

"Fine. I'll come only because I'd hate to worry about you on that hiccupping leaf blower all night."

Her regained humor relieved him.

"Facing your fears to save me. I'm flattered," he teased. "But, you being that brave and all, I still think you should tell Colin about your shoulder and save yourself, or at least your reputation. I'm missing the logic in your choice here."

"I told you, I'd rather prove my ability without excuses," she said, and the stubborn set to her full, kiss-shaped lips was inexplicably sexy. "Anyway, who said a reason has to include logic?"

Who indeed? He didn't push her further. He was beginning to see that sexy stubbornness flowed through Jill Carpenter's veins side by side with her life's blood.

As soon as Chase turned off the Triumph twenty minutes later, Dewey Mitchell stuck his head out of a garage bay and eyed him with mild suspicion. When Jill pulled off the oversized helmet, however, Dewey relaxed and waved. "Oh, hey, Jill," he called. "Got yourself new wheels, I see. Your truck's almost done. Hang tight, be right with you."

"You're a dream, Dewey. Thank you!"

She slid off the bike. Chase followed and stretched. Dewey's shop possessed small-town familiarity except that the place was weirdly pristine—as if everything had been freshly painted and power washed. A solid brick station building stood beside a three-bay metal garage with not a scratch or dent on it; the apron asphalt around the six-pump island all but shone like a waxed floor with not a crack to mar its surface. A tire display flanked by a giant poster of the Michelin Man stood in front of the station's huge picture window. The oldest-looking things in the entire place were the cars lined up beside the garage awaiting repairs—Chase assumed.

"This has got to be the cleanest garage I've ever seen," he said.

"Dewey lost pretty much everything in the tornado." Jill looked around, a touch of nostalgia in her eyes. "Buildings, tools, vehicles, pumps. This place was one of the first things rebuilt. Everything is brand-new, down to the last socket set, and I'm pretty sure everyone in town pitched in to get it done. Kennison Falls couldn't survive without Dewey's shop. Same for the Loon Feather Café three blocks up."

Chase followed her finger up the long, sunny main street. The still-healing scars of Jill's hometown were clear even to a stranger. A low whistle passed his lips.

"I'm sorry, honey. This was bad, wasn't it?"

"Pretty bad," she agreed.

A patchwork of empty lots and freshly refaced storefronts marked the continuing restoration.

"The Loon Feather's up where all that new plywood is. It's kind of the heart of town, everyone's favorite restaurant. As long as Dewey's and the Loon are back, the town is back. The saddest losses are the trees. The street used to be lined with gorgeous old maples."

The boulevards did look shorn and ragged, like a child who'd taken a scissors to her own hair with disastrous results.

"I've never been through anything like this. Were people hurt?"

"Nobody! Amazing, isn't it?" A combination of pride and sadness lit her eyes. "Tough Midwesterners in a resilient little town."

"Small towns do have a special kind of bravery."

"This is a good place," she agreed.

Chase pointed at a vending machine beside the station door. "What can I get you, I'm after bourbon myself, but I doubt I'll find that for a buck in the machine."

"Never know. Dewey's pretty good at having what his customers need." She reached for her striped bag and extracted a wallet. "Anything cold sounds wonderful."

"Got it." He waved off her money. "Sit over there on the grass. I'll be right back."

He leveled his gaze at her when she opened her mouth. For once, she let his directive stand and headed without protest for the slice of freshly sodded lawn at the far end of the driveway. It took him only two minutes to rejoin her with two dripping Coke cans.

"Sorry. Nothing stronger than a couple little ol' Coke colas, but this'll get rid of the dust in your mouth," he said.

Her fingertips grazed his knuckles when she reached for the Coke can, sending a zing through his skin. Was he imagining that her eyes lingered on his hands? Was it wrong that this attraction on his part wouldn't let up? Yes. *Callous bastard.*

"We don't hear 'Coke cola' used that way very often."

"You all say pop up here?"

She nodded. "Pop," she said, at the same instant she snapped open her can with a satisfying hiss and fizz. She tipped it to her lips, and her throat bobbed sweetly while she guzzled like a pirate. The delicate-tough contrast intoxicated him.

"So are a lot of people in town still rebuilding?" he asked to distract himself. "Like David?"

"Oh, right. My boss, the traitor." Her elegant, girly brows puckered in on each other. "A lot of people are still waiting, yeah, because they won't do what David did and hire Connery."

"Because of the gravel pit project you told me about. Rigby says the hostility around here is veiled but real."

"You asked this Rigby an awful lot of questions."

"I sort of had to since the opportunity came up." He fixed his eyes on hers to gauge her reaction. "I came from Memphis to take a job with Connery Construction."

She took several seconds to process his news. "Seriously?"

"He's a friend of my granddaddy's."

"Who? *Duncan* Connery? The man who runs roughshod over rules and regulations?" She certainly didn't veil her animosity much.

"Wait now. How do we know this?"

"From all the times he's ignored opposition to the project. From all the dismissals his lawyers get within hours of complaints and injunctions being filed."

"Could it be there isn't as big a problem as people think there is?"

Her eyes were now clear windows into muted frustration. "Don't say that too loudly around this town."

"I'll keep that in mind." He appeased her with a smile. "Look, I'm not on any side here, but I came to do an honest job and seem to have kicked up a hornets' nest."

For a moment longer the stubborn set to her jaw held firm, but slowly it softened. "Sorry."

"No. It's a good thing to be passionate. Obviously the town has gone through a lot, and I suppose there's not much stomach for being charitable."

"Exactly. They've seen enough land ripped up to last generations. The idea of ripping up more and maybe harming the state park a mile away doesn't sit well with most of us."

Chase sighed inwardly. From the viper pit of Memphis, Tennessee, to the hornets' nest of West Nowhere, Minnesota. He sure knew how to pick 'em.

"Okay, Jill, I think she's passed inspection." Dewey was a tall, muscular man, roughly Chase's own age, with quick eyes, a broad-cheeked face and mustache, and a flat but pleasant Minnesota drawl. "Joey's givin' the bumper a little last shine. Interior still smells like burgers 'n' fries, though. I can put one of those little trees in there if you want."

She wrinkled her nose. "Nah, Dewey, thanks. I'll scrub 'er out and stick a saddle or two in there. That'll fix the smell. What do I owe you?"

"Heck, it only took us fifteen minutes to hook 'er up and pull her free. Thirty-five bucks?"

"That's all? Dewey, don't short-change yourself."

"I'd be outta business if I did that."

"I was honestly expecting more."

Chase listened with interest. Thirty-five dollars was equivalent to nothing. Dewey's tow truck across the driveway was state-of-the-art, and who knew what his costs had been to rebuild. Clearly Dewey took friendship more seriously than profit.

As if he'd heard Chase's thoughts, Dewey impaled him with stern eyes. "And who's this?"

The question hung in the air with neither a welcome nor a threat, just the expectation of an honest answer. Chase stuck out his hand.

"Chase Preston," he said. "Turns out, helping Jill was fortuitous for me, too. How much do you know about motorcycles?"

"Some," Dewey said, cracks forming in his skepticism. "That's a beauty you got there."

"Thank you. When you and Jill are finished, I'd appreciate you taking a look at it."

Completely won over by the request, Dewey shook hands.

Jill held a blue credit card out to him. "Here you go. Doesn't hurt nearly as much as I'd feared."

"We aim to please. C'mon, Jill. Let's get you on your way."

Dewey headed toward his station door, Chase's disappointment flared at the thought of losing his last excuse to stay with Jill.

"Hey," she said, hesitating before following Dewey. "Come to dinner." The words appeared to surprise her as much as they shocked him. "Come home to dinner, I mean. I owe you a very big thank-you, and I can forgive you for consorting with the enemy long enough to hear the motorcycle story you promised."

A zip of happiness shot through him despite the warning in his brain. "That's awful nice of you, but, you know, I could tell you the story right here, and you could go take care of that shoulder."

"What?" She scoffed. "A little ice. A shower before bed. What's a good story without food? There's a catch, though."

"Oh?"

"I live at home, with my mother and my sister. We're a little dysfunctional."

Her lips turned up, but a second of embarrassment flickered in her eyes.

"Now tell me what a stubborn little girl like you is

doin' living at home," he teased. "Not that there's a thing wrong with it."

"For most of the year I'm a dirt-poor student," she said without hesitation. "I usually live at the university, but I'm home to work for the summer. For now that means suffering the indignities that entails."

She's a student?

Oh hell, how young was she?

"And your sister? Same thing?" He asked the question with no small amount of trepidation. How big was this hornets' nest he'd disturbed?

"No, no. She's a physical therapist. The apartment building she lived in was another casualty of the storm, and the new place she's buying isn't done yet. Lucky us, we got her back. We really should be a sitcom."

He very nearly turned her invitation down. At the same time, his curiosity suddenly went wild. Olympic hopeful *and* college student? That made her more than a shallow dreamer and deeper than a stubborn personality.

"Okay," he said, before he could stop the words. "I'd love to come."

For the first time her dazzling smile terrified rather than thrilled him. She followed Dewey, her hips, hugged by the fitted breeches, swaying with unaffected ease—damn feminine and sexy, but strong-strided, purposeful, and as far from flirtatious as a girl could get.

Girl. A younger girl. A college coed. What on God's little green Earth was he thinking?

Chapter Five

CALLING TO LET her mother know there'd be a guest for supper had been tantamount to assembling the Spanish Inquisition—readied for the occasion by Martha Stewart.

"My goodness! Who have we here? Welcome!" Her mother came forward with such effusive familiarity when Chase entered the kitchen, Jill expected her to kiss him outright. Instead, she took his hands and squeezed them as if receiving an old friend.

"Mother," Jill said. "This is Chase Preston. Chase, my mother, Elaina Carpenter."

Chase returned her greeting with equal warmth, surprising Jill with his lack of discomfiture.

"It's nice to meet you, Miz Carpenter. I can't thank you and Jill enough for the invitation."

Elaina raised a pleased and charmed eyebrow at the accent, but got no chance to reply. Dee, never one to be upstaged when a man was involved, pushed forward and placed one elegant-fingered hand on Chase's forearm—a seductive twist on her mother's familiarity.

"Isn't this a lovely coincidence? Seems we get to have our meeting of North and South after all."

Jill hid a sigh. "You've met my sister Deirdre—"

"Good to see you again, Dee." Chase seemed plenty at ease with her, too.

A trace of Dee's signature perfume clung to her, despite the time she'd spent in the barn. All Jill smelled on herself was horse. With little lingering notes of cat dander from the clinic this morning.

"Jill, however did you manage to snag the man with the best accent in town?" she asked.

Jill pinched the bridge of her nose to keep her eyes from rolling. "Why, I set my snare out on County Road Eight and snapped him right up."

Chase chuckled. "Easy as swervin' to miss a pup in the road."

"Sounds like you two have a good dinner story to tell." Elaina gestured like a maître d' to usher them toward the dining room. "Homemade spaghetti. We're all ready for you."

Her mother could make a gourmet meal out of water and napkins, and the homemade spaghetti sauce showcased that skill—to Chase's vocal delight. Dee lived up to her reputation as well, monopolizing each new discussion topic and coaxing the story of Chase's afternoon from him as if Jill had merely been a mule—delivering him to their dining room for Dee's pleasure. Long ago, Jill had accepted the fact her sister didn't like her. She'd never known why there'd been animosity between them ever since their father had left home over ten years earlier, but it was now the normal state of things. Today, however, something was dragging her back toward the dark, early days of jealousy.

Maybe her out-of-character resentment had to do with the throbbing in her shoulder, or maybe the idea that Dee had done better than she with Colin Pitts-Matherson, but if she was honest, it was the fact that her knight, now off his silver-and-red iron steed, sat entranced, seemingly unable to resist the siren call of Deirdre Carpenter.

"I didn't know you could still ride a forty-plus-year-old motorcycle." Dee rested her delicately pointed chin on her manicured hand. "Dewey thought there might be a problem?"

"Actually, he couldn't find anything. We're going with the bad gas theory. He fiddled with her a little and she ran all right on the way here."

In fact, Chase and Dewey had talked motorcycles for nearly twenty minutes the way, Jill supposed, she and David talked horses. Annoyed with her infantile inner pout, she squelched it.

"You promised me the bike's story you know." Her stomach danced a little when he replied with a grin. "I think it's time to find out about its Minnesota connection."

"I'm originally from outside of Lexington. My daddy's family's been there five generations. Poppa—my grandfather—was only in his early fifties when my grandmother died. He left the family farm for a year and a half and found his way north, to a job with a construction crew. He bought a used Triumph and spent a little over a year getting his act together before finally deciding there was no place like home.

"When I recently found myself out of work, Poppa set me up with his old construction friend, handed me the Triumph keys, and pointed me here. About now, though, I'm thinkin' the good Lord just needed me to experience this spaghetti."

"Oh, of course, I'm sure that's exactly what happened." She accepted the compliment in good humor. "What does your family do in Kentucky? What led you away?" Elaina asked.

Something shadowy flickered in Chase's eyes, but his smile held. "I believed it was principle when I was young and self-righteous." He set out the words carefully, as if afraid he'd put them in the wrong order. "I was a little bit of a disappointment to my daddy, since I was the oldest but walked away from the family business. I come from a long line of tobacco farmers, and there are very few left in central Kentucky. Daddy's a holdout, and wants to keep it that way. The life was very good to his family. But I couldn't do it."

"You didn't like farming?" Dee asked.

"I liked the farm. I spent time with Poppa. Helped him more than I did Daddy. But I didn't like the idea of growing tobacco. Still don't."

"You were enlightened for a kid," Jill said quietly.

"My folks didn't call it enlightened. Daddy called it disrespectful. And since the Prestons have been farmers all the way back to Scotland generations ago, he said if he hadn't been there at my very beginnings, he'd think I was the milkman's son."

He caught Jill with a suggestive wiggle of his brows.

"You're letting us ask an awful lot of personal questions," she said.

"Figure I owe y'all a little background since you've taken me in not knowin' if I'm an ant farmer or an ax murderer. And I really do appreciate a good meal, Miz Carpenter. Thank you."

"It's Elaina, please. And cooking for compliments is always worthwhile."

She rested her elbows on her crisp blue tablecloth, clasped her hands beneath her chin, and frowned a little at Jill. She was a quirky parent, most interested in having her daughters look on her as a young, very with-it mompal. She was as organized and pristine of habit as an operating room, but, once in a while, she couldn't quite keep the inner mother fully at bay.

"Are you all right, Jill? You're moving like something hurts."

She was? Jill shot a quelling look at Chase, who seemed primed for an I-told-you-so.

"It's nothing." It wasn't nothing, if the steadily increasing stiffness in her body was any indication. The lack of movement was hurting her. She needed to loosen up again. "Dragon got spooked and jumped around a little. He nailed my shoulder and it's a little stiff."

"You girls and those horses." Her mother had never been a horse person—that love had come from adventurous Julian, their long-gone father. "One of these days something's going to happen. You need to finish vet school and stop this riding nonsense."

A tangle of emotions vied for attention—anger, defiance, defensiveness. Jill almost missed the incredulity on Chase's face.

"You do realize that if I become a vet I'll be a horse vet." She rotated her shoulder and grimaced in spite of herself. "I wasn't riding when this happened."

"I know." Her mother sighed. "I worry less when you're up at the U."

That was a standard lament. Raising an Olympic rider held little appeal to Elaina Carpenter. It wasn't lucrative, which would have been the only reason to consider sports as a job—and it required participation on a mother's part. You didn't need to continually cheer for a veterinarian.

"Sorry, but I have to backtrack here." Chase pinned her with deep blue interest. "You're in vet school? That's pretty damn, sorry, dang impressive."

"She just finished her second year," Elaina said. "I think it's been her calling since she was a kid. Our little animal lover."

"That's me." She rubbed her temples with a grimace.

She did love animals. She liked vet school. She loved to ride. Her life was a smorgasbord of fabulous choices.

"I'm impressed," Chase said, and the truth of his admiration shone in his eyes.

"Speaking of impressed." Dee reentered the conversation. "How did you like Colin today? I admit, I was skeptical when I heard he was coming, but I was super-impressed. He told me I had potential. How's that for surprising?" She gave a self-deprecating chuckle.

Jill was done. She pushed her chair back. "*I* had a crap ride. He told me to work on my hands and my posture."

To her credit, Dee looked honestly surprised. "Wow, I'm sorry."

She wasn't, but she made the sentiment sound good.

"Your sister was too stubborn to tell him about her injury." Chase pushed his chair back, too, and tossed Jill a hairy eyeball warning-teasing kind of look. "She's thinking of admitting it next time she sees him." Her jaw dropped at his audacity, and then he turned his blasted Elvis look on her again. Her stomach did an unexpected flop. "Now, how 'bout I help with the clean-up before I leave you lovely ladies? I have to get on to Northfield and find a motel."

"Chase?" Their mother's attention returned to him, her concern over Jill's day exhausted. "I have an idea for you. We have a small guesthouse out back that's fully set up for visitors and completely private. We'd be happy to have you use it. Sounds like you've had a long trip from Memphis. We'd get a chance to hear more about what you do."

"Oh, I don't think so, Miz Carpenter." For a moment, Chase looked like a dog cornered by bears. "That's awful nice, but I can't impose."

"Don't be silly!" Dee's eyes lit with ulterior motives. "It's a wonderful idea. Trust me, the guesthouse is much, much nicer than any hotel."

"I have no doubt."

To Jill's surprise, Chase found her eyes and asked her what she thought as clearly as if he'd spoken. No way was she going to let on about the flutters in her belly, but her growing bad mood slid magically away.

"It's entirely up to you. I'll tell you the same thing I did earlier, I'd feel much better knowing you didn't have to ride that overgrown weed whacker into the sunset tonight." She bit her lip to keep from laughing at his momentary speechlessness.

"Well then." He recovered. "I guess that settles it."

"Excellent!" Elaina stood. "How about we get you settled, Chase? Then I've got time to get us some dessert."

"I'm happy to clean up." Jill said, and stood too quickly. Pain radiated over her shoulder. She sucked in her breath.

Chase pointed at her. "You should be icing that shoulder."

"There's a bag of peas in the freezer, I'm sure." She fixed Chase with a warning glare. It was one thing to tease, another entirely to hover. He conceded with a reluctant shake of his head. His black bangs flopped into his eyes.

Dee smiled at Jill, but it was strictly for Chase's benefit. "Thanks, sis. Since you're doing fine, Mother and I can show Chase around."

"My mama would threaten me with a hickory switch if I left before chores. Growing up with all boys, even the South was liberated in her world."

"Hickory switch?" Dee formed an obvious sexy O with her perfect lips. "I need to hear more about that. Sounds a little kinky."

Chase hesitated.

"Go." Jill gestured for him to follow.

Sending him off with Dee was preferable to having him fuss like a fishwife over her injury. The last thing Jill heard was his bourbon-rich Kentucky drawl. "I could be mistaken, but you seem a touch dangerous, Miss Dee Carpenter."

"Oh good! You noticed!"

FIFTEEN MINUTES, A tour of his lodgings, and countless come-ons later, Chase watched Jill surreptitiously from the kitchen door. He'd finally ditched Dee, a witty, smart girl with more moves than a foxtrot and seemingly less shame than a streetwalker. How Jill could be such a complete opposite he didn't know, but she tugged at him with an old-soul compatibility and layers that were softer and more complex than his mama's heirloom quilts.

"Hey there, Olympic vet girl," he called at last. "I hear I can find water around here."

She turned a little stiffly from the sink, and her eyes, brightening as she took him in, warmed him with a welcome. She still wore her close-fitting breeches and a pair of bright blue-and-purple socks that rose halfway up her slender calves. She opened a cupboard filled with glasses. "Of course. Help yourself."

He leaned against a counter and crossed his arms. "Confession time. I don't need any water. I came to make sure you're all right."

"Chase, I'm fi-ine." Her voice lilted in a mild warning. "Let me give you a hand with these dishes."

"Don't be ridiculous. You're company."

"I like the company right here fine." That sent her brows momentarily toward her hairline. He picked up a towel and chuckled. "You're a lot different from your sister. I don't think she was much interested in the motorcycle."

"I will guarantee she wasn't interested in it. She's into hot cars and hot guys. Hence the barrage she sent your way."

"I think that hot guy part was a compliment."

"Don't let it go to your head. You're okay, for a rescuer of women who swerve into ditches."

He liked how she teased him and how easy it was to tease her, as if they'd been friends a long time.

"So how *do* two sisters get to be so different?"

"Dee would say it's because she's our mother and I'm our father."

"What if I asked *you*? Are you like your father? Sorry." He backed off at her startled expression. "That was personal."

"No, it's okay. Nobody talks about Dad very often, that's all. Julian Carpenter is almost as unpopular in this house as Duncan Connery. But, to answer your question, I suppose I was a daddy's girl until he left. None of us has seen him in person for three years. He lives in Chile of all places, and climbs in the Andes. I honestly don't know if I'm much like him anymore."

"Sounds like you hope you aren't."

She leaned against the counter beside him, her features tight but unreadable. "Being like him would not be a compliment. Dad left us. No real warning, no apologies. He was a normal high school science teacher and then, one day, poof, he quit. He'd built a dream life for his girls, all the niceties we could want, but turns out it was all a lie, a way to appease his conscience so he could move on once he told us he'd never been truly happy."

"How old were you?"

"Fourteen. Dee was sixteen."

"I'm sorry, Jill, that's really rotten. But with the things you've got planned—I don't see that part of him in you."

"My mother does a little bit. She thinks I have out-of-reach dreams just like he did. The Olympics? The biggest pipe dream of all."

"It's an enormously focused dream, isn't it? Not like a flighty person could achieve it. And you're a vet student. That's a pretty solid goal, too."

"Ah, but what if I were to *quit* vet school?" Her brows shot up in a challenge. "That would prove Mother's point, and Dee would have proof that I'm no more than a tomboy who can pound nails but not polish them."

"Hey. I don't see any tomboys in here."

He drew her eyes to his and held them. Immediately he realized his mistake. The remark had taken on a far more intimate tone than he'd intended, and two rosy spots bloomed on her cheeks.

"Thank you."

She reached for a pan and grimaced.

"Did you put ice on that like you promised?"

The rose color on her cheeks deepened, answering the question.

He didn't say anything, just located the freezer and boldly pulled open the door. It took only seconds to locate a bag of frozen vegetables.

"You're the most hovering worrywart of a man I've ever met," she grumbled.

"Good. Clearly you need someone to hover."

"Of all the gall—I don't either."

He laughed at the peevishness in her voice and wrapped the frozen bag in his towel. He stood behind her and, without permission, pulled the neckline of her polo shirt out with his left hand and slid the makeshift cold pack down her front with his right. Gently he pressed it to her shoulder.

"Tell me where exactly where it should go," he said.

Wordlessly, she encircled his wrist and guided the placement of the veggies. For several seconds they stood, her scent in his nostrils, her chest rising and falling beneath his hand, her fingers light on his skin. When his body threatened to give away his physical reaction, he withdrew, leaving the frozen peas behind.

"Now behave and hold that there." His voice rasped slightly. "I'm taking over the washing."

She ignored him and picked up another towel. "I can hold this on and wash, too. Here—dry if you have to help."

"Would you stop fighting me at every turn? I've washed a lot of dishes in my time. Be a little like your sister. You don't see her in here helping."

"She would if she knew you were here to charm."

Her undertone of animosity was hard to miss—just as it had been that afternoon at the barn.

"You know, Southern men work hard at proving they're the ultimate connoisseurs of a woman's charms." He glanced at her. "Take it from a Southern man. I know which Carpenter sister has the charm."

For several long seconds she remained silent. "Thank you," she said at last. "That was a nice thing to say."

Chapter Six

JILL STARED AS Chase plunged his hands—the same hands that had taken charge of her care moments before—into hot, soapy dishwater. Liquid tremors, still assailing her from his touch, pooled in her stomach and rippled into her core, where they swelled into pleasure that settled in her abdomen and lower between her legs.

Which should have embarrassed her. The truth was, it was more than a reaction to his sex appeal—which he had in abundance. She simply couldn't remember the last time someone had stepped in and fixed things for her with no strings attached. He'd been doing it all afternoon.

He talked, but she did little except listen, spellbound, to his accent. Words rolled into each other, knocking rough edges off the sounds so sentences emerged like polished stones from a lapidary's gem tumbler. It was an indulgence to accept the guilty pleasure of his company.

"Oh, for crying out loud, Jill, you've hijacked our guest."

Dee swept into the room, sucking all the pleasure from it and glowering as if Jill were a scullery maid seducing the prince consort. Chase, up to his forearms in suds, simply pointed an elbow toward another dish towel.

"There's been no hijacking, this was my idea," he said. "How 'bout you grab that towel and help? We're almost done."

Dee's clouded eyes darkened further, but she took the towel as ordered. It didn't take her long, however, to forgive Chase. She chatted with him like a lover, teasing and flirting. Chase allowed her to go on but said little until he pulled the stopper from the drain.

"Done," he announced. "I say we throw in these towels."

Jill didn't expect the weight of his arm as he flung one around her and the other around Dee. It sent a spasm of pain through her shoulder and she groaned. Chase dropped his hold like a dead weight.

"I'm sorry, honey. I'm so sorry."

"It's just tender." Jill looked away.

The pain subsided, and she reached beneath her shirt to adjust the nearly thawed bag of peas.

"That probably needs to be replaced." Chase motioned to Dee. "Could you help by throwing some ice in a plastic bag?"

She didn't say a word, just thinned her lips and opened the freezer. When she'd dug out an actual cold pack, she handed it Chase, not to Jill, but then stood, arms crossed, mouth drawn into a sulky bow. Dee's competitive animosity had begun so many years before that Jill barely remembered being friends with her sister. They had been once upon a time, but except for rare, unexpected occasions, Jill had lost her big sister the same time she'd lost her father.

"Where does it hurt most?" Chase pulled her thoughts back.

Tentatively, Jill rotated her arm and touched the muscle pad below the front of her shoulder. "Here."

Once again, Chase reached from behind and slipped the pack down the front of her shirt. His breath warmed her neck, musk tickled her nostrils, and fresh shivers ensured the cold pack had much more to douse than the heat from the injury.

"Good?" he asked, after adjusting it.

She nodded despite his bossiness.

"Are you two quite finished?" Dee demanded.

Her mother pushed through the café doors that hung between the kitchen and dining rooms in time to see Chase withdraw his hand. "Ahem, do I need to ask what's going on?" Her impish smile proved she could tease with the best of them.

"Chase is playing doctor with your youngest," Dee said. "Of course, not the way I'd have chosen."

She swept around their mother and out of the kitchen. Mortified, Jill would have gladly melted into the floor. "Is there anything in the world my idiot sister won't say?" she mumbled.

Chase stared after Dee wan-faced, as if Bad Bart had stalked out of the saloon after threatening him.

"I'm so sorry. She can be a little over the top."

He shook off whatever had affected him. "Aww, she's

not a problem. She's just quick enough to take a person aback."

Despite his smile, the intimacy they'd momentarily shared had vaporized.

Her mother deftly redirected the subject. "I made some brownies when I got home. And I've got your room ready, Chase. You can move in any time."

"Thank you more than I can say," he replied. "What can I help you with?"

"Nothing." Elaina pointed at the door. "You two go, sit."

By the time Jill's neat-as-whiskey mother and hyper-flirtatious sister managed to stretch dessert into two hours of work stories, questions, and pleasant but innocuous chatter, Chase couldn't figure out how Jill had sprung from their gene pool. While they rambled, Jill sat quietly, more and more of an enigma. She didn't even try to compete for time with her sister, whose life-as-a-physical-therapist stories were admittedly funny, but who owned the room from bamboo flooring to vaulted ceiling. When Elaina finally got up to take away the long-empty dessert dishes and, blessedly, took Dee with her, Chase wanted to grab Jill and run for cover.

Jill rose from her chair, too. She didn't hide a grimace as she straightened, but once she stood in front of him, she grinned. "She has her sights set on you."

"Lucky old me," he said.

"I don't *think* my sister is as loose as she sounds, but I could be wrong."

"She likes digging at you."

"And vice versa, sometimes."

"It's a wonder you ever learned to speak."

Her eyes flashed in fun. "Hey, credit where it's due. Dee can weave a good story—embellished sometimes, but entertaining."

She rotated her shoulder and stretched her head and neck to one side and then the other.

"Does it hurt a lot?"

"No," she said too quickly, and her slight pallor disappeared under a quick flush. "Okay, yeah, it aches. Would it be rude of me to leave you to the guesthouse? It's after eight. I need to shower, make a few lesson plans, and get up early."

"Of course not. You sure you can't sleep late?"

She nodded without complaint. "Gotta be at the clinic at seven-thirty, work until one, and be at the stable by two. Full day."

He frowned in sympathy, grasped one of her hands, and squeezed. "Thank you. I never expected a day like this."

Her fingers tightened in response, and she raised her eyes, rich and hot as expensive coffee, and full of something that jolted his senses like a triple shot of caffeine. "Hey, no. I made it through today because of *you*. I'm only sorry to abandon you to my family."

"I've protected myself against far worse. Time to pack it in for me, too, anyhow."

"Good idea." She tilted her head slightly toward the doorway where Dee was returning.

Ignoring his conscience, he touched a kiss to her cheek in front of her ear.

"You're not leaving?" Dee's eyes, suddenly a bright, scheming hazel, flitted between him and Jill.

"I am. Wednesdays are my long days."

Unexpectedly, Jill's eyes lit, too, but hers were like a wood sprite who'd come upon a good prank to pull. Jill picked up a pen from a table and took Chase's hand. Bending until her hair and breath brushed his palm, she made short, ticklish strokes. Gooseflesh advanced up his forearm.

"My cell phone," she whispered. "In case."

For the first time all day, she rendered him speechless. With a last good-night, she headed for the stairs. Chase stared at the number on his hand, feeling socked in the gut. He had no business with a beautiful woman's phone number inked on his palm. He hadn't come here for anything like this.

And yet, she left a gloomy cloud in the room with her departure. Already planning his escape, he faced Dee.

"I told Mother I'd get you settled," she said. "Come on, I'll show you the idiosyncrasies of your house and turn on the back garden lights. It's the prettiest part of the house at night. Very romantic."

"Garden," "night," and "romantic" formed a combo he wanted no part of.

"Dee. I don't need a tour."

"Okay. C'mon, then. We'll get you tucked in."

Dear God, get him safely to his door, he thought. This

girl was something he simply couldn't figure out. "Lead on," he said, and the sultry look she adopted gave him the sense of tripping—right after Eve into the trunk of the apple tree.

REMOVING HERSELF FROM Chase's immediate presence came nowhere near to removing him from her mind. Every time Jill closed her eyes, his face was there. His kiss beside her ear had been meant in friendship, but it had branded her, clinging to her skin as if it had physical properties.

Her life was in jumbled and knotted disarray. She had no time for herself, much less a man, but for the first time in a very long while, despite a list of what should have been utter disasters, today no longer felt all that disastrous. And it was his doing.

But who was he? She had nothing but a small handful of facts. Born in Kentucky, two brothers, a motorcycle, a lost job in Memphis. That stopped her. A job as what—a volunteer? How vague was that?

Heck, he very well *could* be on the most-wanted list. But she knew he wasn't.

She rubbed her throbbing shoulder absently and looked around her room, decorated in her favorite blues, purples, and teals. All her life it had been a haven filled with books, a parade of small animals and fish, rocks, music and, after he left, postcards from her father, although when he'd never fulfilled his promises to return, she eventually thrown those away. In fact, the only thing of her father's that mattered anymore was the pillow-filled window seat overlooking the yard, one of the many things he'd built before leaving—a window seat for her, an old-fashioned, built-in dressing table and wardrobe for Dee, a fairy tale backyard for his wife—all created to prove that, despite his deceptions, deep down he cared for his family. That had been the biggest lie of all. Julian Carpenter had been a talented doer. He'd just been a lousy stayer.

There were no hamsters or guinea pigs or parakeets in her room anymore. And no dogs. She missed dogs more than she missed Julian—he'd taken "his" with him when he'd left. The inside of Elaina's pristine house had never been friendly to slobbery canines. Besides, a vet student with two jobs had no time for pets.

She dug her teaching calendar out of the striped bag and toted it to the pillows of the window seat. Her private nest welcomed her, and she found a position that cradled her sore shoulder and let her mind drift. Her eyes strayed to her father's elaborate gazebo. What would he think about his daughter's infatuation with a passing motor-cycle man?

He was Julian Carpenter. He'd tell her to follow her bliss.

It had clearly worked for him. He'd been following it for almost eleven years now.

When the backyard lights flicked on, illuminating the flagstone path that led to the gazebo, pond, and two giant weeping willows, Jill pushed aside her father's memory and searched for movement. To the left stood the small, blue-

and-white guesthouse Julian had bought from a friend, over Elaina's vehement protests, but the neat little three-room cottage he'd created had been well-used over the years.

Chase's appearance didn't surprise Jill, but Dee's did. They stopped at the door and stood for a long time, Chase against the frame with his legs casually crossed at the ankles, Dee animated and gesturing. Jill's heart went out to him. Dee could talk the paint off a wall, and he was likely stuck. After ten minutes, however, she actually considered he might need rescuing.

Before she could gather herself to leave, however, she caught Dee tugging on Chase's arm and leading him toward the garden. Jill frowned. When they reached the largest willow, Dee parted the cascading branches, and, to Jill's dismay, Chase ducked through the makeshift doorway. He stood still while Dee climbed into the white-painted tire swing she and Jill had loved since childhood. His arms remained crossed.

Jill begged herself to turn away, but growing dread held her sickly fascinated. After moments, Dee stopped swinging, extracted herself from the tire, and stepped purposefully to Chase. Slowly, she slid her hands up his chest and clasped them behind his neck.

Her nose flattened to the glass, nausea roiled, and she waited for the train wreck. It came like clockwork in the form of a deliberate kiss. When Chase lifted his arms, Jill spun away at last. She pulled her calendar hard to her chest to hold in the pain and, for a few seconds, closed her eyes and gulped air as she had when Dragon had slammed into her shoulder. Then, as suddenly as it had formed, the constriction in her chest burst, and fiery anger engulfed the pain.

"You are an idiot!" she chastised herself, and slammed a fist so hard into the pillows she hit the wood beneath them. "'Take it from a Southern man,' he says."

She stood and paced the room, her mind working furiously at damage control. She had no claim to Chase Preston. He'd kissed her cheek. He'd kissed her sister, too. Why not? Dee had as much right to flirt with him as Jill did.

There was no reason to be upset. No reason, for God's sake, to be jealous.

But she was. She placed her fingers against the spot near her ear he'd kissed and fought a mortifying burn behind her eyes. She never cried. What on Earth was worth crying about here?

Banishing tears, Jill nonetheless let the day's disasters crash in on her. She could still feel Chase's gentle ministrations in the kitchen, but the memory made her stomach hurt.

After a shower failed to soothe either the deep ache in her muscle or the hollow one in her belly, she forced herself to check the now-empty yard and crawl into bed. But there was no sleep to be found. She lay awake in a sore, stiff lump. Angry. Hurt. As rigid as the tree under which Chase and Dee had kissed.

DEE ALREADY SAT at the kitchen table the next morning when Jill arrived, aching and sleep-deprived. Her sister looked a model of elegance, even in the plain navy slacks and white polo shirt of her clinic uniform. With coffee mug in hand, she lifted perfectly plucked brows casually, like the cool girl preparing her abuse of the school geek. Jill ignored her, but standing at the toaster in stocking feet, worn Levi's, and an old chambray shirt hanging open over a yellow tank top, she felt like rumpled laundry.

"Good morning." Dee's fake cheerfulness drifted like a toxic cloud across the room. "How's that shoulder after playing doctor with your motorcycle man yesterday?"

Jill caught the fast, ugly retort on her tongue before it escaped. The poorly concealed smugness in Dee's eyes proved she would love to see Jill blow. "Heck," she said instead. "You should know that was nothing. Being nice is what he's good at, Dee. Right? He was pretty nice to you in the yard last night."

Dee's smile vanished. "Excuse me?"

Jill went back to her toast. "It's a private window and a public backyard. You should think about being a little more discreet."

The room instantly went cold and silent.

"Good morning, ladies."

Both of them jumped. Chase leaned against the kitchen jamb wearing jeans that hugged his hips and a Kentucky Wildcats T-shirt that fit a little too well. Erratic beats hammered inside Jill's chest over his freshly shaven skin and water-slicked hair. She dragged her gaze from him, annoyed at her mutinous hormones for still finding his shoulders so broad in the bright blue T-shirt, and his thighs so hard beneath the denim.

"I thought you'd be sleeping late." Dee's voice held a surprising dusting of frost.

"I figure I'd best be on my way. I have an interview at nine and I didn't want to miss saying good-bye."

Jill reached into the cupboard for a juice glass. Without warning he stood behind her.

"How's the shoulder?"

Her stomach flip-flopped at the subtle dash of spice emanating from his skin.

"Just peachy." She stepped away from him and reached for the refrigerator door. "OJ?"

"Sure." He took the container she proffered, puzzlement clouding his eyes.

She got him a glass and picked up her uneaten piece of toast.

"I hate to say it, but I'm running late. I'll eat this on the way." She forced herself to smile. She really wasn't angry. Really. But if she didn't have time for a man in general, she definitely didn't have time for a player. "Thanks again for everything. Good luck."

She stopped in the hall to pull on her paddock boots. Chase followed and touched her arm as she straightened and reached for the garage door. His eyes held familiar concern.

"Hey. Are you really okay?"

"Chase." She met his eyes, hers resolute. "I'm fine. So from this moment on you're off the clock. You can stop worrying."

CHASE STARED AT the back door for long seconds after it closed behind Jill's swinging ponytail. Her coolness thoroughly bewildered him in the wake of their warm friendship. Dee smiled a little too knowingly.

"What am I missing?" he asked.

"I think she's a little miffed at us." She gave her coffee mug a satisfied smirk. "She has a window that looks out onto the backyard."

A spasm of chagrin twisted Chase's gut. "What? Oh, that's great. And I suppose now she thinks we . . ." He glanced toward the door.

Dee stepped in front of him and placed a hand on his chest. "Don't feel sorry for her. She'll milk this for sympathy and then be over it. Are you sure you haven't changed your mind?"

He removed her hand, not particularly gently, annoyance sparking into anger.

"You're really somethin'. You almost caught me off guard last night, and that was my fault. I don't think you're really this kind of girl, Dee, and I'm giving you the benefit of the doubt because we sure don't know each other. But you listen up close. I'm not some stray ol' pup that responds to treats and games."

Chilliness infiltrated her eyes, and she strode from the room without another word. Chase sank into a chair. Moments ago his day had actually held potential. Now, between the two feuding sisters, he'd just lost half the "friends" he'd made in Minnesota.

He wished Dee's assessment of Jill's behavior was

wrong, but he knew it wasn't. Dee was at least partially right. Jill would be better off if he walked away—if he ignored the number she'd written on his hand. But he'd bragged that Dee had no effect on him—and she absolutely did not. But she'd come on to him like a stampede last night, and depending on what Jill had or hadn't seen . . . No. He knew exactly what she'd seen, and she now thought he was a class-A jerk.

He rubbed his temples. He'd been away from Memphis only five days and already his not-so-brilliant plan was falling apart. He shouldn't have listened to his brother. He should have fought through the pain and stayed at the clinic to pull his weight.

The buzz from his cell phone filtered through his back pocket to his backside, jolting his black musings. He fished the phone free to find Brody's name lighting up the screen. The coincidental timing of his brother's call made him stare until realization cracked across his emotions like a bullwhip.

He didn't want to answer. He didn't want to return to the Marian-Lee Clinic even over the phone. In fact, he didn't ever want to go back—not to the crack babies, the bullet wounds, and the strung-out punks. Not to Clara and life without Tiana.

"Oh God."

The words slipped into the empty room, but they weren't a prayer. They were a curse or an accusation—or maybe both.

The phone stopped ringing. That made him a coward as well as a runaway. He couldn't be sure his brother hadn't had an important question, but more likely Brody was simply checking up. Chase set the phone on the table with no intention of calling him back.

The block he'd resolutely put on his memory the past week evaporated, and the exposed pain spilled out so fresh it could have been dealt that instant.

Clara Washington, strong and proud-featured, had earned every one of her coffee-brown crow's-feet with worry and hard work at far too young an age. But her eyes knew laughter as well as hardship, and more often than not it was laughing eyes she turned on Chase. Laughing when he promised she would outlive him, and when he proposed marriage for the tenth time and she told him he'd be wise not to get fresh with an experienced older woman. Clara, God help him, was his favorite.

Except for Tiana.

Chase had brought the girl, whimpering, sickly, and eight weeks early, into the world. His first delivery after opening the clinic. Although the child's heroin-addicted mother hadn't survived, Tiana's grandmother, Clara, had nurtured the miracle baby into a vibrant, talkative nine-year-old.

Who was dead.

His own ego had cost that precious, spirited child her life.

At the Carpenters' safe, pleasant kitchen table bedecked with sunny daisies, his phone announced a new voice message with a bright electronic burble. Chase fit the heels of his hands into the hollows of his eyes, pressing until lights danced behind the lids. For three days he'd convinced himself these memories could be controlled—that he'd been able to leave them in Memphis. Now, like a shipwrecked man finally washed ashore only to find his haven devoid of any help, Chase knew he controlled nothing.

He picked up the phone and slipped it into his pocket.

Chapter Seven

LESS THAN AN HOUR later, Chase's world had gone from black to green. Every shade of it, painted on waving grasses, surrounded hills as far as he could see. He searched the empty landscape and bit back a curse with monumental effort. His mind assured him it wasn't possible to get lost three miles from a town—despite it being a pinpoint on a map—but his mind told him something different.

The Triumph had started acting up again, now wheezing like an emphysema patient, which worried him considerably more than being lost did. He craned his neck to find anything familiar in the sea of wild grass and maze of gravel roads from which he couldn't seem to find an exit. Twice he'd hit the same dead end—a ten-foot chainlink fence marking someone's very private property.

He stared at his grandfather's scrawled directions on

the piece of paper in his hand as if this time they would yield results. Sighing, he jammed the useless note into his jacket pocket and lowered his visor. Planting a pivot foot, he throttled up slightly to turn. The Triumph gave an ugly moan and died halfway around the arc. Worry blinked awake in his gut. He straightened the bike and stomped the starter. The engine mocked him with a whirr. He tried twice more and got the same.

"No." He groaned aloud.

He jabbed down the kickstand, dismounted, and removed his helmet. Kneeling with dread, he checked the spark plugs and leads that seemed unchanged from when they'd been tightened at the station yesterday. One more attempt to start the Triumph failed yet again.

He stood beside it, drove his fingers through his hair, and kicked at the road, spraying dirt and tiny stones at the Bonne's engine. Helplessly, he turned in a circle. How the hell did he get out of this mess and get to his interview in an hour and fifteen minutes? His mind scrambled for a solution.

The only immediate answer was to call Duncan Connery and get the meeting postponed. He dug his phone out of an inner jacket pocket and flicked it on. All that showed up where his signal bars should have been was the dread no-service circle-with-a-line-through-it.

"You have got to be kidding me!" he shouted at nobody.

He considered removing the bike's engine covers right there on the dirt road. He knew his way around the inside of the Bonne. But the engine was too hot.

He lowered himself to the hillside. *Give her a chance to cool down. She'll start; she will.*

After fifteen minutes, Chase sent the most positive vibes he could muster to his motorcycle and swung one leg over the seat. Six stomps later he leaned onto the handlebars and buried his head in his arms. A fried coil, a burnt-out cylinder ring—there were a number of potential culprits. But he didn't want to start thinking about what it would take to find parts for his granddaddy's baby. They would not simply be lying around.

With no choice but to hike, Chase pushed the bike into the grass, slung his duffel bag over one shoulder, and set off, keeping his mind blank but his eye on his cell phone. It wasn't until he'd gone at least a mile that he came to a crossroads—two gravel lines intersecting the grass—and his phone screen awarded him two bars of service. Stopping in his tracks before he could lose them, he found Connery's phone number in his contacts list. Five minutes later, he'd explained his situation to Connery's secretary and made arrangements to call as soon as he knew when he'd arrive. He hung up, slightly relieved, although he had no way to get himself the twelve miles to Northfield.

But now what? He couldn't even get hold of Dewey Mitchell at the service station—he had no wireless connection to look up Mitchell's number.

"Nice cluster, Preston," he said out loud.

It was almost funny. He, a man of a thousand contacts in Memphis, knew no one here. He trudged forward three steps, then stopped again.

Except he did know someone.

His heart raced as he looked at his palm, almost able to feel the gentle scratching from her pen. He'd washed away the ink, but not before entering that number in his phone. Of course, based on events this morning she might not answer at all, but he dialed anyway.

"Hello?" Her voice flowed through the phone, and he sent up a prayer of thanks.

"Jill? It's Chase."

She replied with dead silence.

"Preston?" he added.

"As if I could forget."

He tried to ignore the frost on her words. "I'm real sorry to call you, but I seem to have run into a little trouble, and I'm hoping you'll give me Dewey Mitchell's number."

"Oh dear. What happened?" For an instant the warmth he remembered returned.

He could almost, maybe, hear the line thaw as he related his predicament and explained the black hole he'd fallen into.

"I'll call Dewey," she said simply. "Hang tight, I think I can tell him right where you are." She hung up with nothing more.

Sure enough, it took only fifteen minutes before he heard a motor. He stood, amazed, stomped dust off his boots, and waited. It nearly knocked him on his rear when a metallic-tan Suburban led a dusty cloud tail straight toward him. Although he'd never seen it on all four tires, he'd have known The Creature anywhere.

"Hello." She stopped beside him and leaned out the window.

"Well, pat my head and call me surprised."

He could tell it took some effort for her not to smile. "Yeah, we seem to have perpetually bad timing. Dewey says he's sorry. He's out on another delivery. I couldn't make myself leave you stranded. We'll meet him at the station."

"That was awful nice of you. I'm sorry you had to leave work, though. I'd have been fine."

A tiny shrug lifted her good shoulder. "I owe you a couple. C'mon. Get in. Show me where the motorcycle is so I can give Dewey exact directions."

The ride was silent, slightly strained. When they reached the Triumph, Chase happily left the confines of The Creature. He tried to start the bike again, but it was unquestionably dead.

"And you made me get on that thing." Jill shook her head.

"She had me fooled. I didn't think there was anything wrong," he admitted, angry with himself and annoyed enough with Jill that he kept his eyes from straying to hers. "I'm sorry I endangered you."

"Hey. I was kidding."

At that he met her eyes. Her stance had softened, but her brown eyes still kept him at a distance. His calm finally gave out.

"You wanna tell me how I'm supposed to know this morning *what* you're thinking? We were doing fine last night. This morning I'm in an igloo doghouse. You kidding about that, too?"

"I think you maybe got the wrong idea about . . . things yesterday."

"Things? What things?" He waited for her a second and changed his mind in a rush of irritation. He didn't have the time or the desire to play games with a girl he barely knew. "No, forget that. I know exactly why your fur is all ruffled, and I refuse to pussyfoot around you."

Her spine stiffened, and she made no effort to hide an angry frown. "You don't owe me any explanations."

"You're right, I don't owe you anything." The words obviously confounded her. "But I do respect you, and I'm selfish enough to want your respect in return. You saw your sister kiss me last night. I'm sorry you did."

"I'm sure you are." She crossed her arms stubbornly in front of her chest. Despite *looking* like a teddy bear in a snit, somehow he knew not to take her anger lightly.

"The kiss would have ended the same way regardless. About two seconds after she tried starting it."

"Chase, this is your business. It doesn't have anything to do with me."

"But I shot off my mouth about Southern men. And that's what's at the core of this. Admit it."

For the first time she looked away. He tugged gently on her good shoulder to make her look back.

"I don't like excuses," he said. "I'm a big boy, and I should have known what Dee planned to all along, but I didn't believe it until it happened."

The hardness eased from Jill's features, and a knot in Chase's gut loosened.

"She's a piece of work, my sister."

"Regardless, it was no kind of kiss. Trust me, after last night Dee won't be giving any stirring eulogies at my funeral."

Jill's eyes closed in acceptance and reopened, warmed to gentleness by soft flecks of golden light. Her sheepish smile sent a flush coursing through his body, as unexpected and unnerving as a chill during a fever.

"I'm sorry. My day had gone so badly." Her voice, soft in contrition, only fanned the heat in his body. "When I believed Dee had managed to do what she does best, make a fool of me and get her hooks into a handsome guy, I chose to believe my bad luck was holding and you were actually a jerk."

"I'm a jerk often enough." He started to reach for her arm, started to make a joke about her handsome guy line, but he decided touching or teasing her was a bad idea this soon. He stuffed his hands in his pockets. "So what now? Where are we really?"

"At one time this was going to be a housing development." Her eyes roamed the surroundings, and the slight breeze sifted through her ponytail. "The paths winding through here were planned as residential streets. But the company funding the quarry project bought up all the land within the past year, put up the fencing, and is ready to make all of this into access roads. You're at the heart of the controversy, mister."

"That explains why my directions were wrong. They're old. How'd you know where I was?"

"We ride here," she said. "It's a great place to take the horses out and let them gallop. If it's any consolation, you were headed in exactly the right direction. At a brisk walk, you'd have made civilization in an hour."

"How long to walk to Northfield?" He grimaced.

"Oh! Your interview." She looked at her watch.

"Postponed until I can get there."

"Maybe it's for the best. Fate keeping you out of the hands of the enemy."

He glared at her despite the teasing quirk of her lips. She held up her hands. "Kidding. Kidding. Let's go. We'll find a way to get you to Northfield."

They headed back to the intersection where Jill had found him. She slowed and stopped on the side of the road.

"If you're willing to take two minutes, I'll show you something."

"What's two minutes out of an epic adventure?" He sighed.

Jill led him across the intersection from The Creature and up a rise in the road. "Look."

Spread beyond the Suburban was the section of land Chase had just escaped. He could see dark impressions slicing and curving through the rolling terrain that marked the roads he'd been winding through. The view left him stunned.

"No wonder I felt like a trapped rat."

"Yeah. Now turn around."

He obeyed. A quarter of a mile away lay an oasis of trees flanked by more flawless fields. A spot of glistening water lay in the middle of a fenced pasture. Dotted through the idyllic setting were buildings, including a house and barn.

"Nice."

"A little local color for you. In truth, *this* is the heart of the quarry fight. That farm belongs to a man named Robert McCormick. He owns six hundred and forty acres, and most of them are in the middle of the future quarry. But he's refusing to sell. He's lived here all his life and is quite elderly. People who know him say he's pretty much a loner nowadays, and there are rumors he's run the quarry people and the Connery people off at gunpoint. I don't know if that's true."

"Have you ever met him?" They returned to the corner of the intersection.

"Weird, but no. He's only a crotchety hermit to me. But, tell you what. He's my hero."

"I wonder why that doesn't surprise me in the least."

For the first time in hours—no, in *ever*—he wanted to laugh at the situation. How could he not? He'd broken down in a crazy little town that was in a crazy fight, and now there was a crazy hermit farmer man, and a girl he was crazy to care about. Life was freakin' hilarious.

"I like the troublemakers." Her brows rose along with the corners of her mouth.

"Very funny."

Jill started toward her truck, but Chase put his arm out to stop her.

"Hold on, listen. What's that?"

A low rumble from the direction of the stashed Triumph grew in volume until its source came suddenly into view—a forest-green Lincoln Navigator bouncing over washboard ridges a little too fast for Chase's liking.

Jill squinted. "I'm not sure. Regardless, they'll be turning left to the main road. We'll just wait for them to pass."

The Navigator gunned closer. Jill waved at the sole occupant, but the man gave no indication he saw her. His jaw worked furiously into the phone he held to his ear, and he headed for their corner with careless speed.

"Watch out!"

Chase literally stepped in front of Jill seconds before the driver spun his powerful SUV around the corner and missed them by inches. The driver sped on, clueless, his Lincoln spewing pebbles sideways like bullets. One struck Chase's lower leg, another must have stung Jill.

"Hey!" she hollered, and rubbed furiously at her thigh.

Chase coughed on swirling dust. "Are you all right?"

Anger sparked from her eyes, but she didn't seem to be in pain.

"I'm fine. You wanna see a jerk? There goes one right there."

The Lincoln finally had to slow as the uneven road bed ascended. Pictures of Tiana flashed into his brain, and Chase's blood surged with rage. He'd had it to the red behind his eyeballs with drive-bys. He gauged the distance to the Navigator and grabbed a fist-sized rock.

"Wait. Chase, what are you thinking?"

"I'll be right back."

He sprinted after the vehicle, closed the twenty-foot gap in seconds, and hollered out. The fortyish-year-old man still held a phone to his ear, and Chase's next two shouts went unheeded. In desperation, he halted, took minimal aim, and pitched his rock. It flew squarely into the vehicle's green door. The vehicle's nose dove. The driver's elbow, balanced on the open window frame, shot up, and the phone disappeared from his hand.

"I'd get out if I were you," Chase ordered, gasping.

The man grabbed his phone, growled something unintelligible into it, and tossed it to the side. The third of his body visible looked like an athlete's. His brown hair was blown into disarray, and when he peeled off an enormous pair of sunglasses, dark eyebrows formed a single angry line across a harshly handsome brow. He exploded from the car, his nostrils flaring. Nevertheless, Chase faced him squarely.

"You'd better have a damn good reason for that stunt, man."

Chase took a step forward. "I think it's you who has the explaining to do, since you were six inches from having hit-and-run charges leveled at you."

"What the hell are you talking about?"

"About you taking that corner back there at about thirty-five miles an hour, when the speed limit should be fifteen. My friend and I were nearly hit."

"I never saw you. You must have had time to move before I reached you."

"Not good enough."

The man's fists flexed several times, and a pulse throbbed visibly at the open collar of his white dress shirt. His creased green trousers matched the hue of the Navigator. "What are you doing here anyway? This is private property."

Jill reached them, her face mirroring Chase's anger. He couldn't afford to fold this hand no matter how weak it was, so he shot Jill a look pleading with her to play along, stilled his breathing with effort, and bluffed for all he was worth.

"That's right. And I know as well as you do that Robert McCormick has no love of dickering. We're on our way there, and I don't want to be the one to tell him you've been trespassing."

"You punk. You don't know Robert McCormick."

Chase stuffed shaking hands into his back pockets. If this ruse worked he wouldn't believe the luck until his dying day. "Is that so? Shall we go on ahead and ask him?" The man said nothing. "This is Jill Carpenter, by the way." Chase filled the silence. "At the very least the lady deserves an apology."

He glared a moment longer, then stiffly inclined his head. "My apologies, Miss Carpenter."

He climbed back into the Lincoln and yanked the door closed. Chase stifled a groan. He'd been too angry and focused on the man to notice the stylized house-and-tree logo he'd seen at the stable yesterday. Over the words "Connery Construction" was a fresh two-inch dent and a feather pattern of scratches.

"I want your name and address," the driver growled.

"Make an appointment with Mr. McCormick. He'll be glad to give them to you."

A final tense glaring match glued them in place for several more long seconds. "I'll find out who you are, I promise you that," the man said.

"Sooner than you think," Chase replied under his breath.

When the Navigator had backed around and disappeared, Jill stared after it, rubbing her shoulder absently.

"Wow," she said. "My hero again. Thanks for saving my honor, but that was rash."

"Really. You noticed." The adrenaline rushed from his system. He wanted to sink into the grass and simply let it grow over him. "He was an ass, but I didn't do myself any favors."

"I saw the logo. I'm sorry. I'd laugh, but I know it isn't funny."

"Hell, he could be Duncan Connery for all I know." The thought sent Chase's stomach into a sick roil.

"Hey, are *you* all right?"

"Not so much. I shot myself in the foot. It doesn't feel all that good."

"You actually did a nice thing, you know." Her fingers on his upper arm soothed, as did her eyes, peering at him in concern. "You can make this right. I'm sure of it."

He should tell her. Tell her how bullies and creeps who drove by with weapons far stronger than this guy's rude words made up his world. But then he'd have to tell her how minor throwing a rock was in the list of his transgressions.

With a deep breath and a redirect, he dismissed her thanks. "How's that shoulder? You didn't hit it again, did you?"

"It didn't feel all that great running up here, but I'm fine. Let's get you out of here."

"Maybe I will cancel that appointment."

"What, and let the jerks of the world win? I say go find him and push him down."

He wanted to tell her the jerks of the world almost always won. Instead, he forced a smile that felt anything but cheerful. "He was a big ol' guy. What if he pushes me down?"

She winked, as blind to his bluff as the Connery man had been. "I'll hold your coat for the fight."

Chapter Eight

CHASE PARKED THE CREATURE in an oversized space at the drab industrial park and shut off the engine. For all Jill's denigration of it, the Suburban drove well, but he would have been grateful had it driven like an Asian elephant. At Jill's insistence he'd dropped her at the clinic and taken her truck to his appointment. The only downside to her kindness was that now he had to return to Kennison Falls, something he hadn't planned on doing. Find a hotel and stay the heck away from the little town that revved up his volatile emotions—*that* had been his plan.

Instead of being one more nondescript cement-block structure, the brick-and-glass home of Connery Construction blossomed like a rose in the industrial desert. A luxuriant lawn lapped up against the building like a cool green pond. A carved wooden sign, flanked by profusely blooming wild rosebushes, bore the parent version of the Connery house-and-tree logo. Chase winced when he passed it.

The company's lobby was to interior design what the exterior had been to landscape architecture, dominated by forest green blended with artsy pastels, pale oak, and potted plants. A young receptionist greeted him with practiced friendliness.

"May I help you?"

He nodded. "I'm Chase Preston. I called earlier to change my appointment with Duncan Connery."

She lifted a phone receiver. Chase rubbed his damp palms down the sides of jeans until she looked at him.

"Mr. Connery had to leave for a short while but he's due back any second and is expecting you. You're welcome to wait in his office. His secretary at the end of the hall will get you settled."

He'd been out. With a sinking heart, Chase guessed exactly where the man had been.

"I appreciate it," he lied.

Compared to the rest of the building, Duncan Connery's office was unpretentious and gave away nothing about the man himself. By the time a cheerful voice hailed him, Chase was so wound up he jumped.

"Mr. Preston! My apologies for keeping you waiting."

Chase stood and sagged with relief when he met the jovial and completely unfamiliar eyes of Duncan Connery. Tall, distinguished, and fit, he cut a youthful figure for a man approaching sixty-five. Chase extended his hand, hoping it didn't telegraph his tremble of relief.

"I'm the one who was late. Thank you for rearranging your schedule."

"No trouble I hope."

"Yes sir, with a motorcycle. I'm afraid this one's past her prime by a fair amount."

"Wait." Connery's smile widened. "Not a Triumph? A '75 Bonneville 750?"

"Yes, sir."

"You mean to tell me it's still running?"

"Actually, at the moment no."

"By God, he did it, didn't he?" Connery circled to his desk chair and motioned for Chase to sit again. "I remember thinking when your grandfather bought that old bike it was a foolish thing for a fifty-plus-year-old man to do. We all teased him viciously. Apparently, it's on its way to outlasting him, just as he vowed it would."

Connery's easy conversation soothed Chase into relaxing. "When I was a kid he let me help tinker with the engine, but the rest of the family thought, like you did, it was an impractical toy."

"I'm close enough to retirement now to admit I was dead wrong about judging 'old men' and their toys. If it keeps you young I'm all for it."

"I don't think anyone knows for sure what keeps Delaney Preston young," Chase said.

"So he's doing all right, your grandfather?" Connery leaned back in his chair.

"He is."

"What is he, seventy-seven or -eight now?"

"Seventy-eight, yes, sir."

"He was one of the best foremen my father and I ever had. If he runs his farm anything like he ran the crews, he has a hell of a good operation."

"He still oversees everything with a sure hand."

Duncan Connery crooked his eyebrows into bushy question marks. "Which brings us to you, the young Mr. Preston. Delaney tells me I can expect no less a performance from his grandson."

Inwardly Chase squirmed. "You must have learned to take my granddaddy's superlatives with a grain of salt."

Instinct told him this was a fair-minded man who deserved to know about the rock.

"What brings you north, Chase?"

At least he'd practiced this answer. "Looking for a change. I lost a good friend in Memphis, and it was painful to stay."

"I'm sorry to hear that." Connery contemplated him a moment. "Like I told Delaney, we always need good men. And we have endless work. We can't keep up with all the rebuilding jobs since a pretty severe storm hit last summer."

"I heard about that," Chase acknowledged.

"We also have a big new project in the works. I'll be glad to take you aboard, but, obviously, you'll have to start at the bottom on a crew. It won't be as easy there as it is with me. Nobody swinging a hammer these days remembers your grandfather."

"Bottom of the ladder is fine with me."

"Excellent! Let's get you over to personnel—"

"Hang on, Mr. Connery. Before we go that far, there's

something I have to tell you." He leaned toward the man's desk, rubbing his palms on his thighs again, like a kid in the principal's office. "You deserve to hear this from me."

A scuffle of feet and exchanged greetings in the hall made Connery raise his hand. "Hey, Jim, c'mon in here! Excuse me, Chase, I'll hear you out, but I want you to meet your likely boss as long as he's making a rare trip to his office."

Connery stood as his man entered the office, and Chase's luck ran out. The angry driver had added a green sports coat bearing the now-infamous logo on its breast pocket, but his thick brows and furious eyes hadn't changed.

"This is Jim Krieger, the foreman on that new project I mentioned," Connery said. "Jim, this is Chase Preston. You'd remember his grandfather Delaney, I think."

Chase and Krieger dropped their hands simultaneously, and bewilderment grew on Connery's face at the grim stare-down.

Krieger loosened a clenched jaw muscle. "I wonder if Delaney realizes his grandson belongs with the Twins—as a pitcher." He barely controlled his envenomed words.

Connery's posture stiffened. "This is the *boy* you encountered today?"

Krieger's meager control evaporated. "Ask him how the hell his friend McCormick is." His fingers curled palmward, transforming large, strong hands into knuckled weapons. "You son of a bitch. What game are you playing?"

"Hold on." Chase's glare didn't waver. "Before I let the

insult to my mother pass, I wonder if your boss knows how you nearly got my friend and me seriously injured."

"You lying punk. I refuse to be responsible if you haven't got sense enough to get out of the road when a car is coming."

Chase's remorse vanished along with words of contrition he'd been ready to offer.

"All right, Jim." Connery looked at Chase. "So you admit throwing the rock?"

"Yes, that's what I was about to tell you. And I'm sorry it happened, but right this minute I can't honestly say it wouldn't happen again. Your man Krieger here had a phone glued to his ear, took a gravel corner at least twice as fast as was safe, and wasn't about to stop even though his window was completely rolled down and I called to him three times."

"This is serious, Chase." Connery's features hardened into solemn lines.

"Yes it is. I'm glad to say neither the young lady involved nor I was hurt."

"Don't even consider hiring this lying asshole." Krieger spat the words.

"Enough." Connery stretched an arm in front of his foreman as if to forestall an attack. "We're going to sort this out, right now. I'd like to know exactly what happened."

Chase squared his shoulders. "I can tell you in less than sixty seconds. When he took that corner he didn't use a signal, we had no idea he was turning at us, and he missed us by six inches." Chase narrowed his eyes. "When he didn't stop, I got his attention the only way I could. I had to force an apology from him. I have a hard time respecting that."

Krieger's eyes bulged as his arrogantly handsome face went scarlet. "You've got the balls to talk about respect? Tell me what you plan to do about the vehicle you damaged."

Chase barely had to consider his reply. "Right this moment I plan to ignore it and walk away." He straightened his shoulders. "Mr. Connery, I believe I know why my grandfather calls you friend, and I regret this for his sake. I apologize for damaging the truck. Personally, I think we're even, but I'll get you my contact information as soon as I have it."

"Now, hang on. I don't know yet about the truck, but I do know it's a mistake for you to leave."

"No doubt you're more than right. I didn't inherit a lot of my granddaddy's cool head, but, unfortunately, the good Lord gave me double of his stubbornness. This is a matter of principle, Mr. Connery. I appreciate what you were willing to do as a favor." He started to turn.

"No." Connery stepped from behind his desk. "I know you aren't a kid, but I won't willingly allow you leave. If I sound like a dictator it's because I told Delaney I would keep an eye on you. As long as there's work for you here, you should take it. We can discuss whether any compensation is due for the truck. You need to stay put or we'll both have your grandfather to answer to."

Despite the truth in Connery's words, Chase stood poised to leave. He did not have to stay no matter what the man had promised Poppa. He did not have to stay and work for an ass like Krieger, and every impulse told him to leave. But the truth was, some of this was on him, too. If he hadn't thrown the damn rock, he wouldn't be in this position at all. Besides, Duncan Connery wasn't the only one who'd promised Poppa that Chase would stay put in Minnesota and not run headlong into the unknown.

He released an audible breath.

"I'll stay under one condition. I will not work for him. Put me on the job you're taking at Bridge Creek stables."

"What the fuck, Duncan?" Krieger bellowed his indignation. "Are you going to let this kid dictate your business to you? He's a vandal and a liar. I swear to God, he looked me straight in the eye and told me he was a friend of Robert McCormick's. Challenged me to walk with him to the old man's goddamn front door. We don't want someone who can lie that easily."

Krieger's stare tore into Chase like a lightning bolt.

"If you use that language around women and elderly folk, I'm glad I kept you away from McCormick this one time, even if I had to lie to do it. It doesn't take much imagination to swear at me. A lot less than to apologize when you're in the wrong."

"Enough," Connery said. "Chase, how do you know about the Bridge Creek project?"

"I happened to meet your man Jeff Rigby there yesterday. I figure I could work with him fine."

"Then that's what we'll do. When we're done here, you'll go on down to personnel and take care of the paperwork. I'll have Jeff get in touch when it's time to start. He's looking at next week, is that soon enough?"

"Yes, sir."

"You're making a monumental mistake." Krieger's anger intensified. "I haven't worked for you thirty-five years to have my reputation laid low by a hotheaded punk who was trespassing where he doesn't belong."

"Who said anything about your reputation? Hiring Chase has nothing to do with you, Jim. I owe loyalty to a lot of people."

"It's your company," Krieger said tightly. "I'm just the guy you pay to keep things running. But I am not responsible for Sandy-fucking-Koufax here. Don't ask me to bail you out of the messes he makes."

He took his turn to try and leave, but Connery stopped him, too.

"Stick around. We have a few things to discuss. Chase? My secretary will take you on to personnel. If you don't hear from Jeff in a day or two call me. And come back here after the first week. We'll discuss how this is working for you."

"Yes, sir. I can do that."

Chase brushed past Krieger, who didn't move a quarter of an inch to let him pass easily.

"And Chase?" Connery added. "No more rocks."

He paused a moment, too riled to make a reply that wouldn't get him in deeper. He nodded. "Let me know about the truck."

"I KNOW IT seems impossible, Rebecca, but try it once more. Let the horse push you out of the saddle to post."

Jill's voice remained cheerful after nearly an hour, but Chase could see small chinks in her armor of patience. The bitter-faced teenager astride a rangy gray gelding named Roy made no attempt to follow directions and continued her seat-slapping ride around Bridge Creek's arena. Chase believed without a doubt the girl could have passably posted the trot. The only instructions Rebecca Barnes had followed the entire lesson, however, had been ones that kept her on the horse.

The paperwork at Connery had taken longer than he'd expected, and by the time he got The Creature back to Jill she'd been done at the clinic. He'd brought her here to the stable, and he'd been too fascinated to leave.

He marveled at her reservoir of calm expertise. Within the first ten minutes of Rebecca Barnes's lesson, Chase had decided she needed a little less leather and a lot more hickory slapping her behind. Although the girl hadn't spoken twelve words, it was abundantly clear she'd mastered the art of rude behavior.

Jill requested no more of her than bare-bones beginner work—basic walking and trotting to assess her experience. Yet Rebecca's looks were insolent, and her answer to nearly every question an indolent shrug. Her black riding breeches looked new, but her knit T-shirt was faded and skintight, and the worn, blunt toes of her ankle-high Doc Martens barely fit in the stirrup irons.

"Stretch your leg long, Rebecca, and lift your toe. Don't hang on the reins for balance."

Neither Rebecca's seat nor her hands changed that Chase could tell. When Roy and his passenger trotted past the gallery of padded folding chairs at the end of the arena, Chase finally caught an exasperated eye roll from Jill.

The only other spectators, Rebecca's mother and sister, had paid Chase little mind during the lesson, but Jamie divided her time between studying her sister and staring around the arena as if memorizing every detail. Occasionally her eyes met Chase's, and then she would offer a shy smile or rub her palms self-consciously on the plastic arms of her wheelchair.

He'd been curious from the moment he'd seen Jamie the day before, even though he'd vowed to leave professional curiosity behind. But kids and families were his specialty. They were the reason he'd gone to medical school. And they were his Achilles' heel. When Jamie's halting glance got to him at last and he stood to go greet her, his heart skittered around his chest like a nervous rabbit's. He didn't have to tell them who he was, yet it seemed as if the pair could see through him right into the darkness he carried.

"Good afternoon, ladies." He directed a smile first at Anita and then Jamie. "We didn't get to meet properly yesterday afternoon. I'm Chase Preston, a friend of Jill's. I didn't want you to think I'm just lurking."

Even though he was.

"I'm Rebecca's mother, Anita. This is her sister, Jamie."

"Very nice to meet you both. It's good you all are here to cheerlead."

"Becky was pretty excited about the first lesson," her mother said. "We had to watch."

Chase looked away to hide astonishment. If this was Rebecca showing excitement, he couldn't imagine what her lack of interest would look like. Anita Barnes, however, didn't seem to think she'd said anything strange.

"Okay, Rebecca. Walk him now." Jill's voice echoed slightly in the spacious metal building.

Rebecca's immediate response might have been relief, but her features flicked so quickly back to boredom that Chase doubted his eyes. Jill, on the other hand, gave him a smile that sent his stomach into lazy, cheerful rolls of pleasure. He'd studied her during the lesson, an exercise that hadn't dimmed his budding crush in the least. She'd exchanged jeans for a pair of cocoa-colored riding breeches and removed a blue sweatshirt, leaving a yellow tank top. Slender legs and flared hips had emerged, just as they had yesterday, from the baggy denim of her jeans. Along with shapely arms and full, rounded breasts, the body her riding clothes revealed definitely did not belong to a tomboy.

She was more than a pretty woman, however. What compelled him was her mastery over contrast. Although her legs and arms were toned and muscular, they were feminine. Although she moved with decisiveness, her tread barely left prints. And she stepped out with the bravado of a platoon, her soft commands echoing with authority.

"Bring him into the center now."

Rebecca continued walking. Jill's patience didn't waver, but a hard, calculating eye followed the teenager's progress.

"She's trying on purpose to make her mad," Jamie whispered to Chase, her face grave, almost sad.

Chase tried to find the resemblance to Rebecca, but although they shared the same cute-pretty features there was little else. Jamie wore a red Aéropostale T-shirt, faded jeans, and shiny white Nikes, and her brown hair tumbled in waves past her shoulders. She looked as scrubbed and fresh as spring.

"Why do you say that?" he asked.

Rebecca's dramatically eye-linered eyes and the green-swashed hair spiking from beneath her helmet commanded everyone's attention as she passed by again. For the first time, Jill raised her voice a notch.

"Bring him *now*, Rebecca."

Rebecca obeyed at last, albeit as slowly as if she needed ten yards to stop a train.

"She wants to see if she can blow the lessons. She always tries to see how much she can get away with. I wish she wouldn't do it here."

"Jamie," her mother warned.

"Are you an older sister?" Chase asked diplomatically.

"We're twins—fraternal."

"Ah."

Becky swung her leg over Roy's croup and dangled above the ground on the left side of the saddle. Jill supported her to the ground, gave her some quiet instructions, and stood back. Rebecca mounted and dismounted four times before Jill made a cursory nod of her head.

"Enough for this time," she said, matter-of-factly. "Walk him now, three times each direction of the arena."

With that Jill approached the audience of three. If she was fed up it still didn't show.

"So how did she do?" Anita Barnes's confident voice said she already knew the answer.

"Oh? We'll make a horsewoman of her in the end. Jamie, what did you think?"

"It's so great. I wish my sister appreciated it."

Jill cocked an eyebrow but said nothing and rubbed unconsciously at her injured arm. Chase fought a rush of warmth and the urge to massage away the soreness.

"I'm sorry." She looked into his eyes "This isn't very exciting for you."

"Hey, I could have left any time. I enjoyed it." When Anita looked away and waved for Rebecca's attention, he leaned forward. "Six times around the ring?" he whispered. "The horse isn't even sweating."

Jill's smirk told him all he needed to know about her understanding of passive revenge. She took a chair next to Chase, and sullen Rebecca began the punitive trudge.

"I would never have guessed you to be a petty woman." He chuckled.

"Proves how much you have to learn." She folded her arms and stretched her legs.

But by round three, Rebecca dragged, and Jill clearly lost the heart for carrying out the full sentence. She stopped the teen, and after showing her how to check the gelding between his forelegs for temperature, declared Roy sufficiently cooled.

"You can unsaddle him and brush him down," Jill told her. "Tired?"

A shrug.

"What did you think?"

"Pretty boring. Am I done now?"

Jill's back stiffened, but once again, she betrayed nothing in her voice. "You know what? I think we're *all* done."

Chapter Nine

JILL STOPPED AT the door with the others, allowing Rebecca to lead Roy into the barn alone. Part of her feared that if she had to spend another minute in Becky Barnes's presence she'd throw her over a knee. The girl was a pint-sized pain in the world's ass. The only things that had kept Jill composed were Chase, sitting attentively at the end of the arena, and Jamie, hanging on every word like she was studying the law.

She set a hand on Jamie's shoulder and handed her a horse treat. "I want to make sure you aren't worried about being in the barn after yesterday. Roy is a far different horse than Dragon is, but even so, let's teach you and Becky how to introduce him to your chair. Whatcha think?"

"I'm not sure about this." Anita clamped her fingers over one handle of the wheelchair.

"Mom, jeez, I'll be fine."

"I understand," Jill said, and she honestly did. "But I promise, I won't let Jamie get hurt."

Anita slowly let go of the chair, and Jill walked beside Jamie as she rolled through the doorway. Roy and Rebecca were the barn's only occupants, both standing semi-slumped in the aisle.

"Hey, Becky," Jill called. "Would you lead Roy slowly back down here? I want you to help him meet Jamie before she moves toward him."

For once, although she scowled, Rebecca did as she'd been instructed. She stopped a foot in front of her sister, and Roy barely blinked an eye. He sniffed a chair wheel, snorted once, and nosed Jamie's lap. She stretched a hand to the big gray's pink muzzle, and he lipped the treat from her palm. "What a good boy," she murmured. The simple act clearly put her in ecstasy.

From behind her, Chase found his voice again. "How long has she been in a wheelchair, Mrs. Barnes?"

"A year and a half. She's adjusted well."

"She seems like a good kid."

"They both are." Anita's reply was slightly sharp, slightly defensive. Chase dropped the line of questioning.

Becky made the job of unsaddling and grooming far more time-consuming and complicated than it needed to be, but it was worth the annoyance to watch the pure pleasure in Jamie's face when Roy allowed her to roll right up and brush his sides and legs. Becky resolutely ignored her sister, keeping to her own side, huffing with rolled eyes when Jamie exclaimed over anything. Jill let the little tableau unfold without interference, only giving instructions on where to put equipment and tack. Nonetheless, she kept an eagle eye on the dynamics between the Barnes twins and their eerily familiar animosity.

Half an hour later, Roy rolled in his pasture and the family rolled out of the stable yard in their blue van. Jill leaned against a gatepost, exhausted. Her shoulder throbbed. Her neck had a permanent tension kink. "That," she said, to Chase, who leaned backward against the fence, "was a little bit of awful."

He hooked his boot heel on the lowest board and looped his arms over the top one. "You have the patience of a sitting mule. That child, in my humble opinion, needs a hard look at my mama's switch."

"Hah, I was thinking the same thing. Wait. A sitting mule?"

"When a mule decides to sit she can stay there a long time, no matter how people harass her."

"Thank you so much—I think."

"Definitely a compliment. Are you going to survive Becky Barnes?"

"Disagreeable as she is, yes. But, truth to tell, I doubt these lessons will last long enough to matter. I predict Becky quits within the month."

"Maybe so. Nonetheless, I was impressed. You talked to that child as if she wasn't spoiled even a little bit."

"Yeah." She snorted with only a tinge of derision. "The dumb thing is, the child has enough natural instinct to follow the fewest instructions possible and still keep from killing herself. It's not all that easy to do—like purposely singing badly. She could be a nice little rider if she chose to be. I don't think she will."

"If not, it won't be because of you."

"Wow, aren't you the sweet one? Say? How'd the interview go?"

For the first time he shifted uncomfortably. He swung around to face her and hooked the fence rail with one arm. "Truth? Looks like they'll be puttin' me right here in your hair, working on David's new arena."

He could have broken out in a song and dance and she wouldn't have been more surprised. Here? Working for Connery right in front of her? It shouldn't matter in the least. She barely knew this guy. In fact, she'd barely forgiven him for almost being a jerk.

"Oh? How'd that happen?" she asked, more acerbically than she'd intended.

"Tell you what. You let me take you to dinner, because it's my turn to thank you, and I'll give you the whole story."

How had this man turned suddenly from stranger-passing-through to a fixture in her life at the one place that was her haven?

"Go on a date, Mr. Triumph? Really?"

"Sure, what the heck, let's call it a date. What do you say?"

"I have four more lessons to teach," she warned. "I won't be done until seven-thirty or eight."

"It'll be true dinner then. I can pick you up in your truck when you're ready."

He made her laugh so easily. "That's just weird enough I have to accept. Pick me up right here. Do you care if I smell like a barn?"

"Honey, if I get close enough to tell that, it'll make up for the entire rest of this day."

The accented innuendo rolled over her, numbing the last of her misgivings like ten massaging fingers of Kentucky bourbon. She swallowed. "Yeah. What you said."

FIVE HOURS LATER, more than a little bemused, Chase stood beside Jill in front of a gleaming cage inside the Loon Feather Café. She crooned to a small white cockatiel that fluffed its feathers and scrabbled along its perch in excitement.

"How . . . howdee," the bird squeaked. "Howdee stray-jer."

Behind the white bird, a slightly larger, pearl-gray cage mate let out a long, happy wolf whistle. Propped against the outside of the cage was a hand-lettered sign: "Cotton's new phrase—'Welcome, come in.'"

"Oh, good girl, Cotton," Jill cooed. "Welcome, come in."

Cotton, evidently the white bird's name, cocked her head. Jill glanced at Chase.

"These little ones are the Loon's official greeters, almost more iconic than the restaurant itself." She bent to the cage again. "Welcome. Come in."

"Wekkum-ku-im." The bird's chirping words were close.

"Try it," Jill urged. "Everyone is required to help teach

Cotton her phrases. She learned 'howdy stranger' last year. Now it's a Loon Feather tradition."

"Oh, I think you're doin' a fine job without me." He scratched the back of his head self-consciously. "Does the other one talk?"

Jill laughed. "Lester? He has his own way of communicating. You'll see."

Lester, at the sound of his name it seemed, warbled a second wolf whistle and launched into a hearty rendition of "The Colonel Bogey March."

"He's like the Hogwarts sorting hat," Jill laughed. "You're either Colonel Bogey or Andy Griffith. Welcome to the Bogeys."

Chase shook his head and allowed a breathy laugh. "I don't understand a thing you're talking about."

"You will. Come on. Talk to Cotton and let's go get some pizza. Told you, the owner's husband makes a mean pepperoni."

With a skeptical look around the large waiting area in the café's new entryway, Chase bent a little closer to the cage.

"Welcome. Come in," he said quietly.

Cotton gave him a confused stare.

"It takes her a little time to get to know you," Jill said.

Twenty minutes later, Effie Jorgenson, the Loon's proprietress, set a sizzling pizza between them on a calico tablecloth at the Loon Feather Café.

"Sure you don't want a nice cold beer with this?" She cocked a brow at Chase, who only shook his head. "The Coke is fine, Miz Jorgenson. I'm the designated driver."

"Told you I'd be happy to drive." Jill hefted her own glass of Diet Coke.

"It's all right," he replied. "Nothin' better than soda—ah, pop—and pizza."

Jill took a small edge piece of the pizza and fixed him with quizzical eyes, obviously knowing most red-blooded men figured it was beer that went with pizza like chocolate went with milk. He avoided her implied question and moved a large center piece of pizza onto his plate.

"So," she said, dropping the beer topic and returning to what he'd told her on the drive to the café, "the coil is shot. But it's fixable, you say?"

He nodded, blowing on his pizza. "The good news is, an engine as old as the Bonne's isn't complicated. I can fix it. Bad news is, the coil is a little tough to find. Most vintage parts are in use, and there aren't many lying on stock shelves."

"So what's the plan? Buy a nice, safe car?"

"Bite your tongue."

"Sorry."

She nibbled carefully at her hot crust and tested the temperature of the sauce with the tip of her tongue. The sight of it slipping delicately between her impishly upturned lips sent a little depth charge to his lower belly, where it exploded into warmth and heaviness.

"Dewey will search his contacts." He forced away the unwanted physical reaction. "I'll go online. Maybe someone on eBay or a bike site will have a lead. I'll find one; it might take a little time." He picked up his fork. "I'll find a rental car temporarily, book a room, and go from there."

"You know the guesthouse is available," she said with an easy, welcoming shrug. "Why not stay with us? We'll keep Dee out of your way."

At that he allowed a rueful chuckle. He hadn't meant to piss Dee off. "She sure was spittin' mad this morning. I reckon I took care of keeping her away all by myself."

"Not many people turn her down."

"Aw, c'mon, you make her sound like a successful streetwalker."

"No. She's actually pretty choosy. But when she chooses, most guys jump."

"Maybe if I'd met her first . . ." He pointed his fork at her with a wink. "You're a tough act to follow."

"Better watch that slick tongue. You're on my hit list, you know. Working for the bad guys the way you do now."

"Does it really bother you?"

"Probably more than it should, because it sounds like it's his father's fault. It's the principle."

Chase remembered his brief encounter with the owner of the stable. He remembered his endless, not-so-brief encounters with his own father over the years. "Sometimes it's easier to face the wrath of an angry mob than fight your parents one more time."

She cocked her head. "Is that what you're doing by taking the job? Appeasing your grandfather?"

"Yup."

"Okay then. Not much to say to that, is there?"

"Look. Poppa's a good guy. A good man. He's strong in his faith, strong in his principles. I grew up closer to him than to my own father. So, yeah, I disappoint him as little as possible."

"How long have you lived in Memphis, away from your family?" she asked, and finally popped her small piece of pizza fully into her mouth.

"Ten years."

She reached for a larger piece and did a poor job of hiding her surprise. He knew she was trying to do some kind of math. In Memphis, when dealing with street kids, looking younger than his true age was a plus. Here, probably not so much.

"You must have moved when you were pretty young."

"I moved when *you* were pretty young," he teased.

"You aren't that much older than I am."

"How 'bout I tell you after the first kiss?" There was no reason not to tell her how old he was. But she was so cute when he razzed her—about anything. Now she sputtered.

"My mother definitely warned me about boys like you."

"And you should listen to your mother."

He sank his teeth into his own piece of pizza, and the cheese and sauce seared into the roof of his mouth. "Dang!" He dropped what was left of the piece onto the plate and reached for his Coke.

"Ouch." She leaned forward. "Burned your mouth?"

"I thought I'd cooled it enough." He reached for his Coke.

"You can't be very old or wise if you don't know to bite into hot pizza."

He laughed at her prying, holding his hand to his

mouth to keep in the cold pop cooling the burn. "Sneaky as a weasel stealin' eggs, aren't you?" he said when he'd swallowed.

Jill's laughter bubbled free yet again. "Does everyone from Kentucky talk like that?"

"Prestons from Kentucky do."

"Your family sounds close."

"We have our issues like every family does. Told you Daddy and I didn't always see eye to eye. He's hanging on by his fingernails to a lifestyle that's going extinct, but don't get me wrong, he's a good man, too. We've made peace over the years."

"So, you went to Memphis to do what work?"

The light atmosphere sank into the darkness of reality. Just as with his age, there was no reason not to tell her what he did—what he'd fought so hard to become all those years ago.

I'm a doctor.

It was the truth. But he could hear her inevitable praise and the questions that would follow. Everyone had a doctor-god complex before learning the realities of the profession.

What kind of doctor was he? What kind of clinic did he work at? Why was he here?

Why was he running away from such an important, fulfilling job?

And he'd have only one truthful answer he could give. Because Tiana was dead. And it was his fault.

He didn't know the answers to those questions. And he'd made the pact with himself before leaving Memphis. He wouldn't relive any of what had happened for anyone else until he could do Tiana justice in the telling. He hadn't even told Poppa everything. The story he'd fabricated, vague as it was, was his only protection. Not even an earnest woman, with eyes that seemed at this moment as if they could swallow his fears and heal the pain, would hear the truth.

"I worked with a nonprofit," he said, the words still careful on this first time through the half-truth. "They help administrate homeless shelters, boys' and girls' clubs, soup kitchens. I'm a professional . . ." He scratched at his ear and then shrugged. "A professional volunteer."

"You're a crusader. That's cool."

He literally snorted. She used the word as a compliment. His brother Brody never meant it in such a positive way.

"I," he said, picking out a piece of pizza with deliberate care, "was a grunt. A drone. And it was time for a change. But now you. Near as I can tell you have about twenty jobs."

For a moment she frowned at the change of subject, and then she, too, shrugged. "Two jobs and school. I stay busy, but it isn't twenty jobs worth of bad."

"Vet school, though. That's impressive. Have you always wanted to be a vet?"

"Never, at least early on. I just liked working in a vet clinic. Ben Thomlinson, my boss, has been the champion of vet school. It took him years to convince me."

"Are you glad he did?"

"I am. I think I'd be good at it—like Ben has always

said I would. I have a standing job offer from him for the day I graduate. And you heard how happy it would make my workaholic mother."

"Are you worried about what your workaholic mother thinks?"

She frowned. "Of course. And about what Ben thinks. The same as you being worried about your grandfather."

"Touché. All I meant is that I watched you pretty closely today. You're a natural teacher. What's would be wrong with that, for example?"

"Nothing. Nothing's wrong with wanting to make the U.S. Equestrian Team either, despite what my mother thinks." She met his eyes, and the rich, deep brown of hers, along with a tiny, self-conscious grin tugging on the corner of her mouth, slammed him with the attraction that was becoming too familiar. "Why do you think I want for that to happen? Serve her right."

This time, Chase bit his pizza carefully, letting his tongue judge the heat before taking the bite.

"There," he said. "That's the damn-the-torpedoes spirit I've seen in you from the start. That's what'll take you wherever you want to go. Only you can decide when to listen to the people around you. Sometimes you just need to listen to yourself."

"Who are you really? A Triumph-riding psychologist?"

"Hardly. Just someone with no opinions," he replied. "And you don't need any more opinions, so c'mon, eat up. If I'm going to book that room at Hotel Carpenter, I should check with management before they close the front door."

"Heck, if that happens, I am authorized to act on behalf of management."

"I always say, life's about who you know." He winked, glad to be through the reality check unscathed, and raised his glass in a salute.

"ISN'T THIS THE same road where I found you in a ditch?" Chase peered over the steering wheel at the road, dark since they'd stretched dinner until after ten o'clock.

"Good memory."

He tapped his temple. "You don't forget your first rescue."

He glanced at her pretty profile, amazed at how protective, excited, guilty, and plain old turned-on like a teenager he felt around her. Yet the unconscious, sexy sweetness she exuded also fueled guilt that had burgeoned at dinner. He had no business getting close to her, not with the past he'd refused to reveal. But he was stuck with the Connery job for now. And her radiant personality, along with the anticipation of hearing what unexpected thing she'd say next, made it impossible to keep his distance.

"Stop! Stop!" Her sudden cry sent a surge of panic into his bloodstream. Her face pressed against the passenger window and she cupped her eyes with her hands. "Chase, Stop!"

He jammed on the brakes and steered The Creature to the shoulder. "What the—?"

Jill was out the door before he'd come to a full halt.

He was gonna strangle her. *This* kind of unexpected wasn't what he'd meant. Grumbling, he got out and found Jill squatting behind the truck with an outstretched arm.

"C'mere, sweetheart. Come on, baby. It's okay." Her voice had taken on the same soft cadence she'd used on the bird Cotton. She looked over her shoulder. "Get low," she whispered. "He's nervous. Or she."

Chase hunkered into a full squat. Peering past her hand, he saw the black-and-white dog. It sat just off the road, head lowered, eyes unblinking.

"What are you doing?"

"It's her. Him. The dog."

"Dog?" He paused. Then he understood. "Hold on. The dog you went into the ditch for?"

"Exactly. He's got no collar, and he's filthy, but I don't think he's hurt."

The dog had a delicate black head with a white stripe that ran between two huge, amber, Border collie–like eyes, a white chest with long, slender legs like a pointer, and flared, pointy-tipped black ears shaped like bat wings. Chase's heart melted in spite of himself, and he held out his hand alongside Jill's. To his shock, the dog stood and made its way slowly to him, tail wagging between its legs. Once he touched its head, the tail came out from its fearful position, and the gentle eyes warmed and brightened.

"It's a girl," Jill said. "And she likes you!"

The dog put her nose in Jill's hand.

"And you." Chase scratched along the mutt's slightly bony spine, and she arched into his touch. She let Jill fondle her crazy little ears. "What the heck do we do with her?"

"I can't leave her; she looks so thin and hungry. Plus she's still here, right where she was yesterday. Doesn't that say we were meant to find her?"

"I don't know about that."

"We have to take her home. Tomorrow I can bring her to the clinic and have one of the small animal vets look at her. But . . ." She hesitated, biting her lower lip. "You might not want to get involved. This will have to be covert." Her eyes caught his with a warning twinkle.

"Okay . . ." He waited for her explanation.

"My mother does *not* like dogs and hates them in the house." She sighed, letting the stray lick her hands. "My dad had a dog, but it had to live outside."

"You're saying what? We have to sneak the dog past your mother?"

"Pretty much." She looked up at him sheepishly. "You can run now. I'll hold no grudges."

"Heck, honey, what's the worst that can happen to me? I won't get the room."

"The room!" She scratched excitedly at the dog's ba-twing ears, and the lithe little body wriggled in pleasure. "She can stay in the guesthouse. Mom won't be going in there tonight."

"I . . . suppose that's true."

"Last chance to back out."

He laughed, resigned. "What kind of a friend would I be to abandon you now?"

A smart one, he thought, but didn't say so out loud.

Chapter Ten

THE DOG WEIGHED fifty pounds tops, but with her shoulder still painful Jill couldn't quite get herself and the dog into her truck alone. She offered to drive, but Chase insisted the job of holding the mutt fell to her and hoisted the little stray onto Jill's lap. Once they were all safe in the truck, it became immediately clear the dog had been somewhere other than civilization for a long time.

"Whoo-eee. She stinks enough to kick a rat off a gut pile."

"Eeew, that's disgusting." Jill's laughter shook the dog, and the odor of dank hair wafted through The Creature's interior.

"We aren't gonna hide the fact we had a critter in that room if the dog smells like this all night."

"And all the guest house has is a shower. Not too good for bathing a dog."

"Let me know when you've got a plan, Miss Greenpeace. You're head of rescue operations. I'm just the driver, and I like it that way."

"Gosh, thanks a ton."

No interior lights shone when they pulled into driveway close to 10:30 p.m. The Creature's windows were fully down and the dog sat on Jill's lap with her head hanging ecstatically out in the wind.

"Did we put 'em all to bed?" Chase asked.

"Doubt we'll be that lucky," she replied. "Mother reads before turning out the light. Dee could be anywhere."

"We could give the dog a shower in my room."

"We could, I've done dog showers before. Got a bathing suit with you?"

"Why would *I* need one? It's your dog. You've saved it twice now." His lip lifted in the now-familiar curled-lip smirk, and it made her laugh. She was back in high school again, sneaking in after curfew, and suddenly having the most fun she'd had in months.

"If I'm in charge then she gets a proper bath. All you have to do is help me sneak her into the bathroom upstairs. Got any experience as a cat burglar?"

"I stole my share of apples when I was a kid, but I've never broken something *in*to a house before."

"Heck, I've been sneaking animals into the house all my life. Mostly bugs and baby rabbits and stuff."

"Then why are we worried?"

"I didn't say I was usually successful."

"Great."

One light over the sink softly illuminated the kitchen when Chase carried the pungent dog into the house.

With her finger against her lips, she ushered Chase up the stairs and peered down darkened halls for a clear coast.

"C'mon," she whispered. The dog gave a tiny whine and Jill wrapped her fingers gently around her muzzle. "Shhh, baby. Don't get yourself tossed out now. Here." She held the bathroom door open. "Stick her in the tub, and I'll get some towels."

The only towels she'd get away with using were from her mother's rag pile, and the two she selected would have been decent in almost any other home. A line of light shone from beneath Elaina's bedroom door, but she was as far from the bathroom as any room on the floor. Dee's light right next door was more worrisome.

"Everyone's still awake." She knelt with Chase beside the tub. "This has to be the quietest dog bath we've ever given."

"Not a problem." His whisper came close enough to touch her cheek. "Since it'll be the first dog bath for me. If the farm dogs needed cleaning, we threw 'em in the creek."

"You did not." She muffled her laughter in one arm.

"Might turn a hose on 'em if they refused to swim."

She slapped at Chase, wincing when the turning motion tweaked her shoulder. "Stop it."

"You oughta be the one taking a hot bath."

"Is that your official prescription, Doc?" She eyed him in exasperation.

The grin fled his face, and his arm froze on the faucet knob. "Just making sure," he said quickly, and the moment passed before she could wonder about it out loud.

With the first spray of water it was clear the dog wanted none of it.

"Whoa, there, baby." Chase grasped the wet, scrambling animal tightly, and Jill took over the sprayer. "We aren't gonna hurt you."

In a scrabble of toenails against porcelain, the dog attempted her escape. Chase managed to keep her in the tub, but barely.

"She's slippery as greased owl shi— Oops, sorry." He laughed when Jill swiped at his arm again. "C'mon, girl, let's get this done." His voice soothed, and the dog stopped fighting if not shivering.

Jill squeezed a bead of fruity shampoo from a pink bottle along the dog's back. With her good arm she worked soap into the short, wet hair. The suds turned brown and then black.

"Yuck," she said.

As the dog resigned itself to its fate, Chase released it with one hand and scrubbed along with Jill. Several times he brushed over Jill's knuckles, the back of her hand, or her fingers and appeared oblivious when it happened. But with every touch the room and her cheeks grew warmer. The unexpected knock on the door sent her heart into her throat.

Chase grabbed her soapy hand. "Don't panic," he whispered.

"Jill? Are you in there?"

Dee. Jill's pulse danced in chaotic circles between her nerves and the thrills scooting around her belly. She took a calming breath. This was silly. She was a grown woman in her own bathroom, and this was just a dog.

"I'm fine, Dee," she called.

"I'm not deaf or stupid," her sister called in a hoarse whisper. "I can hear both of you. What's going on?"

"We're naked in the shower, Dee. For crying out loud." Jill reluctantly pulled her hand from Chase's and wiped it on one of the towels. In three steps she opened the door a body's width, reached for Dee's bathrobe sleeve, and yanked her into the bathroom. Her sister blinked.

"Hullo, Dee," Chase said, slightly preposterous-looking in his Wildcats T-shirt soaked down the front and his arms full of pitiful, wet dog.

"What the crap? What is it with you two and washing things?"

"Dee, shhh?" Jill begged. "This is the dog I almost hit yesterday. She was still on the road tonight, and I couldn't leave her. I'll take her to the clinic tomorrow, but she reeked so badly we couldn't let her wander through the house."

"Elaina will murder you."

"Unless we can get her to the guesthouse for the night. C'mon, it's not her fault."

"Jillian? Deirdre?" Their mother called from the hallway. The jig was up. "What's the fuss?"

Dee fixed her eye on Jill with a superior smile. "Nothing," she called back. "Jill's washing dirty horse boots in the tub again."

Jill's breath left in a whoosh.

"For goodness' sake, Jill, can't you wash that horrible stuff at the barn?" her mother called. "Clean out that tub thoroughly."

"I will."

The bedroom door down the hall closed with a solid click.

"Well done, Miz Dee," Chase said.

"Yeah, thanks." Jill said sheepishly. "I owe you one."

"Oh, you bet you do." Dee studied the full scene. "I didn't do this for you. You were right, she's a cute little thing, and she doesn't deserve Elaina's wrath." Dee reached out one forefinger and ran it down the dog's white striped face.

"I still appreciate it."

When the dog was finished, Dee and Chase got her wrapped into towels while Jill struggled to clean every speck of dirt and strand of hair from the tub. Once she was satisfied it would pass Elaina's inspection the next morning, Chase picked up the dog again. Dee kept watch.

She'd *definitely* owe her. Deirdre Carpenter didn't do her sister favors for free. Ever.

They let the dog go in the small main room of the guesthouse. She shook vigorously and scooted back and forth between Chase and Jill as if she couldn't decide who her favorite was.

"I need to go find her something to eat," Jill said. "She at least needs water."

The little house was stocked with bare necessities—plates and utensils, pots and pans, a few bakeware items.

Jill found a square cake pan and filled it half full of water. The dog lapped it nearly dry in two minutes. Jill filled it again and the dog finished over half.

"You were parched clear through, weren't you, pooch?" Chase scratched her wing ears.

"She looks like a little cockeyed angel," Jill said. "Are you a little angel dog? Or do you just have angels looking out for you?"

"Sounds like Poppa." Chase gave a yawn and stretched his legs long on the floor, where he sat with the dog nearly in his lap. "Says it's perfectly true everyone has angels. Don't know that I've ever heard him weigh in on whether it applies to dogs."

"It must to this one. The way she was standing in that road the other day not moving, I could easily have hit her. And then to still be in that spot, alive, over twenty-four hours later? Shall we call you Angel?" Jill patted the dog's damp sides.

"Aww, don't name her." Chase groaned. "She must have owners."

"Somewhere, but I doubt they're from town. If she was missing, there'd be signs and her people would have called the clinic."

"But you name her, you'll wanna keep her. I know this about girls."

"Oh, is that right, smart guy? And where would I keep her? I told you my mother doesn't allow dogs in the house."

"I'm just sayin'."

"Well, you keep talking. I'm going to find her some food. I'll be right back."

Angel started barking the moment the door closed, and Jill heard Chase take up a calming baritone croon. Excitement shimmied through her at the rumble of his voice. The shivery memory of his hand around hers in the tub sent a little wave of guilt washing over her pleasure. She had all but ordered Chase to help her, and he didn't deserve to be entangled in this covert operation. Elaina really would be angry if she found out.

Jill searched the fridge for leftovers or sandwich makings. She came up with two pieces of meatloaf and three hard-boiled eggs, along with a cup of leftover peas. She carried the gleanings to the guesthouse, and Chase opened the door, laughing.

"I'm sorry, but you can't leave again. She spent the entire fifteen minutes you were gone whining and staring out the window."

"My goodness!" Jill set the food on the small table in the kitchenette—one of three perfectly decorated spaces in the tiny house. "You missed me, Angel? Did you miss me?"

Angel smeared her face with kisses and shoved her head beneath Jill's hand for petting. But as soon as she'd gotten a good dose of attention, she stopped begging and settled beside Chase on the couch, as if there'd been no problem at all, to watch Jill fill a bowl with the food. When she finally tucked into the makeshift supper, both humans were momentarily forgotten.

"What a strange little thing." Jill plopped beside Chase on the couch while Angel gobbled. "It's almost like she's doing things on purpose. Watching and plotting and ex-ecuting."

"Okay, don't anthropomorphize."

"Woo, Mr. Triumph, you got yourself a big vocabulary."

"I grew up around a lot of animals. Real men aren't allowed to turn dogs into people. Chaz Preston Animal Behavior 101."

"Who's Chaz?"

"My daddy. Short for Charles. As is Chase for that matter."

"Seriously? You're a Charlie?"

"Goes back to Scotland. Firstborn Preston boys have been Charles with a clunker of a Scottish middle name for six generations."

"You have a bad middle name?" She wriggled closer to him, teasing. "Whisper it. I won't tell."

"It's not bad, just very old-fashioned. In me own case," he adopted a passable brogue, "ye'll be callin' me Angus, lassie."

"Angus! I love it." She giggled her approval, letting his semi-embarrassed smile warm her. "Charles Angus. It rolls around kinda nice on the tongue."

"Until kids at school find out and start calling you Where's the Beef?"

"You made that up!"

"Why would I do that? It was hurtful and painful and it made me cry." His eyes shone with humor.

"It made you tough and sarcastic. Like the boy named Sue."

"That's it."

"Whatever all it did to you, it also made you sort of nice. A lot of the time. So, thanks, Charles Angus."

"You're welcome Jill . . . ?"

"Jillian Michelle. After *my* father, in fact. Julian Michael."

"Here's to fathers." Chase bumped knuckles with her. She didn't make the caustic retort dying to come out.

The weight of the day closed in around her like fog over moonlight. The call from Chase this morning, her unwarranted anger, the rock-pitching incident, and the Connery employee's monumental anger. On top of everything, the memory of her lesson with Becky Barnes floated into the mix.

"What?" Chase asked.

"What what?"

"You sighed, or groaned or something."

"Did I?" She yawned. "I was thinking about Becky. She makes me groan. What did I do to deserve her?"

"I think it really is, what could she possibly have managed to get right so she deserves you. You kept a kid who wanted to be anywhere but on a horse, on a horse. You showed pure patience in the face of one major piss and vinegar act."

" 'Mule,' I believe, was the word you used." Jill cocked a sardonic eyebrow.

Chase leaned sideways and nudged her with his shoulder. "Mules are okay. Don't let anybody tell you differently. And it's possible you're just the mule to give Rebecca Barnes a swift kick in the behind."

Jill's head buzzed with the affirmation. David told her all the time she was a good teacher, but David was, well, David. Proper British over-politeness in a good-looking, hardworking package.

"I usually like teaching. This afternoon I came close to changing my mind."

"Aw, don't give up yet, honey. Think about it, you might teach that girl to sit a horse someday. And heaven help her if she happened to learn a little respect along the way."

The compliment warmed her to her toes and astonished her with its positive breakdown of a job she'd always considered mostly goofing off. If she had to make money to pay some bills, what better way than sloughing off real work to boss around people who wanted to ride horses?

"You're a nice guy, Preston."

He wriggled as if trying to escape the compliment. "You're not so bad yourself."

"I have to get up at the butt-crack of dawn again tomorrow. Look." She scooted forward on the couch. "I don't need my truck while I'm working—at either job. If you're willing to take me to the clinic in the morning and to the stable at around one-thirty, you can have The Creature for the day. Maybe you can track down the coil for the Triumph?"

"I don't want to take advantage of you that way."

"What advantage?"

"You're sure? I *could* head over to Dewey's, then, and see what he's found. Do you all have a library in town that would have a computer?"

"We do, but you can take my laptop."

"Jill." His fingers wrapped around her upper arm, and she lifted her eyes to his. "Don't put yourself out for me. Your family has gone above and beyond."

"We're small-town hicks, Chase. We don't know any better."

For long, heavy seconds she couldn't turn away, and she searched his face. The eyes she'd found deep and welcoming, from the moment she'd seen them through The Creature's window, now held hers with familiarity. And yet, beneath the surface blue she saw a wall, as if he'd fortified all access points to his inner self.

"I should go. I—we need to leave by six-twenty. Up to you."

He stood. "I'll meet you in the kitchen."

Her eyes met the collar of his T-shirt six inches away. By tilting her head up she could trace every crease of his throat with her eyes and follow the planes of his jaw and chin to the ends of the dark, thick hair curling behind his ear. The air filled with possibility, and the small space between them crackled with static. A herd of something trying to be light and feathery but tramping around more like uncoordinated rhinos congregated in her stomach.

"All right," she said. Her throat squeezed tight with desire around the words.

Despite the caution in his eyes she could sense his body tensing to match hers. Almost imperceptibly he lowered his head and she stupidly longed for a kiss, wished for what he'd said her sister hadn't gotten.

"You're a lifesaver. You know that," he said, and brushed a thumb pad over the top of her cheek, branding it with an icy-hot touch. He straightened, the fantasy moment dissipated, and the heat from his touch turned into the heat of mortification. What was she thinking? She took a quick step backward.

"It's been a good couple of days for lifesavers."

She took a few steps toward the door, and Angel lifted her nose out of the water dish, concern in her eyes.

"Don't worry, girl," Jill said. "I'll be close by. You stay here with Chase and he'll . . ."

Angel emitted an almost inaudible whine. By the time Jill opened the door, the dog built to three loud, piercing woofs.

"Hey, you've gotta help us out here." Chase knelt beside Angel. "I don't want her go either, but that isn't how this works. And if you wake up the mistress of this place, your name is homeless again."

He didn't want her to leave?

She knelt beside him to kiss Angel on the nose. The dog wiggled between them, happy and quiet. "I have to go," she said. "But I'll see you in the morning. Promise."

Promises didn't hold water, apparently. Once the door closed between them, the little dog howled. Jill scooted back in, and Angel's tail wagged her entire body.

"This is nuts," Jill said. "Normally I'd let her bark it out, but my mother would be here quicker than the FBI."

"Maybe if I was the one to leave? And bunk on a couch?"

He tested his theory by grabbing a pillow and heading for the door. As soon as he disappeared, Angel's sharp, continuous barking brought him back.

"Oh great. What did I get myself into?" Jill groaned. "Two adults held hostage by a mangy dog."

Their eyes held for a long minute, but no brilliant solutions came to her. She only found it easier and easier to ignore the problem and simply stare at the lovely man she'd dragged—along with his motorcycle and a slightly psycho stray dog—into this mess.

"Okay," she said at last. "I'll sit here until she falls asleep, then I'll sneak out."

"You really haven't ever had a dog, have you?" he teased. "They wake up if a bread crumb changes position."

"Then I guess I'll have to be quieter than a bread crumb."

She curled into a corner of the sofa. Chase took the other end, and Angel, still damp from her bath, hopped happily between them. She didn't beg for petting or cuddling, she simply laid her head on Jill's feet, wedged her tail end against Chase's outer thigh, and sighed.

"Oh. My. Gosh." It was as if the dog had some weird plan.

"You're going to end up keeping her."

"A needy thing like this? She requires a family full of children and other dogs."

He grunted.

Jill rested against the arm of the couch and took in the modern, earth-toned decor. She'd have gone for the more clichéd north woods cabin look, but Elaina was not into pine trees and moose. Georgia O'Keeffe and Laura Ashley were her muses. The effect wasn't particularly masculine, but at least frilly fabrics had been kept to a minimum.

"You must be awful tired," Chase said. "You haven't stopped moving all day. Want something to drink? There's a water pitcher in the refrigerator, or I saw hot cocoa mix and some tea."

"Are you going to have something?"

"I'm not a tea man, but I'll heat some water for the cocoa if you like."

"Perfect."

He eased from the couch, and Jill closed her eyes. Angel shifted and Jill stroked her head rhythmically. Nothing hurt. Nothing pressed on her body or her mind. Chase didn't ask her what she'd done today, what she was doing tomorrow or next week or next fall. He shuffled pots in the kitchen, and it sounded safe and comfortable.

SHE OPENED HER eyes to a dim room. Warmth from a thick quilt cocooned her. Quiet snoring from the end of the sofa filled the room, and she cocked her head to see Angel curled like a little husky at her feet. Chase was nowhere to be seen. Struggling to her seat, she winced slightly at the stiffness in her shoulder and squinted at a mug on the coffee table in the middle of the floor. That's when she heard it again. The voice that had awoken her.

"No." Chase spoke softly, urgently, a note of despair in his voice. "She can't be gone. You're the . . . Brody . . . have to save her." His voice trailed off into unintelligible syllables.

Jill stood, curious but confused. Who was he talking

to? Someone in his sleep? What time was it? She pressed the glow button on her watch and read 2:15 a.m.

"This isn't our place anymore." Chase mumbled again. "Didn't want. My fault. Brody . . . failed."

He was curled into a loose ball on his side, fully clothed, on top of the bed quilt. Nothing moved, he didn't thrash like a victim of nightmares supposedly did, and the only indication he was dreaming was a slight tic around his closed eyes. A deep frown.

Carefully she touched his shoulder. "Chase?"

"Huh?" Like a trap snapping shut, his hand shot out and clamped around her wrist. She screeched. "What the—" he began, and bolted upright. "Jill? What's wrong?"

"Oh Lord, I was about to ask you the same thing. You scared the crap out of me." She looked down at her wrist and he followed her eyes. When he realized how tightly he held her, his fingers sprang open.

"Sorry! Sorry." He released a huge sigh and raked his hand through his hair. "You can't sneak up on a guy from the hood."

"The hood?"

"Memphis. Where I lived, it wasn't cool to startle someone."

"I'm really sorry, too. You were . . . mumbling in your sleep. I was making sure you're okay."

He rubbed his eyes. "Was I saying anything interesting?"

"You were trying to save someone."

He went still. She stroked the side of his arm. "Is everything okay?"

"Fine." He relaxed again. "I, ah, lost a friend recently. I think that must have been the dream."

"I'm so sorry. Is that why you left Memphis?"

"One of the reasons."

"Want to talk about it?"

The spark she was growing to love in his eyes returned. "No. You know how it is—your memory playing games in your sleep. I stopped needing to analyze dreams a long time ago."

"Okay."

His glib explanation didn't match the words she'd heard him calling out from his sleep, but she wasn't about to play Freud with his nightmares. She shouldn't be here.

The bed creaked as Chase swung his feet off the mattress and stood. Softly he kissed the top of her head, causing her pulse to stutter. "Thanks, though."

"I'm sorry I fell asleep."

"Why are you apologizing? You were tired. I was tired. The dog stayed quiet. We're all good. Cost nothing but a cup of hot chocolate, and that's reheatable."

"I, should, uh, try to go back to the house."

"Okay."

"Don't know if the dog will like it."

He shrugged. They tip-toed to the living room. Angel, just visible in the light spilling through the windows from the moon, cocked one doggy eyebrow but remained silent. When Jill reached the door, she hesitated.

"Everything's really all right?" She ventured the question again.

"It really is."

"Good."

The house, the world seemed ethereal in the dim light. She had to work hard to keep from kissing his cheek the way he'd done to her crown—it didn't seem that inappropriate. But it was. "I had a very nice night," she said instead. "Sleep tight for the rest of it. If the dog goes crazy, call my cell. I'll come back."

"Here's hoping she does," he whispered, and flashed Elvis at her.

She snorted and opened the door. Angel didn't make a peep.

Chapter Eleven

JILL ENTERED SOUTHWATER Vet Clinic the next morning with Angel padding obediently beside her on a makeshift collar and leash.

The clinic, housed in a beautiful log and fieldstone building, occupied several acres half a mile from Main Street. Over thirty years, Dr. Ben Thomlinson had built his dream facility with three other veterinarians, exceptional skill, tireless dedication, and a savvy eye for the future. He'd trained that eye on Jill when she'd first wandered into the clinic as an all-knees-and-elbows eleven-year-old, treating her childlike fascination for animals with tolerant amusement.

He'd given her odd jobs that she'd performed eagerly for no more pay than petting the dogs, cats, and horses. Over the years, as her home life had disintegrated, Southwater had become a haven. Odd jobs had turned to real responsibility, Ben's tolerance to affection, and his affection to respect and love.

Because of her special affinity for horses, it hadn't taken long for him to christen her the practice's horse whisperer, and he planted the idea of vet school early on, although she hadn't taken to it immediately. As a teen, she'd focused purely on her riding. But he, her mother, and old-fashioned logic had worn her down. Riding horses for a living carried very few chances for success. A stellar recommendation from Ben Thomlinson, one of the top equine vets in the state, however, had helped her gain admission to vet school. And that would take her to the future.

Jill remembered clearly Ben leaning over his perpetually cluttered desk two years earlier and handing her a check that had more than covered her first year's books and supplies. "Go," he'd said. "Learn what's new. Then come back and teach me."

As it turned out, she loved vet school. Until the moment David had mentioned his father's unexpected move to the United States from England. At the possibility of riding with Colin, Jill hadn't blinked at the thought she might leave the university.

Nobody quit vet school.

Did she really want to quit? Did she *have* to quit?

What she did know for certain was that she didn't want to tell Ben quitting had even crossed her mind. He'd been cheerleader, confidant, and surrogate father. She'd sooner poke her eye out than hurt him. Now, every time she entered the clinic, she dreaded her first meeting of the day with her mentor, certain it would be the moment he read the future in her face.

"Morning!"

She jumped three inches and put her hand over her heart. "Ben! I didn't figure to see you here."

She meant on the small animal rather than the equine side of the clinic.

"I heard you were coming in with a stray. Had to see your newest rescue project."

Heat crawled up her face until she saw him nod at Angel. Jill mentally kicked herself. He didn't even know about Chase.

Ben had been a handsome man in his youth. Now, nearing sixty, his long face was craggy, his eyes heavy-lidded and adorned with the crow's-feet and tracings of late middle-age. As usual, his horn-rims had slipped down the bridge of his nose, giving him a professorial mien.

"I found her on the road. She's an awfully nice dog. The girls in the office are going to help me get the word out."

Ben squatted and let Angel greet him with wiggles and enthusiastic kisses. "She's a pretty little thing. Some-one will claim her, give her a good home." He stood, and caught her eyes with something like regret. Her pulse quickened. "I got some other news last night, too."

"Oh?"

This was a small, small town. Had he finally run into David? Or Colin?

"I received a call that Dr. Hardy, Dennis, up in Northfield, got viral pneumonia, of all things, and it actually landed him in the hospital."

"No! I'm sorry." Jill had never been so cruelly relieved over someone's bad news.

"Yes. The thing is we'll be taking his emergency calls this week, starting with two big appointments today. So, I have to ask you a huge favor. You know Robert McCormick?"

"Everybody knows of him. Of course."

"Did you know he has horses?"

"No way, seriously? Crabby Robert McCormick with the shotgun?"

"Yeah. He's Dennis's client. Turns out he has a mare due to foal any day, and Dennis has her on sulfa for a puncture wound. McCormick lost, or spilled—I missed the story—his bottle of tablets. I said you'd play delivery service."

Angel barked and sat, wagging her tail as if she thought it was a marvelous idea. Jill, on the other hand, frowned, mild dread forming in her stomach. "Gosh, thanks, Ben."

"All you need to do is hand him the bottle, look at the wound, and run." A roguish tic threatened at Ben's mouth. The evil man. He was palming the task off because he didn't want to do it either.

"You're the worst boss ever."

He patted her bad shoulder, and she managed not to wince, although it hurt less today. He'd only fuss if he knew about an injury. "Soon you'll be the doc, and you can order people around, too."

She nodded, a little guiltily. "And if I do ever become

one, I'm going to be nice and never give my techs the crappy jobs."

"I'm writing that down somewhere," he said. "Gotta run. I'll leave the sulfa on my desk."

"Good. If I can't find it then I don't have to go, right?"

"I'll clean off a spot."

DEWEY MITCHELL MIGHT have been unassuming in nature, but he was clearly the man to know in Kennison Falls. After a mere hour sitting beside him at his computer in the cramped office of the Garage and Gas, Chase experienced countless interruptions from people who flowed through the station for gas or service, or who simply stopped by to jaw about life, and was beginning to think of the man as a benevolent earl. Dewey spouted his laconic opinion on every subject, and employed a young man of about fifteen named Joey who seemed to regard his boss as something of a hero. In fact, although he seemed anything but soft, Dewey had no enemies as far as Chase could discern.

"I've checked pretty much all my connections, and nobody has that part sitting in inventory." Dewey sat back in his plain wooden chair and pointed at the computer screen. "But, like you saw, most everyone thinks they can find one sooner or later. And we got that '78 coil there on eBay. If all else fails."

"You've given up a lot of time for this." Chase stretched his own legs out next to the desk. "I appreciate it. You sure you don't mind keeping the bike here?"

"Nah, it's no problem. And this is like a puzzle to solve now. Have to find me that coil. I have a reputation to maintain, after all."

Chase huffed out a laugh and stood. "I don't see that as a problem. I could make money running your fan club."

"Don't want a fan club. Got too much other stuff to do. Besides, here's the guy with the fans. Don't ask him for an autograph, though. We don't let anyone bother him when he's home here."

A tall, jeans-clad figure strode across the driveway, a green ball cap pulled to his eyebrows. Something familiar in the man's jawline kept Chase's eyes glued to the door until the figure entered and filled what remained of the small space.

"Dewey!" he called.

"Gray." He nodded. "Welcome home. How was California?"

"Insane. I'm very glad to be here. Hi there," he said to Chase.

"Chase Preston, this is Gray Covey. Gray, Preston here is stranded in town with a busted motorcycle."

Chase couldn't help his momentary jaw drop. Every woman in Memphis over age twenty swooned over this guy's singing. What on Earth was he doing here?

"Man. Sorry to hear that." Gray extended a hand.

"Thanks. Dewey's working on it. Nice to meet you, Mr. Covey. Wouldn't have expected to see you in a place like this."

"Bah. It's Gray," he said. "I married a local girl, and they've had to take me in." He laughed. "I ran out to the lumberyard and told Abby—my wife," he added for Chase's benefit, "that I'd stop here, too, and order her feed and shavings."

"Sure thing," Dewey said. "Usual amounts?"

"That'd be great. Hey, I ran into Ray from the barbershop. He said things are heating up with the gravel pit again and there's a protest meeting or something being planned?"

"I heard rumblings about it," Dewey agreed. "I think they're talking about something at the VFW hall in a week or so."

"There sure is something fishy going on," Gray said.

"Seems to be, but nobody knows what. Personally? I think it's that Krieger dude."

"Krieger?" Chase asked.

"Works for Connery Construction. Pretty high up," Dewey told him. "There's something about him. He's in charge of this project, and he's got a smart-ass answer for every question we ask."

"I know the guy. Sort of," Chase admitted, with a little trepidation.

"You *know* him?" Dewey asked.

"I, ah, *met* him under unpleasant circumstances. We aren't friends."

"Welcome to the club." Dewey snorted.

"Don't welcome me too quickly." Chase lifted a brow. "I just took a job with Connery Construction myself."

"I see. Dangerous thing to do around here."

"So I've heard. Duncan Connery is a friend of my grandfather's. He seemed like a decent sort of guy."

"Connery is a damn wimp." The adamant statement

constituted the harshest thing Chase had heard Dewey say. "He defers everything to Krieger."

Gray shrugged. "I told Ray I'd be at the meeting." He looked to Chase. "This is my new hometown, and it's a nice place. I'd hate to see anything hurt the people and businesses here. All they're after is the truth."

"Amen," Dewey added.

"I've gotta run." Gray gave Chase a quick, sly grin. "You know, since you'll be working there, we could make you our spy, Preston. You hear anything from the big office, let us know."

"Will it keep me from being lynched around here?" Chase took the suggestion as he assumed it was intended, and laughed.

"It might," Dewey said.

He and Gray finalized a delivery time, and as they were saying good-bye Chase's cell phone buzzed in his pocket. He waved to the singer and stepped away from Dewey's desk, looking at the caller ID. When Jill's name flashed, his heart lightened.

"Hey there," he said.

"Are you deep in your search?"

"Just finishing with Dewey. No part yet, but we have some leads. What's up?"

"Could you pick me up an hour earlier than we'd planned? I have a favor to ask."

"Sure, ask away."

"Oh, uh-uh, not on the phone. I'll never see you again if I ask ahead of time." Her voice picked up the sparkle that set his pulse to pounding.

"And that's supposed to entice me? Wait. Do you need rescuing again?"

"No. Do you?"

"No. Sounds like we're in the clear. How's the dog?"

"Everyone loves her. She doesn't have a microchip, so I've contacted the humane society in Faribault and listed her on an online pet-finder site. Eventually I'll put a lost-and-found ad in the closest papers. We'll see."

"Don't bother. You're going to keep her."

"Will you stop that?"

Just over an hour later, The Creature rattled along the all-too-familiar gravel toward Robert McCormick's farm. Chase's memories of James Krieger's damaged green Navigator and the resultant fury grew more vivid the closer Jill drove to the rise. He cringed. Throwing that rock had been such a phenomenally stupid thing to do.

"Here we are." Jill distracted him with a touch to his arm.

Once again they faced the sloping, curving driveway descending to Robert McCormick's farm. The road made a gentle curve to the right around a stand of oak, and three hundred yards away stood the house, a barn, and a silo. The spot of blue he'd seen yesterday became a crystal blue pond sparkling like a gemstone.

"I admit it." Chase sloughed off the memories. "I might stand my ground over a piece of land like this, too."

"It is lovely," Jill agreed.

Minutes later, however, when they rolled into the farmyard and stopped near the house, he could see why she'd enticed him into this trip by saying, "I need a bodyguard." Up close, the charm of McCormick's setting gave way to a shabbiness that couldn't be seen from the hill.

Chase swiveled his head slowly from side to side.

"I don't believe these buildings have been painted since World War II." Jill said. "I knew the farm was old, but this borders on decrepit."

"Kind of sad."

"Let's get this over with."

They approached the farmhouse slowly. It had once been stately, with two full stories, a massive three-sided porch, and gingerbread scrollwork adorning eaves and corners. Now the clapboard siding was grayed and chipped, and a massive rust stain veiled one side behind a metal downspout. Chase followed Jill onto the deck, skirting rotting boards to reach the door.

No one answered any of Jill's reluctant knocks, and her eyes filled with dismay at the crumbling outbuildings surrounded by battle lines of tangled grasses.

"Holy handyman special, Batman?" she ventured.

"Holy bucket full of ugly, Batgirl."

They made for the barn, which bore its own degenerated paint job—traditional red faded to cracked pink. Cobwebs festooned its windows, gaps and buckles marred the siding, and no doors protected the hayloft opening. The main doors were open, too, leaving a dank hole to the interior. A stray breeze carried the faint, acrid odor of ammonia.

"I'm scared to see what the innards of that barn look like." Jill's voice dropped to a whisper. "What kind of poor horses live on a place like this?"

Without warning, a lithe, elderly figure emerged from the barn's maw, a green rubber garden hose slung in a coil over his left shoulder and a large, galvanized bucket in his right hand. He saw them and stopped like he'd slammed into a force field. His eyes darted between them, finally locking in like radar on Chase. The old eyes were piercing and darkly colorless.

"Who are you?" His voice threatened like a thunderstorm.

"Mr. McCormick?" If Jill was nervous her voice hid it. "My name is Jill Carpenter, I'm a vet tech from Southwater Clinic in town."

"Where's Hardy?" For the first time, Robert McCormick locked in on her, too.

"Dr. Hardy is ill, in the hospital. He asked if we'd deliver your sulfa, check your mare, and ask if you have any questions." At McCormick's skeptical look she added, "I'll treat your girl with kid gloves. I've worked with horses a long time."

"Hunh." McCormick gave a derisive snort. "You ain't even been around a long time." He gave Chase another long, curious stare and turned for the barn with a scowl. "Well, come on then. You the assistant's assistant, young man?"

Chase placed a reassuring hand at the small of Jill's back. "No, sir, only a friend."

"Hunh," the old man repeated. "Thought maybe they sent two for safety."

Jill's mouth popped open. "Great. A mind reader," she mouthed.

McCormick was built like Popeye, short but powerful with a barrel chest, strong muscular forearms, and slim hips. He walked with a slight geriatric stoop, but his step, though a little bowlegged, was brisk. Profuse white hair curled from beneath a smudged baby-blue baseball cap that sported an ancient Allis-Chalmers logo, and his jeans fit loose and long in the legs.

"Mare's in here." McCormick set his bucket and hose on the floor when they entered the barn, and Chase gaped in amazement. The filth he'd fully expected was nowhere in sight. In fact, the interior of the barn gleamed and smelled of nothing except sawdust and redolent hay.

"Don't slip on the floor," McCormick warned. "I just hosed it down."

The cement walkway dividing the barn in half was, indeed, glistening wet. To the right, metal pipe stanchions lingered from old dairy days. The left side, however, had been rebuilt into four roomy stalls with scrubbed pine sides, classy black vertical top bars, and sliding doors. McCormick stopped in front of the first, largest, stall.

"In here. Name's Gypsy. She's big but friendly."

Jill pressed her face to the bars of the door, and Chase heard her intake of breath. She'd told him to expect a worn-out old pet. When he joined her, however, what he saw was a magnificent mountain of black and white.

"Holy Budweiser, Batman," he whispered in her ear and received a soft elbow in the ribs.

Jill breathed out. "Mr. McCormick, she is stunning. I had no idea you had a Clydesdale. This is no pet, she must be worth a fortune."

Clearly Robert McCormick found that reaction pleasing. For the first time, a smile deepened the creases in his face.

"You're wrong, she's a pet all right. Plain spoiled. Like her partner here." He stepped to the next stall where another animal stood, ears pricked. This one, however, was light golden brown with a bronze dappled rump, white mane, and wide white blaze. It was slightly smaller than Gypsy, but the beautiful horse was still huge. "That there's Belle."

"A Belgian!" Jill nearly squealed, all traces of nervousness or quietness disappearing.

"You know something about horses, don't you, missy?"

"Some. But judging from these two beauties, so do you."

McCormick uttered one pleased grunt and went to Gypsy's stall door to unlatch it. "Sulfa is for a gash Hardy stitched up about five days ago. It's on the left flank."

"I'll look at it and take her temperature if that's okay."

Jill pulled a digital thermometer from her pocket and stepped into the stall. Gypsy towered over Jill by eight inches and her belly was like two rain barrels tied together. But she lowered her massive head and nickered, thrusting a velvety-looking muzzle into Jill's hand. Jill stroked the wide nose and let the mare softly lip her palm.

"She ain't afraid," McCormick said.

"I don't believe she is," Chase acknowledged.

"When's she due?" Jill ran her hands over Gypsy's sleek, swollen sides.

"Hardy says any day."

She didn't reply, but continued stroking the mare everywhere—down both forelegs, around her hindquarters, down each rear leg. Without hesitation she shoved the mare's haunches around until the neat, stitched line on her left flank faced outward. "This looks perfect," she said. Finally, she reached under the horse's enormous belly and stroked Gypsy's swollen teats.

"When do *you* think the foal will come?" she asked.

"Still a week, at least." The old man grunted again.

"I agree," she replied, and stood to give him a thumbs-up.

"You a vet?"

"Not yet, but I am in vet school."

She turned her attention to taking Gypsy's temperature, and McCormick turned his to Chase. The man and his perpetual frown seemed to have taken an instant dislike to him. Chase cleared his throat and rapped against the open stall door.

"Did you build all of this yourself?"

"If the door latches when we leave I'll admit it."

"I'm impressed. These stalls weren't built very long ago."

"You sayin' it's not bad for an old man?" Chase finally met McCormick's stare.

"That's exactly what I'm saying."

A permanent furrow had taken up residence on McCormick's forehead.

"That accent says you ain't from around here but seems sure I know you."

"Mr. McCormick, I've only been in Minnesota a couple of days, so I know we've never met, sorry to say. My name's Chase Preston."

The old man took an offered handshake with a firm grip but no loss of bemusement on his face.

"Yah, well . . ." He shrugged, then gave the stall door a fingertip caress. "The carpentry is all right, but the hardware? To this day none of the latches work smooth."

"But they are rock solid."

McCormick froze in place and then began to chortle. "Rock, that's it. Been wonderin' if I was getting senile like people claim." Chase's heart tripped nervously. McCormick cocked his thumb toward Jill. "It's the lady doc here confused me. She looks different today. Longer hair or some damn thing. But you." He leveled his gaze at Chase. "You're the young upstart who pitches rocks at trucks."

Chapter Twelve

CHASE'S GUT CHURNED beneath his belt. Robert McCormick erupted into full-throated laughter.

"You were there?" Chase's question came out like a ragged surrender flag.

Robert McCormick wiped his eyes. "Saw every second."

"Mr. McCormick, look, I, ah . . ."

The old man shook his head to ward off Chase's apology. "I go for a walk every afternoon, you see. Yesterday, when I got to the line of trees up the hill, I saw Krieger's damn car and then caught sight of you runnin' next to it. Next thing I knew, you heaved the rock and the fun started. I could barely keep myself hidden."

Jill removed the thermometer and stepped forward.

"Mr. McCormick, I am sorry," she said. "We weren't—"

He lifted a hand to halt Jill's apology, too. "Best damn performance I've ever seen. But you took a mighty big chance with that whopper you told, boy. I guess you must not know my reputation."

"Oh, believe me, I'd heard." Chase wished McCormick would finish dressing him down so they could just leave.

"I almost walked out and played along, but it was much more entertaining to wait and see if Krieger called your bluff."

"Hey, I expected a rear end full of buckshot as it was." Chase stared back, annoyed with McCormick's obvious glee. "Do you even own a shotgun?"

"Sure. You ain't supposed to point one at people for fun, of course, but I tried it once, and now everybody thinks I'm meaner'n a ruttin' boar. I don't mind, it keeps away most of the riffraff."

In complete astonishment, Chase suddenly realized McCormick wasn't the least bit angry.

"That whole thing went a little too far. I am sorry."

"Hell, you saved me from another meeting with Krieger. That's worth a lot. What was your name again?"

"Preston. Chase. You do know James Krieger?"

"He comes by every now and again with the gravel pit's latest offer for my place. We don't care for each other much."

"I'm sure not his idea of a birthday party either," Chase said.

"When I die, the highest bidder can do what he likes with this place. I got no children. It's too small to be any use for farming anymore. You know those gravel people offered me $750,000 for this place? Almost makes me wish I needed the money. But I'd rather be a pain in everyone's ass until I'm cold in the ground. How's the horse's temperature?"

Chase let relieved laughter bubble free. The man was half-crazy blunt, yet wise to the world.

"It's 100.5. Normal."

"That's good then. Anything else you need her for? Otherwise, I'll put 'em out now you've seen her."

"I'm done. Thank you."

Chase watched with Jill in bemusement as McCormick opened the stall doors without further words. Once Belle and Gypsy had ambled to their pasture, McCormick led the way out of the barn, still content with the silence.

He didn't speak until they stood by The Creature. "Do you get yourself into trouble often?" he asked.

Chase had no idea how to answer. He'd run from trouble in Memphis, and now he was living with trouble in Minnesota. Trouble in the form of a young, beautiful woman and messes that seemed to compound by the second.

"I don't try to find trouble," he said, and that was more than the truth. "But in this case, I'll tell you what I told Krieger. I regret what happened, but I'd do it again."

"That's my boy." McCormick shot him a wink as conspiratorial as any Chase had seen between gang members.

"You're encouraging him?" Jill tossed up her hands immediately after the outburst. "Forget it. I'm sure glad you two have hit it off so well."

"Hell. I'll be nice to anyone who gives Krieger a slap upside the head. Like I said, best show I've seen in a while. You visiting in these parts or are you staying awhile?"

Chase chafed at the question. He was close to getting out of here with his skin intact—he could hardly tell the curmudgeonly old man he'd gone to work for the enemy.

"I'll be working in the area, but I don't know how long," he hedged.

To his great relief, McCormick nodded. "Who gets paid for this trip?"

"Dr. Hardy will take care of the sulfa," Jill said. "There's no farm call—I'm only a messenger."

"I guess you'll do as a messenger. You were right. You know some about horses."

"Why thank you! And I always want to learn more. Mr. McCormick, would it be all right with you if I came to see Gypsy's foal after it's born?"

"Come see it, sure." He shrugged. "Next week it oughta be here, you said."

"Wednesday."

"Tuesday." He ambled off. "Keep outta trouble, young feller."

"Yes sir. A pleasure meeting you, Mr. McCormick."

"Hah, been a long time since I heard that one."

Relief flowed so strongly through Chase as they pulled away that he didn't dare speak for fear of breaking some sort of spell. Surely he wasn't getting off this easily. He relished the reprieve selfishly enough that they reached the main road before he realized Jill hadn't spoken either. She concentrated on the road, her hands tight on the wheel, her face unreadable.

"Hey." He touched her knee. "I think that went fine. Everything okay?"

A misty smile played on her lips. "Yeah. It was just hard."

"Hard? Heck, what you do when you ride is hard."

"This is hard because when I meet people like this, I can't believe I'd consider leaving school."

"Well, honey, leaving school isn't a done deal yet."

"I don't know if the possibility of working with Colin Pitts-Matherson still exists. He hasn't said boo to me since the lesson two days ago. Before I learned, six months ago, that Colin was coming, I'd written off the whole Olympic dream thing. Now David's got me going again. But so does Ben."

"Why do you have to choose?"

"If I was going to have a shot at the Olympics, I'd have to go where Colin goes, and riding at that level means twelve- to fifteen-hour days, seven days a week. At the very least I'd have to postpone school. I could probably take a year off, but if it was longer—like Olympics in two-years longer—I'd have to reapply to vet school. I *might* get back in, if I still wanted to go."

"Sounds like what you have to go with is your passion."

She was quiet a long time before she sighed. "I'd love to be selfish. Do whatever the heck I want and damn what's left behind. Be like my father, you know? But people have done a lot of amazing things for me over the years. David has invested an incredible amount of his time and attention to help me reach my riding goals. And Ben . . . he's done nothing but support me and believe in me for half my life. I can't flip him the bird and walk away without guilt."

"Following your own dream does not constitute flipping him the bird, Jill. Everyone gets help in life. That doesn't mean we're beholden to those who give it."

A small spot of flame ignited in her cheeks. Here was another contrast—she might be stubborn, but she was a people pleaser at heart. The only times she'd fully stood up for herself was with Becky Barnes and whenever she sparred with him. It was *that* Jill Carpenter—the one dangerously attractive to him after only three days—he wanted to see stay front and center.

She reached to adjust a temperature control, and as her hand floated back to the wheel, Chase caught it, threaded his fingers through hers, and squeezed. She stiffened in surprise, but then soft skin melded with rough, and she squeezed back. Instantaneous fire raced through his veins, and his composure fled. When was the last time holding a girl's hand had made him senseless?

"All I'm saying is that you can trust yourself." He feathered his thumb along the length of hers, marveling at her delicate knuckles and flawless skin. She squeezed out another battle array of goose bumps along his arm. "I've been watching you, Jill Carpenter. You're no dumb chick. You can figure it out all on your own."

"You have kind of a slick tongue, mister."

"Yeah," he acknowledged. "But this time it happens to be telling the truth."

WEAKNESS GRIPPED JILL as Chase stroked her hand. The past twenty-four hours had been like a never-ending

Tower of Terror amusement park ride. From finding the dog, to the surprise that was Robert McCormick, to these . . . earthquake tremors caused by Chase's thumb, the day had been lifting her up and dropping her like a rag doll without pause. She didn't want to be attracted to Chase, although fate seemed hell-bent on keeping them together. He was either the scariest drop on the ride, or the guy running it who kept everything safe. She didn't have the emotional strength to figure out which it was.

They rolled into Bridge Creek and Chase let go of her fingers, but the shivers remained. Next to the barn, Jill exited The Creature and handed Chase the keys so he could check on Angel and then make arrangements with Elaina to rent the guesthouse until he could find a coil.

"If it isn't my sister and the drifter."

Dee and Colin appeared from around the barn, Dee swaying inappropriately close to the famous instructor. Jill tamped down the jealousy that tinged her irritation. Could she go *nowhere* without Dee materializing out of thin air?

"She's supposed to be at work," she grumbled. "Is she really this shameless?"

"She's just flirting," he whispered. "It seems to be what your sister does best."

He placed a finger on the side of Jill's jaw and gently turned her face to his. The earnestness in his eyes took her aback, as did the perfect angles of his face and the sexy stubble on his chin and cheeks. She swallowed, as stunned as if she were seeing him for the first time. "This doesn't have anything to do with you." He slid his fingers to the point of her chin, tilting her head upward, giving her no choice but to accept the calm sense he was talking.

"I know that."

"Good. Then go do your thing. Let Dee do hers. Don't put yourself down a notch from her."

"I don't!"

She pulled away indignantly, but a tiny wave of shame rolled through her. She *did* compare herself to Dee too often. She'd never be as beautiful, as flirtatious, as fun. Even Colin was smiling. Despite that, these feelings of resentment were unusual.

"I'm surprised to see you here," she said, feigning friendliness. "You're not working this afternoon?"

"I took a shift at the Faribault clinic this evening, so I have a couple of hours now. Given any more dog baths lately?"

Jill held back a retort. "About that," she said instead. "I can't thank you enough. The dog is safely at Southwater, and Mother is none the wiser. Chase is headed over to check on her."

"Ah yes, hello, Chase. Still slumming around Kennison Falls?"

"Not a bad place to slum. Hullo, Dee."

Dee touched Colin lightly on the arm. "It was interesting chatting with you, thanks for the insight. I'll see you on Friday."

"Very good."

Dee passed them without another word, leaving Jill

face-to-face with Colin. "Hi," she offered. "Are you set-
tling in?"

"Yes, quite. There are some lovely riders here. Good
horses as well. But I'm very glad to have run into you."

"Oh?"

"Tell me, how's that shoulder?" His narrowed eyes
were one step from reproving. "And don't bother denying
you were injured, my girl. David spilled the beans."

Heat crawled up her neck, and one of Colin's eyebrows
arched in amusement. His shock of wavy brown hair was
shot with distinguished threads of silver, and his broad
face was regal with straight, handsome features. His
drive-the-female-students-wild accent was a fair amount
heavier than David's, but his gene pool was clearly where
David had gotten *his* good looks.

"I'm sorry I didn't say anything. David wasn't supposed to say anything either." She looked Colin straight
in the eye, determined not to act like a wimp, despite the
fact that he intimidated the crap out of her. "I figured,
incorrectly, that making an excuse was not the best way
to impress you."

"Your stoicism is admirable, but it was foolish." Colin's voice was stern but not unkind. "Riding injured can
cause accidents and worse injuries. And you aren't doing
your horse any favors either. When do you feel you'll be
ready to ride again? For a proper lesson?"

Dumbfounded, she could barely catch her breath.

"My shoulder is stiff but no longer terribly sore. Tomorrow or Thursday?"

"Put your name in my book for Thursday."

"I will! Thank you, Colin. I appreciate the second chance."

"I took the liberty of watching you teach a bit yesterday," he said. "You've a very good eye. Perhaps more patience than I would have." A brief smile toyed with his lips but didn't linger. "Now that I know you were riding with a handicap the other day, I can see you did a competent job with your seat. If you can translate your teaching into riding, as David still insists you can, you've got strong potential."

"That's very kind of you."

"It's not about kindness. I'm looking for working students who are dedicated to advancing. You've got a bit of grit about you. We'll see what we see."

He gave her a nod that finished their conversation, and strode off across the yard, and a slow boil of excitement rose in her belly. It swelled until it broke free in the form of a smile busting dopily across her cheeks. She fisted her hands, did a little running step in place, and spun toward Chase. In three strides she launched herself at him and planted a huge kiss on his cheek.

"He's giving me another chance!"

His arms clamped around her waist, and he pulled her off the ground. "I am definitely not above an I-told-you-so."

"Go for it, I don't care."

"I take it your day just got easier?" Chase continued holding her in strong arms two inches from another kiss.

The kiss. Foolhardy. She hadn't stopped to give it one

rational thought, and now she didn't know whether to be embarrassed or kiss him again.

"Much easier."

"You'll wow Colin next time."

"Hi, Jill!" A bright young voice hailed her from across the parking lot.

Jill pulled away to see a lithe, pretty blonde teenager standing beside a two-horse trailer.

"Hi, Kim! Hi, Abby!" she added as the girl's mother stepped from the driver's side of the towing car.

She leaned toward Chase. "Now there's your opposite to Becky Barnes. Kim is a great young rider with the best attitude you can imagine. Despite being related to a very famous person, by the way."

"Abby," Chase said. "Hey, is that Gray Covey's wife? I met him this morning."

"It is. Gray's a great guy. And Abby and Kim could easily be terribly snooty, but they aren't. Becky needs a few lessons from them."

"If only, right?"

"I have Kim and two more lessons after her. Then I'd like to ride—something easy."

He hesitated as if about to question her choice, then nodded. "All right. I'll go run my errands and check on the dog. Anything else I can do for you?"

A surge of gratitude welled at his restraint and his question. She didn't ask for help; she usually gave it. "No. You've been great. Thanks for being around today."

"Hey, I got a kiss from a pretty girl. Don't need any more thanks."

"Yeah. Sorry. Got a little carried away."

He grasped her gently by her good arm. Without pre-amble, he brushed her lips with his, sending shockwaves into her belly. The kiss held no weight, only feathery elec-tricity. The shock dissipated in seconds, leaving a sweet, tingling burn.

"Don't be sorry."

CHASE LOOKED AT Angel beside him on The Creature's passenger seat. It had taken a little sweet talking to con-vince the receptionist at Southwater Vet Clinic he was springing the dog on Jill's behalf. Angel had helped, but now, sitting in the passenger seat as calm as if she'd never in her life thrown herself against a kennel door to get out of it, she alternated lolling her tongue out the windy window with throwing adoring looks in Chase's direc-tion.

Jill had already bonded with the dog, but why was he encouraging it? She couldn't keep the dog in her room and he certainly wasn't in a position to keep an animal. Elaina Carpenter had seemed willing to give him almost any kind of deal he wanted on accommodations for the next week, but he doubted she liked him enough to allow stray pets in the pristine little house. Angel grinned dog-gily, and his doubts fled. Her presence made him undeni-ably happy, even if it wasn't a smart kind of happy.

Once at the barn he clipped the cheap leash on the cheap collar he'd purchased just for this outing. He hadn't thought of his own clinic in hours. Perhaps he was simply numbing his mind with nonsense so he didn't have to face reality, but dang it. Wasn't that why he'd left Memphis in the first place? If it took a stray dog to change his focus, so be it.

"Hey, you!" Jill appeared like a vision, leading a gleaming, dark brown horse, sturdily built and tacked up in a secure-looking Western saddle rather than the horn-less little slabs of leather most of her students used. "Oh my gosh. Angel!"

She barely spared Chase another glance and squatted, still holding the reins. "Typical," he said. "Never try to compete with a dog."

"That's right. How did you spring her?"

"I told the receptionist we wanted to show her around at the stable and see if anyone recognized her. I said she'd probably be back later tonight."

"You're so clever." She stood and ran her hand down the side of his arm. Goose bumps fanned across his skin. "Thank you for bringing her."

"You look like you're heading out."

"I got through my lessons, and I figure I'd better at least get my butt back riding before Thursday. This is another of my horses, Sun, and if anyone can rehab me, he'll be the one. Wanna come?"

"It's been twenty years since I've been on a horse."

"Then you're ahead of anyone who's never been on one. Come on, you don't need your own pony, we can share this one."

"Whoa, hang on. You'd make that poor horse carry both of us? And what about the dog?"

"Sun is a big, strong quarter horse; he could carry us both all day." She contemplated the dog, who cocked her batwing ears and gave an eerily human smile. "Let Angel off the leash and see how she does."

"She could disappear again." The idea troubled him more than he cared to admit.

"I don't think she will. She likes us. C'mon, turnabout is fair play. I had to ride your metal horse. Mine is flesh and blood."

If he was looking for distractions, this certainly beat all. He'd ridden his aunt's horses enough times to get tossed off once or twice, and he didn't want that at his age. But Jill's smile was almost as eager as Angel's, and she was right. She'd been game about the Triumph.

"Well, Sun old boy." He patted the horse's sleek neck. "I've been invited on your date with the pretty girl. Is it okay with you?"

Jill giggled at him and kissed Sun on the blaze between his nostrils and cupped her hands around his muzzle. Grasping his top and bottom lips she made them move. "Yes. It's fine with me," she said in a low, ridiculous voice. "I would be honored to carry you."

"You know you're goofier than a monkey with a mirror, right?"

He might just as well have told her she looked like a princess. Her pure, childlike grin pushed a spike into his pulse. As he unclipped Angel's leash he wondered if this ride was such a good idea after all.

Chapter Thirteen

JUST PAST TWILIGHT, Jill halted Sun at Bridge Creek's outermost pasture. Angel, who'd traveled the trail as if born to it, sat as if commanded beside Sun's forelegs. Behind her, on Sun's broad rump, Chase shifted. She was *almost* used to the bulk and strength of him and *almost* over the shivers his arms around her waist sent zipping down her spine. But whenever she stopped marveling at the sensations, he would speak, and his rolling, accented baritone ratcheted the desire right back up again.

"This is quite a spread."

"David has worked hard. Bridge Creek is one of the premier facilities in the Midwest. Maybe you'll be here for his big show in August."

Her stomach bounced a little in anticipation. Would he be? She shouldn't care since she'd know the man four days. Or was it three? Or was it a week?

"That'd be a premature guess, ma'am."

She smiled to hide the tweak of disappointment at his equivocal answer and changed the subject. "You stayed on pretty well for that long ride. You'll look great as a bowlegged cowboy tomorrow."

"Hope so, because that's definitely what I'll be come morning."

She threw a grin over her shoulder and urged Sun forward again. Chase rocked against her, and a new round of thrills danced jigs in her stomach.

They walked the fenceline for several minutes until Chase gave a snort of amusement. "We're being followed."

She glanced into the pasture at their shadowy equine stalker and halted again. "Slide off, I'll introduce you."

"This guy looks like a carbon copy of Sun." Chase reached for the other horse's muzzle.

"This is Cassidy. Isn't it uncanny? I've owned Sun since I was nine and he was five. When I found Cass through a Thoroughbred rescue, I couldn't resist her. Their dark liver chestnut color is rare enough, but even the blazes give the same twist over their left nostrils. Cass is the horse that put my mother over the edge. Who needs three horses? And she's right. I really can't afford them, but who would I get rid of?" She scratched Cassidy's cheek. "Not you, would I, love?"

"It's hard to miss how you light up around horses. You were in a little bit of ecstasy when you caught sight of that huge horse at McCormick's this afternoon."

"Yeah. She kind of blew me away. I really like it when I see a kid taking lessons suddenly fall in love with horses, too. It happens all the time."

"Oh, I see. You're no more than a drug dealer creating junkies to support your habit."

He was quick. Completely unexpected. And perceptive. She *was* a dealer—a proselytizer. If more kids took up riding and the care of horses, schools and streets would be safer places. Rebecca Barnes was a case in point. The child needed a solid dose of barn work to take her mind off sneering and shrugging.

"C'mon, we should get back. The barn's probably deserted by now." She checked the cinch on Sun's saddle and then mounted easily without too much protest from her shoulder. "Step up on the bottom fence rail and climb on."

As Chase settled behind the cantle, Jill's stomach gave a lurch and excitement spun immediately into a whirl of desire that traveled low and settled securely between her thighs. Electrified and embarrassed in equal parts, she concentrated on not letting him know how hot her face felt or how liquid and boneless her body had gone.

Once back at the barn, Chase took it on himself to give Sun a thorough brushing. Jill watched him while she finished with the tack, wondering how it was possible he could be the sexiest man who'd ever groomed a horse. He leaned into the task, naturally following the contours of Sun's body, scrubbing hard over the big muscles, lightening his touch over the tender spots. What would it feel like to have him take such care with her?

The memory of their lip brush that afternoon sent one spasm of pleasure deep to her core. When it didn't break up but nestled there, begging for more hot fuel, she gave Chase the okay to quit, afraid to watch him any longer.

Together they let Sun into the pasture with Cass and the others, and Chase fell into step beside her as she headed to the barn for a last check. His quiet presence continued firing all her nerve endings into a frenzy. She longed for the courage to touch him and see what happened. But the courage wasn't there.

At the end of the barn walkthrough, he leaned against an open, empty stall door.

"All done?" he asked.

"Yup, lights out."

"Ready to head home?"

"Sure," she said, her emotions churning in disappointment.

"Do you *need* to go home?" he asked.

Disappointment slid toward shivery hope. "We should take Angel back."

"I could tempt the fates again and smuggle her into the guesthouse again."

"You'd do that?"

"I hate to stick her back in that kennel. And neither of us has eaten. Do you always eat this late?"

Disappointment flared again. Drat his perfect gentleman's manners. He wasn't suggesting anything but food.

"Too often. Luckily, I know a few late-night spots. And I'd love to not put Angel at the clinic."

"Then it's decided."

"Okay."

Reluctantly, Jill found the light switch near the door and snapped it. Blackness robbed them of sight.

"*Muwahaha.*" His disembodied voice echoed. "Beware of bogeymen."

"Heck, what good is having a big, strong, Southern biker around if he can't protect you from bogeymen?" Her eyes began to focus in the dim light. "Where's the dog?"

"She was right here."

"Angel?" Jill called. "C'mon, girl. Let's go get you something to eat." She'd responded to her new name all evening. Jill frowned.

Chase gave a soft, staccato, dog-calling whistle. Angel stuck her head out from a stall a third of the way down the aisle. "There she is. C'mon, girl."

Angel disappeared into the stall.

"Weird," Jill said, and headed down the aisle.

At the door to a freshly bedded, empty stall they found Angel curled beside a mound of sweet, fragrant hay, staring up as if expecting them.

"Silly girl," Jill said. "You don't have to stay here. We're taking you home. Come."

Angel didn't budge. She rested her head between her paws and gazed through raised doggy brows. Chase led the way into the stall. "Everything all right, pup?" He stroked her head.

Jill reached for the dog, too, and her hand landed on Chase's. They both froze. Slowly he rotated his palm and wove his fingers through hers. The few minor fireworks in the car earlier had been nothing compared to the explosion now detonating up her arm and down her back.

"I've been trying to avoid this since I got off that dang horse." His voice cracked into a low whisper.

"Why?"

He stood and pulled her to her feet. "Because I am not a guy someone as young and good as you are should let do this."

"You've saved my life and rescued a dog. Are you trying to tell me I should be *worried* about you?"

She touched his face, bold enough in the dark to do what light had made her too shy to try.

"Maybe."

The hard, smooth fingertips of his free hand slid inexorably up her forearm and covered the hand on his cheek. Drawing it down to his side, he pulled her whole body close, and the little twister of excitement in her stomach burst into a thousand quicksilver thrills. Her eyelids slipped closed, and his next question touched them in warm puffs of breath.

"If I were to kiss you right now, would it be too soon?"

Her eyes flew open, and she searched his shadowy eyes, incredulous. "You're asking permission? Who does that?"

"Seemed like the right thing."

"Well, permission granted, now hush."

She freed her hands, placed them on his cheeks, roughened with beard stubble, and rose on tiptoe to meet his mouth while he gripped the back of her head.

The soft kiss nearly knocked her breathless with unleashed power. Chase dropped more hot kisses on each corner of her mouth and down her chin, feathered her nose and her cheeks, and finally returned wondrously to her mouth. Again and again he plied her bottom lip with his teeth, stunning her with his insistent exploration. The pressure of his lips and the clean, masculine scent of his skin took away her equilibrium. She could only follow the motions of his head and revel in the heat stoking the fire in her belly.

He pulled away at last and pressed parted lips to her forehead. Stepping carefully backward, he took her along, their escalated breathing syncing in the dark. Chase backed into a corner of the stall, slumping slightly for balance, and she settled against him, belly to belly, thigh to thigh, her breasts crushing against his torso. Gripping her bottom, he urged her hips closer, and desire rushed to the pulsing spot between her legs.

His touches became offerings, smoothing over the swell of her seat, caressing her sides, sliding up her spine. With the sparest motions he brushed loose wisps of hair from her face before bending to mate their mouths once more.

This time there was no chastity from either of them. When his head angled, she eagerly allowed his warm, arching tongue between her lips, and he tasted good— something far more exotic than anything she'd ever tried before. They started their dance of acquaintance, tasting and turning, learning the steps together. He teased and tantalized her, drew her into his mouth, and let her explore. She pushed into him and groaned as their kiss fanned her desire.

But although each giddy step made his physical pleasure more evident, he never pressured. Jill knew without question she could break away any moment, and Chase would honor the choice. She pressed all the closer and sent inquisitive fingers delving into his thick black hair, fingering it, combing it, and learning its textures before trailing to his cheeks. She stroked the corners of his mouth, riding along with the thrust of his tongue. More thrills scattered like buckshot through her body. She pressed against the length of him, gasping in pleasure at the fit of his arousal against her, weak from the power they were discovering.

"Hey there, kid . . ." He pushed her away for the first time.

"Kid, is it now?" Out of breath, she set her forehead against his chest. "Did I age you with that kiss?"

He struggled for breath, too. "You're a kid, all right, even though you sure don't kiss like one." He touched his lips once again to hers, but then pushed and held her far enough away that she couldn't reciprocate.

Sighing, she struggled for a way to discover what had gone wrong. "What's going on all of a sudden? You aren't exactly the two-thousand-year-old man."

He straightened, a wry smile on his sensuous lips. "One thousand maybe."

"Now, now, you promised to 'fess up about your feeble age after the first—"

He set his forefinger against her mouth. When he spoke, his attempt at levity barely came through. "I thought that was a safe bet."

"What possible difference could your age make?" She scuttled forward and rocked her hips once more into his hard length. "Under the circumstances?"

His sigh mixed with a groan. "I'm thirty-eight, Jill. You're twenty-five. Tell me that doesn't make a difference."

Jill was grateful the dim light hid her features while she calculated. Thirteen years. The revelation stunned her, not because he was too old, but because he truly was older than he looked. Chase's hands dropped dully to his sides.

"Wait." She caught his left hand and found the fingers clenched. After hugging them to her cheek, she kissed his knuckles. "It doesn't make any difference at all. Did you really think I'd care?"

"You probably should."

"But why? I'm an adult. You could have told me you were forty-eight or even sixty-eight. It wouldn't have changed what I felt when you kissed me."

"That's the danger," he added quietly. "My life is a can of worms. I'm not your basic Disney material."

"Do I look like Snow White to you?"

"No. You look like her kid sister to me."

A tiny flash of irritation pulsed through her. "That's not fair. Did you kiss me just to see what kissing a kid would be like? You don't seem like the type."

"Of course not. I kissed you because you're smart, you're beautiful, and you've shocked the hell out of me by turning me on since the moment you licked ketchup off your T-shirt in that stupid truck of yours. But I shouldn't have acted. We might not know each other well, but I have figured out you aren't the kind of girl who wants a one-night stand."

Her irritation couldn't keep its grip in the face of his

sincerity, warped though it was. "I must be, because I don't know about you but I sure wasn't expecting life commitments from this, Chase. Two consenting adults—or one adult and a decrepit old man—making out in a barn. That's all that was on my mind."

He finally allowed an easier smile, and he tugged on her hand as he slid down the wall to sit in the soft, fresh shavings. She settled beside him, resting her hand on his thigh, a sense of power flowing through her as he shifted, looking uncomfortable.

"It's simple to you," he said. "But we're very different. You're fresh and optimistic. I'm jaded and pushing forty. A fairly tarnished forty."

"A knight in tarnished armor. Pull a worm from the can, Mr. Preston. It's about time I got a little background out of you."

She traced a pattern on the denim stretched across his thigh while she waited for him to speak. He'd listened to her plenty, but it was true—he'd shared very little about his own life.

"Among other things my past harbors an ex-wife."

His sudden admission caused a pang of jealousy. She nearly laughed as it dissipated. Jealous of someone who three seconds before hadn't existed?

"Is there a current one?"

A mild chuckle pierced his discomfort. "No."

"Good. That's sort of the real issue, don't you think?"

"The important thing is, it matters a lot to me what you think," he said. "I got married for all the wrong reasons. I was very young, she was beautiful, and we were hot-stuff college seniors. But we never talked about whether our goals were the same. In the end, she wanted glitz, and I was happy to grub hard at anything. I clung to the marriage for four years because my family believes marrying someone means making a commitment you don't walk away from. In the end, I made her be the one to leave."

"I'm sorry."

She understood his pain over a failed marriage, but something about the depth of his distress didn't feel right. This had happened long ago, and she wasn't discussing a future with him. An ex-wife was no reason to freak out over a kiss.

"This bothers you, doesn't it?" he asked.

She blinked, mystified. "It absolutely does not. What bothers me is the big deal you're making out of all this. There's an age difference between us. It's hardly unheard-of. As for the ex-wife, really, it would have been a little unusual if at your advanced age you'd never been married." She couldn't resist poking at the little wound—it was silly in her mind. "C'mon, Chase, it's like you're confessing sins, not telling me about your life."

"You really do get to the heart of things, don't you?"

"Sometimes, you have to strip things down and look at them for what they are. I'm not always good at it either. But I'm happy to show you how dramatic you're being over a harmless little kiss."

She shuffled to her knees, rustling the shavings, and straddled his thighs.

"I don't think—" he began.

She stopped him with her mouth against his, and

after a few seconds he groaned in response. But when his hands finally rose to her arms, it was to push her away yet again. He set his forehead against hers.

"We need to not do this, Jill. I'm sorry. I was wrong to take advantage of you."

"Dang it!" She scrambled off him and to her feet, her heart pumping with disappointment and a smidge of anger. "Since when is a mutually enjoyed kiss—a freaking great kiss, by the way—taking advantage?"

He held her by the shoulders. "But there are reasons I can't do this to you. To anyone. I'm kicking myself for forgetting that. You're a girl a person could fall into and get lost forever—willingly. But I didn't come here to fall in love."

"Who's talking about falling in love?" Her voice rose.

"Nobody. That doesn't mean it would be hard to do."

The words sent her stepping back in surprise. She swallowed her anger but couldn't quite ignore the rejection.

"You're a godsend of a friend, Jill," he continued. "Can we just stick with that for a while? Please?"

"I . . ." She turned away, her disappointment almost physical. Angel stood, stretched, and trailed across the stall to stand between them. Jill knelt and wrapped the dog in a hug, willing herself not to cry like a rejected high school prima donna. Chase placed his hand briefly on Jill's head. "Of course we can be friends," she forced herself to say into Angel's coat. "That's what matters."

Chapter Fourteen

BRIGHT, EARLY-JUNE SUNSHINE woke Chase Saturday morning. As he had the past two nights, he'd dreamed fitfully about the few sweet moments in the stall at Bridge Creek, where things had been as uncomplicated as Jill had described—two people, drawn to each other, sharing no more than kisses. To be sure, they'd been incredible, sex-drenched kisses, but teenagers in a parked car would have gone farther.

He'd had to stop them.

Things *were* better this way.

He threw off his sheet and sat up. Liar, he told himself. Things sucked. Behind the explorations—chaste enough to satisfy a preacher—there had been frightening power. And he couldn't afford to play with such fire. He'd left Memphis to make a solitary journey. It had to be solitary until he figured out where it led. And that knowledge was as elusive as ever.

Angel padded through the door, and the next thing he knew she'd launched onto the bed. After bestowing two kisses, she settled beside him, rolling to expose her belly.

His mind calmed.

"G'morning, mutt," he crooned, laughing as her back leg twitched while he scratched.

They'd never returned her to the clinic, and there'd been no response to any of the ads for a found dog. Jill kept insisting they'd find a good home for her, but Chase already knew there'd be nothing but devastation if Angel had to go anywhere.

Thoughts of Jill brought pangs of regret. She'd taken his plea for friendship completely to heart. Her flirtatiousness had stopped. Her teasing held no innuendo. Her warm cheeriness had gone generic. She was being, as requested, a perfect friend.

Oh yeah. It sucked big-time.

So did his guilt. He caught sight of his cell phone on the bedside table and closed his eyes. He hadn't dealt even minimally with the mess he'd left behind in Memphis. He hadn't called his brother back, or let his parents or Poppa know he was safe in Minnesota. He'd shoved Memphis and Kentucky away as unremittingly as he had Jill.

On a typical Saturday morning like this, the Marian-Lee Clinic, two miles from Graceland, would be an insane asylum of injuries, colds that had gone too long unattended, and, on a rare day, a welcome baby visit. Saturday mornings had turned into the only times Chase enjoyed his job—the only time families took back the free clinic and gang members slept off the previous night's territory wars. Brody and Julia would be running ragged unless they'd managed to find help.

Fueled only by shame, Chase reached for the phone. The smooth, slim piece of technology would connect him in mere seconds to the world he'd left, yet it felt like lead in his hand, as if it physically contained every mile between Memphis and Kennison Falls. He turned it on and found a missed call from his mother and four more from Brody. Fresh guilt assailed him.

Deliberately but reluctantly he scrolled to Brody's number. With his finger poised to dial, he tried to imagine any way the conversation would not be agonizing, or any question his brother might ask that Chase could even answer for sure. Was he all right? Did he have a timetable for being gone? Did he know that Clara Washington was doing fine? Did he know they missed him?

He touched Brody's name on the screen, and with that small action his breath began suffocating him. *You know it wasn't your fault, Chase.* Brody would say it. He would probably mean it. But Chase couldn't bear to hear it one more time.

He hung up before the signal went through.

Angel whined and literally crawled into his lap. Chase buried his face in the dog's short, curly hair. She licked his face.

"Aw, shit," he said. "Don't you start trying to make me feel better, too."

SUMMER SATURDAYS WERE notoriously busy at Bridge Creek, and Jill normally loved the bustle. Today, however, she sat on David's office chair, swiveling idly while her mind raced. Her second-chance lesson with Colin the day before had been a stellar success. He'd been tough and quick to correct. But he'd praised her thoroughly.

"David didn't exaggerate your abilities," he'd said. "I'd like to work several times a week through June and see where we are."

He hadn't asked, he'd told, as if in his mind her internship had begun. A dream had literally come true. And yet, now that the first flush of excitement had faded, so had the thrill. That made her furious—and sad. Working with and for Colin promised to make for a glorious summer. Why, then, had the shiny promise dulled?

David and Chase had been unequivocal in their excitement. David she understood. But Chase? She didn't know why he cared this much. She'd known better than to fall for him, or lure him into that kiss. But like a dope she'd done both, and look what it had gotten her. A friend. One with the bluest eyes, thick black hair, an intimate sculpted mouth.

A gloriously hard body.

Stop that.

She was obsessing. She never obsessed over men. And why pick someone who would barely talk about himself to go all moony and stupid over? At first she'd been furious with him for ending their incredible night in the barn the way he had. Now she was simply . . . confused.

Chase Preston was flipping her life on its head. And for no productive reason she could see. She picked up a note in David's unique European handwriting letting her know an hours-long group lesson with a troop of Girl Scouts had been canceled. Suddenly she had a fully free afternoon, and she should have been ecstatic with the extra time to work her own horses.

Instead she wanted to leave. To see if Chase was at the house with Angel. To see him.

Her memory returned to the long, hot kiss and Chase's hot, hard body. Shivers sluiced through her belly.

Half groaning, half growling at herself in annoyance, she rose from the chair and stomped from the office. This was ridiculous.

The idea to turn off the main road on her way home struck like random lightning as she approached the road leading to Robert McCormick's. She dismissed her first urge to take the turn as proof her world had been up-ended. When she found herself hitting her brakes and careening onto the gravel road, she changed the self-diagnosis to certifiably cracked.

If anything, McCormick's farmyard seemed shabbier. Nervousness danced through her stomach. The man did have his reputation, and this time she had no reason to be here. She searched the farmyard without luck and nearly decided to leave before she found Robert McCormick laboring with a hand hoe in a twenty-five-foot garden plot behind his house.

The corn plants he weeded stood about six inches tall. Most of the rest of the garden was weed-free and sown

with a variety of vegetables in various stages of growth—
feathery carrot greens still only four or five inches high;
purple-tinged beet seedlings; a row of young but usable
lettuce; short, bushy potato plants; and full-grown pea
plants clinging gracefully to a trellis of chicken wire. The
immaculate garden-for-one delighted her.

"Mr. McCormick?"

A grunt accompanied the quick straightening of the
old man's agile body. Mistrustful eyes squinted from beneath the bill of the battered, baby-blue Allis-Chalmers
cap.

"I didn't mean to startle you. Do you remember me?"

"Oh, it's you."

The piercing eyes softened, and McCormick stooped
again over his hoe.

"I'm sorry to bother you."

"You and that young feller of yours got to be the sor-
riest pair I know. First he comes 'round this morning
nearly apologizing for having hair on his head and now
you. You ain't got to be so damn sorry."

Jill didn't know which surprised her more, McCormick's gruff welcome or the news that Chase had been
there. She ventured closer and stood at the garden's edge.

"Chase was here?"

"Yah, 'bout ten this morning. Nice young fellow.
Helpful. Moved a little hay for me. You here for Hardy
again? I didn't call."

"No, I'm afraid this time I came on my own. I, ah,
wondered how Gypsy is doing. How you're doing."

"You rehearse that line?" He looked over his shoulder as if he expected her to wriggle under the accusation.

"No." She laughed instead. "I guess you and your big horse just made an impression on us."

Robert McCormick smiled, and an amazing transformation took place. Lines eased away and an ageless handsomeness possessed his face.

"Nobody minds decent company, young lady," he said. "But you'll have to talk to my hind side till I finish this corn and get my peas."

"Please, let me help with the peas?" A surge of silly excitement struck her.

Surprise glazed McCormick's eyes. He grunted. "Suit yourself. Bucket's over there."

Jill carried an old shallow pail to the long row of plants she'd earlier admired and knelt beside the bulging little pods.

"First time I had help pickin' peas since my Olive died."

"When was that?" Jill asked gently.

"Nineteen-eighty."

"I'll bet it seems like yesterday sometimes."

Their gazes met across the garden before each turned back to work.

McCormick's conversational skills surprised her. Interwoven with blunt, acerbic observations, he shared bits and pieces of his history on the farm and laced his stories with unexpected wit. By the time ripe peas filled the pail and the corn had been weeded, Jill knew he'd been born on the farm, married his high school sweetheart, Olive, and, by age twenty-five, taken over the farm and bought the land from his own father.

His only son, Karl, had died in Vietnam. Robert had farmed all six hundred forty acres until Olive's death. Now he grew enough hay for his horses, gardened for himself, and bred one mare each year to sell the foal and live off the profit. Jill marveled at his vigor and tenacity and told him so as she helped carry garden tools to the barn when the work was done.

"I ain't had it no better or no worse than most folks around here." He brushed off her compliments. "It was hard losin' the boy. And hard when Olive passed. I don't know why I'm still doddering on, but I'm plain mean enough that I don't want that damn fool Krieger or his boss to get their way too soon or too easy. I'd like to live a little longer just to enjoy being a real pain in Krieger's ass. Excuse me."

Jill could only laugh as they checked on the two huge mares in the pasture behind the barn. Gypsy, enormous with the foal whose birth was clearly imminent, still trotted thunderously to the gate at the call from her master. Beside her, mere inches shorter but positively petite in her non-pregnant state, Belle sought attention, too, impatient but knowing her place in the two-horse pecking order. After she looked at the nearly healed cut on Gypsy's flank, Jill patted both horses in a reluctant good-bye.

She followed McCormick through the barn to the house where he produced a pitcher of lemonade and two glasses from a dorm-sized refrigerator tucked into a corner of the decrepit porch.

"Got me this refrigerator so I can get lunch without trackin' through the house. I don't clean like Olive did." He took a swallow of the lemonade and pursed his lips absently. "I don't make lemonade like she did either."

The liquid burned its tart citrus tang down Jill's throat, and tears stung the backs of her eyes. It was the best lemonade she'd ever tasted.

"Then Olive's lemonade must have been pure heaven, Mr. McCormick."

Once again the remnants of youthful handsomeness eased onto his weathered face. When she finished her drink, Jill stood.

"The time has flown," she said. "I really should go. But if you're sure you don't mind I'll see you again when the foal is here."

"Ya, sure. Suit yourself." Jill wondered why he put on such a crotchety act and why so few people ever got past it. "'Preciate your pea pickin'. It wasn't necessary."

"I enjoyed it. And the lemonade."

He grunted in acknowledgment and spoke without looking at her. "Been a long time since I shared it with someone."

Feeling oddly tender at the awkward compliment, Jill touched his shoulder.

"It's peaceful here. I wish there was a way to hang on to places like this forever. I'm glad the contractors think what they think of you. I won't tell them they're wrong."

"They ain't all wrong," he growled.

"Whatever you say." She winked at him. "Thanks again."

What a messed-up day, she thought as she drove from the old farm. The place that should have been her safe haven had driven her away, and an old man supposedly the scourge of the county had made her feel more at home than she did, well, at home. Then there was the puzzle that was Chase's visit to McCormick. The whole soft-hearted image of Chase doing sweaty chores for a man he barely knew left her utterly confused. Chase was strong and decisive, yet secretive and aggravating. Was he a hot catch or some sort of fugitive?

At the speed limit sign on the edge of town, she slowed her mother's little Accord, which she'd borrowed so Chase could have The Creature, and when Dewey's garage came into sight, Jill moved at a near crawl, searching the parking lot. Chase had planned to spend part of the day working on the motorcycle. It was only three-thirty, but Dewey's place was locked up tight.

She rolled on past the beauty and barber shops facing each other across Main Street. On the next corner, the small, once-pretty library building was still boarded up, and empty pedestals guarded its door. Jill and everyone in town mourned the half-sized lions that had perched atop the columns before the tornado.

A block later, she nearly slammed on the brakes in the middle of the street. A crush of cars filled every parking spot and curbside space around the Loon Feather, including Dee's little red Miata parked directly behind

The Creature. It took five minutes for Jill to find a spot of her own, and when she pushed open the new etched-glass café door to find out what was going on, a buzz of voices hit like a wave.

"Wekkom kom!"

"Hi, Cotton. Welcome, come in," she said absently, moving curiously into the restaurant.

The Loon was filled nearly to bursting. Every chair was taken and tall stools from the bar had been brought into the café. Jill scanned the crowd in amazement. At the far end of the room, Mayor Sam Baker stood in a small hub of people. It didn't take long to find Elaina, Dee, and Chase seated at a table near the front.

She passed Effie and her husband, Bud; The Sisters, Gladdie Hanson and Claudia Lindquist; and finally reached the table where Chase bent close to Dee. Her sister nodded vigorously, and Jill suppressed a twinge of jealousy.

"What's this? Someone throwing me a surprise party?" she asked.

Chase's head popped up. "Hey! I'm glad you're here!"

It was more of a welcome than she'd expected. Unsurprisingly, Dee only scowled. Chase stood and pulled out his chair.

"Sit. There are more chairs by the back door." He left and returned before Jill had finished greeting her mother. "They said you usually work late on Saturday. I didn't hold out any hope you'd make it."

"I had a big lesson cancel. But make it to what? I have no idea what's going on."

"An impromptu meeting, I guess. I'm only here because Dewey dragged me along. I guess there's some sort of new information about the gravel pit?"

"Look at you, involved in small-town politics already."

"Oh no. I don't plan to be involved at all."

Sam Baker broke away from his group, and while the others blended into the crowd, the mayor raised his hands for silence.

"Thank you all for coming. This is not a decision-making meeting, so I'm a little surprised at the crowd. Proof how hot this topic has become." Sam was a fireplug of a man, short, wide, and powerful. He'd been mayor since Jill's high school years, and he wasn't likely to be replaced any election year soon.

"We heard tell the gravel pit they been sellin' us is only a fourth the size of what it really will be." Stanley Severson, who owned the local pharmacy, wasn't known for his subtlety or his patience. "Heard it straight from the gravel pit people themselves. I want to know what you're planning to do about that, Sam."

"Oh c'mon, Stan, sit yourself down and hold your horses." At the firm, kind voice behind her, Jill smiled. Gladdie Hanson, seated next to Stanley, literally tugged him into his chair. "You know Sam can't do anything on his own. That's why we're here."

Gladdie's sister Claudia Lindquist patted Stan on the shoulder. "Give the mayor time to be mayorly," she said.

A mass chuckle rippled across the room. Gladdie and Claudia held almost as much sway in Kennison Falls as Sam did. If they said to sit down, you sat down.

"The Sisters," she whispered to Chase.

"Your mother was telling me about them."

"We do seem to have some conflicting reports," Sam told the assembled group. "I called Duncan Connery this morning, and he claims all his paperwork is in order. That the gravel company signed off on the square footage we were told about. I don't see how I can call him a liar without proof."

"It doesn't matter. The *original* size of the pit is too big." A voice rang from the back of the room.

"We've read study after study saying any size pit will harm the groundwater and erode land in the park," called another. "How do we stop this crook Connery?"

"Now, wait." Dewey stood. "Connery has taken on a job and he wants to complete it. Just because we don't want him to do it, doesn't make him a crook."

"Aw hell, Connery doesn't care," Stan shouted. "He just wants to make money. And he'll make about twenty loaded trucks a day's worth if he's allowed to go through with this."

"Maybe he's trusting the person gathering his information," Dewey said. "That's the person you need to find, to discover if anyone is manipulating facts."

"Nobody is manipulating facts, Mr. Mitchell."

The small crowd turned to the booming voice behind them. Jill's mouth dropped. The man from the Navigator sauntered into the room, his confidence, his unwavering, piercing gaze that took everyone in, and his imposing good looks cowing all but the feistiest locals.

"Good evening, Jim," Sam said. "You're willing to

admit to these good people that you, not Duncan Connery, are the foreman in charge of the Sandhurst Aggregate pit project?"

"I have no reason not to admit it."

"I'd love to have you stand up and tell these good folks whether or not there's any truth to the rumors they've been hearing."

"I will be happy to answer any questions as honestly as I can." Krieger's voice no longer boomed but held an eerily calm reassurance. "I am in charge of the Sandhurst project. And I can tell you there is no manipulation of facts going on."

"So, the projected output of the pit remains at the tonnage level our town council was told it would be six months ago?" Sam asked. "There's no truth to the rumor that the amount of gravel taken on a daily, weekly, and monthly basis is actually going to double or triple, and increase the amount of waste product or the amount of heavy truck traffic through town?"

"Mayor Baker, anyone is welcome to visit the Connery offices and go over the paperwork. You contact me to set it up. Or name a date here and now."

Krieger was too smooth, too confidant. He made Jill's skin crawl for no other reason than he was a little too well-oiled. As if he'd come here to say these precise words—like a Storm Trooper relaying a message from the Empire.

The mayor opened the floor and attendees bombarded Krieger with good questions, which he fielded unhesitatingly without answering anything at all.

"He's awfully good at diversion," Chase whispered.

They hadn't spoken much since the night in the barn. Tonight, Chase was a different man, tense with a warrior's excitement, as if he knew how to fight battles just as well as he knew how to kiss a woman. The mixture made him even more enigmatic. More desirable.

Forty-five minutes later, the meeting broke up. To Jill's surprise, Chase had a crowd of people around him before Krieger had left the building.

"You must be the motorcycle man Dewey's been telling us about." Gladdie shook his hand with her natural warm enthusiasm.

Chase smiled, perfectly comfortable. "And you're one of The Sisters, Mrs. . . . ?"

"Gladdie," she said, brushing off any formality. "I understand you work for Connery Construction?"

"Yes. My grandfather knows Duncan Connery. That's how I came to get a job with him. I don't know Mr. Krieger very well, however."

"Nobody knows him *very* well."

"Not too fast, Gladdie." Stan Severson spoke over her head. "You're new here, young man. Krieger might not be *well* liked, but he's familiar adversary. You thinkin' to play both ends against us, don't."

Chase regarded Stan solemnly but with a glint of amusement. "I appreciate the warning, but I promise you I'm no double agent."

Stan harrumphed and walked away.

"Don't mind him," Gladdie said.

"I don't know, Chase. I disagree with Stan." To Jill's

shock, Gray Covey stepped up and clasped Chase's hand. "I still believe what told you earlier. You *should* be our double agent. I think we need one more than ever."

"Amen," Gladdie replied. "I wouldn't trust Jim Krieger were he planted in my garden up to his dang neck."

Chase laughed and clapped Gray's arm. "Tell you what. If I decide on a break-in, I'll call you two for backup."

Jill still got a little tongue-tied around Gray. She'd never quite gotten used to the fairy tale surrounding Kim Stadtler's mom, Abby, marrying the famous singer. On the other hand, Gray was the reason Jill had faith her town would accept Chase, too. They'd made Gray one of their own, taking his fame and the media circus that sometimes surrounded him in stride. If they could protect him, they could forgive Chase working for Connery Construction.

She had.

Disregarding their new pact to be friends only, she smoothed the front of the plaid button-down shirt he wore open over a plain white T-shirt and mimicked herself. "Look at you, making inroads into town already."

For the first time he looked uncomfortable. "No, ma'am. I'm just trying to blend in."

Chapter Fifteen

CHASE HAD NEVER been so happy to start a job as he was Monday morning. The weekend had turned into an exhausting marathon of hiding the dog, fighting disappointment over Dewey's coil find not fitting the Triumph, and avoiding the weird, newfound notoriety in town. Word of his arrival and job with Connery had spread, and he was suddenly far more noticed in Kennison Falls than he wanted to be. Gray's double-agent joke wasn't funny any longer.

Work on Bridge Creek's new arena began without fanfare. Chase appreciated his new boss Jeff Rigby's patient approach to teaching, and picked up the routine easily. Lunch hour came quickly.

Minnesotans thought eighty degrees hot for the beginning of June, but after ten sticky Memphis summers, Chase found it downright balmy. He and his new co-workers settled around the base of a tree near the work site and scarfed their lunches like teenagers. The boring peanut butter sandwich, the quart of milk, and the four cookies he'd packed into a cooler that morning weren't nearly enough, which surprised him. It had been years since he'd manually labored hard enough to crave huge lunches.

Genuine surprise swept through him when Angel jogged unexpectedly around the barn and yipped at the sight of him. After only a week, the black-and-white dog looked shinier and healthier, and she'd attached herself to Jill and Chase as if they'd raised her from a pup. Angel's presence meant Jill was also around. After letting the dog enthusiastically add the other three men to her list of admirers, Chase followed her around the barn toward the other arena.

The first person he met was Jamie Barnes seated in her chair outside the arena. She shaded her eyes against the glare of sunshine and grinned when she recognized him.

"Hi!"

"Are you banished?" He sat in the grass beside her and checked his watch. He still had thirty of his forty-five minutes.

"No, I left." Jamie's eyes grew stormy. "Becky is such a butthead I can't stand to watch."

"I'm sorry. What's with Becky today?"

"Jill called and asked if we wanted to come early. I'd have jumped up and down but Becky's just snotty. She does things wrong on purpose to make Mom mad."

"She wants to make your mom mad?"

Jamie shrugged. "Becky hates that Mom's making her

do this. She's never been into sports, even though she used to like horses. She's the brainy one. I liked softball and gymnastics, and I used to horseback ride and stuff."

"I'll bet you're still athletic."

"Not exactly." She cast her eyes downward.

"Jamie, I'm not tryin' to mess with you . . ." Chase caught the street slang, and a finger of guilt poked into his consciousness. How often had he begun dealing with a young person using those words? "I just know there are a lot of sports for kids who think they're stuck in a chair."

Jamie said nothing, and Chase kicked himself for opening his mouth. He couldn't have things two ways. He'd left the clinic behind for this very reason—to keep from getting involved with any more of the world's Jamies.

Or Tianas.

His brow beaded with sudden sweat. He'd kept her face from his memory for days, but now it came to him in full detail followed by the image of her slender, knobby little body—so broken, forever stilled.

Let her go, Chase. It's over now. You've done all you can.

"I keep busy. I take piano and clarinet lessons." Jamie's voice overrode his brother's words and dragged him mercifully back into the present. "We go way up to Minneapolis to a place called Courage Center. There's cool stuff there, but I wish there was a clinic and activities closer. I don't like riding in the car for hours."

Although it went against his very nature to squelch the desire to help, Chase kept his response noncommittal. "Can't blame you for that. So, think about what you really want to do."

"I wish I could ride."

"Even that's not impossible. You never know." Did he catch a flash of surprise in the girl's eyes? Hope? It pained his broken heart to drop the subject, but he did. "How long has Becky been in her lesson?"

"Twenty minutes."

"If you don't want to go back in there, we could take a quick walk before I need to get back to work, check out the place. I'll ask your mom if it's okay."

With Anita's permission they visited paddocks and wandered through the main barn, making easy conversation for the next fifteen minutes. When the terrain grew uneven, Jamie allowed Chase to push her chair. Most of the time, however, she preferred to manage it herself, proving her athleticism was still intact. At last they stopped at the paddock nearest the arena. Jamie craned her neck trying to see over a cross board in her sightline, and he knelt to her level.

"Good thing these fences aren't made of lead, hey Supergirl?"

"Huh?"

"You wouldn't be able to see through them."

She rolled her eyes, but when two horses ambled slowly toward them, Jamie's scoffing turned to giggles. She straightened in her chair and arched her back to reach for one front pocket of her jeans.

"You still have sugar left?" Chase asked incredulously.

She'd been materializing lumps from her pockets the whole trip.

"Sure."

"Here, lemme angle your hotrod chair better."

Jamie giggled, and Chase swung her sideways. She held the sugar out to one quizzical mare, who lipped up the cube, chewed it noisily, and allowed her forehead to be scratched as she nosed for more goodies. Jamie tugged on her forelock and rubbed the flicking ears. Leaning forward, she kissed the horse quickly before it yanked its head away.

"They smell so good."

"Whoa." Chase wrinkled his nose.

"Don't you like horses?"

"Oh, I like horses fine. Never got into smellin' 'em for the heck of it."

"I don't wash my hands for a long time after I pet them. Then I can pretend I have one of my own."

"Jamie, we're gonna have to find y'all some normal friends." He checked his watch. He had fifteen minutes. "We should go see if your sister's finished."

They were in time to watch Rebecca dismount and begin the tedious walking-out process. Her dispassionate features gave no clue as to how the lesson had gone, but the plastic smile on Jill's face told plenty. His heart reacted to her as it always had, and he regretted holding back from her.

Jamie wheeled toward her mother, and Chase took a seat on one of the folding chairs.

"Having fun?" he called quietly.

Jill's face cleared. "Hey! Are you ever a welcome sight."

"Sounds like things maybe went smooth as river rapids."

Jill sent a guarded glance toward Jamie, and lowered her voice. "I'm going to kill her."

"I'm sorry, honey."

Rebecca finished her circuits grumbling. When Jill gave the okay to quit, the girl exited, and three minutes later wielded a brush carelessly over Roy's coat. "God, you gotta pamper these stupid horses," she said angrily.

Jamie, at the big gray's head, glowered. "Just grow up, Becky."

Becky glared right back. "Who's talking to you?"

"You should realize how lucky you are and quit being such a biatch to everyone. Especially the horse. What did he do to you, anyway?"

"Shut up. It's not you being forced to do all this stupid work."

"Yeah? I wish it was me." Tears glistened at the corners of Jamie's eyes. "You're so ungrateful. I'd give anything to ride that horse, and all you can do is complain."

"Oh, listen to that," hissed Rebecca. "Always making people feel sorry for poor wheelchair Jamie."

"Girls . . ." Anita cautioned, far too mildly in Chase's opinion.

"I hate you." Jamie spun her chair and rolled angrily away.

Anita sighed, stroked Rebecca's arm, and watched

Jamie wheel out of the building. Fury sparked in Jill's eyes.

"Go talk to Jamie, Mrs. Barnes," she said with amazing calm. When the woman left, Jill whirled to Rebecca, her voice brittle. "You, young lady, owe your sister an apology."

For once Rebecca showed true emotion. "Why? Because she's a poor little thing stuck in a wheelchair? Because you feel sorry for her like everyone else does?"

"Of course not. Because she was right. You have been on your worst behavior all morning. Maybe there's a reason for that, maybe we can talk about it. Whatever you want. But I won't let you take out your frustrations on the people and the animals around you."

"Why don't you just let me quit lessons, then? They weren't my idea in the first place, and I hate them."

Chase watched the anger drain from Jill's face. "You aren't doing jail time, sweetheart, you can quit whenever you want. But it isn't lessons you hate. I don't know what it really is, but let me tell you what I do know. Under that anger I see potential—and not only for riding. Now, I mean it, you never have to come back again, but you do have to finish this lesson. And that includes apologizing to your sister."

After Rebecca had given an emotionless apology, Chase pulled Jill aside to say good-bye.

"What a pair," he said. "Hard to believe they're sisters, much less twins."

"Oh, I can believe it." A flash of irritation crossed her

face and realization dawned—like a two-by-four across Chase's brow. There was nothing frivolous about Jill's connection to Jamie or Rebecca. "Thing is, I don't know what to do with her," Jill continued. "Even my sister at least responds to the animals."

"She seems like an impossible case, honey, but she's not. She has some walls, but you're doing fine. Look, I hate to leave when Miss Becky has you down, but I have to get back. First day and all. Can we finish this later?"

"Of course, I'm sorry. How's it going?"

"Good. The crew is friendly. I'm out of shape, though."

"Poor baby."

Her impish teasing returned, and his attraction slammed him and made him take a determined step back. "How late do you work tonight? Need me to take the dog?"

"I'm done by six-thirty or seven. She can stay."

"Would you consider coming with me afterward and showing me someplace I can grab a couple things for work and some groceries? Dinner'd be on me."

"You're offering food? Sold! We could go to North-field. There are bigger stores and a nice Chinese place."

"My favorite."

"Then it's a date. I'll tell Mother not to expect us home."

A date, he thought as he headed back to work. He wished she hadn't used the word. He wished he hadn't secretly intended exactly that.

The evening was sunny and still hot when Chase, Jill, and Angel strolled to Northfield's charming downtown center with a heavy brown bag of food. Park benches ringed the grassy triangle, and an actual popcorn wagon did brisk after-dinner business. Two young boys on inline skates thwipped past. Locals held hands and window-shopped from storefront to quaint storefront; children ran freely along the main street.

It was absurdly different from the world Chase had left. Marian-Lee Avenue, Memphis, was to Division Street, Northfield, what a porcupine was to a pussycat. There was probably a tough element in Northfield—there was in every town. Here, however, it was unwelcome in the open. In Chase's part of Memphis the good people hid while gangs ruled evenings like this. On Division Street life turned at the hands of the seasons. On Marian-Lee Avenue life often turned at the point of a switchblade. Those differences brought home ever more painfully to Chase the reasons he'd left Tennessee.

They settled onto one of the benches, balancing cartons and napkins. Jill delved into the bag for egg rolls. "We probably should have gotten all finger food for eating without a table."

With her first bite, egg roll crumbs cascaded down Jill's shirtfront. He laughed and brushed the crumbs from her shirt. The simple gesture was way too intimate, and it sobered him. "This is a nice town, too. It's . . ."

"Midwestern?"

"Non-violent."

"That's kind of heavy for a nice night."

"Memphis has some pretty rough edges. In a town like this, a person could almost forget."

"Hey. Is everything okay?"

"Of course. I just never intended to come to Minnesota and stay. But after a week I'm afraid you were right—I'm getting sucked in."

"Like with Jamie Barnes?" She bit again and Angel went after crumbs on the ground.

"What do you mean?"

"You're smitten with her. And she thinks you walk on water."

"You're crazy." But she wasn't, and he sighed. "Okay, it's true. She does get to me. She's the kind of kid who'll never tell you what's really going on inside. She'll smile, she'll adapt, she won't make waves. At least she yells at her sister."

Jill's eyes widened. "You're serious."

"Jamie and I got to talk a little today. She's the horse-crazy one. She meant it about trading places with her sister." He worried the inside of his lip and then asked, "Do you know if there are there facilities around here for handicapped riders?"

"There are a couple of organizations."

"Or. Could you teach her?"

She chewed a moment on the nail of one slender finger. "I wonder."

"Any idea what it would take?" Chase couldn't believe he was spearheading this after his vow to stay uninvolved.

"I'd have to do some research and talk to David this week."

"Jamie's face would light the city if you told her she could mount up."

She squinted at him. "This is what you do, isn't it? Help people. Help kids?"

After warning himself all week, here he was, hoist on his own petard. He sighed. "I like kids. I saw a lot of broken ones over the years. You don't work in Memphis without seeing a lot of broken things. And I hate to see Jamie feel like she's broken when she isn't."

"I know you ran away from something," Jill looked up at the clear cerulean sky. "But you're honest and caring. You could work around here, you know. Kids need help everywhere."

Honest. The word burned his conscience like acid. The idea of her discovering his secret horrified him, but he had no right to be dishonest—to hide what he was and what he'd done. One conversation—that was all it would take. But if he didn't like who he was, how could she? He was here for the summer and probably no more; that much he'd semi-decided. He didn't want to spend it without her friendship.

"Let's start with Jamie," he said lightly.

Jill reached into the take-out bag and pulled out three fortune cookies. "Look! One for you, one for me, one for Angel? Even though she's already had her own egg roll."

He considered a moment. "We could bring it to Mc-Cormick. I kind of liked surprising the old guy."

"Now, do you see what I mean, Mr. Preston? I think the people who get you as a friend are very lucky. What a great idea."

THE GLOW OF early twilight masked some of the farm-yard's scars when they arrived at McCormick's. With

Chase at her side, Jill didn't hesitate getting out of the truck, although she kept Angel close. McCormick liked horses; she didn't know about dogs. They found him behind his house doing, of all things, his laundry. The sight of the sprightly farmer, clothespin in mouth, reaching for a work shirt off the line, was so comical Jill announced their presence with a laugh.

"Looks like you need a maid," Chase called.

McCormick looked over his shoulder and tugged an old-style wooden pin from his lips, spitting as if he'd bitten the end off a Cuban cigar.

"Or a wife."

"Can I help?" Jill moved toward the clothesline.

"You're too young, girlie, but I appreciate the offer." He tossed the shirt in the basket on the ground and moved to the next article on the line.

Jill joined him and pulled a few socks from the line. "How are you?"

"Pretty good considering it was washing day. You can see how much I love it. I'm getting it done early."

"Olive taught you a lot about home ec, I see," Chase said.

"Hah. The only thing I remember about hanging clothes is that the socks went on one line, the shirts on another and the trousers on another. Made no sense to me, but I suppose that's how it's done."

"Come on then, let's get finished," Chase said, pulling a pin from another shirt. Within minutes the lines were empty.

"Can I help fold them?" Jill asked.

"What, did you come here to work?"

"Sure."

"No," Chase countered. "We brought you your fortune."

"Cookies," Jill added as Chase pulled them out of his shirt pocket. "There's always an extra."

"Oh. Well, gimme the one that says I'll meet a nice Norwegian widow who does overalls."

Jill giggled again. "Are you sure I can't help?"

"No, no. Set down, I'll just put these by the door."

Once on the holey porch, McCormick pointed to three ancient Adirondack chairs and they all sat. Jill held out the three fortune cookies. "I was serious. Pick one."

"Lotta nonsense," McCormick said, but chose thoughtfully. "Thank you."

The crackle of cellophane filled the air, and three cookies snapped simultaneously.

"Boring," said Jill. " 'You will know the future when it has come.' "

"Mine says, 'Help me, I'm trapped,' " said Chase.

"It doesn't either! Let me see." Jill snatched the slip of paper. " 'No man is born wise.' Ooh, let's analyze that one."

"Goes to show what horse hockey this is." McCormick grunted. " 'A tall, dark stranger will fulfill your needs.' Do they make tall, dark Norwegian widows?"

"I suppose. Chase, are you Norwegian?"

"No, ma'am. Scottish on one side. Ancestors on the *Mayflower* on the other."

"Phooey, doesn't look like any of us is getting a rich

fortune tonight. So, Mr. McCormick, how's Gypsy? You know that's really why we came." She winked at him.

"Females. Bond quick as flies to flypaper."

"Fine. If that's how you feel, you boys can sit here while I go visit my soul mate."

She stood and tripped lightly down the porch stairs. The dog followed. Neither man moved a muscle.

Gypsy pressed her massive face against the bars of her stall when Jill called her name and unlatched the door. As always, the beautiful mare's sheer size took Jill's breath away. The sleek ballooning sides, the flawless mane, tail, and fetlock feathers, and the vivid black-and-white coloring all added to the horse's power.

"Hurry up and have this baby," she murmured as she pushed in beside the horse. "You look like you're about to pop."

The huge horse lowered her muzzle, snuffling into Jill's hand and nuzzling curiously at Angel, who sat calmly in the open door. Jill drew in the familiar musty scent of horse and talked on, petting and admiring her, finally pulling her head close and blowing softly into one enormous nostril. In return Gypsy snorted and cocked one ear, staring down with intense interest.

"She likes you." McCormick's voice surprised her.

"I like her. Mr. McCormick, this is very forward, but if I give you my phone number, would you, maybe, give a call when the foal comes?"

"Yeah, yeah," he said brusquely. Jill swore he tried not to look pleased.

Deeper twilight had settled once they got outside. Along with the dark came battalions of mosquitos. Everyone swatted as they headed for the porch.

"Come on inside, and I'll get paper so you can write down your number," McCormick said. "You two want some lemonade, or a beer? Wash down them dad-gummed cookies."

"If it's the lemonade I heard about, I vote for that," Chase said.

Just like the barn's interior, McCormick's home showed none of the neglect evident outdoors. The kitchen was a spotless, warm hodgepodge, one where nothing matched but everything fit. The living room was equally eclectic with faded pink cabbage roses on the drapes and deep maroon leather on a well-used recliner. Beside the chair was a generous pile of Louis L'Amour Westerns. More framed photographs than Jill could count stood on various end tables.

"Look, Chase." Jill picked up one picture of a younger Robert McCormick beside a woman with graying brown curls and deep crow's-feet. The eyes harbored an impish light.

"This must be Olive?"

McCormick nodded and proceeded to recount a story for nearly every photo, including the ones of his son, Karl. Eventually they all sat with their lemonades, McCormick in the recliner, his legs elevated and slack-hipped, Chase and Jill on two cushions of a saggy sofa, Angel at their feet. The old man seemed starved for his captive audience and reminisced for nearly an hour before there was a lull. Chase checked the time and broke the satisfying silence with an astonished whistle.

"Dang!" He showed the watch face to Jill. It was nearly eleven. "I hate to say it, but we need to go. We both have work in the morning."

McCormick followed them into the black night, and all three looked up. A vivid smear against the luminous sky marked the Milky Way, and awe engulfed Jill as the stars pulsed and seemed to push closer to Earth, as if it were they who gathered to peer down upon the three puny Earthlings.

"This is a good place, a safe place," Chase murmured. His head craned back, exposing a jutting, very sexy Adam's apple. "I remember Mama telling us when we were young how any place where you could see clear up into heaven had to be good. She hated it when I moved to Memphis. 'But can you see the stars come down?' she always asked. She meant like this." He scratched the back of his head in slight embarrassment and then extended a hand to McCormick. "Thanks for the hospitality."

The old man cleared his throat gruffly. "Nothing to thank me for."

"Goodnight, Mr. McCormick," Jill said. "For the lemonade if nothing else."

"Thank you for the fortune. Next time just bring me the Norwegian."

He walked them to The Creature, and Jill caught sight of a fence she'd never noticed jutting from the far side of a small shed.

"What's that gate?"

"Old chicken yard. It's oversized, but as we got older Olive tired of chasing her stubborn biddies around the whole yard."

"How big is it?"

"Oh. Mebbe sixty-five, seventy feet long and half that wide. I made it big enough so Olive thought the damn birds had running room. Only woman I know who cared whether her chickens got enough exercise."

"The more I hear about Olive the more I like her." Jill touched McCormick on the shoulder. "Next visit you'll have to give me a tour. There seem to be stories everywhere."

"You come," McCormick said, still gruff. "You c'mon back, too." He looked at Chase.

"Thank you, sir."

"Sir?" McCormick snorted. "Hell, call me Robert."

They drove a long way in silence before Jill finally looked at Chase, staring pensively out the passenger window. "You're awfully quiet. Everything all right?"

To her shock, he threaded his fingers through hers and squeezed. Her stomach did happy and very confused flips.

"Each visit reminds me a little bit more of home."

"You sound awfully wistful for somebody who left the farm voluntarily."

"I knew long ago I didn't want to be a farmer. But the lifestyle always had its appeal."

"You said you're really close to your grandfather. Does Mr. McCormick—Robert—remind you of him?"

Chase chuckled. "Not even a little. Poppa is one hundred percent smooth, Southern, church-goin' gentleman, and Robert McCormick is calloused, cynical, Midwestern work ethic. I just appreciate old people—they know a lot more than I do."

"You're nice, and smart, too." She smiled in the dark.

"I kind of wish you'd stop saying things like that— Hey! Cut it out!" His disheartened tone grew into a chuckle and then a laugh as Angel lapped at Chase's ear from her spot in the seat behind him. "Crazy dog. What got into you all of a sudden?"

"She's agreeing with me."

"Yeah, well, you both need to stop." He nudged Angel away with his shoulder, squeezed Jill's hand again, then loosened his fingers. "And I'm sorry. I said I wasn't going to do this anymore. I promised we would be just friends."

She refused to let his hand free.

"Let's say we're friends with hand-holding benefits. I'm not reading any more into it."

His hand tightened into hers. The butterflies in her stomach belied what she'd told him. Angel rested her head on the console between their seats.

Jill pulled into the driveway and parked where Chase could take the dog around the side of the house without being seen. They sat silently, and neither moved. He ran his thumb back and forth along hers, and electricity bloomed like static off a big old balloon rubbed on thick carpet. Jill's pulse raced.

Nothing preceded his kiss except a slow movement toward her and heat from his breath on her skin. Nothing touched but their lips, locking, opening, and exploring hungrily. His head bobbed with hers, and her stomach slid toward the reactivated throbbing point between her legs. When he pulled away, the parting made a succulent sound in the dark.

"Aw, hell," he whispered. "I don't seem to be very good at keeping promises, do I?"

He trailed a finger across her jaw, opened the door, and slid out, then patted his leg for Angel to follow.

Chapter Sixteen

JILL FLOATED UNHAPPILY from sleep fifteen minutes before her 5:30 a.m. alarm went off. She dragged the covers over her head and drifted along with the wisps of a dream.

Chase kissed her until Jamie Barnes flashed past them bareback astride a magnificent black-and-white stallion. Every few seconds she passed the gate from Robert McCormick's chicken yard. Rebecca wedged herself between Jill and Chase yelling, "This is so stupid, Jamie, you're the only woman I know who cares whether your chickens get enough exercise."

Jill's eyes flew open, and she sat straight up. Sleepiness vanished, and she hugged her knees to keep from laughing. It wasn't hard to figure out the inspirations for this dream. Seventy by forty feet was just big enough for a functional riding space. The idea was cheerful if insane.

But, by the time she got to breakfast Chase had already borrowed Elaina's car and gone, leaving her cheeriness faded.

She settled for the anticipation of seeing Chase at lunch, but it lasted only until she learned he'd worked all morning, then gone to a Connery company meeting. Bummed for a second time, she distracted herself by scoping out the stable's familiar outdoor and indoor arenas with an eye for Jamie's needs. She didn't like the outdoor since it had no fence or rail, and the potential for runaway was too great. She didn't like the indoor arena because the space felt too cavernous for a rider with limited control.

All of a sudden, the prospect of Jamie riding seemed far-fetched. Too many barriers seemed insurmountable. She didn't have the foggiest clue how to teach a physically challenged rider. That was Dee's area of expertise. The whole endeavor would take a lot more thought.

When Chase wasn't in the guesthouse after eight when she got home, Jill finally started worrying, wondering if he'd been hurt and nobody knew whom to contact. Or, she wondered if he was avoiding her, running scared after their kiss last night, as he'd done once already.

She didn't know how to reach the part of him he kept hidden from the world. When it came to support and tenderness of her, he could out-Casanova the great Casanova. When it came to himself, however, he was guarded as Area 51—hiding who-knew-what behind the half lover, half warrior she could see on the surface.

A fugitive? A deadbeat dad? A drug runner? An undercover cop? A werewolf? She'd considered the most fanciful possibilities. Nothing made sense. He couldn't be a bad person. On the other hand, nothing less than something bad would make a person toss back every deserved compliment he received like it was an unexploded grenade.

Jill padded around the kitchen scrounging halfheartedly for dinner. When the phone rang, she ignored it, hoping her mother would answer. On the fifth ring, however, she grabbed it, exasperated.

"Hello?"

"Jill? Is this Jill?"

The gruff old voice startled her. "Mr. McCormick?"

"Yah. Say, I think there's a problem with the mare." His words came out understated in comparison to the agitation in his tone.

"With Gypsy? What's wrong?"

"She's been in labor all afternoon I think, but she's not right."

"Did you call Dr. Hardy?"

"He's still out sick, so I called your Thomlinson fellow's clinic. Their vet is on another emergency and will come when he can. I was thinking you know horses pretty good."

"Of course I'll come if you want me to, but you know I'm not a vet."

"I've seen you with her. Maybe you'll have an idea."

"Okay. Keep her calm. I'll be there in ten minutes."

"Good. That's good."

The worry in his voice set her heart aching. She knew exactly what was at stake for him.

"Robert? Take care of yourself, too. Gypsy will be fine."

"Yah, me. I don't worry about me."

"I'll be right there."

She grabbed her paddock boots from the back hall and stuck her foot in one of them, hopping to get it on. "I'm going out," she shouted toward the living room.

"Bye. Have fun," came her mother's disembodied voice.

After jamming on her second boot, Jill paused a moment to decide if there was anything she should bring with her. There was nothing. She made for The Creature, her laces dragging, Angel behind her, and just as she opened the door, Chase pulled in beside her. Angel howled in happy greeting.

"Hey." His quiet voice held questions and apologies, but she couldn't think about anything except her task.

"Mr. McCormick called. He thinks Gypsy's in trouble and he can't get a vet."

"Oh no."

"I doubt there's anything I can do, but I told him I'd come. Ride along?"

"Of course."

"What could be wrong?" Chase asked when they were under way.

"Any number of things or nothing at all. The foal could be positioned wrong, or Gypsy could be having trouble dilating. I just pray everything's okay. I think this horse means an awful lot to him."

"I know you're right." He nodded and closed his eyes.

"Are you okay?" she asked. "Or are you praying to all the angels again?"

"Got one angel right here." He stroked the dog's head. "But you can't have too many in a situation like this, I suppose."

"Good point. I, uh, missed seeing you around today."

He was quiet for so long Jill feared what he would say. "I was avoiding you. Sort of."

"Ouch."

"You have to know by now you scare me to death. I can't control myself around you no matter how hard I tell myself to behave."

The hurt that had started to build dissipated with a rush. "Two kisses don't constitute bad behavior, Chase. They constitute two kisses. Extremely good kisses, I admit, but it's not like you have to marry me now. It doesn't work that way in this part of the country. Does it in Memphis?"

He finally laughed, his deep, nasal chuckle filling her with relief. "All right," he said. "I got it. No strings. No expectations. Friends with stolen-kisses benefits."

Jill's heart, heavy over Gypsy and Robert, lightened with the briefest swell of joy. Chase's acceptance of this simple relationship was the first time he'd let his guard down. The first time he'd trusted her with a part of his real self.

"My fling with a bad-boy biker."

"I, uh . . . sure. Okay." He shook his head. "Speaking of that, we found a coil. That's really where I was, with Dewey making sure this one will fit. It will."

"That's fantastic! How long until it's fixed?"

"A day or two. I'll do the work. Dewey's not really a motorcycle guy, but he agreed to let me work on it at his shop."

"I'm so relieved for you. You must feel great."

"I do. But most important right now is Robert."

With no more light conversation, Jill drove straight to the door of McCormick's barn, and she and Chase were out of the truck almost as she threw it into park. They jogged in and found Robert leaning against the bars of Gypsy's stall. He turned, peaked and unshaven, and put a finger to his lips.

"Turns out I'm an old fool." He pointed.

With Chase pressed next to her, Jill looked into the stall and gasped.

As babies went, the foal was enormous. As Clydesdales went, it was every bit the newborn—still wet and unable to stand, and only mildly interested in attempting the feat. Gypsy stood over her baby, her coat dulled with sweat and her hind legs stained from the delivery. With long, efficient strokes of her tongue she performed the instinctive act that would not only clean the foal but coax it into rising.

"Never, ever been such a worried old cuss before," Robert said. "I should have known she just wanted to be left alone. Soon as I returned from callin' you, here he was. It's a colt."

Relief, excitement, and awe bubbled in Jill's stomach, which only moments before had churned with anxiety. Impulsively she wrapped Robert's neck in a hug. Awkwardly he patted her back.

"Sorry to make you come for nothing."

"Nothing?" Chase grasped the farmer's hand. "This is a huge relief."

"I'm *glad* it was nothing. Oh, Chase, isn't he beautiful?"

She hugged him, too, and he dropped a kiss on her head. In his embrace, Jill marveled at the sudden sense that all was right with her world. An easy hour passed while they watched the colt struggle miraculously to his feet, nurse, and collapse back into the straw to sleep.

Robert replaced the soiled bedding, and when mare and foal were settled, his tired face registered supreme contentment. Jill linked her arm through his as they left the barn.

"They okay for the night now, you think?" she asked him. "I can call the vet and tell him not to come until tomorrow. He can check the colt then."

"That'll be fine. I'll be up a couple of times to check anyhow."

"You be sure you get enough rest, too," Jill said.

Jill waited for his normal acerbic retort. Instead he patted her hand. "I will."

Once at the house, Jill faced the farmer again. "Now that we're not worried, can I ask a favor?"

"Could I stop you if I wanted to?"

She laughed. "May I see that old chicken yard you were telling us about last night?"

He shrugged. "Go ahead. Ain't nothing but a big weed patch."

The enclosure was as perfect as it had been in her

dreams, not too big for a rider with imperfect control, but big enough so a horse could perform all three gaits. With its three-foot-high chicken-wire fencing it would be an unorthodox riding arena, but it was right.

"Robert? I have a crazy proposition for you."

Chase, who'd wandered off to check out a mostly whole shed, reappeared. "Robert?" he echoed. "I have one, too."

FOUR DAYS LATER, Chase almost liked his life. He whistled as he wiped grease off his hands and surveyed the Triumph, with its new coil, standing whole on a drop cloth in Robert's old granary shed.

"You sound happy." Robert appeared behind him, a bottle of beer in one hand, a lemonade in the other. He handed the lemonade to Chase. "You sure you aren't far enough along to celebrate with a real man's drink? You and your girlie lemonade."

Robert had taken wholeheartedly to both Chase's request to use the farm as his fix-it shop and Jill's to turn Olive's chicken yard into a riding arena. The old man's friendly camaraderie, completely contrary to what everyone thought of him, kept surprising them.

"Alcohol makes me work slower," Chase said. "Besides, I'm about to fire her up and take a test run."

His heart pounded in anticipation.

"Well, hell, boy, let's hear it."

Chase tossed his rag to the ground and nodded. "Wanna ride?"

"I ain't crazy. You get the bugs outta her first."

A buzz from his pocket cut off Chase's reply. His mood soared highter. It had to be Jill.

"Hi there," he answered, grinning at Robert, who was convinced he saw more between them than there was.

"Call the paramedics and restart my heart. You answered the phone. Hello, grandson."

In the moment it took for his smile to disintegrate, Chase's mouth went as dry as if someone had stuffed the work rags down his throat. "Poppa?" he rasped, as warm joy collided with deep dismay.

"Yes. It's me. Am I getting you in the middle of something?"

"I, ah, I had to make some repairs to the Triumph. She blew the coil. I just finished replacing it."

"Really? I'm sorry, son. And you found a part? That's not easy." His grandfather's deep drawl rolled smooth and easy, and did not sound like it came from a man nearing eighty.

"It did take some doing. What about you? Everything's okay there?"

"Fine, fine, except we're all concerned about you."

He hung his head. He'd continued ignoring calls for the two weeks he'd been in Minnesota. He'd likely have ignored this one had he been paying attention.

"I'm sorry. I haven't had a thing to say. I sent Mama an e-mail that I was fine."

"You can't hide from us forever. I'm livin' proof we'll stalk you." The humor in his voice was reassuring. Poppa had always been more easy-going than Chase's father. "I was spurred this time by a talk with Duncan. He called to tell me he's pleased with your work."

"He called for his scheduled check-in, you mean."

"Somebody has to let me know you're still breathing."

"Poppa." His admonishment held only half strength. "I'm a big boy. Grown up a long time ago. If I was in trouble I'd let you know."

"And you're not in trouble? Duncan says you're in a feud with Jim Krieger. Something about throwing rocks? Now, it sounds like Jim has been looking into you."

"What the hell?" Chase cursed. His grandfather had built a reputation on commanding respect without ever raising his voice, much less uttering a hell or a damn or a vulgarity, but frustration had always brought out, in Chase and his brothers, the pointless game of trying to rile him. It never worked. "What kind of bullshit is that?"

"I had to drag every word out of Duncan by claiming inconsolable parental worry. All he said is Jim doesn't trust you. But Duncan does. I'm simply making sure you're all right."

"What happened to letting the good Lord and His angels worry about me?"

"I'll turn it back over to Him now that I've heard your voice."

"You do that. I'm perfectly fine. And forget about my feud with Krieger. Part of the deal I made for not walking out on this job was that I wouldn't have to work with a first-class jerk."

"Jim Krieger might be a jerk, Chase, but you are not."

"For God's sake, I'm not a child either."

"Nor are you yourself. Don't burn bridges until you know you'll never have to cross them again. And preferably not then. Never know who'll need to cross them looking for you."

"Stop it," Chase said, with irritation but not conviction.

Poppa laughed. "We all have our crosses to bear, Chase-boy. I'm yours. Don't forget you're up there to figure out what you want."

"You think I can forget why I'm here?" Chase lowered his voice, pain slicing through him. "Believe me, I wish I could."

"You mustn't forget, son, that Brody, Julia, and everyone at the clinic might be worried, we here might be worried, but you need to solve this for yourself. This isn't about dealing with guilt. You have nothing to feel guilt over. This is about physician heal thyself."

Chase had nothing to say. His grandfather rarely resorted to being pedantic, but when he did get full of himself, there wasn't much arguing with him. He was wise to an annoying fault.

"I am working on it, Poppa. Not much more I can say."

"Then I have only one more request. Please call your daddy."

"He'll only say I told you so." His father had been the original naysayer when Chase had left for Johns Hopkins—a place Chaz considered worldly and highbrow that would only lead Chase to heartache.

"Your papa doesn't call a swan a biddy hen anymore, you know that. Tell him in your own voice you're fine."

"You're right. I will. I promise."

"You know I love you, son. We all do. You're a good man, a gifted man. What happened to that child wasn't your fault. What the clinic has become isn't your doing. And the roadmap you have to follow wasn't drawn by Rand-McNally."

"No more angels, old man." He wanted to hang up. But he also wanted his grandfather's voice in his ear until all the pain disappeared.

"Fair enough. You know if you need a thing in the world, I'm here."

"I do, Poppa. I do."

He ended the call and stood still, feeling as bruised as if he'd gone fifteen rounds and lost on points. He'd completely forgotten Robert waiting behind him.

"Someone checking up on you, I take it?"

Chase wiped his face as if replacing a mask. Angel wandered in from wherever she'd been exploring and rooted against his hand, giving one little lick. How the dog knew exactly when she was needed, Chase could not figure out.

"Home," he said. "You're never grown up as far as they're concerned."

"You ain't running from the law, are you?"

"No." Chase shook his head. "I swear. Nothing like that."

Robert bent slightly and wriggled his fingers between Angel's ears. "Didn't you say the place you're staying now has problems with dogs?" The question seemed out of the blue.

"Jill's mother doesn't like dogs in the house."

"If you needed a place you could both stay, I got me a spare bedroom. Only a thought. Wouldn't cost anything if you helped me fix my porch."

Chase stared, nearly dumbstruck. The number of problems that would solve, now that he had his own transportation, was huge. The temptation made him giddy. Only one thing niggled his conscience.

"Robert, you have no idea how enticing that is. But there is something you don't know."

"That right?"

"I've never told you that I work for Connery Construction."

The information stopped Robert for a long moment. He pulled off his cap with one hand and scratched through his thick, white hair. "How well you know Krieger?"

"I don't know him at all. I just have my opinions."

"Are they the same as mine?"

Chase almost chuckled. "I believe they are. I don't think he likes me either. That was my grandfather on the phone. He's knows Duncan Connery, and I guess Krieger has not taken kindly to my . . . insubordination."

"Anyone insubordinate to Jim Krieger is welcome here." Robert replaced his cap. "You in any kind of position to spy?" He gave a faintly naughty smile.

Chase answered with a puzzled frown at the third time spying had been suggested. "I don't think so."

"I believe the man is up to no good," Robert said. "There were other plans for different projects, and Krieger steamrollered 'em. I think he's got a personal stake in this gravel thing. I don't know enough about how it all works. I just know I'm not sellin'—not to him."

"You're a strong man, Robert. My newest hero. I'd be more than happy to help fix that porch. Let me ask Jill if she minds moving the dog here. It's really hers."

"I'm not sure, but I think that dog has some sort of plan for you two."

"That makes no sense at all."

"Most things in life don't."

Chapter Seventeen

"Now that's exactly what I wanted. Excellent!" Colin's voice rang across the arena.

Jill leaned forward in her saddle and slapped Dragon's neck as he cantered away from their last combination of fences. "Excellent" was ultimate praise from the Englishman, whose acknowledgment of a job well done was usually a more-or-less satisfied grunt. Jill slowed her horse, her heart still flying. The exhilaration of jumping well gave her a high that had to be better than anything a junkie could get from crack.

Not until she halted beside Colin in the center of the arena did she notice her audience by the doorway. Several of her students gave her a thumbs-up, and the Barnes family stood in a tight little knot. Since Becky's lesson wasn't for an hour, their presence was a surprise. A bigger one yet was the sight of Chase's muscular frame, slouched comfortably several feet from the girls. Jill's pulse skipped happily.

In the two weeks since Chase had moved to Robert's, life had settled into a routine built around him. She practically lived at Robert's, too—feeling guilty the man had taken on two boarders instead of one. But Chase seemed . . . happy. He courted her like an old-fashioned lover, surprising her with flowers, holding hands while they talked, stealing sizzling kisses when Robert wasn't looking.

And the heat in her body intensified every time she saw him. Standing at the arena door now, in his faded jeans and a crazy cowboy hat Robert had dug up from somewhere, Chase made such a contrast to the proper breeches and riding helmets everywhere around him that he stood out like a mustang in a herd of Lipizzaners.

"I've got a few things I'd like you to consider." Colin pulled her attention back to him.

"Sure."

"You've done two advanced shows, you said?"

"We finished in the top half both times. It wasn't perfect, but not abysmal either."

"That's fine. We'll get him there. I'd like you to think about doing two more shows this year. I have one in mind for September in North Carolina. You could do it on the way to Florida, where I'd really like to have you join me at the new barn for the winter. I need a working student, and I think we could get you and this young man"—he patted Dragon's neck—"ready for Rolex."

Jill swallowed her shock. The Rolex Three-Day was

the United States' most prestigious eventing competition. The best of the best made it to its four-star course in Kentucky.

"I'm thrilled you think we're ready."

"You are. You've maxed out the training facilities in this part of the country. I keep trying to persuade David to move his operation, but he has fallen for this area, I'm afraid. It's very nice, but no more conducive to year-round training than is most of England."

With that, his request sank in. Colin Pitts-Matherson wanted her to move to Florida. It was the request she'd wanted from the start. A million thoughts raced through her head. She really would have to leave school. She'd get to leave Dee. Have to leave her mother and Ben. Robert. Have to leave Chase.

A lump like swallowing a giant ice cube slid painfully down her throat.

But Rolex. And, maybe, the Olympic Games. But it would still take an incredible amount of work. And so much luck.

"I'm honored, Colin. I hope you know I'd love to work with you. Please, may I think about your offer? I would need to make quite a few changes here."

"Of course. Of course. You're in vet school, are you not?"

"I am."

"You are a talented young woman," Colin said. "There are difficult sacrifices required for any career. But trust me, you can have one as a rider and trainer."

Not be a vet? How did she really feel about such a prospect? Over the years she'd downplayed her acceptance into vet school—told everyone it had been Ben's dream, not hers. But now she was invested in school—in the process. She enjoyed forgetting about classes in the summer—but to not go back?

And yet, she was being offered a chance to reach a goal shared by every girl who'd ever dragged on a pair of breeches and sailed over a cross-country jump with her horse. She'd been dreaming about the Olympics since the age of eight. And here it was, the pot of gold in sight.

Her audience became a small entourage when she led Dragon into the barn. Well dones flew at her, and Jamie Barnes stared moony-eyed from a distance, as if Jill had grown a halo.

"He's pretty."

The voice behind the compliment nearly bowled Jill over. Becky, her hair glowing green today and her T-shirt still too tight, stepped to the horse with her normal hostility missing.

"Thanks, Becky."

"Why do you call him Dragon? He doesn't look that tough."

Jill laughed and stroked her fingers over the lightning-shaped slice of white between her horse's eyes. "He's tough out on the cross-country course. He snorts and attacks the jumps like they're big castles. His show name is Flash Dragon."

Becky didn't reply. She studied him as if for the first time. "Is he the best jumper in the barn?"

The hint of awe was so infinitesimal it was like a high-frequency whistle, nearly inaudible, but Jill heard it.

"It's kind of vain to say, but he's one of them," she confided. "Would you like to get to know him a little better? You could walk him out for me."

Becky's mouth opened and closed guppy-like—as if Jill had willingly handed her the keys to a sports car she wasn't quite old enough to handle. Jamie's eyes, from across the aisle, turned to saucers of disbelief—tinged with more than a little envy.

"Okay," Becky said.

Jill snapped a lead rope onto Dragon's halter and handed it to the girl, who moved off past her mother, Jamie, and Chase.

"You're letting her go alone?" Anita started to follow. She was a quiet woman but always a bit jittery in her watchfulness.

"I trust her to be safe," Jill promised. "Colin's there, and if there's one thing Becky knows how to do it's walk out a horse."

"Can I go watch?" The wistfulness wasn't hard to identify in Jamie's small voice.

"Of course," Jill said.

"I'll take you," her mother added.

"Mrs. Barnes, could I talk to you first?"

Anita swiveled her head, her frown tremulous, but at last she let her second daughter go.

"She's quite a horse lover, too, isn't she?" Jill nodded toward Jamie.

Anita adjusted her owlish glasses. "Yes. I've tried to keep her from coming and getting envious and depressed, but she insists. At least she has a lot of other interests."

"She's always welcome here."

"I know, I appreciate that. But the question is whether it's in Jamie's best interest. The most important thing is for her to accept her limitations."

"I know a physical therapist," Jill said, carefully omitting that she and the therapist were barely on speaking terms. "And I have an idea. I'm sure you've heard about equine therapy for kids with special needs. Riding holds a lot of benefits for someone like Jamie. If you were interested, I think we could get her up on a horse."

Anita's brow furrowed, and her eyes darted to the arena door where Jamie had rolled out of sight. "I don't know. Jamie's a child who gets her hopes up so high that she's hurt when things don't turn out as she imagines. She wants to gallop away across fields, not do pony rides around a ring with other handicapped children."

"It might not hurt to ask her."

"Let me speak to her father, and I'll get back to you if we're interested."

Jill forced a patient tone she didn't feel into her voice. "That would be great, Mrs. Barnes. I'd really love to help her ride."

Anita smiled tightly and broke away to take up watch over her girls.

"That went over like a lead balloon." Jill whispered to Chase, who leaned unobtrusively against a stall. "Why wouldn't she jump at giving her child the desire of her heart?"

"That child's in a wheelchair and she's just nervous." Chase pulled her close, resting his cheek on the top of her head. She melted into his hold. "It's out of your hands for now, give her time."

Jill shivered from the thrills he sent twirling down her spine like little sparks on a fire pole. "I won't give up."

"If you did I'd be worried."

He kissed the top of her head. Warmth flowed from that simple touch and heated up her desire so quickly that she looked longingly down the aisle to the stalls. They'd never repeated that night—not here in the barn. Kisses, yes. Stolen and exciting, but still almost chaste, as if Chase was protecting her from something.

She ran her hands down his long, strong back, and the sparks inside her gathered into a mini conflagration in her belly. When he squeezed back and held her tightly to him, her knees nearly lost their strength. Tilting her head up, she waited for him to smile, to wrinkle his nose, to do any of the adorable things he could do with his beautiful features to make her drizzle inside even without a public display of affection. Instead, he shocked her by slipping a short, hot kiss onto her lips.

"It stinks, but I have to get to work," he whispered, his breath feathering her nose.

"Yeah."

Vet school, teaching, and the Olympics be hanged. She wanted Chase Preston. She didn't want to miss him if she left. She wanted to strip away his reserve—not to mention his jeans—and learn what it would be like to fully have his trust, to love him, to make love to him.

He released her.

"The arena's coming along," she said, flustered by the

fantasies and searching for a way to hide it. "You guys do nice work."

"It's fun work, now that I'm in shape."

"Oh yeah, you're in shape all right. Roaring up on that motorcycle every day lookin' tough."

Which was pure understatement. She was starting to like that stupid machine. Chase made James Dean on his bike look like a dud.

"Tough as Silly Putty around you." He took a few steps, then hesitated. "What was Colin jawing about at the end of your ride?"

The conversation returned to her with a jolt. "About going with him to Florida in the fall."

"Hey, that's exactly what you want." His gorgeous eyes and mouth, his whole expression, remained unnervingly neutral.

"I always thought so." She bit her lip. "Now that he's asked, it's a little scary."

"It's a huge opportunity, honey, but a big decision, I know. Okay, see you tonight."

She stared, confused by the abruptness of his departure after the slow heat of his kiss. She couldn't read the reaction any better than she could read her own feelings at the moment. It was far too early in their fledgling relationship to be worried about what Chase thought of her career plans, but his switch to cool offhandedness stung anyway. She'd wanted him to grab her into a bear hug with the excitement he usually showed over her accomplishments. Or she'd wanted him to beg her not to go.

How stupid.

It *was* too soon for such expectations. Too soon to be imagining such things as stripping off his jeans. And way too soon to think Chase felt more like home than anyone or anyplace had in a long time.

As the Fourth of July approached, any decision about whether to leave with Colin remained unmade. Nobody mentioned it; nobody pressured her. For the first time in her life she wanted someone to tell her what to think or do, and everyone who normally had opinions on top of opinions had come down with a severe case of opinion laryngitis.

On Sunday evening two days before the Fourth, Jill squatted in the pasture behind Robert's barn running her hands up and down the legs of Gypsy's month-old colt. He'd been unofficially christened T.N. Tatters after the old clown because Chase said he was so floppy and comical nothing else would do. Since Jill unequivocally refused to name him Bozo—or Ronald McDonald McCormick—Tatters it was.

The foal was still disproportionately leggy but he was no longer uncoordinated. And he was as friendly as a curious puppy. While Jill lifted his feet and fondled his hooves, Tatters lipped at her hair and ears, making her laugh.

"You're horrible," she said, pushing his baby muzzle aside, only to have him poke it into the back of her neck. "Stop it!"

"You're pretty handy with the little fellow."

She set Tatters' hoof down and looked up to Robert leaning casually against the pasture fence.

"I'm just spoiling him," she replied, and headed toward the old farmer. "Developing all sorts of bad habits."

Tatters trotted after her, butting her gently in the rear. Robert chuckled.

"He thinks you're his pasture mate, that's all. And don't think I can't see gold when it's in front of me. I got me a real horse trainer gentling this colt. He'll fetch all the more money when he goes to a new place because he's well started."

"Don't say that." Jill pouted when she reached the fence. "I know he'll be sold but I can't bear to think about it."

"You wouldn't make much of a farmer, girlie."

"Guilty as charged. My farm would be filled with five hundred unsold animals, and I'd be poorer than I am now."

"Don't fret about it. By the time this little boy has to go we'll breed Belle and you can start planning for her baby."

The thought struck painfully that she might not be here for another foal. She blocked the sad suspicion. She'd tell Robert her dilemmas about the future another time.

"I'll bet she has pretty babies, too."

"She's dropped three beauties since I've had her—two fillies and a colt."

"You've been doing this horse breeding a long time, haven't you? You must usually do the gentling yourself."

"I got my ways of halter-breakin' 'em and getting 'em handled. Not like you do, though."

"You sure you don't mind us taking over your peace and quiet, Robert? Your routine? We've moved in almost without permission."

He leaned against the fence and pointed toward his house. "Lookee what's going on around here. I asked that boy to help with my porch. He fixed that and kept on goin' like it's his own daddy's place."

Off between the pasture and the house, Jill could see a half-dismantled old wooden corncrib and Chase ripping at the decrepit slats with a sledge hammer and a crowbar. He'd already razed two dilapidated outbuildings and piled useable wood neatly and burned the rest.

"It does look cleaner in the yard, doesn't it?"

"Hell, this place ain't been mowed neat like this in three years. I'm lucky to chop the crabgrass a dozen times a summer. And you. There ain't been flowers around here since Olive passed. Or a woman cooking dinner. Why would I want my old routine? I figure somebody must be missing *you*—you're the one musta changed a routine."

He was right. Jill had changed her routine. She only went home to sleep nowadays. Maybe this was all a silly, slightly more grown-up way of playing house, but coming to Robert's after work every day, kissing Chase hello, watching him fix up the property, planting flowers, was a perfect life.

"It's only my sister and mother at home. My mother has a plenty active social life without me, and Dee and I don't get along that well, like I've told you."

"What is it with sisters these days?" He shook his head

without censure. "You and yours, the young ones giving you fits at that barn you work at. You should all take lessons from the Nelson sisters."

"Nelson?"

"Oh, they married the Lindquist and Hanson boys."

"Gladdie and Claudia?"

"I don't think anyone ever saw them apart."

"Still don't." Jill laughed. "And, you're right. I probably should be more like they are."

The idea that she and Dee would ever grow older and watch over the town like Gladdie and Claudia was beyond fantastic.

"Yeah." Robert pushed away from the fence and sauntered off slowly, changing the subject as he went. "Anyway, I can't get you or that boy of yours to take a red cent for all this renovation. That's worth a little disruption."

"All right. I know how you could pay me. Has Gypsy ever been ridden?"

Robert looked back. "Been a long while, but yes."

"If you'd let me try her, that would be more than payment enough."

Robert continued walking. "Fine, fine. Whatever you like. Besides, whoever said I like peace and quiet?"

MONDAY, JULY THIRD, Becky Barnes showed up for her sixth lesson of the summer. Not a single week had been canceled despite the mercurial Becky's regular threats, and Mondays loomed like the most difficult jumps in a cross-country course—to be negotiated with extreme care and planning.

After Becky's flash of interest in Dragon, she'd reverted to her uncharming self, and if Jill was confused about her own future, she despaired for Becky's. Between the girl's lack of progress, her sister's clear longing to be with the horses, and their mother's reluctance to address either issue, Jill was ready to suggest throwing in the towel for the first time in her teaching career.

When Becky slouched out of her mother's van, Jill could not face one more minute of watching the girl circle apathetically around the arena. Spur of the moment, she had Becky leave Roy in the pasture and saddle Sun instead. "You and I are leaving the arena behind today," she told her. "It's a holiday, let's go have some fun."

Becky gave no indication she knew fun from cod liver oil.

After tacking up Cassidy and mounting with Becky, they left Anita, clearly skeptical, to wait out the hour with Jamie.

"What do you think?" she asked when she and Becky left the stable yard. "Fun yet?"

"Sure." Sarcasm oozed from the teen. "Definitely the best idea ever."

Jill ignored the rudeness, preferring it to the girl's usual shrug. She purposely gave no instructions except to tell her a little about Sun—how old he was and how long she'd owned him. Slowly, when Becky realized Jill was on the level about no formal lesson, she relaxed. When Cass gave a fresh little crow hop at a bird flying past, Becky actually giggled. When Sun broke into a trot at her command, Becky dropped her heels and posted better than she ever had.

"They look like each other," she said at last, without directly referencing the two horses by name. "How did you do that?"

"Pure luck." Jill hid her delight at Becky initiating a conversation. "Like I need three horses, right?"

"Like you need one."

"That's true." Jill laughed. "Most people would say horses are not necessary to life. That might not be true for me. What about you? What do you have that's unnecessary?"

"Green hair."

A genuine bubble of laughter burst from Jill. She'd never have guessed the child had an IQ over a hundred.

They ambled along the same path Jill had ridden with Chase, and she dared broach the subject of school, fully expecting no response. Instead, Becky answered with a tidy synopsis.

"I like science. I hate English. Math is boring. My social studies teacher last year was cute, but he was a dork, like most of the boys."

Jill nearly tumbled off Cassidy's back in shock. "Well," she said, before the moment passed. "It's okay if seventh grade boys seemed like dorks. They get better with age."

"Maybe like that Chase guy. Is he your boyfriend?"

The question took her complete aback. "Wow. I don't

know that I can call him a boyfriend." But then again, what else would he be?

"He likes you."

Jill stared ahead, inexplicably unnerved. "How can you tell that? You've only met him a few times."

Becky's shrug this time was an honest gesture. "It's obvious."

Jill wondered why the opinion of a troubled teenager should make her heart pound. "I like him, too."

"Yeah. I know."

The ride was an unqualified success. After emerging from the woods on their way to the stables, they flushed a pheasant cock out of the tall grass. Sun, the consummate trail horse, barely blinked. Cassidy, on the other hand, jumped sideways two feet, wheeled, and threatened to wheel and bolt. Jill calmed her and brought her back to Sun's side. Rebecca watched with wide eyes.

"Wow, you didn't fall off."

It hadn't been much of an incident, but Becky had seen it as a feat.

"It's just experience, Becky. You'll learn to be comfortable, too, I promise."

"I doubt it."

"You can do anything you want, kiddo, don't sell yourself short." She took in the slender girl with the round-cheeked, overly made-up face. Becky still stiffened now and then as she experimented with skills she'd somehow picked up over six weeks, but basically she rode more easily than she ever had. The breakthrough seemed like a gift.

"Do you know there's a big horse show here at the end

of August? I think you should make it a goal to ride. You can show Roy. Or Sun," Jill added impulsively.

Becky wrinkled her nose, whether in distaste or uncertainty Jill wasn't sure.

"You don't have to, but I'm willing to help you get there. We'd have two months to get you ready."

"Are you doing it?"

"I am. With Dragon and this one." She stroked Cass's neck.

Becky didn't reply, but she didn't shrug either.

The outing's success ended the moment they returned to the barn. Anita and Jamie waited expectantly, and with the first inquiry from her sister, Becky copped her familiar sullen, closemouthed attitude. With no choice but to ignore the animosity, just as she ignored Dee's, Jill took Anita aside as she had done before and let Becky finish caring for Sun on her own.

"It went really well today," she said. "Without an audience she relaxed."

"A change of pace can be good once in a while."

"So, what do you think? Can we get Jamie up riding, too?"

It had been two weeks since she'd first made the suggestion. Anita's features clouded.

"Yes, that. I did discuss it with my husband. Jamie's gone through so much change adjusting to junior high and watching her friends playing all the sports she can't. She's starting to like the activities up at Courage Center. We, and her doctor for that matter, think we shouldn't throw something new in her path right now."

Jill stomach couldn't have hurt more had Anita punched her. She eked out a calm voice. "I'm sorry to hear that. I'm disappointed."

"And the other thing is, horseback riding has become something Rebecca can excel at without worrying about her sister. We need to keep it as her activity for a while."

Jill swallowed rising anger. The whole argument was ludicrous, even aside from the idea that Becky was excelling at the sport.

"Have you *asked* Rebecca about this? Have you consulted Jamie? That's a young lady who really wants to ride horses again someday."

"Someday I'm sure she will."

Anita simply turned away, closing the subject unalterably.

Jill reeled as if she'd announced a death. In fact, something had died—if only an idea she'd loved too much before she should have let it take root in her heart. She slogged through the rest of the day in a murky, undefined grief, and by the time she headed home, Jill still couldn't figure out why one little girl should mean enough to make her so sad. And so angry.

CHASE STRETCHED OUT on the faded brocade couch in Robert's living room. Thinking about the past two weeks boggled his mind. He kept his demons at bay more often these days by pushing his muscles in the ways he hadn't since boyhood, but he tried not to give them chances to sneak in.

Robert helped, too. He was a quick-minded, non-judgmental companion. But it was Jill who held the key to Chase's slow healing. No woman had ever accepted him this unquestioningly, although she knew there was plenty to question. Keeping his secret for this long curled Chase's insides into knots of guilt that rarely left him. Only his belief that Jill would understand when he finally did explain what had happened in Memphis, kept him searching for the right time.

Robert's tread on the stairs descending from his bedroom caused Chase to check the time. The clock read nearly nine, and he frowned. They'd expected Jill tonight by eight.

"Jill ain't here?" Robert sat in his recliner and reached for his current book. Chase noted the Louis L'Amour Western Robert had read at least twice. The old farmer rubbed his eyes with one hand and tapped lightly on his breastbone with the other.

"Something must have come up. You all right, my friend?" Chase asked.

"Yeah, yeah. Little heartburn after dinner. Gotta go feed the horses, but I'll do it in a minute."

"I'll go. You look tired."

"What? So you can sneak out to go look for the girl? Think you two was already newlyweds."

"I'm warning you, I'm gonna replace those Westerns with romance novels."

"Don't need no damn *romances*, got one goin' on right in front of my twenty-twenty."

A romance he definitely had. Chase lived in a permanent state of anticipation when Jill wasn't around. When she was, he lived in a permanent state of war with self-control. Jill was far more to him after six weeks than a desirable woman, but lately, especially since he'd learned for certain he could lose her to Colin Pitts-Matherson, his dreams about her had lost all the sweetness they'd ever had.

Now they were urgent.

Angel popped her head up as if a squirrel had darted past her nose. Three seconds later she was whining at the door. Robert grunted.

"That'll be the girl now. Get out of here now, you two. Quit yammerin' about romances and go do something about it."

The old man was sharp as a bee sting. Chase laughed and let the screen door slap behind him. He looked toward the horizon and reveled in the flat expanse of navy-blue night sky dipping to the line of silver-green alfalfa. His eye traveled over the farmyard. The pasture pond was full and its banks weed-choked, but other than that, he and Jill had made quite a few changes.

The new deck floor was finished, and a new railing started. Three old buildings were gone. The lawn, admittedly more crabgrass than bluegrass, looked neat and trimmed nonetheless, and Jill's flowers, planted with love and optimism along the house and deck perimeters, had taken hold.

He stepped off the deck and followed Angel around the house. To his shock, he found Jill squatting in front of The Creature, her arms wrapped around the dog, her face buried in the curly hair behind Angel's pointy, floppy ears.

"Can I be next?"

She uncurled herself and smeared away tears beneath her eyes with the back of her hand. His stomach dropped.

"What happened? Aw, Jill, what's wrong."

She never cried, but now she flowed into his embrace and buried her head against his chest.

"There's nothing wrong. This is completely stupid."

"Tell me."

"Anita Barnes axed the idea of Jamie riding, that's all. I don't even know what to say. Her reasons are completely lame-assed."

"Honey, I'm sorry." He lifted her chin and wiped the last of her tears away with his thumb.

"The worst of it is that I care at all, that I'm foolish enough to get invested."

"You'll always care too much, Jill. Believe me, that's what got me into trouble with you in the first place."

"Great. I didn't know you were in trouble."

"Trust me, honey. I'm in old farms, big horses, and problem teens up to my Kentucky red neck. That's before mentioning beautiful equestrians."

"And I have a problem with silver-tongued drifters."

"C'mon. Feed the horses with me and tell me more."

The mares galloped in from the pasture at Jill's call, and Tatters wheeled in after them as if he had ants in his little equine britches. He didn't care all that much about grain yet, but he had his own little foal bucket to play in. Mostly he jigged and squealed for Jill's attention, because next to his mother she was just about his favorite thing in the world.

Chase loved to watch her with him. She clearly spoke his language when convincing him his little baby halter wasn't a torture device, or that walking with a lead rope was a cool game. She climbed into the paddock with him now and ran her hands over every inch of his leggy body. The colt stood perfectly still, as if getting a massage.

"This is what it's about," she said, wrapping her arms around his neck. "Learning from all creatures. Why can't Anita Barnes see her daughter is one of those people who needs animals?"

Chase could hear her tears welling up again. He crawled over the fence railing and pried her gently from the foal, spun her to face him, and gazed into the doe brown of her eyes for only a moment before he lowered his mouth.

Right there in the pasture he let his lips roam loosely, achingly over her, and he pressed the hair back from her forehead with both hands. Their cool tongues touched and played until both grew hot. In response, she feathered her fingers across his stomach, and control edged from his grasp. When he tugged on the delicate skin of her lip eliciting a whimper, a dangerous spark seared through his belly, followed by more in rapid succession as she slid her body against his. The sparks fell onto days and days of built-up, smoldering desire and ignited the deep, unstable warmth. His physical response followed swiftly. Groaning, he cupped his hands over her ears, thumbs on her cheeks, and pushed her head away.

"Stop," he said, his voice in shreds.

"Stop?"

He pulled her through the pasture until he pressed up against the side of the barn. The moment her body joined his he assaulted her mouth anew, and she pressed her hips intimately against the arousal he couldn't hide, eliciting a mewl of delight from her.

Relentless now, his fingers danced to the swell of her breast, drawing approval from deep in her throat. With no finesse, he yanked the hem of her T-shirt free of her riding breeches, slipped his hand beneath the fabric, and searched out fine lace. He pushed beneath that as well to the soft side of her breast. As his thumb found its fullness, desire hardened him more, and he pushed aside the satin and took her hardened nipple between his thumb and forefinger.

Gasping, she trailed her fingers down his cheek, across his shoulder, and to his elbow. He braced harder against the barn, and with excruciating slowness, she brushed around his hip and tried to delve between where she fit tightly against him. Thwarted, she switched directions and circled his leg to grasp the heavy muscles of his seat. He nearly sank straight into the dirt.

"Honey." His voice barely functioned. "You're making me crazy."

"Good." She kissed him again.

"Crazy people do things they regret."

Her whispery kisses slowed. "There'd be no regrets. I'm asking for this, right out loud. I know I'm not as virtuous as you are but don't hold that against me."

He grasped her shoulders, unnerved by her words. "What makes you think I would ever consider myself a judge of your virtue?"

"Prove it. Don't stop yourself on my account."

He led her to the fence and they ducked under it. Safe from inquisitive foals, he found a grassy spot next to the barn and pulled her to straddle his lap. Her softness against his head was like putting a match to tinder, and he thrust against her.

"I will stop us," he said, leaning for her mouth. "Because we can't play with this kind of fire simply because we hurt about something else. The act of love changes everything—including futures."

"At least you admit to the fire."

"Oh, Lord help me, don't ever doubt that."

She placed her mouth carefully on his and kissed him with the most deliberate, thorough tongue dance he'd ever experienced. "We can play without making a whole bonfire," she whispered, and stroked herself against him, arching at the top with a cry of surprise.

He groaned in surrender and dragged her hips down, rocking beneath her until they found a rhythm that made her whimper in anticipation.

"Okay, baby," he whispered. "Make it feel good."

She shattered around him mere minutes later, sobbing out her release and clinging with spaghetti noodle limbs. His own painful desire didn't matter anymore as the simple magic of an old-fashioned technique overwhelmed him. He stroked her hair.

"I lied. I think that was a bonfire," she said, shuddering and smiling.

She rose up and eased off his lap. He kissed her and she lingered, finding a spot cuddled up to his side. Surely, with a firm touch, she cupped him and stroked down his length. "Your turn," she said into his ear, and the hot words shot straight to a spot beneath her fingers.

"Honey, you don't—"

"Shhh. Oh yes. I absolutely do."

She took control, finding the zipper of his jeans and rasping it down to release him. Giving up the last misgiving, he closed his eyes and sank back to let her hold him, and take him dancing on the lip of a volcano.

Chapter Eighteen

TRUST WAS A funny thing. It could be present and not present at the same time. Jill held the two-by-two railing post for Chase, smiling at the top of his head while he pounded, loving that she knew how thick his black hair was beneath her fingers. She loved how well she knew his soft Southern accent in her ear. Loved how he trusted her to touch him so intimately and explore that trust with her all week.

And yet, he remained hidden. She saw the shutters on his emotions more clearly now that they'd shared almost as much physical closeness as they could. *Almost*, because the trust to share himself completely was *not* quite there.

Still, he was her champion. He might not rave about going to Florida, but she never doubted he would build her up, remind her to trust herself, tell her how smart and talented and caring she was no matter what got her down. Like now. Helping Chase with the new porch was nearly cathartic enough to let Jill forget how Becky had taken a graceless, although not dangerous fall from Roy that morning when she'd yanked too hard on his reins and pissed him off, then proceeded let Jamie have it for "always being in the way with that stupid chair."

Jill was running out of ideas for reaching the girl. It really was almost time to cut bait.

At the unexpected crunch of gravel beneath car tires, Angel, lying at Robert's feet on the new porch decking, jumped up and let out a series of warning barks. Jill's heart sank at the sight of Jim Krieger's Lincoln Navigator rolling to a halt outside the chicken yard. They hadn't seen him in three weeks, but Krieger emerged into the warm evening sun, bringing a chill.

"Hell's bells," Robert cursed. "Ain't we got fun now?"

"Good evening, Mr. McCormick."

"Krieger," Robert acknowledged, without rising from his chair. "You're still in the trespassin' business I see."

"Now, now, I'm here to give you an update. You're important to us, Robert." Krieger spoke as if dealing with an addled nursing home patient.

"I still don't want your money, so spare the update and leave."

Krieger spotted Jill and Chase and his eyes widened. "Ahhh. I find you here after all, Preston. You're on my list, too. We have a little unfinished business."

"None that I know of," Chase replied.

Krieger's superior smile sent annoyance oozing through Jill's body. "The decision has been made to push ahead more quickly with the start of the project," Krieger said. "We're preparing a petition for the state that will allow the powers that be to declare eminent domain here. I think you need to accept reality, Robert, and take our offer before you're forced to take the pittance the state will offer."

"Don't make me ask you to leave again." Robert's reply was almost nonchalant.

"Your stubbornness might seem admirable," Krieger said, "but if you continue you'll find out you were very foolish." He stared at Chase. "Since you two are *such* good friends, why not talk some sense into the man?"

"He's talking plenty of sense to me," Chase said. "And I see they did a fine job on that truck door, so since I paid the bill weeks ago, I can't see that we have anything else to discuss."

"You talk pretty bold for a man with so much past."

Jill couldn't put a name to what she read on Chase's face. Controlled fury? Fear?

"Oh? Why don't you share what you think you know about my past?"

"As a matter of fact, I will. I know the Memphis PD is looking for you right now."

Jill's breath caught. The Memphis police? The skin around Chase's eye tightened, and his face lost half a shade of color.

"You don't know what you're talking about," he said.

Krieger shook his head, a smirk solidly in place. He looked toward the porch. "Oh, Robert, Robert. You're not only foolish about money but about people, too. Watch yourself. This one isn't what he seems." He turned for his car. "And do let us know when you change your mind about selling. We don't have much time."

After Krieger drove off, Robert was the only one left in a good mood.

"Son, you're worth a hundred shotguns!" he said gleefully. "I love how you best him."

"Was he serious?" Jill asked, and spun Chase to face her, grasping his upper arms.

His face was such a blank mask, Jill's heart only pounded harder. What *was* this man she was falling in love with hiding?

"You told me you weren't running from the law," Robert said. "I still believe you if you say it ain't so."

"It isn't so."

"So Krieger is making things up now?" Jill moved her hand to his face and stroked it, begging him to answer.

"I doubt he's making it up." Chase sighed. "I told you I worked in a bad part of Memphis. I saw things. Who knows what the police could want." For a moment he seemed unreachable, but suddenly he softened, and to Jill's utter relief wrapped his arms around her. "I'll call my brother. He'll know what's going on. I sure don't."

"Really?"

Because if he was in trouble, she was in trouble.

"Really."

She knew the wall he could erect in front of his emotions. This time it wasn't there. She sighed. "Robert, what about eminent domain? Isn't that serious?" she asked.

"The man is all wind, girlie. He's played that hand before. He knows they don't need my place for access, but he thinks I'm a fool. I'm not. I have a lawyer, too, and I've seen the plans for this gravel pit. If it's the size they originally said it will be, then the only reason they could want my land is to expand. Eventually they'll get the farm, but if I have my way, it won't be until my name is a burr so deep in their fannies they'll need surgery to remove it."

"Mean old coot," Chase said, laughing outright for the first time.

"And proud of it."

"Stupid gravel pit," Jill said. "Wish *we* could buy the farm and continue the standoff longer yet. Robert, just live another eighty years, and I'll save the money."

Chase waited until Jill had gone home to call Brody. She had every reason, every right, to be unnerved by Krieger's accusation, and Chase had promised her he'd solve the mystery first thing in the morning. But he wasn't about to wait. He'd ignored his brother's calls until now, but he had a few choice words for Broderick "Brody" Preston he wasn't sure he could control. Jill didn't need to hear them.

Rat his whereabouts to *the police*, had he? Rotten snitch. He'd probably sweet-talked Poppa into giving him Connery's number. How else would Krieger have known?

The police had to be looking for him in regard to Tiana's murder, but he'd already told them everything he knew. Brody had worked on Tiana after the shooting. They should be talking to him.

When he was certain Robert, too, had headed off for bed, he wandered toward the barn and punched in Brody's number. It was close to 11p.m. in Memphis, but Chase didn't care.

"Are you effin' kidding me? I was starting plans for your funeral service!" Brody answered with cheerful chastisement, and his voice was as comforting as a back-slapping embrace. To his annoyance, Chase's ire faded ever so slightly.

"Nice to hear your voice, too," he said.

"I'm serious, where the hell have you been?"

"Winning friends and creating enemies. Same old, same old."

"Yeah, enemies like me. What's up with never returning phone calls?"

"I told you I wouldn't answer until I was ready." Chase let his aggravation swell again. "And speaking of enemies, what exactly were you thinking siccing the Memphis police on me? You *gave* them Connery's phone number?"

"Whoa! What are you flappin' your gums about? I didn't tell them anything."

"C'mon, somebody did. Poppa wouldn't. You're the only two who know where I am."

"You live in a dream world," Brody said. "Mama practically beat it out of Poppa." He chuckled. "Hey, you know, I'll bet they got to Mama. She probably told 'em to contact you and then carry on fetchin' you home."

"Oh, that's terrific. Then they are after me."

"They aren't *after* you, grits-for-brains. They've finally got Chuckie D. and Louis Franto in custody, Louis flipped on Chuckie as the shooter, and the detective has some questions before the arraignment."

Deep in his heart Chase had known it was something this straightforward. He'd wanted a reason not to need

Brody, but he found his anger ebbing away, under the balm of his brother's cheerful voice.

"I'm sorry. I just needed someone to blame. I'll call and holler at Mama."

"Yeah, you do that." Brody's chuckle broke to a laugh.

"Tell me how it's going otherwise," Chase said. "You all right?"

"We're holding our own. I took your suggestion and got Levon Benson to fill in for you. He's working out."

"He's not the surgeon you are, but he's tough and talented," Chase said. "Good move. You listened to me for once."

"You had a good idea for once."

Chase leaned against the side of the barn, closing his eyes and smiling.

"So." Brody's voice lost its teasing edge. "Does this call mean you're ready to come back?"

"No."

"Clara asked about you."

"Clara would ask about Jack the Ripper."

"Knock it off. How many times do we have to say it? You didn't pull that trigger. Get your shit together and figure it out."

"Working on it, Brody."

"Look. The police will manage with what I told them, you don't have to call. On the other hand, you could do little Tiana a big favor by contacting the detective."

"I'd have done her a bigger favor by being the hell where I was supposed to be that day and not leaving her alone on those steps."

"You know the truth. Tiana was in the right place but at the wrong time."

For the first time in weeks the memory flooded into Chase's mind and wouldn't leave at his command. He held his breath against the searing pain and pictured the lifeless body, a skinny doll against stark white exam table paper. Vials and boxes and blood-soaked cotton strewn like macabre confetti on the floor. Brody's hand, firm on his arm, guiding him away, urging him into a chair. "It's over, Chase. I'm so sorry."

"Chase? Man, you there?"

"I know, Brods, I do know. I'll call. Do you have a name?"

"Ashland, Ashmore. Yeah, Ashmore, He's not a bad guy."

No. The bad guys were in custody. This should all be over. But it wasn't. "Thanks. Can you text me his number?"

"I can. Chase. You really okay?"

"I'm fine. I'm working hard, and I've met some good people. I don't know what the next step is, but I probably won't be here past the end of the summer."

He swallowed against a sudden hollowness in his gut. Did he mean that? Was he planning to leave in another six weeks? The idea twisted him up with a mix of relief and dread.

"Good. Don't friggin' ignore the phone from now on, okay?"

"Don't bug me like a mother then, okay? I've got to go, got work in the morning. And I know I woke you."

"Easy day planned tomorrow. Unless something blows up."

"Here's to nothing blowing up. I'll talk to you, soon. Sorry I called to jump on you."

"Love ya, man. Let me know if you need help with that detective."

"Sure."

JILL CAME UP with one last desperate trick for Becky Barnes. If it didn't work, she . . . well, she didn't know what she'd do. It seemed silly for the girl to keep wasting her parents' money on pointless lessons, but the thought of giving up sat like a stone in Jill's stomach.

Thursday, Jill stood with Robert in the barn, neither speaking as they waited to launch their plan. The old farmer stared meditatively at his big Clydesdale, as nervous as Jill was. She heard the crunch of gravel and raised her brows.

"Show time," she said.

Robert grunted.

Outside, an unfamiliar silver Saturn pulled up in front of the house, and a confused Becky exited the passenger side, peering around like a lost tourist. Surprised at not seeing Anita or Jamie, Jill studied the man who got out from behind the wheel. When he saw her, he offered a boyish smile.

"Hi," he said. "You must be Jill? I'm Michael Barnes, Becky's dad and designated driver. Anita and Jamie had a conflicting appointment. I have to zip back to work, but Becky says she's fine until my wife gets here."

"Well . . . sure." She had Becky to herself again? Jill sent a prayer of thanks upward. This was working out better than she'd hoped when she set up the special lesson. "We'll be great."

"Terrific, thanks!" The exuberant Michael ruffled the spikes of Becky's orange hair and she scowled but didn't pull away. "Have fun, Becs. See you tonight. Sorry I have to run."

A moment later the tornadic Michael Barnes was gone. Becky glanced nervously around, her defiance non-existent in the face of Robert's intimidating old farm.

"*This* is where I'm riding?" she asked.

"Yup. But don't judge the book by its cover. The first time I saw this place I did, and I was dead wrong."

"What am I doing here anyway?"

"Like I told you, I have something special for you to try."

Special and, Jill hoped, a little intimidating. The experiment about to take place left Jill's stomach in nervous free-fall. Chase was at work, although she wished now he was here. The girls liked him and he was wonderful with them. Her heart still broke over the story he'd told about seeing a little girl killed by gang violence. Such a simple but awful reason for the police to be looking to ask questions. That was another reason she wanted him nearby—he'd been pretty quiet since talking to the detective in Memphis.

She pointed Becky toward the makeshift riding arena. It had been mowed and scraped until it was passably even.

"That's where we'll be working. Take Angel and check it out. I'll be your groom and get your horse for you today. She's my surprise."

Robert had Gypsy haltered and ready. He looked jumpier than Jill felt.

"Robert, is this cruel?"

"No. You got to get her attention right off. Go through it like you planned."

He handed Jill the lead rope.

"Okay, little girl," Jill murmured. "I'm counting on you to work your magic."

Gypsy nickered softly.

It wasn't possible to tell whether Becky's eyes widened more in fear or awe when Jill led the enormous horse into the sunny yard.

"Becky. This is Gypsy."

"Is this a joke?" If Becky's eyes could have spit flames, Jill and Gypsy would have been roasted.

"Absolutely not."

"Right. This is a lesson horse."

"No, but there's a lot she can teach you. C'mon, get to know her. I promise she's a baby."

Becky clearly had no clue how to deal with a beast that towered over her by a foot and a half. Gypsy lowered her muzzle to snuffle Becky's hair then blew a welcoming snort. Becky jumped ten inches.

"It's all right. She only wants to get to know you. Go on, give her a good pat."

"Seems like she could get to know me pretty good in one bite."

Amazed again by the humor, Jill laughed. "Guess we're fortunate she's not carnivorous."

Becky stroked Gypsy's neck for several seconds. Jill pulled some carrot pieces out of her jeans pocket. Offering one to Gypsy, she handed two more to Becky.

"Give her these, and you'll be friends for life."

"I don't have a death wish."

"How come you aren't this funny at our regular lessons?"

"This is a funnier place."

"Well, I like it. But you'd better feed Gypsy the carrot before she takes it from you herself."

With her entire arm trembling and her jaw clenched, Becky offered her palm to the huge horse. Gypsy's muzzle dwarfed the girl's proffered hand, but with a lipping motion as gentle as a breath, the mare removed the carrot and devoured it in two muffled crunches. Becky fed another, and Jill handed her Gypsy's lead rope.

"Tie her up over there. Let's get her groomed."

Becky took a breath to object but closed her mouth, leaving only skepticism in her eyes. Like a docile puppy, Gypsy followed the slender teen. Jill and Robert followed the horse.

"Becky," Jill said, when Gypsy was secured with a release knot. "This is Robert McCormick. He owns Gypsy and this farm."

Rebecca eyed him, and he returned the unblinking appraisal.

"Howdy," he said at last, in the gruff voice Jill now knew so well.

"Hi." Becky had never sounded less petulant.

With a marked lack of lip, Becky performed the tasks Jill assigned. She groomed the mare, standing part of the time on a sturdy two-foot cube Robert had created years before for the task. With Jill at her back, Becky lifted each massive foot, picking out what little straw and manure had caught in the grooves beside the frog. She fumbled valiantly with the huge bridle Jill handed her, and finally accepted help. She didn't balk or complain until Jill announced that it was time to ride.

"Ride?"

"Sure. This is a riding lesson."

For the first time since meeting him, Becky looked to Robert as if he could save her from Jill's madness. "On her?"

"Jill here's been doin' it all week," he acknowledged.

"You're trying to get back at me." She spun to glare at Jill.

"Get back at you for what?"

For the first time Becky's anger found a voice. "This is retarded. Nobody rides horses this big."

"Don't say retarded, please. Why not?"

"Because you can't get your legs around a dumb horse like this."

"You can, though. It's really a pretty cool feeling."

"Fine, you split your pants. I'm not riding her."

Jill choked back laughter despite the sassy-as-a-five-year-old tone. "Why, Becky?"

The girl kicked at the dirt with a booted foot and looked away.

"Becky?"

"Okay, what do you want from me? I'm scared to ride her, does that make you happy?"

Her voice quavered, and although her face looked ready to crumple, her eyes remained dry, and her chin tilted upward in defiance.

"Yes, but not for the reason you think." Jill set her hand on Becky's shoulder, and the girl looked away. "You want to know what this is really about? It's not about revenge or humiliation, but it is about humility. At least you admitted that you're scared. You told me how you feel, and that's more than I've gotten from you in two months.

"Maybe you think your feelings are none of my business, but I care about them, and I'm concerned when they cause you to act apathetically around horses. It's my job to keep you safe. You don't realize it yet, but you could climb on Gypsy and ride like you do every week at our lessons. You could kick her and bounce on her and she'd ignore you. But she's got you buffaloed with her size, and suddenly the tables are turned."

"So it is teach-Becky-a-lesson time after all."

"Teach Becky a lesson, yes. Get even with Becky, no."

"I'm not here to learn lessons about life. Everybody's always trying to teach me about life."

"But you're here to learn how to ride, and you can bet your boots I'm using every trick I can to see that you do." Becky said no more and Jill raised her brows. "Ready for a leg up?"

"I'm not riding her."

"You are, sweetie, but you don't have to do it alone

if you're nervous. And I don't blame you for being nervous." Once again Becky's eyes could have lasered Jill to smolders had they been weapons. "I'll give you a boost and come right behind you."

Jill waited. "Fine," Becky said at last. "All right? Fine!"

In seconds the slight girl was settled astride the eighteen-hand Clydesdale. Jill mounted the box, grasped Gypsy's thick mane in front of Becky, and swung up behind her as easily as if the horse had been a toy rocker in a nursery. She put her arms either side of Becky's rigid waist.

"What do you think?"

Becky shrugged. Robert handed up the thick reins, and Jill closed her fingers around the leather.

"Relax, okay? How can you fall off anything this wide?"

Even after practicing all week, Gypsy's incredible breadth still awed Jill. Through the gate, into the make-shift ring, and three times around its small circumference, she did nothing but talk to Becky and keep Gypsy to a walk. She worked to get Becky rocking rhythmically with the movement. At long last Becky's stiffness drained away and fluidity eased into her spine.

"All right! Can you feel how easy it is?"

The teen actually nodded.

"Take the reins now, we'll keep walking."

Becky see-sawed her way through the lesson. With her own hands at the controls she tensed up again until repetition and time bolstered her confidence. She flopped like a boneless doll when Jill took back the reins and sent Gypsy into her ponderous trot, but got the feel for the quicker gait as well. By the time Jill turned the reins to her, Becky was able to laugh when her coordination temporarily mutinied. They trotted twice around the enclosure and, at last, Jill told her to halt.

"You did fantastic. Now go it alone."

"No!"

"At a walk, no faster until you're ready." Jill slipped off Gypsy's back. "Go ahead."

At first Rebecca sat, no more than an uncoordinated passenger. Slowly, finding patience from somewhere she had no idea existed, Jill talked Becky back into relaxation, and elasticity returned to her body. The magic, when it occurred, was nearly visible. Becky connected herself mentally with the horse, and, in that instant, her riding became effortless.

"Yes!" Jill whispered in triumph. "See that, Robert? She's got it." He nodded.

It wouldn't matter if Becky did nothing else right the rest of the afternoon. She understood how to ride a horse. The skill would come if she wanted it to. If Becky quit after this lesson, she would take something away with her that she hadn't possessed before this afternoon.

"Trot her now," Jill called.

Becky obeyed. Not prettily at first, but confidently. After a couple of circles, Jill stopped her and met her at Gypsy's side. "Okay, c'mon down."

She knew Becky had no clue what prompted the little hug, because it elicited a scowl. "Why do you think that ride earns you an A-plus?"

"Because I was stupid enough to do it."

"That got you a C."

"Then I have no idea."

"For effort, Becky. For fifteen minutes you let go of your anger and you listened, not as much to me as to the horse."

"Big deal."

"It is a big deal."

There was more she wanted to say, further she wanted Becky to come now that this smallest of breakthroughs had occurred, but she turned away, made a pretense out of studying the horizon, and forced herself to wait until her adrenaline rush tapered off.

The grooming process was silent, but Becky took the lead rope herself when it was time to go back to the barn. Jill fell into step beside her. "Want to do this again sometime? I'd like to keep working Gypsy, and if you want to and your mom agrees, you could come help. Kind of freebie lessons now and then."

Becky gave the smallest of nods. Jill didn't want to lose the tenuous connection she could barely feel. If they could keep it growing, Becky might make it to the horse show in August after all. The idea of bringing her along that far before Jill had to leave—if she left . . .

If? Her thoughts careened off track. Of course she was going with Colin. She just hadn't made a big deal of it yet. She had goals to reach this summer first. She focused back on Becky.

"Plus, I think you're ready to start jumping."

"On her?" The wide eyes returned.

Jill laughed. "No, no. I promise you a regular horse for that."

"I want to jump."

It was the closest to eagerness Jill had ever seen.

"S'pose that youngster's gonna be glad to see his mama," Robert mused.

"Youngster?" asked Becky.

"Robert, why don't you introduce her to our little clown," Jill said.

Tatters was used to short intervals away from his mother, but he squealed and kicked up in relief the instant Gypsy came into view. She whinnied back, loud as a siren.

"Oh!" Becky squealed, too, before she could stop herself as the big baby barreled up to the gate and halted in a frenzied crow hop.

"Rebecca Barnes, meet T.N. Tatters," Robert intoned. "Let them get their kicks out and then you can go in and play with him. He likes his ears scratched."

When Becky warmed to him, she allowed smiles Jill had never even glimpsed before. Jill stepped to the fence with Robert.

"Thank you," she said quietly.

"No thanks necessary."

"We have a long way to go, but it's a first step. Can I bring her back?"

"I think you should."

Jill's chest constricted, seeing his protective watch over the girl in the pasture with his horses. How could she have grown so fond of the old curmudgeon? But she knew how. He was an old fake. For all his tough shell, his heart was soft as Tatters' fuzzy baby coat.

Chapter Nineteen

CHASE HADN'T COME into the Connery offices to answer phones. He arrived, frustrated after three unsuccessful attempts earlier in the week to reach Duncan Connery by phone, to find out why nobody would say exactly where his boss had gone.

He walked into chaos.

An explosion at an abandoned warehouse had destroyed an adjacent Connery project and left half a dozen employees injured. Duncan, he finally learned, was not just out of the office, he was out of town, and Krieger had been the boss to race to the scene. The receptionist was out sick, Duncan's secretary, Jane, was trying to fill two positions, and phones were ringing off their hooks. The instant Jane saw Chase's able body, he was the new receptionist.

It took him nearly an hour to get control of the phones, but before he could get a breath, a kid of indeterminate youth wearing a lightweight gray jacket that read "Quik-Qurrier" approached the desk.

"Delivery for James Krieger," he announced.

"I'll sign for it, he's out of the office."

The kid handed over a clipboard. Chase scribbled his signature on the log sheet, the delivery boy thanked him and left him holding a thick packet.

Krieger.

Chase scowled. The man was like a rabid bloodhound. He was still spreading the police rumors around town—Chase knew because he'd received the small-town glares and questions to prove it. He'd been trying to reach Duncan to explain the situation and see about getting Krieger to ease up. No such luck, apparently.

Chase sighed and took advantage of the lull to stretch his legs and take the envelope to Krieger's office. The man had clearly left in a rush since his window was open to the July breeze and papers had fluttered across his desk. Chase set the envelope down, closed the window, and saw several sheets of paper that had landed on the floor next to Krieger's chair. He retrieved them with barely a thought.

The name "Sandhurst Aggregate" dominating the top of the first page stopped him. Beneath the letterhead was a short note. "Jim, here are the traffic assessments—one for your office and one for the meeting. When Connery signs both we're good to go."

Chase drew his brows into puzzled folds. The note was paper-clipped to two copies of a report. A memory niggled. At that impromptu town meeting weeks before, someone had said there were rumors of false traffic as-sessments for the gravel pit. Whatever that meant.

He glanced around the office and looked back to the reports. He hadn't taken the suggestions to spy remotely seriously, but numbers hovered directly before his eyes:

KENNISON FALLS PIT

Acres: 62

Cubic tons per year: 250

Estimated traffic load: 5–10 trucks per day

Life expectancy: 3–5 years

Chase scratched his head. This had to be something Krieger was planning to present to the town council. But it looked straightforward.

He turned to the second copy of the report. It seemed identical to the other. Then the first discrepancy caught his eye. He studied it for a moment and didn't believe what he saw. Every word on this report was the same—headings, dates, categories. But the numbers were differ-ent. Very different.

KENNISON FALLS PIT

Acres: 120

Cubic tons per year: 500,000

Estimated traffic load: 15–30 trucks per day

Life expectancy: 10 years–Indefinite

What the . . . ?

He stared at the papers for another nerve-wracking

minute, and when he finally dropped them into the pile on Krieger's desk, his hands shook. He had no real idea what the separate papers represented, but something was definitely wrong. He read the cover letter again. ". . . one for your office and one for the meeting . . ."

One for the office, one *different* one for the meeting. Fury raced through his veins. Something rotten in Kennison Falls didn't begin to describe this. He knew exactly which report Krieger intended to show the good citizens of the tiny town.

The question was, did Duncan Connery know about this? He couldn't possibly. The man Poppa had sworn by wouldn't be party to such fraud. Chase ignored the ringing lobby phone and marched down the hall to Jane's desk. He wasn't playing spy now. It was time to find out exactly where the head of the company had gone.

REBECCA IN ALL her awfulness had returned.

Friday, with her mother sitting in a canvas chair and her sister's wheelchair pulled fully up to the half fence of the chicken yard, Becky let them all have her obnoxious attitude with both barrels, comfortable enough with Gypsy now to afford that much inattention. Jamie actually offered heartfelt encouragement, to which Becky only made snippy, rude replies. Anita put on blinders to the bad behavior and called out, "You're doing *great*, baby" every few minutes. Jill didn't know which, mother or daughter, she wanted to throttle more.

She ended the riding lesson ten minutes early and

left Rebecca in Robert's hands with the one last activity they'd cooked up just for fun. He was going to teach her how to harness Gypsy as if they would be driving her. She felt guilty abandoning the old farmer, but he was the one who waved her out of the makeshift arena and back to Anita and Jamie.

"Hello, ladies."

At the very welcome greeting, her heart began a happy zigzagging dance. Chase kissed her unashamedly on the mouth. Jamie crowed with delight.

"Chase!"

"Hey, darlin'!" He pulled Jamie's chair away from the fence, knelt in front of her, and brushed her nose with his forefinger. "How the heck are you?"

"Good." Jamie flushed prettily.

Angel bounded from the arena, barking and worming her way between Chase and Jamie. She put her paws on the girl's lap and licked both their faces. Jamie twisted away ineffectually but squealed happily.

"What you wearing today, Milk Bone perfume? That dog's like to lick your tan clean off."

Jamie squeezed Angel like a teddy bear, and the dog melted into the snug hold. "It's 'cause you love me, don't you, Angel girl?"

"So, how's the rod?" Chase patted one of her chair wheels. "Did you ever get to play basketball in her like you told me about?"

"Yeah. I wasn't very good, though. She doesn't spin very fast."

Chase tapped his chin. "I been thinkin'." He continued in the affected Dogpatch-ese that always made Jamie laugh. "We could easy 'nuff hitch old Gypsy to this little rod of yours, give you one of them lo-oong buggy whips, and set you right off up the driveway. You'd be like a souped-up monster truck, you know? With a gigunda engine on a little bitty truck body. Wouldn't matter if you could spin on a dime, you'd impress the pants off'n everybody you pass."

Jamie giggled infectiously. Chase joined her, and they progressed together to belly laughs.

"I find it a little insensitive to laugh about her handicap." Anita's voice wavered into the moment like a stone tossed into a bright pond.

"It's okay, Mom," Jamie said, her laughter fading. "It's funny."

"Mrs. Barnes, I apologize," Chase added quickly. "There was no disrespect toward Jamie intended. You know that, Jamie, right?"

"'Course!" She shot him a quizzical look.

In that moment Angel chose her next task. Wagging her tail furiously, cocking her delicate ears, she sat in front of Anita Barnes and pawed gently against her thigh. She yipped, ran a few steps toward the pasture, stopped and looked back and then barked again.

She repeated the exercise once more with Jamie.

Chase peered incredulously at the dog. "You know," he said, not quite able to conceal his wonder. "I do believe she's talking plain as day. Telling you there's someone you might like to meet in the pasture."

Anita hesitated, but Jamie shoved her wheels into

motion before her mother could say a word. "It's the baby! Gypsy's baby! Becky told me. Mom, come on."

Anita nodded, more relaxed again, and she followed her daughter toward the barn. Jill sought Chase's eyes and he shrugged.

"Why do I feel like we dodged a bullet?" Jill asked.

"Mothers should be protective of their kids," he replied. "I got a little warning, that's all."

"For what? Being great with her daughter? Why are you so understanding of her?"

He pulled her close and rocked her in his embrace until she relaxed into his hold.

"You're giving these girls so much, honey. Don't give up. Mama Bear isn't the problem."

They left Jamie and Anita to their own devices and watched the end of the harnessing lesson. With no idea what magic Robert possessed, Jill could only stare dumbfounded at the honest-to-goodness pleasant look on Becky's face when they were finished and led Gypsy from the pen.

"I'm testing you next time," Robert grumped at the teen.

"Okay."

Okay? Jill caught Robert's eye and he winked at her.

And then the green Navigator bumped into the driveway for the second time that week. The smile vanished from Robert's face.

"Son of a b—"

"—bicycle," Chase cut him off, casting an eye at Rebecca and at Jamie, who rolled around the corner of the barn with Anita.

Krieger parked, got out, and strolled to their odd knot of personalities, flicked amber, tigerish eyes over Anita Barnes, nodded to Robert, and glued his eyes on Chase. "Got the day off, Mr. Preston?"

"I do. Finished a whole project for the company, what do you think of that?"

He'd been in an upbeat mood since spending the day answering phones, of all things, at the Connery office the day before. Whatever the reason for his good humor, Jill couldn't miss the definite change in his attitude toward Krieger.

Krieger extracted a white envelope from inside his sports coat. "Robert. I'm glad you have witnesses. This is Sandhurst's final offer for your property. The amount is far more than this place is worth."

"Don't matter what it is. Take it back with you."

"I'm afraid I can't do that. I'm just an agent making a delivery."

"I ain't allowed to say what you really are." Robert snatched the proffered envelope.

"All right, Krieger. You've made your *delivery*." Chase stepped between Krieger and Robert.

Krieger's cold, gold eyes iced as he backed away. "You stopped the Memphis police from phoning, but if you get in my way, you'll be steamrollered. You wouldn't want the lovely young ladies in your life to see something like that." He indicated the girls with a little sweep of one finger.

"Of all the nerve . . ." Jill stormed in front of Chase, but he grasped her by the elbow, gently holding her as

Krieger shot them a gloating grin, got in his car, and backed away.

"Forget him, Jill, he's an ass," he whispered.

"Are you going to sell your farm?"

Chase did a double take. Becky Barnes stood before them, big round eyes trained on Robert.

"Did you hear me say anything about selling to that snake in the grass, young missy? No. They can build around me until I'm a cold, festering lump of clay in the ground."

Becky snorted and turned her color-swashed—purple today—head away, but not before she shot Robert with something that looked like admiration.

"GREAT JOB. HE's coming right along." Colin patted Jill's leg as she removed it from her stirrup and let it dangle along Dragon's side. Colin's praise rejuvenated her exhausted body. After the lessons at Robert's earlier in the week, and today riding four horses, teaching five lessons, and dealing with Colin's intensity, she'd unequivocally proven there was no such thing as perpetual energy. At least the lesson, although tough as always, had been worth it.

But she'd had enough drama. It was Saturday and she was ready to go home. She had just enough energy left to find Chase, drag him somewhere she could hold him, and pretend life was settled and white-picket-fence perfect. Maybe enough energy to try shaking something loose in his head filled with outdated chivalry and make crazy passionate love to him. The thought of playing house under crisp, cool sheets with him flushed her with desire as hot as the July days.

After hopping off Dragon and bidding Colin good night, she led her horse into the barn. In the middle of untacking, she nearly ran into David.

"Hey!" she said. "Coming to ride?"

He rubbed his chin, clearly uncomfortable. "I wish I were. Have you got a moment?"

"Sure? Something wrong?"

"Did anything happen with the Barnes girl at McCormick's place yesterday?"

"No." She bit her bottom lip, thinking. "The smallest little thing with Chase and Anita. I let Robert show Becky how to harness his mare. Jim Krieger showed up. Nothing."

"I just got off the phone with Mrs. Barnes. She's going to stop bringing Rebecca to riding lessons."

David might as well have yanked out her tongue. Jill literally could not speak.

He put a hand on her arm. "She thinks, and mind I only quote because I don't believe her for a moment, that you have to have reached the limit of what you can teach Rebecca because you're resorting to such unorthodox methods—like using dangerous draft animals. She feels Jamie needs to be away from a horsey environment. And there was some story about her girls having a terrible row over the horses once they were home. She won't have them fighting every time Rebecca rides."

"But she's wrong." Jill barely got the small words past

the clog in her throat. "I'm only starting to see glimpses of the progress Becky could make. And Jamie . . . Jamie would need so little and she'd be ecstatic. She's the one who loves it here."

"I'm truly sorry, love. I think you really care for that student."

"Yeah." She had no idea what else to say.

"I'll have another chat with Mrs. Barnes in a day or two. Don't take it too hard until we get it sorted. I simply wanted to make sure you hadn't noticed an inciting incident."

Jill was beyond lucky to have David in her corner. But there was little comfort to be had even from a kind boss when it felt like the world had just ended. Then again, since when did she care? Hadn't she been wishing Becky Barnes out of her life since week one?

Chapter Twenty

SHE FOUND HIM polishing the Bonneville. Jill stood for a long time in the doorway of the shed, so quiet even Angel didn't seem to notice her. Chase bent over his task, his broad back muscles flexing beneath a tight white T-shirt as he caressed the red gas tank with his rag. Khaki cargo shorts bared his strong, sexy calves and ankles, and as he reached forward and back his seat muscles tautened and relaxed with his movement. Tension shot right into her belly, and a stab of hard desire dove for the low, low spot between her thighs.

Good grief. She'd clearly been obsessing more than she'd realized. His spectacular body almost took away the hurt from her talk with David.

"Boo," she said at last.

He jumped as if he'd been hit from a pea shooter.

"What the . . . ? Holy crap, Jill. You snuck up like a ghost."

For the first time she could remember he didn't wear the warm smile he always had for her, and the guardedness in his face took her aback.

"I'm sorry." She took in his features more carefully and frowned in concern. "I was admiring you working."

As if he suddenly realized where he was, his face cleared and he sighed. In seconds he held her.

"No, no, I'm sorry. I was so lost in thought it took me a second to figure out reality."

"Is everything all right?"

He kissed her forehead. "I thought everything was terrific, but I had a chat with Duncan Connery today, and now I'm not sure. C'mere."

He led her to the Triumph, where she perched sideways on the seat. He sat on an upturned bucket beside her.

"Now you have me worried," she said.

"No, no, it's nothing like that. It's Krieger. I found some doctored documents in his office this week. Two very different sets of tonnage estimates for the gravel pit. I think he's pulling exactly the bait and switch everyone fears, and I don't think Connery knows about it."

"But you talked to him. Didn't you tell him?"

"I did. But it turns out he and his wife went unexpectedly out of town to be with their daughter, who is gravely ill. He's basically handed the reins to Krieger for the next month, but he said he'd look into what I found. Today he got back to me and said there was just a mistake in the paperwork and Krieger would take care of it. Says Krieger is tough but trustworthy."

"I don't know. Sounds to me like we know why Krieger is suddenly spurring on the timetable."

Chase nodded. "Yeah. I was thinking the same thing. Great minds, huh?"

"Great minds. So, what's next?"

"I have no idea. I—" He stopped and peered at her. "Hey, are *you* okay?"

"Sure." She looked away, angry to have given her emotions away.

"Aw, honey, I can see that big ol' lie right in your eyes. What are we doing standing here talking about this?"

"I'd *rather* talk about this."

"Nope. This is not important right now." He drew her to a stand and bent until their breath mingled. "Start talkin'."

In that instant Anita Barnes and the canceled lessons ceased to be important as well. Jill thrust her hands into the thick hair above Chase's ears and pulled his head all the way to hers.

"In a minute," she whispered.

He groaned his assent and slanted his lips across hers, sending a blast of heated desire through her body. She delved into his mouth with her tongue for the comfort of his. Hot and firm, it swirled back to explore the soft inner surfaces of her mouth without apology. Her eyes slid shut. A soft moan of pleasure gave him permission to go further.

He broke the kiss, but only to stoop and swing her into his arms. Facing the bike, he had her put one leg over the seat and set her there, her back to the handlebars. He threw his leg over, too, and faced her, looking every inch the bad boy with his smoky eyes and nostrils flared with desire. He pulled her forward, lifting first one of her legs then the other over his thighs.

"I've imagined this every day since the first time you sat behind me."

"You have?" she whispered, dazed.

"Tell me. Are you scared of my Triumph now?"

She wagged her head in slow motion. "You're the one who should be scared."

He chuckled and leaned forward. "Of a bitty thing like you?"

His lips touched hers, but his fingers settled on the buttons of her sleeveless blouse. *Why buttons? Why today?* She groaned in frustration, wishing for a simple T-shirt he could yank off. She tugged on his, sending her fingers beneath it to explore his wide, flat pecs. Hard. Warm . . .

Her blouse fell open.

"I don't think sexy most mornings," she said, self-conscious of her utilitarian sports bra.

"You're wrong. Sexiest kind of bra in the world." He deftly undid the front clasp, and the cups cascaded away. For a second he took her in. "Aw, honey, you're beautiful."

He kissed her again at the exact moment he cupped her breasts and found the puckered tips with his thumbs. Jill nearly melted off the seat.

His kisses sought every inch of her skin, from her lips to her earlobes to the skin on her neck. He pushed her torso gently away and trailed his lips and tongue down her throat to the soft depression between her breasts.

"We aren't going to get walked in on?" she murmured, not really caring.

"He's with Louis L'Amour." The words trailed along her skin. Her laugh morphed to a jagged gasp of pleasure when he grasped one nipple gently between his teeth.

"Let me feel your skin, too," she rasped. He pulled away and shucked off his T-shirt, revealing a soft, dark swirl of hair that took her breath away. "Talk about beautiful."

She scooted forward and lifted herself onto his lap, letting her sensitized breasts crush softly against his chest while she held his head and plundered his mouth. For one short moment she was in power. Then both his hands rested on her thighs and he skimmed his fingers up the stretchy fabric of her breeches toward her core. He reached the soft juncture lines of her legs and her body and feathered long strokes up and down the crease, tantalizing but not touching the aching center of her, over and over until desire spun unexpectedly into immediate need. He'd barely touched her, and he'd taken her to the brink.

She wriggled, which only intensified the heat. "No! Chase. It's too quick. I want us—"

He cut her off with another deep kiss before drawing away. "Shhh."

Watching her intently, his eyes now glassy, he placed one thumb pad softly against the magic spot he'd teasingly avoided. Right through the fabric—one press. Two gentle strokes. And she broke. Into colors and flight and heat and cries of pleasure.

"That's my girl," he crooned into her ear. "Come on, now."

She couldn't stop the tears of release, and he held her for the long, long fall to Earth, his feet braced to keep the Triumph steady, his arms soothing, his breath calming. "No, no," she said finally, her tears finally slowed. "I wanted to wait for you. I wanted it together."

"What?" His humor-filled voice resonated beneath her ear. "This wasn't good?"

"It was perfect. I—"

"It *was* perfect," he agreed. "For me, too."

She wanted to pound on his chest, despite the euphoria that still cushioned her frustration. What was wrong with him? How could it have been perfect? She hadn't even had her chance to pleasure him—never mind making love to him. What was he protecting her from? What was he hiding?

She swallowed the last of her tears and swiped at her eyes. "Your turn?" she asked quietly.

"I'm pretty happy with this turn," he said, and a lump of hurt formed in her stomach. "I want to know what happened before you got here tonight."

She should have felt as if he'd slayed dragons for her, kept her safe and honored—given her everything and asked for nothing. Instead, she was bereft, as if he'd taken the one thing she needed most: him.

Slowly she straightened her torso and her clothing and slipped first from his lap, then the Triumph's saddle.

He caught her hand and made her look into his eyes. "Jill."

An ache in her heart replaced the sweet languor of moments before. "Six weeks ago I met the Barnes family," she said dully. "That's what happened tonight."

A BEAD OF sweat rolled slowly down the bridge of Chase's nose and hung suspended at the tip, like a bubble at the end of an eyedropper. It plopped onto the board he'd just pounded into place atop Robert's deck railing, leaving a perfect wet circle. Sighing, he straightened and cocked a shoulder to wipe his face against a shirtsleeve.

"I should have gone someplace cool," he muttered. "The Kalahari. Or the Amazon rain forest."

Robert knelt several feet away, also wielding a hammer, and replied with a cranky grunt. Chase ignored him except to worry.

It was 11:30 a.m. and, over Sunday and Monday, mid-July had taken a turn for the scorching. He was supposed to start on a new project for Connery at the end of the week. He managed to thank his stars he wasn't off on a scalding job site somewhere.

"Let's break. This is too hot."

"Go ahead, I'm fine." Robert dragged a two-by-six from the stack beside the porch.

"Hey," Chase snapped. "Kill yourself when I'm not around."

Robert dropped the board, stared emptily, and finally shook his head. "Workin' keeps me from thinking. Thinking makes me mad."

Chase looked closely at the old farmer, saw his own

glumness mirrored in the milky eyes, and softened. "You really got hooked on that kid, didn't you?"

The denial was on Robert's lips when he sagged at the shoulders and set down his hammer. "It ain't the girl. Jill was excited, she got me excited. I've never seen her depressed like she's been this weekend. Damn foolishness for a worn-out old man, that's all."

"You're no more foolish than I am."

And he was definitely a fool. He'd hurt Jill two nights ago. It had been unintentional, but she'd surprised the tar out him—the amazing little siren. She'd come for comfort, and he'd known exactly what form she'd wanted it to take. His body still hated him for not giving it. And if Jill didn't hate him, she certainly couldn't have much patience left for his pansy-assed excuses.

But he couldn't let them get that close. Not if he was leaving. Not if it stood in the way of her dreams of leaving. And now the Barnes girls' mother had only deepened Jill's wounds. All his own issues aside, he had no idea what to do about any of it.

Chase ordered Robert to his chair under the porch eaves and fetched them two glasses of ice water. When Robert took his gratefully, Chase caught a pallor beneath the leathery tan.

"Are you okay?"

"Of course. It's too damn hot, and I been swingin' the hammer harder than I should. Shoulder aches some."

"You better quit and take it easy."

"Yeah."

Both men turned to the spit of gravel in the driveway.

Steeling himself for Krieger again, Chase was surprised when a silver Saturn rolled into view.

"I know that car," grunted Robert. "It's Barnes. The father."

A tall, sandy-haired, man with a neat mustache and goatee stepped from the car, his gray-blue eyes searching until they met Chase's.

"Barnes." Robert called first.

"Mr. McCormick, hello. I'm looking for Jill."

"She isn't here."

"Ah. I seem to be one step behind her today, I'm afraid. You must be Chase Preston." He stepped forward with his hand outstretched. "I thought maybe Jamie made you up. You've made a huge impression on her."

"She's a great kid."

"Thank you. In fact, it's my girls I'd like to talk to Jill about."

"Oh?" Robert said.

"I hope to talk her into uncanceling the lessons my wife canceled. Anita is with the twins much more than I am, and I rarely contradict her decisions, but I think I need to now."

Chase thumped Robert on the back. "I promise you nothing would make Jill happier," he said. "She's taken a personal interest in both your daughters."

"I do know that. I've seen noticeable differences in Jamie and Becky since they met Jill. Since they met all of you."

Chase hesitated, but simply couldn't hold his tongue. "Jill won't say this, but I have to. Becky isn't a bad kid, but we've all seen her bad attitude. It's aimed at her sister, but it carries into the lessons. Does Becky really want to keep coming?"

Barnes was silent a thoughtful moment. "She does. And you're not wrong. The attitude is real and she does turn it on Jamie. I've been a pretty absentee dad recently, and I've made Anita handle everything. It's been my way of ignoring reality. Do you know how Jamie was injured?"

"Something about falling out of a tree?"

"A tree house. The girls had an argument, and Becky shoved Jamie off balance. She didn't push her off of the platform; both girls are adamant that Jamie tripped. But Anita got it in her head that Becky had some sort of deep-seated jealousy of her sister. Now she's overprotective of Jamie and overindulgent with Becky, and I believe Becky can't deal with the guilt. I've done nothing to help. My wife and I suffered through this differently."

"Accidents can tear families apart," Chase said.

"This weekend was my wake-up call. I've actually seen sparks of interest when Becky talks about Jill. She's even mentioned some horse show in August. There were fireworks like I've never seen when Anita told Becky she needed to think of some different lessons to take. I had a long talk with the girls, and even Jamie wants Becky to keep riding. So, here I am."

"What about Jamie?" Chase's pulse jumped with anticipation. "Is there any chance you'd reconsider the decision about lessons for her?"

"Jamie? Take lessons?"

Chase's eyes widened. "Your wife didn't discuss it with you?"

"Jamie wishes all the time she could ride again, but this is the first I've heard about lessons for her."

Robert made a rude grunt. Chase coughed to halt the inappropriate words bouncing on the tip of his tongue. "Michael," he managed at last. "I'm giving you a heads-up. Jill is gonna have a pitch for you that'll shame a vacuum cleaner salesman."

The moment Jill arrived that evening, she skipped all three porch steps and launched herself into Chase's waiting arms.

"Hello, my miracle man!"

He hushed her with a kiss, but just as she had done two nights before, she took the kiss over, morphed into the siren that robbed him of power, drove him mad with her skin's natural perfume, and made him hard and aching. She grabbed hold of his neck, lifted herself off the deck, and wrapped her legs around his hips to settle on his hard heat like he'd been made to order for her.

"Is that a saddle horn in your pocket, or are you glad to see me?" she whispered.

"Evil seductress. I am *very* glad to see you."

Her smile widened against his lips until her mouth could no longer shape to the task of kissing him. "Oh, Chase. I meant it about miracles."

"So, you're not angry at me anymore." He feathered her nose, her eyebrows, and her cheeks with more kisses.

"When was I ever?" She pulled back, affronted, then grinned. "You did this."

"Oh no. Michael Barnes came looking for you all on his own."

"But you talked to him about things I wouldn't have said. He told me you are very kind and you know a lot about people. There's always been more to you than meets the eye, Mr. No-Account Drifter."

Chase's gut began its familiar, agonizing curl-up. "Just get them back in the saddle."

"It'll be a week so we can fit into Michael's schedule, but that's all. Next Tuesday for Becky and Friday for Jamie!" She slid slowly down his body, her smile wicked when he groaned.

"It's a good thing Robert spends so much time in the house. He'd be traumatized by your welcome-home ritual."

"As long as you aren't, we're good."

"Honey, I'm traumatized as a lamb in an alligator pond."

"You're as much a lamb as I'm a Girl Scout." She hooked one leg around him this time and rolled her hips.

"I agree, these ain't no cookies you're peddling."

With a sultry wink, she pulled away. "I'm going to see Dee after the lesson tomorrow."

"Really?"

"I'm nervous. I've barely talked to her all summer. Barely seen anyone at home, in fact. Dee's still mad that you ignored *her* cookies."

"Your sister is a beautiful woman, but I never looked twice at what she was selling."

She traced his top lip line with a forefinger. "Dee will know what equipment I need for Jamie. And there's one more favor—this one I need to ask of you."

"I'm pretty much nothin' but your slave after this."

She took his face between her palms. "I cleared everything off my schedule for this weekend. I want you to take me on a motorcycle ride." She rubbed against him like a little cat.

His throat went dry. "Didn't we just try that?"

A self-satisfied smile crept onto her lips. "Why yes, we did. But I mean an actual ride. About a hundred miles north, to some lakeshore property I want to show you. I plan to spend the weekend saying thank you."

Once again her siren song clashed with his fear. This was a bad idea, but he wanted her back on his Triumph with every fiber of his being.

"I'll go under one condition."

"Whatever you want."

"I'm the only one who gets to say thank you."

Chapter Twenty-One

DEE'S BACK WAS to her when Jill stepped into the physical therapy room at the Northfield Orthopedic Clinic. Without designer labels and provocative sways, her sister looked professional—and unfamiliar. Jill's breathing refused to even out, like she was some wimpy kid in a dark alley. She was meeting Chase in two hours for their trip to the lake, but it seemed far away at the moment.

She rapped on the door. "Hey, sis."

Dee turned, her dropped jaw and saucer-wide eyes transcending surprise. "Jill?"

"Am I interrupting anything?"

"No! I . . . no. Hold on." She put away the piece of equipment she held and turned back, her eyes radiating rare uncertainty. "This is definitely unexpected."

"Shocking, right? I should have called, but our track record on the phone . . . Anyway, I need your advice on something."

"Mine? That is hard to believe."

A hint of their natural volatile sarcasm crept into Dee's voice, and Jill struggled to defuse it before it could root. She'd promised herself to beg if need be.

"I know. I'm sorry to bother you."

Dee slipped a professional mien in place. "Don't be silly. What's up?"

"I'm about to start working with a new riding student, but she's paraplegic and I'm hoping you can give me some idea how to handle the first lesson. Tell me about special equipment."

More surprise crossed Dee's face, but her words came out sincere. "I'm not super current on the trends in therapeutic riding, but I do have two patients who go up to We Can Ride. What sort of person is this?"

"A thirteen-year-old girl."

"Don't take this wrong, but wouldn't she be better off at a properly equipped stable?"

It was a legitimate question. "Probably," Jill admitted. "But the situation is complicated."

"You are good at finding those aren't you?"

"Life hasn't been dull lately."

"And how's Chase?" At that Dee's voice exposed an unmistakable edge, and Jill steeled herself.

"He's fine."

"Handsome as ever?" Dee flashed an insincere smile. "My ego took a little beating over him. It's not often you find a man who'll lie to your mother for you."

"Hey, or a sister. I still owe you for the dog."

"And what *will* you do with the dog and the man when you head off for Florida? Send them to school for you?"

Jill sighed hopelessly. Aside from the fact that Dee had neatly bundled every issue in Jill's life into a two-sentence package and tied it with a perfect sarcastic bow, she would never be a go-to sister.

"Maybe we'd both be more comfortable if I talked to someone else."

For an instant she imagined a shadow of remorse in Dee's eyes, but she was all business again before Jill could be sure.

"I can tell you a little bit. But you should visit one of the organizations, too."

"I've made an appointment already."

Dee nodded crisply. "Okay. I assume this lesson is for fun, not therapy. You can use the exercises to give her confidence."

"Do I need a special saddle? I've read about surcingles and pads."

"A plain Western saddle is most secure. A surcingle with handles works for someone with good balance so you can use the horse's body warmth as muscle therapy. Have somebody walk beside her on one or both sides depending on how secure her seat is."

It had been years since they'd shared this many sentences, and it brought on a moment of tenderness. "Dee, why didn't you get into this? You love horses. It would have been natural for you."

Utter blankness swept over Dee's features. "I would never compete with you, little sister."

Jill gaped at her. "Excuse me?"

"Do you really think none of us knows how anything

with horses turns to diamonds and gold in your hands? 'Wanna ride, Jill?' Sure, I'll just win some ribbons. 'Want to teach for me?' Sure, watch my students win, too. 'Hey, try vet school.' Okay, what the heck? I can quit if I get to *go to the friggin' Olympics*. Nope. No way would I have dared to be a riding instructor."

The change in Dee was jarring, like a tremor before an earthquake.

"What in the world are you talking about?"

"About staying off your turf, about staking out my own place in the world where you couldn't compete. But look. You're even invading that. The only other thing I ever did better than you did was attract boys, but only because you had no idea how tiny and cute you were. You've proven that, too. I'm a flirt, but I know they don't come much better than Chase Preston. Congrats on him, too."

"This is ridiculous. Chase has nothing to do with this and I certainly don't want your job." For a moment they avoided each other's eyes. "What did I ever do to you?" Jill asked. "How long have you been keeping all this buried without bothering to get it off your chest?"

"Are you kidding?" Dee poised her jaw like a weapon. "Everything I ever tried you did better. Getting the best grades, having the biggest adventures. It goes all the way back to Dad leaving. You could do no wrong even in that disaster. 'Poor little Jillie, I'm so sorry, Jillie.' On the rare occasions I hear from him it's *still* about you. 'Watch out for Jill. Take care of her.' You even talk to him more than I do."

"You're blaming us on daddy issues?" Jill asked, incredulous. "Look, I talk to him as infrequently as possible, and he tells *me* to listen to *you*. I have little time for our father, Dee. He did a handful of lovely things around the house, and then he walked away. He said he'd always come back and take care of us, and he lied. Instead, he left us in charge of each other. Well, you can just stop worrying about that. It's never been your job to look out for me, no matter what Julian Carpenter told you."

"Why did you really come here today?" Dee asked. "To tell me you wanted to become a physical therapist? Fine, good luck. You won't need it."

"Now hang on!" Jill had had enough. "I came here willing to beg because I haven't got a clue where to start with Jamie. I can't believe you turned it into this."

"Then it's my problem. Forget it."

"After everything you said?" Dee stared past her, lips pressed into a tight line. "If you only knew how small and inadequate I feel around you, you'd laugh yourself to death."

"Don't try, Jill."

"Oh no, you tossed out your bombshell, now it's my turn, like it or not. If I got good grades it was because I could never compete with you for popularity. If I did well at riding it was because the animals in my life seemed to understand me more than the people in my family did. As for vet school, it's no different than what you do here—I would be good at it. And the Olympics? Oh, hah! That's still the biggest pipe dream. Whatever I choose, someone will think it's the wrong choice. My life is a poster for chaos theory,"

"You *really* expect me to feel sorry for such hard horrible choices?"

Jill stared at the floor. Of course nobody should feel sorry for her.

"I've got nothing on your smarts, your looks, your settled career, Dee. To tell me we're victims of jealousy is ridiculous."

"I'm not getting into a who's-got-it-worse pissing match." Dee's voice rose in frustration. "It's past. It's done now."

"What if I don't want it to be done now? For crying out loud, we're sisters."

"Not really in any more than name." Dee thrust the words like an epee jab.

Jill stumbled back. "Are you serious?"

"I have a patient coming any second." Dee ignored her. "I'll get some more information for you along with the name of an expert."

"C'mon, Dee, don't. Don't cut it off like this."

Dee's shoulders sagged, but she braced her palms on the countertop in front of her. "If there was more to be said we'd certainly say it, and not even *this* nicely. Look, I really do have a patient coming."

Jill looked helplessly at the ceiling and drew a steadying breath. "No angry words will ever change the fact that you are my sister and that for some masochistic reason, I love you." She paused and reached for the smallest sliver of humor through near tears. "Maybe this minute not so much."

But it fell flat in a sea of silence. They stood, not look-

ing at each other until Jill had no choice but to walk away,
wishing she'd never come.

THE TRIUMPH ROLLED to a smooth stop in front of a
palace-sized motorhome, and Chase braced his feet, letting the engine idle. This was no simple little RV on a
campground camping spot. This was a land-based yacht
on one of the most beautiful lake views he'd ever seen.

Jill, his snug backstop for the past one hundred and
thirty miles, released her arms and stretched them over
her head. After Chase kicked down the stand and flicked
off the engine, she popped off the bike like a cork from a
Champagne bottle.

"What do you think? Pretty cool, huh? Wasn't this a
good idea?" She chattered like a squirrel on caffeine as
she dragged off the new helmet he'd bought for her. "This
is what my grandparents left to Mom when they died. We
don't come nearly often enough anymore."

"Jill. Jill!" He laughed and took her upper arms in his
hands. "Slow down. What the heck did Dee put in your
tea this morning? It sounds like something questionable
if not highly illegal."

The shadow of pain that flit in and out of her eyes was
unmistakable but gone in the time it took her to lean forward and peck him on the lips.

"No, no, I'm excited to be here with you, that's all.
Come on, let me show you the inside of the motorhome
and then the beach."

He shook his head as she bounded away from him.

She'd been wired ever since her meeting with Dee that morning. Now she bordered on hyper. It was her nature to bounce back, to find the positive, to smooth things over, to please. She'd come as close to full-on depression as he'd ever seen when Anita had pulled the girls from lessons. But this version of her was scarier.

Two hours later, after she'd taken him on a tour of the two-acre, wooded lakefront parcel, cooked dinner, cleaned up, and aired the bedding, Jill's bubble of hyperactivity finally burst. Chase left the bathroom to find the luxurious motorhome empty. He checked the bedroom at the end of the vehicle, taking in the fluffy down duvet cover, the etched-glass storage cupboards, and the built-in side tables. The sight made him both anticipate and dread the night. He wasn't clueless. He'd already pushed his red-blooded maleness to its breaking point. But he was falling too fast in a way he hadn't ever fallen before.

He walked through the beautiful motorhome—nicer than most Memphis living rooms he'd seen in his life— and opened the door into a softly sultry twilight that hinted of welcome rain. She stood, as still as he'd seen her all day, leaning against a rough-barked maple tree, one hand in the pocket of her jeans shorts. Her lean, strong legs shone in the twilight, and the crescent of moon limned her hair in a glow against the lake.

"Hey," he said.

"Time to listen for the loons," she replied, and took his hand.

They wandered closer to the shore. The lake surface gleamed like a huge pewter platter set beneath the moonlight. Chase sat against an old paper birch a solid four feet in diameter, raised his knees, and pulled Jill to sit between them. As she settled onto the mossy grass, the haunting yodel of a loon echoed across the water. She leaned slowly backward and finally relaxed. She felt like safety personified, resting against his chest, nestled into his crotch. He put aside his misgivings about the night. This was peace.

A few stars shone between smoky clouds that slipped across the expanse of heaven. He clasped his hands around her belly.

"You finally ready?" he asked.

"Ready?"

"To tell me what really got you chasin' like a pup after a weasel. I'll fix anything I can, if I know what it is."

"Why do you think anything needs fixing?"

"Jill. You are the least evasive person I know, and you're answering questions with questions. This is about Dee, isn't it?"

Absolute stillness overcame her body. He waited.

"It went like crap this morning," she said at last. "I don't know why I thought it wouldn't."

"You can't let her bully you, honey."

"She didn't bully, she . . . She kind of blew me away with honesty. Dee really does hate me."

"Oh, now, why would you say that?"

She made a rueful little grunt. "Her claim is that the only things she's ever been better at than I am are catching men and physical therapy, and now I'm moving in on both of them. Seems her little geeky sister beat her out of the classiest guy she's ever met. It was the only thing she said that I agreed with."

Chase swallowed the guilt. He pushed Jill away enough to wiggle from behind her and scoot around to look her in the eye.

"She's wrong and I hope you set her straight. You didn't beat her out of anything. You fell out of that car window and kind of into my heart." He kissed her forehead. "And you've been my best friend around here ever since."

"Is that still all we are? Friends?"

"With a few benefits."

She shook her head. "You know what? Not good enough tonight."

Just that quickly, she'd changed the subject, and desire burst over him like water over a broken dam. She traced a path down his jaw in a gesture too simple to be stimulating—but it was. The familiar, insistent throbbing began low in his abdomen, and turned him hard and willing. He tried to keep some self-control, but she placed her lips against his and spoke.

"When I was done with Dee all I wanted was to come to you. She thinks my life is something perfect, but for years it's been a big mess of loose ends. I know it hasn't been long for us, but you make it all come together. I just want to feel like I'm all together tonight."

Her plea snapped Chase's will as if it were one of the brittle sticks on the floor of the woods. He reached for her with a groan. "Be careful what you ask for."

"I'm tired of careful."

With more sweet skill than she'd ever shown, she kissed his lips apart and took his tongue into her hot, sweet mouth. He pulled her onto his lap and released the craving that poised like a panther within him.

She continued her intimate assault until he was no longer master of his body. Her hands floated over his face, his head, his shoulders. Her strong, clever fingers slipped between their bodies to stroke his belly and his inner thighs, and he shifted to give her room.

When her palm cupped him at last, a convulsive swallow turned to groans, and he lay back in the grass, while she stayed upright, seated on his thighs, playing, outlining him through his jeans, exploring until he had to stop her or fear for his control. By pulling her forward, he replaced her maddeningly erotic touch with the coupling of their bodies. Hard beneath soft, his hips undulated, and he drove his fingers into her hair, calloused tips against honeyed silk. Greedily he pulled her soft sounds into his open kiss.

When she arched over him, Chase slowed his rhythmic movement and rolled them to their sides. The buttons of her summer camisole slipped open at his touch, and he feathered kisses downward until his lips met lace and satin. When he lifted the delicate fabric and freed her breast into his hand, the skin was richest velvet to his fingers, her textured nipple, rough and stimulating to his tongue. He wanted to draw with force enough to assuage his need, but he summoned gentleness and, when his tongue circled, she gasped her approval.

She held him to her breast and he laved gently, rhythmically. One hand slid down the flat plane of her stomach, and he delved beneath the waistband of her shorts. Her little spasms sent lightning deep into his body. She grasped at the hem of his T-shirt.

"Off," she demanded.

He pulled his mouth reluctantly from her breast and obeyed. Flattening her palm, she swept across his chest and stopped to send shocks skittering through his system by ruffling through the patch of hair between his pecs. Slowly one finger skimmed down the line of hair on his belly to the button above his fly. She worked it open and spread the denim just enough to give her lips teasing room above the elastic of his boxers.

The breath hissed from his lungs.

Once again, he could only stand her torture for mere moments before he pushed her onto her back where he could hover over her, kiss her forehead, her lips, her cheeks, and circle his fingers around the sweet indentation of her navel. The button of her shorts popped open at his touch, and he slid the zipper, then burrowed once more to the waistband of her underpants. She pulled his head close, sucking her stomach to concave when his fingers found the soft boundary of curls he sought.

"Yesss . . ." The sibilant whisper sent gooseflesh on an assault down his spine and jarred him out of his self-absorbed pleasure.

"Shhh . . ." he soothed.

"I love you, Chase."

The words slammed him like bullets. Everything inside stilled. Goose bumps turned to dread chills. He clung to her as irrational fear stole through him like suffocating smoke.

"I think I fell in love the instant you made me climb on the Triumph. The first time."

How many times had he reminded himself in the past two months that the worst thing he could do was fall in love? He ran down the litany now of why he couldn't love Jill Carpenter. He would leave. She would leave. His real self would disgust her. Although he hadn't physically pulled the trigger, he'd killed a child. A beautiful barely-older-than-a-baby child. If he said the words—if he returned her "I love you," no matter true it was—it would mean he was ready to face what he'd done and stop running.

As long as his growing feelings for her had remained undeclared, he'd fooled himself into believing it was possible to leave without hurting her. But deep down he'd known she was waiting patiently to learn his secrets even though she had no idea what they were. Wasn't that the definition of a woman who'd accept him for who he was?

He withdrew his hand from where it had stilled in its ardent search. She tensed when he rested his lips against her hair, and she waited as she'd been doing all summer. It wasn't fair to lead her on any longer. Although it would be the hardest thing he'd ever done, Chase knew what he had to say. Like a man about to make a cliff dive, his throat constricted.

"You know something?" His voice dropped to a whisper. "I love you, too."

The words embarrassed him, as if he'd spoken too loudly in a hushed room. But after long seconds the panic subsided, and the truth shimmered inside him like sun on his soul. For a glorious moment his reason for hiding held no power compared to "I love you."

He felt more than heard her sob, and he pulled away to see a tear course down her cheek, followed by another.

"Hey, now." He thumbed them away. "Please believe I want you. I want to make love to you all night long."

She quivered. "And yet, there's a 'but' coming."

"C'mere."

He cradled her and stroked her hair. He calmed her but no longer strove to excite her even though his body remained excruciatingly unsatisfied.

"Making love to you will be the best thing that's ever happened."

"Right. Will be." She pulled away and sat up, her big, sad eyes showing the first spark of anger. "I don't understand you, Chase Preston. Tell me who you are."

It was his cue, his chance to stop running then and there, but he didn't. He couldn't do it like this, when it would look like he was using this passion and heat as a way to make her feel sorry for him. Or to cure the wounds her sister had dished out. No, she needed honesty and full disclosure. And the chance to turn him away.

"I'm a lot of things," he said. "Mostly I'm Abigail Preston's oldest baby boy, who didn't turn out remotely like she—or the good Lord—hoped he would."

"Oh *my* good Lord. Preston!" Her voice rose slightly. "That's the stupidest, hokiest thing I've ever heard."

"I'm a hokey kind of guy." He tried a little half grin—the one that always made her giggle. It failed. "I'm not too hokey to know there are some things that shouldn't be between us when we make love the first time."

"Then tell me!" She balled her fist against his chest and beat without power. "What is this bizarre politeness? You're the most ethical, honest person I know, but I hate that right now."

His lungs felt airless. Those words were exactly why he feared telling her. What would she do when she found out how ethical and honest he wasn't?

"I ain't no more special than a hound at the pound, Jill. If you pick me out, I need to make sure you know what you're getting."

"You said 'I love you.' You aren't the kind of guy who'd say it to appease me. I know what I'm getting."

They sat, the ethereal chirps of cicadas and grunts of frogs swelling in the night air. For a long moment he feared he'd gotten this moment dead wrong and she was done, but the loon sang again and a mate answered. Jill bounced up, disturbingly cheerful once more, like she'd been on the trip up and during dinner. Like she was after everything that slammed her down.

"Come on. I need the equivalent to a cold shower." She grabbed his hand. "We're going skinny dipping."

His eyes widened. "Jill . . ."

"Fine—skivvy dipping."

As if that would be any better.

SHE DIDN'T MUCH care if Chase thought stripping to their underwear was ridiculous, inappropriate, or even titillating. She barely thought anything when she reached the lakeshore and ripped off her shorts and the camisole that was still half unbuttoned. She laughed outwardly and smothered the anger and hurt inside. By the time she stood in her bikinis and bra, Chase barely had his shirt off, and he stared a little like a boy at a peep show. At least he wasn't completely immune to her.

"Last one in . . ." she cried, and dashed for the water.

"Hey! Be careful, you. It's dark!"

It didn't matter; she knew the lake with its sand-and-smooth-pebble bottom that deepened gradually. She ignored his warning and let her laughter ring out falsely into the night.

The first splatter of cool lake on her shins and thighs shocked her, but she splashed all the way in, her legs dragging against the moon-sprinkled water until it forced her to slow to a cartoonlike slog. The slight fish-and-algae tang cleared her head of everything plugging up her emotions. Tears welled and she dove, letting the water close over her head and bury her sadness. When she surfaced, she wiped her face clear of water and traces of her crying.

She screeched when Chase rose unexpectedly behind her, his hair plastered into his eyes, his face dripping like a surfacing sea creature.

"Are you crazy?" he asked. "Who runs full tilt into a dark lake?"

"Didn't you just see me do it?" She wasn't sure whether anger, hurt, or captivation ruled her. The perfect diamond of hair on his chest, not thick or furry and not wimpy or thin, glistened with droplets of water. She wanted to run her fingers through it again and move on to his shoulders, hard, but not too rocklike when wrapped around her.

You know exactly what they feel like around you. Tears formed again. What on this side of Mars was wrong with her? She had no reason or right to feel wounded. He hadn't hurt her. He'd said he loved her. Ten sexy hot models kissing her at once couldn't do to her what Chase did with one nibble on her bottom lip. And she didn't *want* ten sexy models—even if they would make love to her and he wouldn't. She wanted to keep coming home to Chase, whether it was here or Memphis or Florida or Zanzibar. She hadn't lied. It was too soon, too fast, too pushy, and, with her disarray of a life, too unfair a thing to do, but she'd fallen in love with him.

"I think I'm figuring out that you turn to insanity when someone pisses you off." Because he was only inches from her, she could see the smile playing on his water-beaded lips.

"Someone pissed me off? I'm not pissed off."

That was now true. She'd narrowed her emotion options to hurt or captivation, and before she could either cry or plow her fingers through that chest hair again, she swept an arm back, cupped her palm, and swished a drenching tsunami of water into his face.

He choked and sputtered. "Why you little . . ."

She dove to the side when he surged forward, but she wasn't quick enough. Like a lithe, handsome dolphin he twisted mid-jump and grabbed her around the waist. The next thing she knew he'd dragged her under water, released her so she could surface, then grabbed her again.

Her laughter broke clean and loud and genuine when he hefted her into his arms and bunched his muscles.

"Don't you dare!"

"You are in no position to request anything." He plopped a soggy kiss on her forehead, rose up, and tossed her as easily as he would have a beach ball.

She flew five feet, her stomach dropping like she'd crested a roller coaster hill, her laughter ringing until she plunged beneath the water yet again. Shooting up off the bottom, she dove at him. The hurt was gone, leaving only captivation. Her fingers dug into what little fleshiness she could find in his side, and he bellowed with laughter.

"Oh no, you don't."

He grasped her thigh and slid his hands over her knee, her calf, and her ankle until he caught her foot and gripped it viselike so he could wiggle his fingers against her arch. She thrashed and screeched, pummeling his chest in desperation to get free. Finally, she pried his right pinky off her foot and pulled on it just hard enough to make him let go. When she had her foot back, she launched her hand for his armpit.

Their combined laughter and their splashes from dogged parries and feints echoed through the dark, sweet air, louder than the chorus of frogs and cicadas. Backs of knees, armpits, bellies, feet, inner thighs—no body part was safe. At last, breathless and choking on laughter, Chase managed to imprison her with his arms, like a zip tie around her entire upper body.

"Little water moccasin, that's what you are." His voice came out a wheeze. "Quick and dangerous."

His accent, seductive as Kentucky moonshine, rolled through her. Any desire to get free and retaliate drained away, leaving only hot, throbbing need in its place. She ached for him but shied away from yet another rejection. Then one of his hands loosened, and he slid it to her seat. With swift decisiveness, he pulled her to him. The water had rendered the thin cotton of his boxers all but nonexistent, and they hid nothing of the long, hard erection now pressing exactly where she wanted it.

"You were right," he whispered. "I hate all that chivalry crap, too."

His mouth came down like sealing wax on a royal decree, and he stamped his mark on her with his tongue and his teeth, nipping, sweeping, claiming her. He flicked the clasp and her bra hung free. He stripped off the lacy thing and tossed it carelessly toward the shore. Together, their mouths still mating in wonder, they pushed down each other's underpants, and both pairs joined the shipwrecked bra.

He was beautiful and hard and slick, and Jill caressed his spine, the swell of his buttocks, and the curve of his seat where it met his thighs. She reached between them and grasped his length under the water, now warm as a hot tub from the heat they generated. He groaned in her ear, and liquid surged from within her until she was sure her every cell, inside and out, bathed in liquefied sensation.

With one effortless motion he lifted her, and the water floated her up until she could wrap her legs around his hips.

"Now I *know* you're happy to see me," she whispered.

"And I would prove it to you this second, but this time we do need something between us."

He nuzzled her behind the ear and carried her from the lake. The hot summer air warmed her wet skin as he strode ten feet across the sand to his discarded jeans. At last she had to slide off, but his hard, proud body thrilled her, counteracting her heat with deep shivers of pleasure. Chase pulled a foil packet from his pocket. She furrowed her brows.

"But if you weren't going to . . ."

"I've lectured a lot of know-it-all young men," he said quietly. "I couldn't expect them to do as I say if I didn't follow the same rules." For a moment his eyes lit mischievously, then he handed her the packet. "Want to handle this?"

The double entendre made her giggle. She grabbed the packet. "I admit I've never had the honor before," she said. "But I'll be darned if I'm waiting for you."

She ripped open the foil and fumbled only a moment before she got it right and rolled the condom up his hard length.

"Perfect," he growled, and she closed her eyes, laughter replaced by shivers.

He kicked his jeans and T-shirt around the ground to make a bed, and seconds later her back was nestled into his shirt. Chase entered her with a molten glide. A cry of pleasure escaped her, and she moved beneath him, closing her eyes as the chirp of crickets swelled into all-encompassing sound. His thrusts were slow and long.

Colors curled behind her eyes, moisture shimmied between their bodies, Chase's breath came hard and fast, and they rocked together until everything exploded, and her orgasm shattered around her. Mere seconds later Chase cried out, and they crashed in waves that had nothing to do with the lake.

She floated to Earth by following his tender kisses back from the clouds. His lips on her eyelids kept them closed, kept her drifting until, at last, she could once again hear the frogs and the breeze and the lapping of the water.

"You changed your mind," she whispered.

"No." His voice filled her ear—her soul. "You changed it."

Chapter Twenty-Two

"I've decided you want to take me into town."

Chase looked up from the construction of his PB&J. "Holy goin' to a funeral, Robert. Where'd you find those duds?"

Robert looked like a dapper earl. A brown tweed sports coat and a white dress shirt, graced with a blue and brown bowtie, were topped off with a neat brown fedora.

"Don't get smart-mouthed. You could do with a few more than two pairs of dungarees."

"Touché." Chase looked down at himself. "Wait. *Dungarees*? What are ya, old?"

"Older than God's mama, and that's a fact. I have an appointment, and then mebbe you can show me that fancy-pants riding hall you been braggin' about."

Chase looked at his friend with sudden insight. "You want to see Rebecca's first day back at riding lessons, you old softie."

"I can drive myself if you're going to insult me."

"Hah! I wouldn't miss this for the world." He folded his bread and bit off half the sandwich. He held out a piece of what remained to Angel.

They took Robert's camel-colored Buick and let the dog hop in and drape her head joyfully out the window. Robert's appointment turned out to be at a lawyer's office. "He's got some information on those eminent domain threats that damn fool Krieger is always throwing around," he said.

Since Robert didn't need help, Chase drove past Southwater thinking to surprise Jill. It had been a whole fifteen hours, after all, since . . . He let his memory send pleasant shivers through his body. It no longer frightened him to admit he loved her. Even so, nervousness gnawed at the edges of his pleasure. She didn't love *him*. Not yet. She loved the hero who'd ridden into Kennison Falls on a motorcycle that wasn't even his. She loved a façade and some false chivalry. Now he needed to change that. He owed her honesty after this weekend.

All he had going for him was a plan—and some fragile faith.

The plan was the easy part—dinner after Jamie's lesson on Friday. The reservations were made, an explanation running in a practice loop in his brain. He *wanted* to tell her now—yesterday would have been better; and he'd tried to start. But her spare moments here and there this crazy week didn't give them enough time. He couldn't drop a bomb on her before a lesson, or in front of the people always surrounding her. She needed time to hear everything and question him, too.

Or run.

The faith that she wouldn't was harder to come by. He trusted that she loved him, but he wasn't above falling back on the angels Poppa always touted. Prayers had worked months ago on Gypsy's foal. Maybe he'd latch on to the tail of a miracle himself.

The Creature wasn't in the Southwater Clinic parking lot. Mildly disappointed, Chase made his way to the Loon Feather, where he and Robert planned to meet.

"How 'bout a treat?" he asked when he and Angel arrived at the café.

She slurped a kiss against his ear and he promised to return quickly.

Cotton and Lester greeted him as usual.

"Welcome, come in." Chase stopped for the required lesson.

"Wekkome . . . in. Wekkome . . . in," Cotton chirped in reply.

"Looks like you have the touch."

Chase started at the voice and spun to see Gray Covey's poster-famous smile.

"Hey, good morning." Chase extended his hand. "I think more likely she's simply got it."

"You heading in or out?"

"I'm after one of Karla Baxter's cinnamon rolls, if there are any left."

Karla, the local high school music teacher, only worked

summers at the Loon and only offered her coveted, gooey rolls when she worked.

"My wife has my son, Dawson, out parallel parking since he's taking his driver's test tomorrow. I am not his instructor of choice. Abby definitely has the touch there."

Chase nodded. "No figuring the power of women."

"Spoken like another who knows."

"Knows but doesn't understand."

"Amen, brother."

They ordered their rolls to go and Gray accompanied Chase back outdoors. They let a wiggling Angel out of the car and stretched their legs out on the Loon's new lawn.

"Wouldn't be Jill Carpenter you're waiting for?" Camaraderie shone in Gray's eyes. "Not to pry. Kim takes lessons from Jill and we've heard, that's all. She's great. Kim loves her."

Chase tore off a piece of roll and set it in front of the dog. "Jill's terrific," he admitted. "Wish it were her, but I'm waiting for Robert McCormick."

"I heard you were staying out with him. I've never met him, but I think he's either very brave or very foolhardy standing up to Connery."

"Robert? He's a good man. Smart. He knows what he's doing."

"I hope he holds out. He may be our only chance."

Chase debated telling Gray about Krieger's double set of numbers, but he was still trying to figure out what to do. He didn't dare spread rumors until he was sure.

"I heard a new song on the radio the other day," he ventured instead and then felt a little silly. Did you talk to

Gray Covey about his music when he was, what, off duty?

"Yeah?" Gray seemed mildly surprised. "It's a little different. Dawson arranged it. Said I needed to modernize myself."

"Impressive. So, he can work with you, just not drive with you."

"You think girls are hard to understand. Try a teenager. I love the kid, both our kids, and this crazy little town to death. But some days like this, I sure don't recognize my life."

"Are you kidding? I came to get away from the big city. Nothing else. Now look at me."

"You met a girl."

"Before I'd reached Main Street."

"Sorry, buddy." Gray shook his head in mock sympathy. "All I can say is, things have a way of working out. Abby wanted nothing to do with my life, believe me. She's a strong, quiet country girl and I'm a . . . well, God knows what I am, but it isn't quiet. Unless I'm here. This place has a way of taking care of a person. It gets to you pretty quickly."

Chase glanced up and down the street. In the few weeks he'd been here more buildings had been restored, businesses were opening back up. The next project he was slated to start with Connery was a new library. And he felt as if he'd always been invested.

"It does," he agreed. "The question is being the smart choice for the girl. I'm no saint—which is pretty much what she deserves."

"Man, you are speaking to the king of being wrong

for the girl. Fortunately, those soft feminine hearts are far bigger than make sense to us. Give your girl a chance—she has a capacity for love and forgiveness you won't believe."

They fell silent. Angel scooted herself between them and nudged Gray on the cheek. Then she licked three times beneath his ear—her way of showing approval. And begging.

"She's getting very spoiled, sorry," Chase said. "C'mon, girl. You've had treats."

Gray slipped her a piece of his roll before she obeyed. "Nothing more fun than spoiling a girl." He winked.

ROBERT CLIMBED OUT of the passenger seat and stared around Bridge Creek farm's neat yard like a man seeing heaven. The main barn stood open and beside it the old arena bustled with riders. Beyond the barn, the peak of the new arena shone against a bright blue July sky.

"Did you ever ride?" Chase asked, as they headed across the yard.

"My pa had a skinny old saddlebred mare he bought off someone who was shipping her to the kill. I was maybe fourteen. Took her to a couple of county fair shows. After she died when I was twenty or so, there were no more useless riding horses taking up space at our farm."

The light of good memories in his eyes belied the gruff dismissal in his voice. As they neared the open door to the new arena, David met them. "Please, come in," he said proudly, ushering them to the tier of four bleachers along one full wall. Opposite the seating, full-wall mirrors reflected the rich, oak-finished interior.

"Damn fancy job," Robert whispered to Chase.

A thrill stabbed Chase low in his belly when Jill floated by, her legs long against Dragon's sides, her hands delicate on the reins, her hips rocking in sync to the horse beneath her.

He couldn't stop the continuing memories of her meshed just as perfectly with him last night. It made her riding sensual and personal and riveting.

"She's a pretty rider," Robert said.

"She's a true horse whisperer, on and off the horse," David agreed.

"She can teach others how to do it, too," Robert mused. "Is she really going to the Olympics? She don't say much about it."

"She certainly has the ability, but the reality of how much time it takes is hitting home. I never had the drive, to Da's disappointment. I think Jill is making up for me a little—never seen my father this invested in a rider."

Lead formed in Chase's gut at the assessment. How could he stand in the way of a dream like this? He wanted to think Jill had looked this happy after their lovemaking, but maybe that was wishful thinking.

Where did he belong?

"I know you've had the Barnes sisters out at your place." David turned to Robert. "It's marvelous you're helping them. And, may I add, that you're helping the whole town."

"Bull wash. What I do is pure selfishness."

"That could well be. But people are behind you."

Robert harrumphed again. "The most important thing right now is that the little girls get to ride, and Jill gets to teach. Only time Jill's any purtier than she is here is when she's trying to knock some sense into those two kids."

The words nearly knocked Chase off his seat. Jill *did* look this happy, this gorgeous, when she was working with the girls. Even when she was furious with Becky, her passion was stunning.

"Hi Chase! Hi Mr. McCormick!"

"Jamie!" Chase heralded the girl's arrival. "We were talking about you and your sister."

Behind her chair, Michael Barnes smiled self-consciously. "Jamie said this is where Jill told them to come today. We in the right place?"

"You are, indeed." David rose. "Mr. Barnes, nice to see you again. Feel free to have a seat—Jamie, you can put your chair wherever you like."

"Want to sit on up on the bleachers?" Michael asked his daughter.

She nodded, set the brake on the wheelchair, and reached for her father's neck. He lifted her easily, carried her to a spot beside Chase, and she used her arms to balance on the bench.

"Never seen you without the rod attached to your behind," Chase said. "Looks good."

"Wait until Friday!"

"Honey, I think we're as excited as you are," he promised. "Where's Becky?"

"Getting Roy ready. She wanted to do it alone."

That was unusual. "Wow. Good for her."

He studied Jamie. Something besides her lack of chair was different, but he couldn't pinpoint it.

Fifteen minutes later, Jill finished. She rode to the short wall in front of the bleachers and swung off Dragon's saddle. "Goodness. A cheering section? Robert, is that really you? Is somebody getting married?"

"You think you're funny, too, don't you, girlie?"

"I am funny."

Her eyes settled on Chase, and her hot gaze shot through him like a lance of fire.

"You almost ready for Friday?" she asked Jamie.

"I'm *all* ready."

"I am, too. What about Becky? Think she's ready to jump today?"

"I know she is."

That was it—the difference in Jamie. Somehow, in the course of three days, she'd lost all caustic animosity for her sister. He really needed to savor this day—it was almost too good to be true.

Chapter Twenty-Three

A FLAWLESS, AZURE sky greeted Jill Friday morning. Jamie's lesson later that afternoon would be a raw experiment at best, but Jill couldn't remember her life feeling so picture-perfect.

Even Rebecca's lesson earlier in the week had been a surprising delight. She'd taken to jumping as if she'd been doing it for months, and Jill was still astounded. Now, the promise of a gorgeous afternoon spent with Chase, giving sweet Jamie Barnes the desire of her heart, drove from her mind all thoughts that anything could ruin her life.

Her only uncertainty came from the pages of notes she'd made while researching techniques for teaching physically challenged riders. She was so far from being an expert, and her main concern was keeping the teen safe. She wished she could magically absorb her sister's expertise for the day.

She dressed for the clinic, grabbed a yogurt and

orange juice from the empty kitchen, and headed for The
Creature. In a fit of goodwill she stroked its side mirror.
The Suburban had run without incident or breakdown
all summer—one of its longest healthy stretches since
Jill had bought it. She tossed her notebooks onto the passenger seat, climbed in, and frowned at a white envelope
taped to the steering wheel. With her brows scrunched,
she pulled out a sheet of paper covered with Dee's
rounded, feminine handwriting.

> *Jill—*
>
> *Yesterday I finally managed to reach a colleague
> who works in therapeutic riding. Here are some ideas
> she had for your first few lessons. Add them to your
> own plans if they make sense. The biggest rule, I was
> told, is don't do too much too fast. I put a couple
> things in your backseat. I need to return them in two
> weeks, but try them before you invest in anything
> expensive.*
>
> *Good luck,*
> *Dee*

The enclosed list was elegantly simple. Several suggestions matched what Jill had come up with, but the
sample first lesson was far less advanced than what she
had planned. Each exercise focused on confidence, not
riding skill, and the wisdom was obvious.

After reading all the notes, Jill craned her neck to
check behind her. There was a wide, leather strap that
cinched around a horse's belly. The vaulting surcingle

sported two solid handles for a rider to grip. There was also a molded plastic saddle seat permanently attached to a heavy foam pad. It had stirrups and a horn but was light, smooth, and free of seams or buckles.

Tears welled in Jill's eyes without warning or hope of being stopped. "Dee," she whispered, and a dull pain from something wounded deep inside eased, as if it had received a healing touch.

CHASE EXITED THE arena, leaving Jill and Michael in charge of the lesson. The past half hour he'd walked on one side of Jamie astride Sun, while her father walked on the other. Side walkers, Jill called them, their job to steady and encourage Jamie as needed. Not that enthusiasm was in short supply. Jamie's face glowed in equal parts rapture and concentration as she gripped the surcingle handles to keep her balance on Sun's broad back. She'd figured it out quickly, though, and all she needed now was her father.

Chase took a spot along the fence not far from Robert, Becky, and Gypsy, whom Becky had ridden for fun. Angel came to sit beside him, and he knelt to pat her, not noticing the Miata until he heard the click of its door swinging open. He turned to the sight of Dee easing her long legs out of the sports car's sleek, crimson body.

Half the summer had passed since he'd seen her. To his surprise, she closed the car door and stood for a moment, looking not cocksure as he remembered her, but hesitant.

The old Dee, right down to the purr, instantly resurfaced, however, when she spied him. "Hi there, stranger."

"Hey, Dee. Haven't seen you since we gave a dog a bath."

"Ah. For which you still owe me since Elaina never found out." She arched a brow. "This is her?" Angel approached and thumped her tail on the ground. Dee reached for her head. "She certainly looks different. What a pretty dog."

"She's a little fatter and a lot sassier. Jill's taken good care of her."

He braced for a caustic reply, but if anything, Dee's pretentiousness faded a little and she pointed toward the arena. "How's the lesson going?"

"Admittedly, we're new at this." Chase paused. "But look—kid can't keep a smile off her face."

Jill had Jamie reaching—up, sideways, cross-ways— and Jamie clearly thought it worth all the effort she had to muster in order to find balance. Dee's gaze came to rest on huge Gypsy standing placidly at the log hitching rail.

"What's up with the Clyde?"

"Creative teaching, I guess you could say," he said with pride. "Miss Becky there is Jamie's sister. This all started with her, and she has a real talent for irritating the good mood out of anyone she meets. But a little girl on a big horse loses her attitude problem right quick."

"A draft horse for riding lessons." Dee returned her eyes to Jill. "She's a good teacher, isn't she?"

He nodded. "A gifted teacher."

"And a good rider. And an A-student. Is she really giving up vet school?"

"She's fighting with that decision."

"Jill's dream is to do what will make everyone else happy."

"I keep trying to convince her to make herself happy."

Dee held his eyes, and her measuring look embarrassed him, until she broke into a grin. "You love her."

Denial was pointless. "Yeah. God help her but I'm afraid I do."

Dee stiffened. "God help *her*? She touches something and it's an instant success. It's always been that way. She doesn't need help."

"You know something?" Chase crossed his arms over his chest and nodded at Jill. "I think you're as stubborn as she is. And you're both scared."

"Of what?" Dee scoffed.

"Look what you did for her today. It wasn't necessary. And you don't have to be here—but you are. You both care, yet you won't give up the hostility, and Jill won't give up the hurt. I think you're afraid you might like each other."

"There's a lot of resentment between us." Dee remained stoic. "I'm not sure I'm ready to forget it all."

"Not ready to forget it or not ready to admit it was never justified?"

"You know?" Resentment tinged her voice. "You're a little prejudiced. After all, she won you. I left you cold."

"When you and I first met, you were all over me like a hound on a hunk of steak, but you weren't showing me the real you. Maybe the biggest difference between you and Jill is that she was honest."

As soon as the words escaped, Chase's guilt clutched at him with familiar tenacity. He averted his face. "Not that I should be lecturing on honesty. It hasn't really been my strong suit this summer either."

"I don't suppose you'd be willing to explain?"

He considered it. Explaining Tiana to someone whose opinion didn't really matter seemed like a great dress rehearsal.

"I would. But it's an explanation I owe to Jill first."

"You aren't wanted for something dreadful, are you?" she teased.

Not wanted, but not a free man either. "No, but a fugitive of sorts."

"Enough. No more cryptic puzzles if you aren't providing answers." She looked back to the lesson where Jamie was laughing. "I've got to get back to the hospital. I just wanted to make sure she—"

"I wish you'd talk to her."

"It sounds like an excuse, but I honestly do have a patient coming that I couldn't reschedule. I'm not sure what to say yet anyway."

"Try, 'You did a good job, Jill.'"

"I will. I'll tell her, I promise."

"Don't let the time get by you. Don't waste any more years."

He walked her to her car and sent her off with a cheery thumbs-up, but the pall of unfinished business hung like Minnesota humid air around him. A huge gap had closed between the sisters, but it was difficult to watch the healing process without wishing for an instant cure.

He returned to the ring and was immediately part of a rowdy celebration. Jamie, still mounted, was outside the arena, chattering like a world traveler.

"Did you see me, Chase? I'm so free!"

"I saw everything, honey. I'm real proud of you."

"I'm prouder of both you ladies than I can say," Jill echoed. "Here, Becky, will you take Sun's reins?"

"Sure."

Chase grinned when Rebecca jumped, then consciously masked her enthusiasm. She continued silently, but couldn't manage to keep a bored look in place. He watched the girls, struck at the irony of Jamie and Becky's relationship in light of his talk with Dee.

Chase spoke little as the girls performed their final tasks, but the warmth of Jill's gaze and the repeated brush of her hand on his arm filled him with confidence and resolve. He was looking forward to telling her everything tonight and, when she reacted as he'd made himself trust she would, figuring out the future. Minnesota. Florida. It didn't matter. He'd follow her, and he never needed to return to Memphis once Jill knew what had happened. He could do other things besides practice medicine— he'd proved that. His stomach danced with trepidation, but he forced away the urge to give in to fear.

As soon as the Barnes's Explorer had disappeared up the driveway and Robert had headed to the house for a nap, Chase grabbed Jill in the aisle of the barn and whirled her into a deep, hard kiss. She joined in eagerly, weakening his knees as she probed the warm secrets of his mouth.

"Was it worth the emotion, this super-lesson of yours today?" he asked when they parted.

"Every bit of it."

"Ready to celebrate? Dinner tonight? A real dinner—no pizza, no fortune cookies, no prying eyes at the Loon Feather. Come with me to the cities. Maybe we'll stay overnight. There's a dive in Minneapolis I've heard about called Murray's."

"Chase! That's one of the most expensive steak houses in the Twin Cities."

"A little pampering after such a big success would be a good thing,"

"I never knew my guy was hiding such a romantic streak," she teased. "What about Robert?"

"He'll babysit the dog. In fact, reservations are made."

"Pretty certain of yourself."

"That's what I'd like you to think."

"If I hustle Sun to Bridge Creek, then run home and shower, I can be back here by four."

"Need help?"

"With the horse or the shower?" Impishly she snaked her arms up and over his shoulders. "One shower *would* be environmentally more responsible."

He growled and grasped her bottom, pulling her against him and lowering his mouth to her ear. "If I thought for a second Robert would sleep soundly enough—"

The snap and crunch of tires on the driveway gravel broke their clinch, and they spun to the most unwelcome sight of Jim Krieger's green Navigator.

"What is *with* that man?" Jill didn't bother to hide her

grimace when the Lincoln stopped and the door opened, depositing Krieger in their path.

"Preston. Miss Carpenter," he said. "Good afternoon."

"It was," Chase replied. "What are you doing here?"

He thought he knew. Krieger had to know by now Chase had brought his suspicions to Connery.

"Protecting my company. Finishing some business with your landlord."

"I thought we made it clear that your dealings with Mr. McCormick are done."

"You don't speak for Robert McCormick any more now than you did before."

"Robert isn't available," Jill said, her voice calm, her face tightly furious.

"You'll excuse me if I knock on the door myself? Robert McCormick handled his business fine before you two started playing watchdog for him." Krieger headed for the porch without a word about accusations.

"He's sleeping." Chase reached for Krieger's arm. "He's eighty-two years old, and he worked hard this afternoon."

Krieger spun and jabbed his finger to within inches of Chase's face. "I am *not* letting you pull shit like that out of the air anymore. Push hard enough and I'll squash you."

"Knock on that door and I'll lay you out before you can squash a bug."

"Never mind." Robert's stony voice stopped the argument.

Krieger smirked. "Nice try, Preston."

"The boy wasn't lyin'," Robert growled. "I don't sleep well with vermin runnin' around in my yard."

"Look, Mr. McCormick, it's come to our attention that you've been to see your lawyer and perhaps changed some things in your will. The company feels that it's our right to—"

"It ain't any of your 'right to' anything." Chase caught Jill's questioning look, but he could only shrug. "How do you come to know what I do in my lawyer's office? That sounds like a lawsuit waiting to happen."

Krieger didn't blink. "We make it our business to know anything that could affect the future of our company."

"My farm don't affect your goddamn company." Robert's voice stretched into a higher pitch like an over-tightened piano wire. Angel whined, slipped through Jill's legs, and moved to sit at Robert's feet. "Now get off of my property."

"I'll leave, McCormick, but don't do anything rash." Krieger slid his oily gaze to Chase. "As for you. I assume you've told these good people about a certain Miss Washington?" He laughed when Chase said nothing. "Oh yes, Mr. Preston. I've had quite an interesting few weeks of research into your rather checkered past."

Chase's head swam dangerously. He could handle Krieger revealing his secret, but having him say Tiana's name was having him too close. A tic pulsed at the corner of his mouth.

JILL SET A hand on Chase's forearm, worried about the hard lines formed in his features.

"That's enough," Robert interjected. "Shut your

mouth, Krieger, and get the hell off my land before I shoot you off. And if you threaten this boy again you'd better damn well have a lawyer in your back pocket." He waved his sprightly arms like a riled banty hen and took three steps toward Krieger. "Now go on. Get out."

The whole sight would have been comical if it hadn't been for Robert's florid face in stark contrast to Chase's pallor. For an instant Jill didn't know who to be most concerned about.

"Robert, Robert," she called finally and tugged on his arm. "He's leaving. It's all right."

"Son of a bitch," Robert spat, not bothering to apologize as he usually did when his language slipped in front of Jill.

"He's all talk, Robert, you've said it yourself."

"You have no right, you hear me? You cheating son of a bitch . . ." Robert ignored her and took one more step toward Krieger, but he was suddenly the pale one, and sweat broke out on his forehead before Jill's eyes.

"Robert. Stop!"

Slowly he shook his head and then rubbed at his chest.

"Robert?" Chase snapped out of his trance and grasped Robert's shoulders. "What is it?"

"I'm fine, just indigestion."

"Come on. Sit down," Chase said firmly.

Jill helped him guide their friend to a seated position on the lawn.

"Stop fussin'." Robert's voice carried none of its normal pepper. He rubbed harder at his left shoulder.

Chase's voice grew calm, almost mesmerizing.

"Robert," he coaxed. "Tell me where you hurt. Don't brush it off. I need to know."

"Shoulder, chest, stomach mostly. Feels like the flu. Damn sudden." Robert coughed and grimaced, then clutched at his stomach and moaned. "Just churned up that hotdish I had at lunch. That's all it is."

"Maybe, maybe," Chase soothed. "Don't worry now, we'll get you some help."

"Don't need . . ."

Leaning swiftly onto one elbow, Robert bent to the ground and vomited. When he was finished Chase laid him flat, then turned him expertly onto one side.

"Jill, there's a blanket in The Creature. Krieger, quit hyperventilating and get the cooler over by the fence."

Jill's first flush of panic calmed. She knew what was happening and she followed Chase's instructions, thinking what they'd do for animal in shock. When she returned with the blanket, Robert lay on his back moaning softly, and Chase had two fingers pressed against his neck. Krieger set the cooler full of water next to him.

"You know exactly what to do, don't you." Krieger's voice, even in the midst of the crisis, held derision and threat. Chase didn't spare him so much as a glance.

"Shut up, Krieger. You stand there until I need you. Don't you move a damned muscle."

Jill unfolded the blanket and spread it over Robert's legs. Chase wet Robert's handkerchief with the cooler water and wiped his mouth, then squeezed some liquid past his dry lips.

"Okay, honey," he said to Jill. "Sit here and keep him

calm and warm. I'm going right over there to call 911. He doesn't need to hear me."

She nodded and bent low over Robert. "You're going to be fine, I promise." She stroked his thick white hair. "Chase is getting help."

Tears beaded in her eyes at Robert's unmistakable discomfort. She pulled the blanket up to his chin and tucked it tight around his body. His forehead was clammy, his hair in disarray. She smoothed it again, and he began rolling his head restlessly.

"Robert?"

His eyes flew open, and he forced one hand free to clutch at his chest. After several desperate gasps, his body went first rigid, then limp. Horrified, Jill waited five, ten, fifteen seconds but Robert's chest didn't rise again. Now she felt the hole in her training. This was a human, not a horse.

"Chase!" she screamed, but he'd disappeared around the house.

It had been far too long since her one CPR course. She begged Krieger with her eyes. "Do you know CPR?"

"From a very long time ago."

Compressions first? Breathing first? She placed her hands on Robert's breastbone.

Chase appeared beside her, and Jill nearly cried in relief. "He's stopped breathing."

"Robert?" Chase knelt beside their friend's ear and shook him firmly. "Robert, can you hear me?" There was no response. "Damn it, Robert, no."

His momentary loss of control sent Jill's head spinning in fear. Krieger squatted beside them, his face no longer its normal mask of arrogance.

"What can I do?" he asked.

"Watch for the ambulance," Chase replied, curt and angry.

He closed his eyes once, took a breath, and when he opened them again, the businesslike look was back. He placed two fingers beside Robert's windpipe and shook his head.

"Okay, look out."

He rose up and placed the heels of his hands precisely one over the other. His compressions were quick, strong, and fluid. Jill's tears flowed at the sight of Robert's chest giving way to Chase's weight.

She lost count of the number of times his palms drove down. At last he stopped, tilted Robert's head back, gave two quick breaths, and returned to the compressions. He went through several rotations before a faint siren wailed in the distance. Krieger trotted up the driveway without being asked.

The sight of swirling red and blue lights heading at them sent a wave of relief through Jill. Two paramedics literally leaped from the ambulance, pulling a dozen cases and bags with them.

"Where we at?" asked one. His partner had Robert in an oxygen mask within seconds and then counted with Chase.

". . . twelve, thirteen, fourteen, fifteen."

Chase rocked back on his heels and pulled his hands away, panting.

"MI," he said. "No respiration, no pulse. Chest pains began approximately fifteen minutes ago accompanied by nausea and vomiting. Down time is five minutes."

"You called this in, sir?"

"Yes."

One EMT ripped open Robert's shirt, unconcerned about popping buttons, and attached two sticky patches to the old man's chest.

"Would you like to handle this part?" he asked Chase.

"I'm out of state. I'll jump in if you need me."

Jill frowned at the odd exchange. The EMTs' deference made no sense. She glanced across the grass to Krieger, whose shock seemed to have dissipated. He cocked a knowing brow at her and she spun away.

The EMT globbed gel onto Robert's skin, lifted two padded paddles from a case, and set some dials. It looked like a TV emergency drama, but everything was all too real.

"Clear!"

Everyone backed off, and Robert's body gave a sickening jolt.

"No change. Raise it to 250. Clear!"

Robert's torso bucked again, then went still.

"One amp epinephrine." The paramedic looked to Chase, who nodded.

Robert received an injection and the paddles came up again.

"Once more. Clear!"

Jill gasped when the monitor began a steady beeping.

Chase closed his eyes. "Normal sinus rhythm," he said. "Check his respiration."

"He's breathing."

Chase stood. He came toward her, but she saw only a stranger. Then he pulled her into his embrace, and she melted, relieved at his familiar scent, his protective hardness, his intimate kiss on her hair.

"Go up to his room, okay? Gather whatever you can find that he might need—toothbrush, shaving things. They'll be taking him in a minute. We'll follow."

"Chase? Tell me what's going on."

"Go," he whispered gently without answering her request.

Chapter Twenty-Four

JILL SCANNED ROBERT'S room in a daze, heartbroken to see his private space for the first time under these circumstances. A worn wedding ring quilt covered a mahogany sleigh bed. Pictures of Olive taken at different times in her life sat everywhere. More of Robert's beloved Louis L'Amours sat on a low chest, and a wrinkled work shirt sprawled on the floor.

Unbearable sadness overwhelmed her when she faced the knowledge that Robert was likely to die.

"No." She spoke aloud and purposefully. "Chase won't let him."

Chase. Her stomach ached in bewilderment. He'd claimed all along he knew first aid, but his actions over the past ten minutes showed he knew a lot more than a Red Cross first aid class could teach a person. She located pajamas in Robert's closet. In a crack-mirrored bathroom medicine cabinet she found a toothbrush, a jar of nonaerosol shaving cream, and an old-fashioned, twist-handle safety razor. She rolled everything into a tight bundle and took a last, helpless look around. On impulse, she grabbed a small framed picture from Robert's bedside table and hurried back downstairs.

Well-ordered bustle ruled the yard. A pile of empty vials and packaging lay near Robert, still on the ground but now attached to two intravenous lines. Angel lay inches from his head, her eyes on him, intent and unblinking. Krieger's Navigator was gone. The EMTs flung straps and blankets from the bed of a gurney. Chase bent over Robert with his back to Jill, and she stopped a few feet from him.

"BP is still low but better," he said. "Pupils are equal and reactive." To her astonishment, he pulled a stethoscope from his ears and handed it to one EMT. "If you'd put in a good word for me, I wouldn't mind talking to the cardiologist and maybe seeing the results of the twelve-lead."

"Happy to."

Chase swiveled his head and saw her. He gave a pale smile. "That was quick," he said.

She stared. Was he an EMT, too? Some sort of paramedic? Her brain wouldn't work.

He kissed her forehead. "They're taking him now. We should put Sun away here and follow."

"Please tell me what's going on," she said. "Chase?"

"Dr. Preston?" a paramedic called, and a shockwave slammed her. Chase's body stiffened. He flashed her some kind of unspoken plea and turned.

"Yes?" he asked, and they drew him away.

Dr. Preston? She reeled in dizzy comprehension. She was an idiot. It was completely obvious. Huge chunks of the mysterious puzzle that was Chase Preston fell into place. But where she should have felt relief there was only debilitating shock.

She'd known he had a secret. She'd suspected it was big. But this kind of big had never entered her mind. As Chase bent over Robert again, and she heard his reassuring murmurs, she told herself he hadn't changed. Except he had. Like her father. Like Dee. Like all of them, he'd lied.

Bald-faced lied.

"Jill?" He looked up. "Robert's asking for you."

She pushed past him and took Robert's hand as they lifted him onto the gurney. As she knelt beside his pale body while they strapped him in, a little relief washed blessedly over her at his wan smile.

"Hey, old man, that was quite a scare you gave us. Aren't you ashamed?"

He grunted beneath the clear oxygen mask, but his eyes held fear. She kissed his grizzled cheek. "Please don't worry. We'll be with you in a few minutes, okay? Promise me you'll show everyone the ornery old cuss we love."

He blinked once. Angel licked the hand Jill held. Robert sighed.

When he was safely aboard and the big metal doors had clanged shut, the ambulance rolled away. Its huge lights circled, and as it picked up speed going out the driveway, the siren hooted and caught.

"They'll take good care of him now." Chase stood behind her.

"You lied," she said quietly. "To me. To everybody."

He tried to pull her close, but she jerked free. "I don't blame you for being upset—"

"Upset?" She took a step away from him. "You bet I'm upset, *Dr.* Preston. You're a doctor? What kind of person hides something like that? "

Chase's arms fell limply at his sides. His voice, when he answered, was colorless. "One would hope a person with a good reason."

Memory overtook logic. Julian Carpenter's voice came clearly through the years. *I have good reasons for this, Jillie. I'd never hurt you.*

"No. You know what?" She focused back on Chase, numbness blossoming into resentment. "If you really are a doctor you took an oath, didn't you? However little you thought of us, you still have moral obligations. If it took Robert almost dying for you to honor your—"

"Stop right there."

Seconds before, Chase had been abject, but now his eyes and words glinted with diamond edges. The gentle hero from the summer was fully gone.

"You be as angry at me for the past two months as you like, but don't talk to me about oaths you will never understand." You want some truth from me? Here you go. In the ghettos of Memphis people die from things a lot scarier than what happened here today. They die from gunshot wounds. From drug overdoses, stabbings, and diseases you've only read about between the pristine covers of magazines and books.

"I've seen things that scare the hell out of my oaths, so

for you to judge . . ." He clenched his fists. "Whatever you think, I did all I could for Robert."

He had. She knew he had. And so his secret was out. He was a doctor. It was a heroic profession, something to cause pride, not anger. So why was she so angry?

Because. She knew of the lie only because of a crisis.

"Since day one you've let me think you're somebody you aren't."

"Yes." His voice finally softened.

"You aren't sorry?"

"I am more sorry than you could possibly know." His back remained as stiff as one of the boards he'd been pounding onto Robert's porch all summer. "You've deserved to know what I really am. I had every intention of telling you. That's what tonight was for."

Did he think she was stupid? "My, how convenient that is."

His shoulders finally sagged. "If we're going to be at the hospital for him, we'd better get moving," he said, ignoring her, his voice weary. "Go get Sun, and I'll toss some hay in a stall."

Angel trotted two steps after him and barked, a sharp, admonishing sound. Chase ignored her, too. Jill fought the urge to follow the stranger he'd suddenly become and . . . and what? Smack the old Chase back into existence? She couldn't because this wasn't the stranger—this was the real man.

Angel trotted to her, and Jill sank to her seat in the grass beside the beautiful dog that had brought her together with Chase in the first place. Angel gazed at the barn, her luminous brown eyes registering an eerily human sadness, then crawled fully onto Jill's lap.

When Jill and Chase left ten minutes later, Angel laid herself resolutely in front of Robert's favorite chair and watched them drive away. Silence choked the interior of The Creature. Jill couldn't shake her anger. She knew not every facet of the Chase Preston she'd loved had been faked, but his impenetrable silence dealt ax blows to her faith. If he was this unwilling to talk now, how could she believe he'd ever intended to tell her?

She parked near the hospital emergency entrance. Once out of the truck, Chase met her eyes cautiously.

"I deserve your anger," he said. "I hoped for something else. I've hoped all summer that when you found out you'd understand. But I get that you don't. Just know this reaction is why I never told you."

"That's ridiculous. You're a doctor. That's not the issue here? Why lie to me on the very first day?"

"Because some things just plain cause pain."

"Yes. Like lying."

He turned for the hospital doors without explaining anything further.

There were few people in the emergency waiting room, just one little boy sobbing loudly while gingerly cradling a distorted right arm. Jill, never squeamish, grimaced and followed Chase to the duty nurse.

"We're here for Robert McCormick," he said. "He was brought in a short time ago."

"You must be Dr. Preston?"

"Yes, ma'am."

"Dr. Harper is finishing his preliminary exam. If you'll have a seat I'll let him know you've arrived."

Their adjacent chairs could have been a canyon apart. Chase slouched into his seat, propped one elbow on the blue upholstered arm, and covered his mouth while he stared at a point somewhere in front of his feet. Jill forced herself to sit still for the next ten minutes with hands clasped like an obedient child.

"Dr. Preston?" A tall, brown-haired man in khaki Dockers, a loosened tie, and a lab coat stood before them. "I'm Theodore Harper."

"Dr. Harper." Chase stood and shook the ER doc's hand.

Dr. Harper turned to Jill. "Jill Carpenter," she supplied.

"It's fortunate you were with him. We've completed the twelve-lead and this was a serious inferior MI. I suspect an LAD lesion, but I'm recommending an angiogram to be sure."

Chase raked a hand through his hair. "Is he a candidate for bypass?"

"There's a good chance. He seems strong. Are you his personal physician?"

"No, a friend. He's normally strong and extremely active for his age."

"That's definitely in his favor. I'll know more when the test is completed. Meanwhile, he's asked for the two of you, and I promised he could see you for a moment. It may help. He seems quite anxious."

"We'll talk to him."

"Where's your practice?"

"A private free clinic in Memphis."

"Well, tip of the hat. That's a challenging environment. I'll have someone fetch you when Mr. McCormick is ready." He extended his hand to Jill. "Miss Carpenter? A pleasure to meet you. Excuse me then?"

Twelve-lead. Angiogram. LAD lesion. The technical jargon swam in her head as meaningless as enemy code. The last person she wanted to turn to was Chase, but he spoke the foreign language fluently.

"What did he say?" She forced herself to be dispassionate.

"They did a more thorough electrocardiogram called a twelve-lead," Chase began, equally clinically. "It's a test that takes readings of the heart from every angle. They suspect Robert has a blockage in a main artery. Sometimes these can be repaired by bypass surgery. The angiogram will confirm the problem."

"Will he be all right?"

"There's no way to promise that. Honestly? He's been lucky to get this far. An LAD lesion has an unpleasant nickname—they call it a widow maker."

Jill's hope faltered. Cruelly, she wondered if his bedside manner was always so grim.

When they were called by a nurse, she led them through a rabbit warren of curtained stations to the one where Robert lay, his eyes closed, his brown forearms stark against the sheets. For the first time ever, he looked his advanced age.

"I'm sorry," the nurse said. "We can only allow a moment. He's very weak."

"We understand," Chase replied.

Jill entered just ahead of Chase, and irrational fear gripped her. It was ridiculous, considering all the times she'd fought unflinchingly to help Ben save a life in a setting not really any different from this one, yet this place was as alien as if she'd stepped into a video game. There were no dogs or horses here. This was a world of sterile smells, vigilant monitors, and desperate hope. This was, it turned out, Chase's world.

"Oh, Robert, dear man." She collected herself and smiled for him.

His face was the color of clay. Blankets covered him to his armpits, and, above them, whorls of silver chest hair caught a pinkish hue from the caress of low lights. Four thin wires snaked into monitors on the wall.

She clasped his hand, and his eyes opened to tired slits. "Jill? Chase?"

"Don't talk," Jill said. "We'll just sit with you a minute."

"I need to tell you."

"Tell me what?"

"About the will."

"What will?" Chase laid his hand on Robert's shoulder.

"I changed my will. Your names are in it now. I want the farm to go to you."

"What?!" They voiced their shock simultaneously.

"You two are . . ." Robert's voice caught, and his pale eyes welled with shiny tears.

"Don't," Jill said again. "We'll talk about this all later. It doesn't matter right now."

"You are the daughter my Olive never had," he whispered. "You"—he raised his far arm slowly and grasped Chase's hand—"you're like another son."

Jill couldn't keep her own eyes dry. "You know we both love you." She smoothed his hair again. "But you can't hand away a piece of property worth that much money. Not to us. Certainly someone will object."

"Krieger already does." A wisp of a smile touched his mouth.

Jill pressed his hand to her lips and allowed a chuckle. "You're a mean old man, Robert McCormick."

"Thank you."

"When you're better we'll argue this out."

He shook his head weakly. "I don't care what you do with the farm, my time with it is up. It was good to me. Just want to give Krieger one last pain in the ass."

"Robert McCormick, don't you dare give up! You're going to fight this to the bitter end."

"I'm just a tired old man." His eyes slid closed.

"Robert?" Panic rose like gorge in her throat.

"It's okay." Chase's words soothed.

After a moment, when Robert's grip remained firm in hers, and the monitors continued to beep, Jill allowed herself to relax. Seconds later Robert opened his eyes again.

"Thank you."

"For what, you old coot?" Chase asked.

"For comin' around the place of a crazy old man."

"It was our pleasure and still is."

"You'll care for my girls, Jill? You'll make sure they have good care, good homes?"

"Of course. With you. You're going to come through this for me."

A nurse returned, smiling but firm. "Time is up. Dr. Harper is nearly ready. I'll show you where to wait, and we'll keep you informed."

Chase stood up still holding Robert's hand. "See you in a while."

"Chase? It's a hell of a thing. They say you're a doctor of some kind."

"Of some kind."

"You—cracked a rib, I think."

"I'm sorry." Chase shook his head sorrowfully. "It's not a gentle thing."

"Thank you for that, too."

"Jill and I were simply the good Lord's instruments today. Go. Get better."

MINUTES SEAMED THEMSELVES into hours and hours crawled past midnight before Jill awoke from fitful dozing on a waiting room couch to see Dr. Harper step through the door. The angiogram earlier had confirmed his diagnosis, and they'd taken Robert straight in for bypass surgery. Now a V of sweat stained the chest of the doctor's blue scrubs, and a haggard shadow hollowed his eyes. Chase, across the small room, snapped to attention, and Jill steeled for the worst.

"Mr. McCormick survived the surgery," Dr. Harper said.

A "but" hung on the end of his announcement. Jill closed her eyes with a heavy sigh, and Chase moved closer.

"There is a complication. He suffered a mild stroke that seems to have affected motor skills on his right side."

"A stroke?" Jill asked in alarm. "Why? How?"

"We don't know, I'm afraid. It may have been ready to occur, it may have been caused by the stress of surgery. It's much too soon to tell if the effects will last, but he's stable now and appears to be strong and resting easily."

"And the prognosis on the bypass?" Chase asked.

"The surgery went well," Dr. Harper said. "If he remains stable over the next forty-eight hours, he has a good chance."

"When can we see him?" asked Jill.

"You can glance in on him now, but morning will be the soonest he'll be alert. Dr. Preston, we'll get a number where you can be reached if there's any change."

"I'll be here tonight."

"You can't stay here all night," Jill shot.

"It only makes sense. They've got an empty bed, and I'll be right here if anything happens. You can stay at Robert's, take care of the animals, and get to work in the morning. Come when you can, and you can keep watch then."

Of course it made sense, but Jill fumed inwardly anyway. He'd pulled away from making decisions *with* her and was now pulling rank—a doctor's rank—to make them *for* her.

"Fine." She wasn't about to argue like a child in front of Dr. Harper. "But I'm not planning to go to the clinic tomorrow. I'll be here as soon as the animals are settled."

"That's fine. I'm sure he'll want to see you."

Even when he was being an ass he was still smooth.

Chapter Twenty-Five

"HOW IS HE?"

Chase looked up to the sound of Jill's soft voice from the doorway. He'd been so engrossed in the soft beep of monitors and the effort of thinking about nothing, he hadn't noticed her arrival.

"He's doing great." He shifted in his chair and glanced at Robert. "He was awake briefly. His vital signs have been good all night. Did you get any sleep?"

"Only because Angel wouldn't let me leave the bed. I think she's the one who didn't sleep."

"You named her appropriately."

Jill nodded and drew close to the bed. Chase's stoic concentration crumbled like a flimsy house of sticks at the sight of her. He wanted so badly to take her in his arms. To wipe the hurt from her face. But he'd disappointed her. He could tell her the story, beg for absolution, and she might give it. But that wasn't what he wanted.

"Oh, Robert." Her tiny gasp wrenched his heart. The effects of Robert's ordeal looked more devastating than they probably were, but his appearance was shocking. His right eyelid appeared to have slid sideways, and the right side of his mouth drooped like melted candle wax. A trickle of saliva drizzled to the pillow.

"That's not him." Tears blossomed in her eyes, and they nearly undid him. She, who kept her cool over injured animals and sass-mouthed teenagers, who could turn a tickle fight into hot, sweet lovemaking, didn't deserve to look so utterly sad.

"He looks worse asleep than he does awake." Chase tried to make it sound like a promise. "He was actually quite with it for a few minutes. I admit he sounds a little tipsy . . ." His attempted smile fell flat.

"He sounded like he'd given up."

"He was in pain, and he was frightened. People who have heart attacks that severe are pretty scared."

She faced him slowly, but only half met his eyes. "You really are a doctor."

"Yes. And I really am sorry this is how you found out."

"I'm sure that's true." She turned away again. His heart fell a little further. "You should go now. You can't have gotten much sleep," she said.

"I did all right."

He didn't want to tell her that the hospital environment had actually lulled him. Familiar sights and sounds hadn't exactly caused homesickness, but he definitely knew his way around this setting.

"Still, you should get a break."

So she wanted him to leave. For the first time, anger poked its head out of Chase's roiling pool of emotions. He was at fault, true. But why was she *this* angry? A snotty teenager with a rude mouth had received more patience.

"Fine. Happy to let you take your turn watching." He stood, holding in a fierce but unjustified need to call her on some kind of double standard. "If you'll let me take The Creature to the farm, I'll come back whenever you want me to."

His voice must have been harsher than he'd intended because she held up her hands. "You're calling the shots, Dr. Preston. Come and go when you're ready."

"For crying out loud," he muttered under his breath.

Jill pulled the key fob shaped like a snaffle bit out of her purse and held it out to him. He took it and watched her continue searching through her bag, her brow creasing ever more deeply.

"Crap," she said at last. "I left my dang phone in the truck."

"I'll bring it back up for you."

"No. I'll come down. He's sleeping anyhow." She sighed.

Chase gave all the monitors around Robert a last glance, then patted him on the shoulder. "Hang in there, old man," he said. "See you later."

The silence that accompanied them to the lobby eroded his anger into deep sadness. When they reached The Creature, his shoulders slumped and he stuffed his hands in his pockets.

"Jill, this is insane. I don't know how to deal with a cold war."

"No, you don't," she agreed tightly. "Why don't you end it?"

"And how do you propose I do that? The secret's out. You chose how you wanted to react to that secret."

She choked on affronted laughter. "You sweet-talk and Southern-charm your way through more than two months, until I learn the secret existence of *Dr.* Preston only because you had no choice but to reveal it. It's increasingly clear you never intended to explain this to me and still don't. Yet you blame *me* for a cold war? Just open your mouth and talk."

"Damn it, I had nightmares about baring my soul to someone I thought would love me no matter what. I'm not about to bare it for someone who's decided to chew me up and spit me out."

"Don't you think I'm the slightest bit justified?"

Just like that, she clobbered him with the only weapon for which he had no defense. The granite keeping him rigid cracked, and his anger vanished. "Yes." He heard his own emotionless voice. "I've always known you'd have perfect justification to feel exactly the way you do."

He pulled open The Creature's door, grabbed Jill's phone from the console, and handed it to her. "What time shall I be back?"

"I have to teach at three-thirty."

"I'll be here by two."

Without a reply, she let him climb into her truck and drive away.

THE ROOM WAS too quiet for noon on the farm. Even the dog, snuggled beneath his arm, didn't move, snore, or complain about being a canine body pillow. After hours of sleeplessness and fighting the memories, Chase gave up. He let Tiana Washington, all knobby knees, mocha skin, and gorgeous, expressive eyes, run freely through his mind. The skinny little girl had possessed Whoopi Goldberg irreverence with Jennifer Hudson dreams. Every time he'd seen her she'd hugged him with abandon, unaware of any stupid etiquette between doctor and patient, and she'd belted out the latest song she'd memorized with fervor that made up completely for lack of finesse. Her quick intellect, fed by the attention lavished on her by her grandmother Clara, had astounded him over the years.

Inevitably, the good memories led to the horrific: Tiana's body stilled along with her voice. Brody making the legally required pronouncement of death. Clara's wide face, devastated and accusatory.

He turned numbly away from the broken grandmother and looked one last time to the table where Tiana lay. An anguished cry broke from his throat. It was not Tiana but Jill lying there—hair disheveled, skin ashen, mouth slack.

"No!"

To Angel's yelp of protest, Chase found himself seated upright in his bed at Robert's, lungs burning from hyperventilation. He blew short, calming breaths into his cupped palms, then hiked up his knees, folded his arms, and buried his face.

When had he fallen asleep?

He'd never put stock in analyzing dreams, but this one was so obvious a five-year-old could grasp its meaning.

He'd lost Jill, too. God knew she more than deserved an explanation, and he was being a jackass to withhold it when he'd been mere hours from telling her the story. He'd just been so certain she'd love him without any explanation. Instead, she was outraged over the mere fact he'd disguised his identity. What kind of revulsion would she feel if she discovered that his secret included abandoning a child to face her death?

He'd never planned or wanted to tell the painful story in the first place. He'd nearly taken a chance, but now he was grateful the words and emotions weren't out there in someone else's keeping.

It was only a few minutes past noon, but he was done with sleep. Fifteen minutes later he held a steaming mug of coffee, his mind calmer but not easy. The old sofa in the living room sagged comfortably beneath him, and Angel lay at his feet. He gazed at all the knickknacks and homey colors that had grown familiar during the past weeks. With a little more luck, Robert would soon sit in his recliner again.

It was time to leave. Time to face what he'd hidden from all summer. It nearly killed him that it had taken hurting a beautiful woman to get to this point.

He'd known he would hurt her. He'd momentarily fooled himself by making love to her and convincing himself she was his elusive "one." But she wasn't. And she would be fine. Once he explained enough to give her closure. Once he left her to pursue the dreams he'd interrupted.

Angel let out a long, doggy sigh and Chase's heart broke at the first realization that he'd be leaving the dog, too. He'd never shed real tears over Tiana, but now he fought them, forcing them angrily away. Out of every crap thing in his life he could cry over a stupid stray dog? He really had been here too long.

The knock at the door startled him. Angel jumped up with one sharp bark and trotted, tail wagging, to investigate. Chase ran a hand through his hair, which needed a good trim, and followed the dog. Surprise turned to shock when he found Duncan Connery standing on the newly finished porch.

"Hello, Chase."

"Mr. Connery. To say this is a surprise wouldn't cover it. How's your daughter?"

"She's hanging in there, thank you. I'll be going back as soon as I can, but I had to come home for now because you were right. The problem you discovered is real. I've worked too hard to build an honest reputation for my company to let this pass."

Chase barely knew what to say. In the midst of all the bad, here was a glimpse of justice.

"I'm sorry, too, about Robert McCormick," Connery continued. "The news is all over town. Any word on how he is?"

"His prognosis is guardedly positive."

"I'm glad to hear that. Do you have a few minutes? I'd like to talk away from the office."

Chase held the door open. "Come on in."

Connery stepped through the door and bent to scratch Angel's ears. "Nice dog."

"Yes, sir. A stray we took in, but she's a special one."

Connery sat at the kitchen table and accepted a mug of coffee.

"I kept your name out of this until today, but Jim Krieger's no fool. He figured it out. His story now is that you concocted all this as a personal attack," Connery said, when Chase sat across from him. "Thirty-plus years of loyalty have made me inclined to believe this is a mistake. But I've realized I have some loyalty to your grandfather, too. I needed to give his grandson the benefit of the doubt."

"I appreciate that."

"I started digging and got some answers from Sandhurst I didn't like. That brought me home. What brought me to you was Jim coming to me this morning with the news about Mr. McCormick. He made a very cold suggestion that we move to take advantage of the man's incapacity without his cooperation. I'm still finding it hard to believe he would think in such callous terms. I guess I've let him run his projects without much oversight for too long."

The man suddenly looked his age. Chase sympathized on a visceral level.

"He'd already been trying to push Robert harder and faster."

"There's a lot of investigative work ahead. If Sandhurst did lie about the scope of this project, then there are environmental impact statements and pollution control agency studies that must have been falsified. If so, I'll pull the plug. I have other developers who shed tears when Krieger chose the Sandhurst project."

"What kind of development might you be talking about? Hypothetically."

"We saw plans for a community center. For office space. For a small housing tract."

"With all due respect, Mr. Connery—"

"Chase, c'mon. About time you call me Duncan."

"All right. Duncan. You could make a lot of people very happy by pulling the plug without any more proof at all. Save yourself a passel of aggravation. There are a lot of things this town needs—a swimming pool, a youth center." He thought of Jamie with a pang. "A local medical clinic."

Duncan massaged his chin. "Forget pressing any charges?"

"Nobody's been harmed yet, far as I can tell. There might be intent for fraud, but it hasn't been carried out. You're the only one who knows how damaging this is for you, but, goodwill goes a long way in a small community."

"Spoken like a true businessman."

Chase hesitated only briefly, then looked his grandfather's friend in the eyes. "If you know about Robert, then you know about my background. Krieger wouldn't have stopped short of telling you about me."

Duncan sat back in his chair. "You must have had a reason for keeping quiet. I told that to Jim several times."

Hell. Chase's heart fielded another blow. Where had that attitude been in Jill?

"That's kind of you," he replied. "I did start a clinic on the south side of Memphis and made it work with grants and fund-raisers. Business isn't my strong suit, but in my opinion, Krieger's way is never right. Folks don't take kindly to dishonesty."

A fresh stab of regret pierced him.

"I, ah, don't suppose you'd be willing to come help me sell that?" Duncan laughed ruefully. "The next town council meeting is in a week. I'll stay here until then, and I'd planned to tell the truth as I know it and let people voice opinions. But I'm going to think seriously about your advice. I sure would like you to be there. The town has sort of taken to you."

Sadness rippled through him. He'd let down enough people. It was tough not to get close to a place like Kennison Falls, but he had nothing more to offer the people here. Time to do the right thing for a change.

"I have to be honest," he said, slowly. "I don't think I'll be here in a week. I'm going back to Memphis."

"Oh." Duncan's eyebrows curved into arches of surprise. "I'm . . . I wish you the best but I am sorry. You know you'll have a job with me now whenever you want one."

For some reason that gave his bruised ego an infusion of comfort. "That means a lot," he said. "If anything changes, can I let you know?"

"I just said you could." He smiled, stood, and held out his hand. "Chase? Thanks more than I can say. You did me an enormous favor."

"I was in the right place at the right time."

Connery turned at the door. "May I ask? You and Miss Carpenter? I was given to understand you're together."

Chase forced a nonchalant smile. "Turns out we were just friends."

"Ah. Isn't that the way it goes sometimes? If we don't see each other before one of us leaves, say hello to your grandfather."

"That I will."

When Duncan was gone, Chase let out a breath he felt like he'd been holding for twenty minutes. He put his hands on his thighs and hung his head.

Yeah. It sure as hell was the way it went. Sometimes.

"OLD MAN, BE happy you're alive." Chase teased an ill-tempered Robert, glaring up at him from a bed at Oakwood Nursing Home. "Therapy will get you home in two weeks, but only if you cooperate. Otherwise you better decide you like puke-yellow walls and rolling bedpans."

"Cooperate." Robert's voice remained gruff, but after another moment he wilted into his pillows, the droop in his face deepening. "I feel like an old, torn pair of pants. Nobody's quite sure if they're worth fixing so they've thrown 'em on a heap until they decide."

"Hey! That one's good enough for the Preston dinner

table. Don't worry, it's only been five days since surgery. You're on the mending pile."

For the first time, Robert allowed a smile. "You're a good boy, Chase."

Chase looked away. "Not always."

"Dumber than dirt sometimes but a good boy. All right, what's wrong?"

Chase found it much harder to form the words than he'd thought it would be. "I'm going home to Memphis for a while," he said.

"A while?"

"I have a practice there with my brother. I've been talking to him, and he needs help. I've been gone a long time."

"Jill knows." It wasn't a question.

"I'm talking to her tonight."

"You two are plain stubborn, boy, you know that? I don't know what's eatin' you up inside, but whatever it is, you won't hurt her without hearing an earful from me."

"I didn't want to hurt her either, Robert, but I already have. The problems are mostly my fault. It's true, I have things to work through she doesn't know about. But she can't forgive me for keeping a secret. She looks on it as one big lie. I can't make her have faith in me."

"You can't give her a chance to develop it if you run away neither."

"It was running away to come here. Facing what I ran from—that's the best favor I can do for Jill. She has big dreams, Robert. She deserves to fulfill them."

There was another silence before Robert heaved a sigh. "When?"

"In the morning."

"When are you planning to tell everyone else?"

"Jill's the only one I need to talk to."

"You better damn well do it. Do you understand?"

Chase nodded miserably.

Chapter Twenty-Six

THE BACKYARD LIGHTS were off at the Carpenter house,
and night shadows painted the flagstone path in hues of
charcoal and blue. Chase followed Jill toward the big willows, their slender leaves luminescent beneath a waxing
moon. Crickets sang up a ruckus, and neon flashes flitted across the patio. Chase stared at the show, wishing he
were young again and had nothing harder to face than
chasing down a Mason jar's worth of fireflies.

"Robert's okay?" he asked when they reached the
gazebo.

"Fine. One of the nurses actually got a thank-you out
of him tonight."

"He'll come around."

"I think so."

Their stilted words only made Chase hurt worse for
what he was about to do. Bubbling water drew his eyes to
a pool planted all around with petunias and moss roses.

The largest willow tree had a gnarled trunk that jutted outward like the bent knee of a royal servant. Its branches cascaded to grass level as if it doffed its hat to welcome a queen. Chase recalled a kiss beside this tree, many weeks before, from a girl he didn't want. Now the girl he did want stood beside him, but there would be no kiss.

He followed her to a white wrought-iron ice cream table and chairs. Her hair swung in a fall of perfect honey-colored silk except for one crimp line at neck level where a band had held it back all day. He longed to feather it through his fingers, knowing exactly what it would feel like, and sadness overwhelmed him.

"You have something to tell me?" she asked quietly.

He nodded. "I've talked to Brody. The clinic needs help. I have to go to Memphis."

"You're leaving?" She straightened in shock.

"Sometime this week. I needed to make sure you can handle Angel and the chores at Robert's. I'm sorry to do that."

"Brody. I suppose he's a doctor, too?" A now-familiar tinge of annoyance filtered into her voice.

"My partner. He's our trauma surgeon."

"Are there more medical people in your family? Your grandfather, perhaps?"

"No. Brody and I are the only black sheep."

"Why? Why did you come here?"

"I was running away. I told you about the little girl who was killed by a gang member. What I didn't tell you is that it happened on the steps of our clinic and the girl was a nine-year-old patient of mine. I . . . couldn't handle the trauma." The words came hard. He'd never told the story aloud. "But it's time for me to face it."

It happened. Just as he'd predicted it would. Her eyes filled with tears. Her face softened.

"Oh, Chase. Why didn't you just say so?"

The tender touch that followed was like a shot of great bourbon on the rocks—cold and anesthetizing, but he removed her fingers from his cheek.

"No. No sympathy. Not now," he said, his voice gruff, his stomach aching. "I only selfishly want your forgiveness for leaving you in the lurch. I'm sorry."

Her irises glistened in pale light that should have been romantic, not heartrending. She clearly didn't understand why he wouldn't accept the apology she'd been waiting to give.

"I—" She stopped as if thinking, then ran the back of her hand beneath her nose and sniffed. "The girls will be disappointed. The big horse show at David's is next weekend, and Becky was going to show off her jumping. Jamie will be our ribbon girl."

"I'm sorry I'll miss it." Regret stung his eyes, and he stood swiftly.

"You'll say good-bye?" she asked.

His heart lay like a broken lump in his chest as he nodded. He reached for her hand. "C'mon. I've got some chores to finish."

When they reached the back door he lingered, holding fast to her hand. He almost gave in—almost accepted her understanding and asked to start over.

He wanted trust. Not sympathy.

He kissed her slowly and, without a doubt, more chastely than any time before, but his pulse throbbed, and his throat constricted.

"Drive home carefully."

"Good-bye, honey. Sleep tight."

"ROBERT? ROBERT DO you know where Chase is? Has he been here?"

Jill didn't even give the poor man a civil greeting when she blew into his room at lunch the next day. She'd sensed something was wrong from the moment Chase had arrived the night before. She'd never seen his eyes as void of animation or heard his voice as lifeless.

Robert lay flat as if the vital force had been sucked from him. Panic rose in Jill's chest.

"What do mean, 'Where is he?'" Robert asked, his eyes closed. "The boy talked to you, didn't he?"

"Yes, last night. He told me he was going back to Memphis sometime this week. Did he tell you something different?"

"I'd murder him if I saw him," Robert muttered. "I didn't think he'd take the coward's way out. He's gone, girlie. He left today."

"Today?" Air left her lungs in a rush.

"He was by here about eight."

Good-bye, honey.

She'd heard. Her heart had chosen not to believe.

Robert roused himself and reached clumsily to touch her cheek. "I'm sorry, Jill."

"He'll be back. Robert? He'll come back."

Robert closed his eyes again. "I don't know. I just don't know."

AN HOUR LATER, David's astute green eyes drilled into Jill's. She hadn't been in the barn thirty seconds and already she knew no plastic smile existed that was strong enough to hide the pain now clawing through her shock.

"Here now, you look a bit green 'round the gills," he said. "Everything's all right?"

"Fine. Crappy day."

He sharpened his gaze. She'd had a crush on David once upon a time. He certainly was worthy of at least a good drool, with his strong nose, classic cheekbones, and wavy, sable hair. Six years her senior, he'd been the epitome of her ideal man—he loved horses, he had a sexy accent, a great body. But, in reality, he'd never been more than a loving friend.

"You've always been a bloody bad liar." He grasped her shoulders with strong hands, and she crumbled. "Aw, there, love."

He pulled her into his arms and wrapped her tightly, and he said nothing until she spent her tears. Although *he* wasn't the least bit uncomfortable, the crying jag mortified her.

"I'm sorry." She wiped her nose childishly with her hand.

"What's all this?" A new voice commanded her attention, and Colin strode down the aisle. "Bit of hanky-panky for the world to see, is it?" He laughed as if he'd just told the greatest joke.

"Aw, right. That's what it is, Da'," David replied irritably. "Don't be daft. Look close and you'll see we've got tears not lust."

"Jill?" Colin's tone demanded she look at him. "I'm sorry, what's wrong?"

"Let's go to the lounge," David said.

"No, no, it's all right," Jill promised. "I'm . . . sad. Hurt. Chase is gone."

"Gone where?" David asked carefully.

"Memphis."

Neither man spoke for a long, thoughtful silence.

"He left for good?" David asked at last.

"I think so."

"Oh, love, I'm very sorry. I like Chase. He's a good man."

"Bollocks that. I'd say quite the opposite." Colin boomed his rebuttal as if he were in a presidential debate. "Good men don't walk away without a word."

Jill forced down her resentment at Colin's edict, telling herself he was only trying to stick up for her.

"Do you know why he left?" David ignored his father.

She nodded miserably and managed a journalistically unemotional recitation of the past weeks' events.

"A doctor, you say?" Colin seemed appropriately impressed until he shook his head. "Well, look here, my girl. You're better off. You've got more time to work now, you see. And you can set your sights on those Olympic rings." He nodded emphatically, perfectly serious, but for the first time, Jill's pulse didn't leap at the thought.

"Da', you aren't helping. Haven't you got a lesson waiting?"

"Always a lesson waiting," he agreed. "Jill, love, don't waste time pining—that's my advice. We'll be leaving in a month, and you'll have nothing tying you down. In my opinion, that lad seems a bit of a tosser in hindsight. A real man would stay and fight if he truly wanted you."

Well, Jill's mood sank further as Colin paced briskly away, he had a point.

David hugged her again. "Ignore him. That's my father in a nutshell. 'Stop whining. Pull up your knicks and focus.' I know how you feel about Chase—it was pretty hard to miss."

"Thank you, that helps." She rubbed the middle of her forehead, where a dull throbbing pressed inward and spread toward both temples. "Or maybe it doesn't. I don't really know what happened."

"I don't know his story," he said. "Still, as a guy, I have to ask, could he have believed there was no point in staying?"

"Of course there was a point! I simply wanted an explanation."

David hesitated. "You know," he said at last. "We males tend to get a rum go in women's books. Strong, self-assured lot that we're supposed to be, it isn't attractive to have one of us sort of come apart at the seams. Not alpha or whatever women call it. But it happens. Or so I've heard." Jill granted him a smile in spite of herself. "Perhaps Chase didn't know if you'd understand him coming apart."

"That makes no sense. I fell in love with him; he could have told me anything."

"He told you he's a doctor, and here we are."

"He didn't *tell* me." Jill fumed. "I found out. There's a difference, and you're supposed to be on my side."

"I'm not taking his side. Just—men do not necessarily have some God-given ability to buck up in every single situation. We'll hole up to protect ourselves—even if we don't admit that's what we're doing." He grasped Jill's forearms, folded defensively across her chest. "I know you still love him. But if *he* doesn't know it, running may have been simple self-defense."

Jill uncrossed her arms. "You're a good and honest friend, David. I don't know if you're right, but telling you helped."

"I'm glad," he said. "But maybe telling Chase would help more."

ANY WISDOM IN David's theory grew muddled over the next week as Jill slogged through the bustle leading up to Bridge Creek's big summer horse trials. She helped ready the farm for the influx of a hundred competitors. She, Michael, and Becky made a success of Jamie's second lesson, and Becky took *two* lessons in preparation for her show debut. Jill took two lessons herself, letting Colin have at her with more nitpicking than usual. Every distraction served to take away her melancholy for a few random hours, but none of it put a real dent in the love and resentment that warred within her, creating a tangled knot of pain she couldn't unravel or ignore.

Worse, Chase had spoiled her with his special brand of strength—the kind she'd never thought she'd need from anyone—and there was nobody else to turn to. David had said his piece. Colin didn't know the meaning of the word "sympathy." Ben barely knew Chase—Jill had made certain of that by avoiding her boss as much as possible all summer. In fact, she still had no idea how to tell Ben about her tangled mess of a life—especially the teensy little fact that she might leave vet school. That would devastate him. She couldn't do it.

As for Robert, her new old friend lost a little more spit and sassiness every day. His physical health improved, but he spoke less about returning to the farm and submitted with increasing docility to the ministrations of the nursing home staff. Jill dreaded the thought of reminding him she'd be leaving, too, come September. He'd invested foolishly in her and Chase. She worried that telling him they were both throwing the gift of his friendship in his face might kill him.

So out of loyalty to Robert, and although Chase's ghost inhabited every corner of the farm, Jill stayed there nights. Hiding away wasn't normal. She'd always gotten her strength from people. But now she drew it from the animals. Angel stuck to her like gray to a rain cloud. Tatters clowned. Gypsy and Belle made great listeners, and she often ate supper in Robert's barn—talking over the day with the draft horses like a certifiable kook.

The truth was, the thought of leaving the horses and the old farm broke her heart, and the reality of a life as Colin's working student and protégée was finally hitting home. She would have to get used to the sixteen-hour-a day life of an athlete in training, and despite dreaming of it for twelve years, the actual prospect was dead lonely.

She resented not having a clear-cut path. Other people seemed to have better handles on her dreams than she did. David. Ben. Colin. Her family. They all knew what was best for her. Chase had been the only one never to voice an opinion on her choices. She was perfectly capable of making her own plans, he'd said. Ironically, he was the one she'd nearly been ready to follow to the ends of the world—without reservation.

But he'd duped her with a person that hadn't existed, and when life got tough, he'd left. Hadn't she learned anything from the other man who'd done that—to her mother. To her sister. To her. Love didn't equal truth. Kindness didn't equal commitment. Lies hid selfishness.

"FIVE, FOUR, THREE, two, one! Have a great ride!"

The cross-country judge called out her instructions, and Becky kicked Roy to a trot out of the three-sided start gate. Her helmet completely hid her cropped hair, and the safety vest she'd borrowed from Jill was a bright blue. With a look of determination Jill had never seen, she set out across the open field toward the first of twelve cross-country jumps.

"Go Becky!" Jamie, pounding an arm of her chair with one fist and pumping the air with the other, urged her sister like a battle cry. Michael placed his thumb and forefinger between his lips and let loose a piercing whistle.

Anita, eyes huge behind her glasses, watched her daughter approach the first jump obstacle—a log barely a foot in diameter, lying on the ground with a brightly filled flowerpot at each end—in silence. Jill's knees went watery. She couldn't have been more nervous had she been the girl's mother. She released her breath when Becky hopped Roy over the log.

"Is that her?"

Dee jogged up, slightly out of breath, and Jill did a double take. Except for a brief thank-you in passing, she hadn't spoken to Dee since their ill-fated meeting in the therapy room. She shook off her surprise, too nervous for Becky to think about residual bad blood with her sister.

"Yeah, it is. Tell me why I'm nervous as if she were skydiving with no parachute."

Dee actually laughed. "Because it feels like your training is on the line. Don't worry—you taught her well. You teach all your students well."

At that Jill couldn't help tearing her eyes from Becky's ride once more. The who-are-you-and-what-did-you-do-with-my-sister begged to be let loose from her tongue, but she swallowed it. Tugging on Dee's arm, she took them several steps from the Barnes family, who were mesmerized anyway. "I've never had a student like her," she whispered. "I've been ready countless times to go to prison for murdering her, and now I want her to succeed so badly it hurts. If she could finish this, I know her confidence would go sky-high, but what was I thinking? She's had, like, three jumping lessons."

"Bah, it's the starter division—she can hang on over the little jumps."

Dee wore her breeches and paddock boots like a Stella McCartney model, but nothing else of the sister Jill knew was recognizable. From where they stood they could see across the fields to nearly all of Becky's jumps. Only two were off behind a grove of trees. Roy carried his rider safely over seven more jumps and then Becky disappeared for the two jumps on her own. Across from her, Jill saw Anita reach for Michael's hand. Her knuckles stood out in anxious relief.

"How are *Jamie's* lessons going?" Dee folded her arms on the fence in front of them.

"Really great. The second one was last week. She's strong and determined."

"I'm glad." Dee nodded, then squinted. "What about you? Has he called? Or anything?"

Jill's breath caught at the shock of the question—and at the shock of her sister asking it. She bit her lip and shook her head. "I didn't expect him to."

"I thought maybe he'd let you know he was all right."

"He barely told me he was leaving. Why would he tell me where he was?"

"It's what guys who love you do." She held up her hand

the instant Jill began a protest. "Yes, he does love you. I know because he told me so."

Images from the lake crashed through Jill's memory. She'd pushed them aside along with as many memories as she'd been able to, but now his "I love you" filled her mind. Filled her eyes with tears. She detested all these stupid tears.

Dee laughed softly and continued. "I had an immediate crush on Chase, I'd have been drummed from the Women Who Breathe Club if I hadn't. But I knew from the start he was perfect for you."

"Right. The man who was *perfect* for me didn't exist. He was the alter ego of a guy who lied all summer and then ran off with almost no explanation."

"He was going to explain."

"Oh, I don't think so."

"The day of Jamie's first lesson, he was nervous about explaining some secret. I couldn't get him to say what it was. He was right—it was a dilly."

"That's ridiculous." Jill's heart pounded in her throat. "If he was going to explain anyway, why didn't he do it? That's all I asked for."

"You know where my opinions always get me." Dee's eyes shifted from Jill to the field. "Maybe you made too much of the secret and not enough of the reason he told it. That reason must be pretty big. I mean, he kept it from the moment he met you—met any of us. Maybe he believed you wouldn't understand if he told you, so why open himself up?"

"Almost everything about him changed in front of my eyes, and he told me I didn't understand him. Why does *he* get the sympathy?"

At that moment, Becky Barnes trotted from behind the trees, and a cheer went up from her family. Michael whistled again. Anita squealed with relief.

Dee gave a hoot. "Look!"

Her sister's unbelievable turnaround was one emotional hit too many for the week. Jill stepped back to Jamie's chair.

"Three more jumps," she said to the girl. "She can do these, we practiced them all."

Indeed, Becky cleared the last jumps without incident, and a final holler went up from Michael and Jamie. Anita threw her arms around her husband. Triumph beamed from all three faces.

"Come on. Let's get to the finish!"

Jamie hauled on her wheels but Michael grabbed the chair handles and pushed her off at a near sprint. Dee followed. Anita hung back and grasped Jill's arm.

"Could I talk to you for a moment?"

"Sure. Of course."

"I need to apologize. I've been worried for so long that Rebecca would never forgive herself for . . . the accident, I've been overindulgent with her. You saw what Rebecca really needed, and I nearly ruined it. Thank you for giving us this day."

Numbness swept over Jill. Some weird spell had been cast over southern Minnesota and changed the biggest pains-in-her-ass into perfect, forgiving people. It wasn't fair. Why would the little things turn around just when life itself had turned upside-down?

"You're welcome. But you've been through something extremely difficult," Jill said. "I can't imagine what it was like. I only had to deal with what was in front of me."

"I'd like to thank Chase, too," Anita added, and again the knife twisted in Jill's heart.

"The girls didn't tell you?" She made her tone nonchalant. "He went back to Memphis."

"No! They didn't tell me."

"If I happen to hear from him, I'll pass on what you said."

"He did a great deal for us."

"Chase?"

"He talked to Jamie's therapist and then he made some inquiries. A colleague of his found the name of a new doctor who wants to see if some new therapies could work for Jamie. We're seeing him next month. Michael just told me Chase is a doctor himself, which explains a lot. We're so grateful."

Pressure so powerful it caused real pain pressed through her chest. He'd even kept this tidbit about her own student from her. She wanted to scream. Chase the wonderful. Chase the saint. Chase everybody's hero.

Everybody's but hers.

The traditional competitors' party midway through the show was always a whole-town affair. In a place as small as Kennison Falls, it was not possible to keep visitors away from a party with music and plenty of food and beer. The jovial atmosphere brought a fresh wave of dejection over Jill. All summer, she'd pictured Chase here at her side. Could he dance? Did he have a decent sing-along voice? Wouldn't he have been proud of her, sitting in first place after the dressage and cross-country phases of the show?

As it was, she barely cared. There were only six people in her intermediate division. Her closest competitor was only three points behind her, so first place could be lost by knocking down one rail during stadium jumping tomorrow. It all seemed silly.

Except in Becky Barnes's case. The child was justifiably deliriously happy—something Jill had never expected to see in her lifetime—over her ninth-out-of-seventeen placing in the beginners' division. For a teenager who three weeks before had looked like she'd fall off the horse if it flinched away a deerfly, Becky could hold up her performance against anyone's.

"Hey, you. I feel like I've been searching for you all summer even though I see you every day."

Ben Thomlinson, present by virtue of being the official show veterinarian, set his loaded plate on the table and eased his long frame onto the bench beside Jill.

"It's been an odd couple of months, hasn't it?" she replied.

He studied his plate for a moment, and a zip of dread through Jill's stomach preceded his next words. "I had a chance to talk with Colin Pitts-Matherson for quite a while. He's a pretty impressive guy. Intense."

"That's pretty much an understatement."

"He told me you're heading for Florida with him in four weeks." Jill's stomach dropped in agonized guilt as he peered at her. "That's quite an opportunity. Were you planning to let me know?"

Not a hint of anger, disappointment, or censure filtered through his words, but her cheeks stung as if they'd been slapped.

"Oh, Ben, I . . ." He didn't make it easy on her by offering understanding. He simply waited while she struggled for words that made sense. "Of course I was. I honestly haven't decided what to do."

Was that true? She hadn't? Of course she had. What was keeping her here?

"Really? You have a chance to work directly with one of the world's greatest Olympians and you aren't sure? I've known you a long time."

"You've put a lot of time into me, Ben. A lot of people have put stock in my vet school career. How can I disappoint you?"

He set his fork down and leaned toward her. His horn-rimmed glasses slid as usual halfway down the bridge of his nose. His features lost none of their unflappable calm. "Jill, I'd be lying if I said I wouldn't be disappointed were you to quit vet school. But I could never be disappointed in you."

The sting of guilt morphed instantly into the shock of surprise. "I don't understand," she murmured. "I can barely breathe without disappointing someone."

"That I don't understand. You've grown up in front of me. I know what you love, the countless things you excel at. I envy your huge heart and your limitless choices in life. But you won't get anywhere until you make your choices to please yourself. You can't make other peoples' wishes come true. Let them find their own ways."

It was what her father should be here saying. She took in Ben's warm visage. For years he'd been more of a father than Julian Carpenter, and yet she'd been so fixated on Julian's abandonment, she hadn't turned to the person right in front of her for advice and understanding.

Just as Chase hadn't turned to her . . .

Were you ever planning to tell me? Her hands flew to her mouth. She'd asked that very question of Chase. What was it Dee had said earlier? *Maybe you made too much of the secret and not enough of the reason he told it.*

"What is it?" Ben touched her shoulder.

"It's all my fault." She leaned forward and hung her head between her knees as if she were faint, but her thoughts were more painfully clear than they'd ever been.

"What is?"

"That he left. I've been so selfish I couldn't see it." She'd wept too many times, and to her mortification, and only a little relief, she outright bawled, choking back only the loudest sounds. Ben gathered her into an embrace. "What kind of horrible person am I?" she asked, curling into him, forgetting he was a boss, forgetting he wasn't her real father. "I didn't ask Ch-Chase his reason for hiding. I didn't tr-trust you to understand me. I'm so self-righteous about how I help everyone else and then I act like a t-total ass."

"You aren't an ass. You're human."

"What am I going to do? I love him."

"Love him?" His brows arched above his glasses frames. "Were you ever going to tell me *that*?"

Laughter mixed with her tears, and she choked while she hugged Ben more tightly. "Can I have a leave of absence?"

He cupped his fingers around her upper arms, and stared pointedly. "How long a leave are you requesting?"

She knew exactly what he was asking. "I don't know for sure. But I think, maybe, just a week. Or ten days?"

"That much I will gladly give you."

Chapter Twenty-Seven

SUNDAY EVENING, AFTER Becky had moved up a spot, finished in eighth place, and snagged a ribbon she called poop brown but hugged like a new teddy bear, and after Jill had retained first place to Colin's enormous satisfaction, Jill found herself at her own door. She'd wandered, lost, in Robert's empty, solemn house, and now she ushered Angel slowly inside. The instant the door squeaked open, her mother appeared.

"Jillie, you're home? How wonderf—Oh my! What's that?"

"Mom. She's my dog. Mine and Chase's."

"Oh! I . . ."

"We won't stay long." She shrugged. "Honestly? I just don't want to keep her a secret anymore. There've been too many secrets. Her name's Angel."

The dog padded demurely to Elaina's feet and sat, fixing her big eyes upward.

"Aren't you the politest dog I've ever seen?" Gingerly, she patted Angel's head.

"Well, well, my prodigal sister!" Dee swung into the room, her eyes bright. "Are you mad at me?"

"About what?" Jill cast her a wary look.

"We kind of ended on unfinished business yesterday. I feel like I lectured you again."

Jill took a deep breath. "I'm a little afraid to say this, because I really like not fighting with you. But what's happening? Why are you being nice to me?"

"I don't know." She cocked her head. "Maybe you, I, said what we needed to say and now it seems pointless to go back. Besides, I watched you teaching Jamie, and my job's not in jeopardy."

"Wow, that's for sure." Jill caught Dee's eye where her smile was reflected, devilish but genuine. "We have fun, but Jamie will need more to do. Would you ever . . . help? Me. Her?"

"Yeah. If you want. I'd be happy to."

Their mother took in the exchange, speechless.

"As for lecturing me," Jill said. "I should thank you. You said some things that made me realize I drove Chase away."

"It *was* a big secret," Dee offered.

"It shouldn't have mattered. I hurt him because I was selfish."

"Have you called him? You could tell him."

"I can't say this on the phone. That would be more cowardly than what I've already done. Besides. If you were Chase, would you even take my call?"

"If I were Chase, I would have fallen for me." Dee grinned. Sobering only slightly, she offered an awkward embrace. "If someone had told me I'd make friends with my little tomboy sister over a man, I'd have called the men with the white coats myself. You need to go get Chase."

"It's only an eleven-hour drive." The idea had been brewing since her talk with Ben, but Dee suggesting it out loud gave her a boost of excitement and confidence.

"You'd *drive*?" Her mother's consternation was clear.

"I'm sure I can dig up frequent flyer miles."

"I'd have to rent a car then. No, I'll have Dewey check The Creature. It's been running like a different truck all summer anyway, and I'll take Angel with me."

"Honey, maybe one of us should come." Elaina's voice still registered concern.

"No, Mom," Dee said, looking at Jill. "She has to do this by herself."

Jill sighed gratefully. It was true. No one could face this with her. Chase might slam a door in her face, but that would be her consequence to suffer. She didn't plan to let that happen.

"You're going where?" Colin stood before her, legs wide, like a general demanding discipline from his troops.

Jill forced herself not to quail. "To the meeting. And then I'm driving to Memphis. I don't know how long I'll be gone."

"You'll miss at least a week of training before the show in Ohio."

"I need to talk to you about that. Colin, I'm not going to the shows. I'm not going to Florida with you. I'm going to finish school first."

"What sort of a rubbish idea is that?" he demanded. "What have we been working on all summer if that's your plan?"

"You've been making me a better rider than I could ever be on my own. You've made me a better teacher, too. I'm a good teacher, Colin."

"I told you you were. Now I expect you to come prove it at my barn."

"I can't thank you enough for that confidence. But it's not what I want."

"Bollocks that. What? So you're going after that bloody idiot you have a crush on? Don't throw away your potential on some drifter."

"I wanted to be an Olympic rider. I did. Maybe I still do. But I've learned that it's a long, lonely road. Eight hours a day on horses. Six more teaching. It would be a dream to do it for fun. That's why I ride. That's why I teach others to ride. I had fun at the show, but what would have happened if I'd come in second or third or sixth? We'd have analyzed what went wrong? We'd have decided who to blame?"

"We'd have worked to eliminate a bloody problem. There are things to work on as it is."

"Do you know what I did this morning? I called the principal of the local middle school—the one who sent Becky and Jamie to me. I asked him if he knew any other troubled kids who needed a horse as a friend."

"I have invested my time and my expertise in you."

"And you will have a hundred wannabes more talented than I am beating down your door in Florida. You know you will. And I have the Barnes sisters. One successful show isn't going to solve Becky's problems. She isn't magically going to turn into an angelic child. She's thirteen. She has issues. She needs consistency."

"Then let her bloody parents raise her properly."

"They're learning, too. We all are."

"I'm disappointed in you." He stood back, his face a mask of British scorn. "David told me you had the backbone for this. Obviously he was wrong."

He walked off without another word and, funnily enough, carried a huge weight with him—one that had been on Jill's shoulders for longer than she'd known him.

THE ENTIRE POPULATION of Kennison Falls appeared to have shown up for the council meeting that night. Rumor was there was fresh controversy about the pit numbers, and Jill wondered how much people knew about the papers Chase had found. If they hadn't heard, she was prepared to bring them up. The crowd spilled into the small park grounds surrounding the township hall. When she eased the freshly tuned Creature into a spot, she turned to her passenger and smiled.

"You ready?"

"One last kick in the ash for Krieger." Robert lisped slightly, but his eyes shone with their old fire—as they'd done ever since she'd told him about her trip to Memphis.

"Let's kick it."

She exited the truck, and The Creature was immediately surrounded.

"There you are!" Gladdie grabbed Jill into a warm hug. "Krieger's just started."

Claudia pulled open the passenger door. "Hello, Robert!"

"Claudia," he replied.

"You look wonderful."

"You lie often?"

She laughed.

Dewey, Gray, and Jill carefully helped Robert into a wheelchair for the trip to the hall, and Jill followed with a walker. She grinned as the overflow sea of bodies parted and some of the people started clapping.

Robert scowled and they clapped harder.

At the door, Robert pushed himself laboriously out of the chair and stood with the walker. Nobody noticed them at first. All eyes were on Jim Krieger and his arrogant self-assurance.

"I will share every bit of information I have," he was saying. "I will also share that the person who found the alleged discrepancy was one Chase Preston, and he is no longer in Connery's employ. In fact, he's left Minnesota in disgrace. I have Duncan Connery's full support on this project."

Robert grunted in warning and Jill put a hand on his shoulder. "Wait," she whispered.

She scanned the crowd. Duncan Connery was nowhere to be seen, and her disappointment spread. Chase had liked the man and insisted his grandfather wouldn't misjudge a friend, but it seemed he couldn't be bothered.

"The council members have our updated packet of information," Krieger continued. "I assure you, Sandhurst Aggregate and Connery Construction have done everything in our power to make sure the town, the people, and the state park are safe and well taken care of.

"You know that if we can purchase the last tract of land we need, we'll be able to build our site far enough from the park boundaries that mining operations won't affect any part of it. You also know that tract of land is owned by Robert McCormick, who, tragically, has suffered a severe illness and in all likelihood won't be living on the property any longer. He's indicating a need to sell at last."

Jill couldn't have stopped Robert had she wanted to.

"If we didn't have proof before that you're a lying Esh-O-B, I'm here to tell everyone we do now." Robert's voice, surprisingly strong, carried through the room.

Krieger's face drained of color. To see the arrogant jerk rendered speechless by an eighty-two-year-old man with a droop to his mouth and a drag to his foot, was like pure movie magic.

"Where did you get your information? The part that says I won't be living on my farm any longer?"

"Mr. McCormick, I—"

"Excuse me, folks. Excuse me, I'm sorry to be late." Jill turned as Duncan Connery hustled into the room. "I just came from a meeting with three members of Sandhurst's board of directors. It ran long, I'm afraid, but I think I can clear up the problems here with a simple statement." He patted Robert's shoulder and eased past him. "May I?" he addressed the council.

"Go ahead, Duncan," Sam Baker allowed.

"Connery Construction withdraws its request for a permit to build a gravel pit on the section of land west-southwest of Butte Glen State Park and south of the town of Kennison Falls."

The floor erupted in chaos and cheers. In the midst of it all, Robert turned to Jill, positively ebullient. "Damn, I'm good."

"Yes, you are, my friend."

"Now why don't you get into that ugly truck of yours and go get our boy?"

"Do you think he'll listen to me?"

"All I know is you're our best chance, girlie. Now go. Those teenagers and their father will feed my girls. Glad-die will get me back to the asylum."

She hugged him so tightly he cursed in her ear and refused to apologize.

Chapter Twenty-Eight

WITH ITS WINDOWS cranked fully open, a rejuvenating morning breeze flowing over Jill's tired face, a floor littered with Diet Coke and Mountain Dew cans, and Gray Covey's newest album pouring from the stereo at a volume loud enough to keep three drivers awake, The Creature rolled into Memphis proper after twelve hours and four pit stops.

Her GPS chattered over the music, excited that she had more than a highway to navigate. Jill followed the directions gratefully to a Super 8 on Elvis Presley Boulevard, several miles from her ultimate destination. Now that she was so close, the urge to skip the motel and head straight for the clinic compelled her. But she couldn't show up with bleary eyes, chip crumbs down her T-shirt, and a dog who'd dutifully kept her company all night and deserved a chance to walk farther than ten feet from the truck.

"We made it," she cooed to Angel, who sat up eagerly as they pulled into the lot. "You were the best driving buddy ever. Let's go clean up and find Chase, huh?"

Angel barked and pawed the door.

Three hours later, just past one in the afternoon, her GPS directed them onto Marian-Lee Avenue, three miles southeast of downtown. Jill's confidence seeped away with every block. The closer she got, the less she wanted to park anywhere and leave the safety of The Creature. Angel, on the other hand, stared out the window with tail wagging in excitement.

Chase's practice was the Marian-Lee Clinic, and halfway between Graceland and tourist-studded Beale Street Jill found it, in the heart of an amalgam of blighted apartment buildings and attempts at rudimentary neighborhood upkeep.

Cool shade trees lined the long, eclectic street. Most buildings were whole enough, but in the sultry summer sunshine the air held a gray quality. Barefoot children in shorts and shattered-knee jeans raced along cracked sidewalks like loose pets. Adults were few and far between, but teens hung in bunches, like Goth bananas, on every corner. Black, white, Hispanic, they gripped cell phones, glaring and punching numbers as she passed, as if she was the circus come to town.

The clinic, on a better-maintained block, was one of half a dozen row houses mid-street. The closest parking spot, however, was more than a block away, and the unconcealed stares she received after taking it bordered on the malevolent.

She wasn't going out there. She'd call Chase and have him come out instead. She might be wearing plain khaki pants and a simple summer top, but compared to the limp cotton and oily leather as far as she could see, she'd be conspicuous as snow in the rain forest. She wished she'd chosen her dirtiest horse jeans.

Without warning, Angel placed her paws on the passenger door armrest and barked. Her entire body shook with excitement as two young boys passed and peered at her, grins breaking onto their faces. A flush of hot shame crept up Jill's face. What kind of lily-white snob was she, kind and accepting but only when people fit into her small-town box? These people lived here. Chase worked here. Her dog didn't care what people appeared to be, she only wanted to make friends.

Still, she wasn't going to leave Angel alone in the truck. Clipping on a leash she'd never used, she led the dog out the driver's door and made sure to lock it. She could be accepting without being stupid. Every single pair of eyes she passed swiveled to her. She garnered two wolf whistles and a "cool dog." Not until she reached the clinic did anyone confront her directly.

"You come on down here to get some tiny lil' problem fixed far from yo' fancy-assed rich family?" A beautiful black girl, maybe nineteen or twenty, sat on the clinic's flight of seven concrete steps. Her jeans clung like denim paint, her toenails in their heeled sandals flamed red, and she filled out a spandex tube top far more flatteringly than Jill would have. "Yo' is, then this is the wrong place. Dudes here be straight as switchblades."

As her meaning hit home, Jill almost laughed, but two tall, intimidating men-teens closed in behind her and cut off any irreverent reply.

"I have a friend who works here," she said simply. "So, no problems."

The two boys eased in closer and leered. "No problems, you say, pretty white girl?"

At his voice, Angel yelped. With no other warning she jumped up against one of the boys, pawing at the belly of his black T-shirt, desperately trying to lick his face. When he jumped away, yelping himself, she went for the other kid. Both boys, shocked, backed away as if she were attacking, and the girl on the steps began to laugh.

"Scared of a friendly dog," she hooted. "Girlfriend, you got yourself the best bodyguard in town if it can make Lamar and Bronte back off. Come here, dog." She patted her knee.

"This is Angel." Jill looked straight into the boys' eyes. "You can pet her."

To her amazement the two tough talkers squatted at her head. "That's a shit-assed name for a good dog," one said.

"Maybe so, but she sort of named herself," Jill replied. She let the tough teens pet the dog for several minutes before she excused herself. "I wish we could stay, but I have to go. It was nice to meet you. Angel liked it."

"Whatever. You best take her if you go walkin'." She didn't know whether it was Bronte or Lamar—but the words formed a clear warning.

"Thanks for the heads-up."

She ascended the steps and tried the handle of a slightly warped brown door. It opened into a sparse foyer smelling of old wood and polish. An ancient Oriental rug, a refurbished park bench, and a sign over another closed door that read "Saunders Clinic," were all that adorned the space. Jill dropped to her knees and threw her arms around her dog. Angel kissed her eagerly, but sat perfectly quietly, the act she'd put on for Lamar and Bronte over.

"Is there a little guardian angel in there? You can't be hundred percent dog." She closed her eyes, relief pouring through her.

She stood again and faced the warmly worn wooden door to her left. Another friendly sign invited, "Come on in."

A hundred questions assailed her. Would Chase be right there? Should she leave Angel here in the foyer? What would she say? What would he say?

"Sweetie, I think you need to wait for me, until I find out if he's here. Will you forgive me for tying you to the bench? It's better than out in the truck, isn't it?"

She threaded the leash through a wrought-iron leg, and Angel stretched out on the floor. With a fortifying breath, Jill opened the clinic door.

The cheery yellow rectangular room stretched away for perhaps twenty feet. An eclectic mix of wooden chairs, half of which were occupied, lined the perimeter, and toys in various states of repair littered the corner to Jill's left. Three small children sat amid the chaos, happily creating more. Several incongruous posters constituted the décor—a prunish Shar-Pei puppy, the Beatles circa 1965, a placard advertising the Cajun band BeauSoleil, and a sun-faded print of Van Gogh's *Starry Night.*

The far wall held another door and a partially open receptionist's window of frosted glass. No receptionist sat behind the barrier, but every face turned when Jill entered. She shifted uneasily, then the far door opened, and a slender, pretty woman with bouncing red curls entered. She wore white pants, blue tennis shoes, and a yellow polo shirt rolled at the sleeves. White block letters on a breast pocket read, "Miss Julia."

"We're ready for Nathaniel, Ellen."

A skinny white girl hardly past her teens stood and reached for one of the children in the play corner. He fussed but the young mother grabbed a truck and handed it to him. The redheaded woman caught a glimpse of Jill and gave a nearly imperceptible start.

"Dr. Chase's door, Ellen." She looked fully at Jill. "Hi, are you here to see a doctor?"

"I think so." Her voice caught in embarrassment. "Is this where I can find Dr. Preston—sorry, Dr. Chase Preston?"

The woman's eyes narrowed studiously, then grew anime-round as if she didn't believe the conclusion she'd reached. Scurrying completely into the room, she closed the door firmly behind her. "That accent," she said. "Tell me you're Jill."

"I'm . . . Jill Carpenter." She glanced around suspiciously. How on Earth would this woman know her?

"Oh my gosh, you're real!" She sounded close to gleeful. "Wait! Please? Have a seat for one second? I promise we'll be right back."

She disappeared, and Jill apprehensively did as she'd been asked. She prayed for strength, knowing Chase was about to come through the door, but before she could tell if any came her way, the door opened again, and Jill looked into a round, full-cheeked face decorated with a dazzling grin. The man would have been completely unfamiliar except for a slender, perfect nose and full, sculpted mouth.

"Jill? I'm Brody Preston. I'm—"

"Chase's brother." She stood, surprised at her relief, and held out her hand.

"We've heard about you." He took her hand in both of his but shook his head. "Aw, shoot, forget the handshake. It's great to meet you." He spread his arms, and she stepped into his brief-but-warm hug. "Did Chase know you were coming?"

His voice lilted with the same Kentucky musicality Chase's did, and his yellow polo shirt matched the woman's.

"No." Her embarrassment resurfaced. "In fact, I'm not sure he'll welcome me. I'm sorry to show up with no warning."

"Nonsense."

The redheaded woman reappeared through the door and leaned around Brody to extend her hand. "Sorry, had to get little Nate settled. I'm Julia Preston."

"Not only our nurse," Brody said with clear pride, "but my best half and almost better 'n an original Preston."

"It's great to meet you, Julia."

"This has turned into a great day!" Brody rubbed his palms together.

"Oh no." Julia shook her finger at him. "This is your I-never-grew-up look. Just you go tell your brother he's got himself a visitor."

"Heck, woman, where's the fun in that? Come on, Jill, I have a great idea."

Brody did indeed look like an impish ten-year-old ready to punk his sibling.

"Wait," Jill said. "I . . . I have a dog. Out in the hall."

Brody and Julia exchanged astonished looks. They turned in unison and chorused, "Angel?"

She nodded mutely. Chase truly had been telling tales. Her spirits rose with the first ray of hope.

"He made her sound like a dog come straight from heaven above," Julia said. "Go. Get her."

"But hurry," Brody urged. "He's in with his patient. We've got a window, but it's small."

"Is he . . . all right?" Jill asked.

"Big brother? Crazy as a betsy bug. Walkin' around like death eatin' a cracker. But I got me a feelin' that's all about to change."

EXHAUSTION HAD SETTLED into Chase's bones like cold into an Eskimo. He should have stayed longer in Kentucky when he'd dropped off the Triumph with Poppa, but instead he'd hurried to Memphis. He still didn't know why he'd been in such a rush. This was his third day back at the clinic, but the fatigue wasn't lessening. In Minnesota he'd worked four times as hard and been energized at day's end. Hardly an hour went by that his weariness didn't remind him of everything he'd left behind.

Julia handed him a chart when he'd finished drying his hands. The folder was crisp and fresh, and the paper inside filled only with statistical information. A new patient. He studied it for a moment and shook his head.

"What's this?"

"A patient folder."

"Hedda Longride?"

"Some of these names," Julia agreed.

"There's no age."

"She wouldn't give a birth year. I figured you're good at sweet-talking these ladies, Chase. That's why I gave her to you."

He leveled a stare at her, but she didn't flinch. "Approximately?" he pressed.

Julia merely offered an irritating shrug. "Definitely wear the lab coat."

His "Dr. Chase" version of the polo shirt was royal blue. Kids responded to the informal dress. But in deference to adult patients, he and Brody had traditional white lab coats. He grabbed his from a hook in his office.

"This is crazy, Julia."

"This is Memphis."

Seconds later, Chase swore he heard her shushing his brother. He gave one final frown to the odd, empty chart and sighed, rapped softly on the exam room door, and turned the knob.

She looked up as he entered. While his heart slammed into his throat, she unfolded her arms and met his disbelief with bright eyes. Her honeyed hair floated in slight disarray around her face as if she'd come in from a breeze, a pretty red top hugged her breasts. It had been barely ten days since he'd seen her, but it felt like a year, and though he tried to tell her she was the most beautiful thing he'd ever seen, he couldn't say a word.

"Hey. What's up, Doc?"

The horrible line literally brought tears to his eyes, and he choked on a laugh. Jill took a first hesitant step. He met her halfway across the floor.

"Aw, honey," he said when she was muffled in his arms. "What are you doing here?"

Before she could answer, something knocked into his knee. Frowning he looked to find Angel, on her haunches, with one paw braced against his leg. He hadn't noticed her. Words had no chance against the enormous lump that materialized in his throat. His arms tightened around Jill, desperate not to let her go. But his dog . . .

"Go." Jill disengaged herself. "Say hello. She's missed you almost as much as I have."

He squatted and let Angel wiggle into his arms. She whined and slathered his ear and neck with rapid, fervent swipes of her tongue. "Silly dog," he managed. "I missed you, too, girl."

When he finally stood, Jill smiled, and the sense of home and calm she'd always generated flowed from her like a hot springs, melting the cold exhaustion from his body.

"I'm here to rescue us. I owe you a rescue from weeks ago in case you've forgotten. And, I came to apologize with all my heart."

"You didn't need to come all this way. You could have called."

Her fingertip lit against his lips like a whisper. "I absolutely could not have. It needed to be done exactly like this."

"There's nothing—"

"Don't." She stopped him again. "Let me finally do something *I* want to do, not what anybody else, even you, thinks I should do. Chase, I can't tell you how sorry I am. I love you, but I know I didn't show you how much I meant it when you needed it the most. It's never mattered what you are. But I made everything about me. I was mad—little-kid-having-a-tantrum mad. My feelings were hurt, and I didn't bother to ask you about yours."

He grabbed her hand and nearly yanked her into his arms, tucking her head against his chest. Swiftly and unapologetically, his body reacted the way it had from the first time he'd held her against him. She'd done it. She'd said the only thing he'd ever wanted her to say. But while his pleasure surged, and she snuggled her soft curves against him causing deeper, sharper shots of desire, his heart remained a lead weight in his chest. His old fear did not magically disappear.

"Honey." He pushed her gently, reluctantly away. "I am happier to see you than I know how to say. But I'm not sure you did the best thing coming to find me."

She wrested herself fully from his hold, and switched

their positions, grasping the lapels of his lab coat with fingers that clamped into fists around the fabric. Fire flared in her eyes.

"Look, buster. I've not only done the best thing, I've done the right thing. And I didn't do it to spend three minutes hearing more evasions. Now you're back to owing me."

His heart finally loosed a few of its stubborn bindings, and he almost smiled at her sexy magnificence. Then she tugged, hard, on his coat and pulled his mouth to hers. Their lips collided and, shocked, he lost his equilibrium to the unequivocal claim she staked. All summer her kisses had never ceased to amaze him with their expert intimacy, but this one reached into his soul and twisted it into surrender.

She gave him no choice but to set aside his fear and let her conduct the kiss like a virtuoso, showing him when to play quietly, and when to surge forward. He followed her lead and kissed her back, softly bitten lip to searching thrust, and tongue to willing tongue. Her mouth finally gentled and then she played, kissing his kisses, tracing his lip with the tip of her tongue and drawing shards of pleasure from the heart he'd thought had been broken.

At last she interrupted the kiss with a sweet succulent sound. "Now. What were you saying about this not being the best thing?"

"Jill. I . . ." His breathlessness took him aback. "I love you, but there's so much—"

"So much you're going to tell me. I know. Tonight.

Let's recreate what you were going to do back home."

At last he laughed. He had no choice. "You're about as stoppable as a freight train with reins, aren't you?"

"I've ridden a few horses like that." She cupped his jaw in both hands and ran her thumbs across his lips. "You just have to be more stubborn than they are."

"Oh, you're stubborn."

For the first time in nearly two weeks, fresh hope flooded him. Maybe she was—

Sharp, gunshot-like pounding on the door split them apart, and he looked up in alarm when the door popped open. Julia didn't apologize.

"OD. They dumped him in the waiting room."

Adrenaline replaced his hope. *Damn it.*

"I'm sorry, honey."

"Go," she said, and pushed him toward the door.

JILL FOLLOWED AT a timid distance, shutting the door on Angel, her bravado subdued to uselessness. The only way to describe the scene in the waiting room was surreal. A large boy, certainly over two hundred and fifty pounds, perhaps nineteen or twenty years old, lay supine on the thin carpet, his olive complexion the sickly color of a dying plant. Brody huddled over him with a stethoscope against his chest.

"What do we have?" Chase stepped to the victim's far side and knelt.

"Probably meth. Possibly Ecstasy. Pupils are dilated,

he's hyperthermic and tachycardic. Pulse is one-sixty. He was barely conscious when two guys brought him in, dumped him, and ran."

Julia arrived with a blood pressure cuff and handed it to Chase, but before he could wrap the boy's arm the patient thrashed and moaned.

"*Todo está bien. No te preocupes,*" Chase intoned. "Can you understand me? Everything's fine. Don't worry. Can you hear me? *¿Puedes oírme?*"

Jill's mouth gaped. Spanish? Would the surprises from this man never cease?"

The kid struggling on the floor babbled and moaned in agitated Spanish before he cried out in pain.

"*Cálmate, hijo,*" Brody said. "Calm down."

It took long minutes for the two doctors to calm the distressed boy enough to get the cuff on him and take his pressure.

"One-eighty over a hundred," Chase said. "And I'm guessing his temp is at least a hundred and two."

"I've got Regional Hospital coming," Julia said.

"He's too out of it to go anywhere under his own power. He's heavy enough that I think we'll take longer to get him moved than he might have. Let's pack him in the cooling towels and hang fluids right here," Chase said. "Get him on Ativan, work on getting that pressure down, and the ride should be here by then."

Brody and Julia shot past Jill. Chase continued talking to the kid in a mix of English and Spanish, holding him firmly as his twitches grew to near convulsions. He met her eyes, but his grim features allowed only the briefest of acknowledgment.

The main door opened, and a wide-eyed mother with two children entered, took a terrified look, and turned around. That's when Jill focused on the six people—four of them children—huddled quietly in the toy corner. They, too, stared wide-eyed at the scary scene, and she knew what she could do to help.

Stepping past the boy, she reached the little group and squatted. "How about if we get out of the way?" she asked, her eyes on the children. "We can go back to one of the rooms, and I have a surprise. Have you ever seen a dog in a doctor's office?"

The kids' eyes widened further for this new, and far more enticing, reason. A woman, ostensibly their parent, breathed with relief. The sixth person, an elderly gentleman, nodded. "Can I come, too?" he teased.

"Depends." She winked. "Do you charge for babysitting?"

He laughed and stood. "No, ma'am."

Julia bustled back into the room, loaded with supplies. She cracked two chemical cold packs and stuffed one under each of the boy's armpits. Chase snapped on a pair of latex gloves. Brody appeared with two bags of liquid—the kind that would be hung from a stand in a normal hospital. Jill gathered her newly minted flock and led them quietly past the intensity.

Twenty-five minutes later, Chase opened the door to the little exam room where the kids were deep in concentration giving Angel a thorough checkup, complete with pilfered tongue depressors, paper towel wrapped around her front legs, and a paper gown Jill had snooped around to find. When she looked up from her conversation with the now-relaxed mother and her new friend Mr. Thomas, she met a pair of blue-sparkling, awe-struck eyes.

"How is he?" Jill asked.

"Stable for now. On the way to the hospital." He gathered himself and stepped fully into the crowded room. He squatted next to the knot of children around Angel, who thumped her tail pathetically. "So, doctors, what's happening on this case?" he asked.

Once it was explained that Angel had a broken leg, a fever, a tummy ache, and an ear infection, Chase shook his head in concern.

"We op-a-rated-ed on her," said the oldest of the four.

"Excellent," Chase said. "And I brought her some medicine. I think it might do the trick." From his lab coat pocket he pulled a piece of what looked like a hunk of bologna. "Fancy lunches," he said to Jill. She laughed. "Okay, Angel, take your pill like a good girl."

Angel was an amazing dog, but even she couldn't resist lunch meat. She shook off her leg wraps and stood, still wearing the gown and causing hysterics in the little ones. She took the treat.

"It's a miracle cure! Well done." Chase high-fived them, and they cheered. "Okay, now who's here to see Dr. Brody?" Two of the siblings raised hands. "Then you all best get out to Miss Julia. She'll fix you up. Mr. Thomas, you're here for that bandage change if I remember. Julia will get to you now, too."

"Yessir," he replied. "Must say, Doc, this here's the most fun I ever had in your clinic."

"We do aim to please." Chase patted the man's shoulder as he left.

When the room had emptied, and Angel had been divested of her embarrassing getup, Chase stared silently into Jill's eyes. Her belly fluttered like a schoolgirl's.

"I don't know what to say to you," he said. "You were amazing, Miz Carpenter."

"Oh, look who's talking," she replied. "I have the worst case of hero worship going on here."

A weary resignation wiped his features free of all other emotion. Taking her hand, he steered her toward the door. "Come with me," he said. "There's something you need to see."

Chapter Twenty-Nine

CHASE WENT LEFT out of the exam room, away from the lobby, and Jill followed, her hand still in his.

"C'mon, Angel," he called to the dog. She obeyed, her doggy brows in a furrow.

Chase led them through an open door to what would have been another bedroom when the building had been a home. The moment she stepped past the jamb, a finished picture of Chase with every puzzle piece in place spread before her. His office.

She could barely take it all in. The walls were a deep ocean blue. A scarred oak desk against the left wall held piles of thick books and a stack of folders. Three heavy wooden bookcases stood against the walls crammed with more books—medical and non—and countless keepsakes overflowing in a sexy, masculine clutter. Two basketballs, a Louisville Slugger, and a pyramid of baseballs sat straight ahead of her. Several intricate model sports cars sat scattered among the books. On one wall hung a poster-sized photo of a middle-aged man with eerily familiar features standing beside the motorcycle Jill knew almost as well as she knew The Creature. This Preston, for he undoubtedly was one, could have been Chase in fifteen years. His face held Chase's sculpted handsomeness, his eyes the same piercing-but-gentle blue. Only the silver shots in his hair and the jowls and crow's-feet of age marked him as a family elder.

She looked from the picture to Chase and suddenly she knew.

"Poppa?" she asked.

He nodded. "Taken in Minnesota."

Warmth and hope spread through her chest. She'd been hearing about this man all summer—Chase's obvious hero. Now the picture connected her with both of them.

Reluctantly, she looked away to scan the walls. She stopped once more on a framed diploma. Stepping closer, she read the scrolled script across the top of the certificate: the Johns Hopkins University School of Medicine. Charles Angus Preston.

Johns Hopkins? Another remarkable accomplishment to knock her off her paddock boots.

Swallowing, she quit roaming the room with her eyes and faced him. "All right. Since you don't seem to want to hear whenever I'm impressed, what am I doing here?"

He walked to a shelf filled with pictures and from the middle of the collection picked up an eight-by-ten portrait. She took it and got drawn into the most animated young face she'd ever seen. The girl's rich skin looked like kissable chocolate, and her two missing front teeth certainly hadn't embarrassed her, since the grin was so wide and pure it could have stopped a war with its sheer friendliness.

"This is Tiana Washington. She's the only girl who's ever proposed to me."

His cracked voice twisted her heart.

"She's the one, isn't she? The one who died?"

"The one I might as well have killed with my own hands."

Her stomach gave a disbelieving lurch at the blunt words. "Don't be ridiculous. I don't know what happened, and I know *that's* not true."

"That's just it. You don't know what happened."

"I saw what you did out front not five minutes ago."

He shook his head vehemently. "What happened out front happens fifteen times a week around here. If it's not an overdose, it's a stabbing, or a gunshot wound, or an infected gang tattoo, or a fourteen-year-old beat to within an inch of his life because he tried to escape the gang initiation he'd once desperately begged to go through. We barely do community medicine here anymore. We're Memphis Gang-Central urgent care. We're no longer what I started this clinic to be."

She shuddered inwardly. While Angel sniffed the room's perimeter, Jill set Tiana's photo carefully on Chase's chair. She put a hand on each of his cheeks and made him look squarely in her eyes. "Tell me."

He took her into a bear hug and rocked her for a few

seconds. Then he drew a deep breath and released it in resignation. "I guess I have to go back to the beginning."

She nodded firmly.

"When I was kid, ten maybe, I begged my mama and daddy to let me join an association basketball league in Lexington. One I could get to after school. They didn't like it much. I was supposed to be coming home and helping on the farm. But Poppa said sports built character and talked them into it.

"That's when I met LeBron Claiborne. He played on my team, and I believed he was the best basketball player in the whole state. He became my best friend.

"My folks were as liberated as people could be in the South back in the dark ages, but the Claiborne family was not only black, they were poor. One step above dirt-poor. Sure, they had a house and clothes and food, but that was about it. And for me to be hanging around a neighborhood like theirs in the heart of the city was not something that pleased my mama much. But I loved the Claibornes' house. They were always laughing and playing games and singing. I don't think they were ever mad or even sad."

"They sound wonderful."

"Mama realized over time she couldn't change our friendship. But three years later, LeBron's daddy fell off their roof fixing a leak and ended up losing a leg. Mr. Claiborne, Oliver, had no insurance, and neither did his wife. She tried to make her housecleaning wages go far enough, but she couldn't afford the medical bills or money for anything like rehab. LeBron's daddy got so depressed he committed suicide a year later."

"Oh, Chase!" Jill's stomach rolled in horror at what that must have been like for two young boys.

"The thing that still angers me most is Oliver Claiborne's death was totally preventable, if he'd only had a place to go and get help and care he could afford. In the end, LeBron, his younger brother, and his sister went to live with an aunt in Louisville. I think their mother stayed to try and earn money, but she finally left, too. Louisville wasn't that far away by today's standards, but back then it might as well have been the moon. Thirteen-year-old boys don't exactly write letters."

"I don't know what to say. It's awful."

"I did find LeBron later. He still lives in Louisville, and he's miraculously okay. But he has no idea where his siblings are. I vowed I would do something to make sure families didn't have to get split up and suffer like that."

"So you started the clinic."

"Yes—my pie-in-the-sky notion that we could fix the world. Let me tell you, I would give my own leg if I could spend the time I wanted helping families like LeBron's. For a while I thought we actually might be doing good work. But now, because of the violence, because we're more trauma clinic than anything, my family practice has dwindled to a quarter of what it once was. Most are afraid to come here except for emergencies."

Frustration had seeped through his sadness, and his voice squeezed tight with anger.

"This has to be about the hardest kind of place in the world to make a change," Jill said. "You can't blame yourself for gangs and violence."

"Remember what you said about riding tough horses? Well, this place is a herd of nightmares, and I was naïve enough to think I could bridle and gentle them."

"You only have to gentle one to be a success."

Chase walked slowly across the room and picked one basketball from its spot on the shelf. "Tiana was the first baby I delivered after I got here. Her mama was an addict who went into labor a full two months early. I couldn't save her. Tiana's daddy tried to take care of her, but he died a year later in a car accident involving two rival gangs. All she had left was her grandmother Clara, one of the kindest, most faithful women I know. Clara turned that skinny, sickly preemie into a spitfire, crackerjack of a kid, and through the years *they* kept coming back. You aren't supposed to have favorites but, by God, they were mine."

He shifted the ball from one hand to the other.

"What happened?" She urged him gently but firmly toward the end of the story.

"Tiana and Clara represented everything I wanted to achieve here. When Brody joined me with his specialty in ER and trauma medicine, we made the perfect team. I got the touchy-feely cases—in his words—and he got the ugly truth cases. For four years we worked on community building. When I told you I'd worked with teens and centers and nonprofits, I wasn't lying. I just withheld some of the truth. But those centers, which we support with volunteer time, are tough, hard-core places. This is the core of Memphis gang territory."

He bounced the basketball, smiled wistfully, and

tossed the bumpy-surfaced sphere to her. She caught it, searched it for some significance, found nothing, and sent it back to him.

"Basketball comes closest to soothing savage beasts around here. It's popular with kids after school and kids who are lucky enough to have avoided the gangs. Most gang members stay away—organized sports are for losers. But once in a while we talk one into giving it a try, and I managed to get my hands on one of the higher-ups in our biggest Latino gang. Eric Spinoza.

"He was reluctant. Big-time. But I was arrogant enough to think I'd help him and get an inside track to the gang leaders if I could just wine and dine him into the fold."

"It sounds like a noble cause to me—"

He shook his head. "Nobody thought this was a good idea. Not Brody, not the staff at the center. And certainly not Eric's buddies. But I met him one afternoon at a bar a block from the center. Good place for a meeting, right? Eric was already two illegal beers down when I got to him, but they were giving him confidence. He wanted to play, he said. He even admitted wanting to get free from the gang. I was thrilled. He was nervous. I kept him talking.

"What I'd forgotten was my promise to Clara that I'd pick Tiana up at the clinic after school. I did that once in a great while when Clara worked overtime. It was pretty rare—but I was always happy to take her. We'd go get ice cream or something to pass the time until her grandma was home. She called it our date."

"And you forgot her this time?"

"I remembered fifteen minutes late. I'd been so busy trying to turn the gangs into my own personal charity that I let her sit alone on the clinic steps waiting. I drove eight blocks in about thirty seconds when I got my head out of my ass. And I drove smack into a horror show."

For the first time Chase's voice cracked. Jill took the ball from him, placed it on the shelf.

"Tiana was already gone when you got to her."

"No. Brody had taken her into the clinic after hearing shots outside and finding her. He was doing his best. He is the best. If anyone could have saved her, he was the one. I missed her by five minutes. Five damn minutes, Jill."

"Why did they do it? Why a little girl?"

"They weren't after her. They didn't know she was there, I'm sure. They were trying to teach me a lesson. Mess with our boy, we'll shoot up your place. They were sticking it to the white man. If Tiana had gone into the clinic she would have been fine, but she was on the steps. She was waiting for me."

Jill understood it all. Chase's horror, his guilt, and the need to keep this a secret.

"I know you won't believe me when I tell you this isn't your fault. But it's not. Still, I know why you left here this summer."

"Tiana died because my egotistic desire has always been more important than dealing the hand I was dealt."

"No! Tiana died because the world can be a truly awful place. You aren't egotistical. You were and are idealistic. That's not a weakness; it's a superpower. Most people don't have the guts to be idealists. It's scary. "

Chase ran his hand over her head and sifted her hair through his fingers.

"God in heaven, Jill, I wish I could believe that. When you say it, I almost do. But tell that to Clara. You see, I lost two people that day. Clara's face is very nearly the worst memory of all. She doesn't think I have superpowers. That much was clear her eyes and in her face. Her trust in me was simply erased."

The edict he pronounced on himself represented the darkest moment in his entire story, but Jill's heart didn't despair, it cheered. She had no clear idea how she'd convince him of the fact, but she knew, as surely as she knew she was taking Chase home to Robert's, that Clara Washington knew something about trust he did not.

"I DON'T KNOW why I'm doing this." Chase growled, staring out the car window.

Jill knew he hid true trepidation beneath the crabbing. She took his hand and kneaded his fingers. From the back seat of Brody's '99 green, the-body-doesn't-look-too-horrible-but-nobody's-going-to-steal-its-hubcaps Honda Accord, she watched the six blocks between the Saunders Clinic and Clara's house pass in a dingy blur.

"Because you love me," she said lightly.

"You have no idea how true that must be."

"Gosh, I think that's one of the most romantic things you've ever said." She laced her fingers through his, picked up their intertwined hands, and kissed his knuckles.

"Oh lordy, Jill, I *am* sorry." Brody laughed from

behind the wheel. "He's always been a little serious, but I'da thought the lessons I gave him about romance would have stuck better'n that."

"Shut up, Brody." Chase growled, but returned the squeeze on Jill's hand.

She'd made this trip once already, yesterday, and she was still star-struck at the memory of the woman Brody had taken her to meet. Chase had no idea Clara expected him, or what was about to whack him upside the head. She smiled tenderly, wishing she could put into words what the mixture of raw courage and vulnerability in his character meant to her. She would never stop regretting what a huge virtual smack to her own head it had taken for her to see it, but she'd sure as heck spend the rest of her life proving she'd never forget it.

"Here we are!" Brody pulled up to a small, white clapboard house on a simple street whose houses held little curb appeal except tidiness.

"Jeez, kid, what are you so hyped up about? This isn't the circus. Ain't like you're getting popcorn and a pony ride."

"No. that'll be from me." Jill kissed him soundly.

"Hey, this is a family cab," Brody said. "None of your kinky, pony ride sex talk."

"Shut *up*, Broderick," Chase said again.

They exited the car and made their way up Clara's short sidewalk to the two-step porch in front of her door. Chase shuffled like a condemned prisoner. Jill propelled him gently forward. Brody whistled the first two phrases from Chopin's funeral march, and at the door, Chase punched him in the arm. It was hard to believe these two men saved peoples' lives on a daily basis.

"Look," Brody said, rubbing his arm. "This is going to be all right. Trust us."

Jill rapped at the aluminum screen door. It took only seconds for the inner door to fly open. Clara Washington wasn't elderly—Brody had said she was not yet sixty-five—but her broad face carried more than its share of work worn creases. Her sun-bright smile encompassed all of them, but her ebony eyes shone with flecks of deepest gold strictly for Chase.

"Hallelujah! Law', son, I done thought you up and flew to the moon." Clara pushed open the screen door. "Now you get your skinny little self in here. It's about time you came to see me."

Chase's jaw worked soundlessly and he looked at Jill. With her pulse beating triple-time on his behalf, she nudged him until he stepped into the house. Brody patted him on the shoulder and closed the screen door behind him.

"Hey, what—"

"You jes' let those two beautiful people go on out into the sunshine and close this door behind you, Chase Preston. You and I need to have a little talk."

"Yes, ma'am," he said, and caught Jill's eye one last time. He looked on the verge of laughing or crying. Or both.

Brody stood on the stoop once Clara's door had closed and cocked his brow toward heaven. "Up to Him now." He took Jill's arm. "Let's go. Clara will send him to the park when they're finished."

She nodded. "I hope forcing this wasn't a bad idea."

"Listen to me, beautiful girl. My brother is ten times the physician that I am. I'm a MASH doc. Life or death, patch 'em up, race the clock. I'm good at that, and I actually enjoy the challenge. Chase—he's the soul and the artist of doctoring. Prevention, families, kindness, diagnosis, bedside manner. But don't get me wrong, he's tough as an old wolf and fights just as hard when he needs to. There are kids alive in this neighborhood because of my brother."

"I believe that."

"But the last year around here has loaded bricks onto his wagon faster 'n a little kid sneaks food to his dog. Tiana was just the last brick. So, believe this, too— anything that will bring my brother back to himself is a good idea. I never thought of making him talk to Clara. Forcing this was a stroke of genius."

"I know he must be a good doctor," she said. "I think he even healed my stupid truck. It certainly has a crush on him. Not as big as mine, of course." Her face heated, and she grinned at the ground.

"And not as big as his on you. C'mon. Let me tell you how I know that."

The dilapidated neighborhood park a block from Clara's house needed repairs desperately, but it shone like a wonderland as Chase crossed the street and headed for the two figures sitting on a pair of ancient swings that still had sling seats and hung from chains thick enough to shackle prisoners.

Chase hadn't seen anything look like a wonderland around this city in years. Now, one bright beacon filled the scarred park with golden light. She didn't see him at first; she rocked the swing in random patterns with her feet and laughed at something Brody said.

He'd miss Brody.

Jill finally caught sight of him and stilled, but everything inside him came alive. Childlike excitement warred with thoroughly adult desire and male reactions.

"Who are you?" she asked, when he reached her. "There's something about you I don't recognize."

"I'm wearing a lotta of things I haven't worn in a while. Gratitude. Happiness. Love."

"You sound like a danged ol' girl." Brody stood, grinning. "I'll be giving you two a wide berth now—"

"Stay." Chase commanded him the way he would Angel—who had stayed with Julia at the clinic as chief entertainer of children. "Close your eyes if you don't like the mushy stuff, but I've got something you need to hear, too."

"I was afraid of this." Brody sat back down on the child's swing. "Clara gave you your balls back."

"No." He searched in Jill's rich brown eyes and saw exactly what he'd hoped to see—unclouded, unequivocal, undeniable love. "She showed me I never really lost 'em. And that you are something else."

Jill laughed and literally jumped at him. He caught her as she wrapped her legs around his hips. "Dang right, I am. I'd have to be to land you." She pressed her mouth to his and tasted like sweet heat and eagerness.

He explored their kiss for the first time without a veil of hesitancy and guilt between them. Love, clear and fresh like a Minnesota stream, poured over him, and he knew without having to ask that all Jill's doubts were also gone. She pillaged him like she'd discovered long-lost treasure, and they kissed a long time as if Brody wasn't there.

"Ahem," Brody said at last. "This really is very, very boring."

Chase pulled his mouth from hers but didn't put her down. "You set up this meeting with Clara."

"I did," she admitted. "I knew you had to be wrong about her trust in you. And? What did she say?"

"In a nutshell? That I'm so damn dumb if I threw myself on the ground I'd miss."

Brody snickered.

"Now why didn't I think of that?" Jill giggled, too. "We could have avoided all this driving and crying and stuff." She slid herself down his body, brushing dangerously against his pelvis. With no reason to hold back, he was quickly turning into an impatient teenager.

However, he pushed her away. There were, unbelievably, more important things than what his body wanted right now.

"There's a lot of *stuff* we can't avoid, honey. Stuff we have to figure out."

"Together," she said. "We'll figure it out together. Hang on." From beside the swing set she dug her phone out of her purse and scrolled around the screen for a few seconds. At last she held it out to him. "From Dee. Just this morning."

The simple text message held his future.

The permit request for the gravel pit was officially withdrawn last night, and Krieger announced his "retirement" from Connery Construction. Sandhurst plans to sell the rest of the land. Robert is happy dancing. Okay, would be if he could. :-)

"It's ours?" he asked, looking stunned as reality hit home. "The farm?"

"Yes."

He glanced to his brother. "Clara also told me it wouldn't be selling out for me to leave the clinic here in Memphis to Brody."

"I could have told you that, you moron," Brody said, a catch in his voice. "You've done more here in ten years than ten doctors. Go. It's time for you to make a family."

"You know anyone who wants a family?" Chase searched Jill's face again and found tears in her eyes and laughter on her lips.

"I'll ask Gladdie and Claudia to give finding you someone a shot. They're the matchmakers. Is it okay if I put my name in the hat?"

"It better be the only one in there fifty times."

"Alrighty then."

"Seriously. I want to come home. Whether you go off to the Olympics or to the university or just see what comes, I'll always be your home."

"No Olympics. That was someone else's dream. I do think the vet school one is mine—why throw away two years of something wonderful? Other than that, I'm my father's child. I have no idea what all I'll find to do. Teach? Start a program for special needs riders? Work in a new clinic with you? But I promise to find whatever it is in Kennison Falls, not South America. Can you live with that?"

"For the rest of my life."

He lowered his kiss to her lips, softly this time. Sure hands slipped around his waist, and Jill's eyelids drooped closed as her head tilted. He slid his fingers through her hair and pressed her for more tongue, more fire, more contact. All fuel for his greedy hunger.

"That's it." Brody huffed and stood. Chase broke their kiss enough to see his brother dismiss them with a wave of his hand. "I do not have to watch this. You two can walk home when the hormones have worn off."

"See you in fifty years then." Chase's grin bumped against Jill's lips. Their noses smashed. Their laughter mingled.

"Aw," she said. "He can come to the wedding before that. Don't you think?"

Epilogue

DELANEY PRESTON SNAPPED off a dry stalk of oatmeal-colored, fall bluestem and popped the slender end into his mouth Huck Finn–style. He'd left his tuxedo jacket on the porch next to Robert, and now the warm October breeze tugged at his fancy shirt and fanned his face. Many things in Minnesota had changed over twenty-five years but not the pleasure of an Indian summer. It was a blessing of a day for a wedding.

Cresting a small hill, his camera in hand, Delaney gazed below to the farmyard that looked like a butterfly emerging from its chrysalis. Three bedraggled outbuildings dotted the yard, but Robert's house glistened with fresh white paint, and the barn sported a new coat of traditional red, at least on the two sides visible from the driveway. Only so much could be done in six weeks, after all. Even with the passel of friends Jill and her sister, Deirdre, had amassed, there'd been more to do before the wedding than paint buildings.

Women could be utterly amazing. Ask them to take time and bake your favorite pie for dessert, and there were insurmountable obstacles. Tell them there was no way to plan a wedding in a month and a half, and they snapped their fingers like magical wood sprites and put on a gala.

No, he amended. Calling it a gala was unfair. The outdoor wedding two hours earlier had been lovely, but there'd been nothing ostentatious about it or the celebration going on now. From his vantage, he could see another spot of beautiful white: his new granddaughter, pretty as a Kentucky primrose, wearing just enough Chantilly lace to honor her brand-new husband's Southern heritage.

His old heart swelled with contentment. Although he was father, Poppa, and great-grandpoppa to enough children that he couldn't come up with an exact number without figuring, Delaney allowed himself an indulgence he'd never speak out loud: the knowledge that his *favorite* grandchild had been granted the greatest gift a man could receive—perfect love.

He snapped his photos, using the color-drenched woods as a backdrop, and they looked beautiful in the new-fangled digital view screen. From out of the tall grass alongside the road, Chase and Jill's dog bounded to join him, still wearing a collar decorated with flowers.

Angel.

He patted his leg, and she came for a scratch between her pointed little ears. She'd been his constant companion since he'd arrived a week before, a presence so comforting, he swore he'd known her for years. Her uncanine-like spirit reminded him of his beautiful Mary—and that was purely crazy. Self-admittedly he was the indulged, overly spiritual Preston patriarch, but he'd never been one to reincarnate folks. He'd tried to explain the peculiar feelings about the dog to Chase, and his grandson had surprised him.

"You don't need to convince me," he'd said. "The dog is inexplicable. No one will ever convince me she didn't lead me straight to this wedding. She startles me often, always being where she needs to be. And she knows."

"Knows what?"

"Whatever needs knowin'. She's Angel."

"*An* angel?" he'd asked, laughing.

"Maybe so."

Delaney ambled back into the yard approached Robert, who sat in a wooden swing beside the front porch, shooing away a jovial woman trying to give him food.

"This is why I don't invite people to the place, Gladdie Hanson," he groused, his voice not exactly soft despite the slight lisp. "They don't mind their own business. You've already stuffed me like a laundry hamper, now take this away."

Robert, too, had shed the tuxedo coat Jill had pressed him into wearing, and the woman, Gladdie, gave one of his exposed suspender straps a minuscule snap. "You look like skin and bones, so don't Gladdie Hanson me, Robert McCormick. You can't turn down my apple crisp, and you know it. Put some meat back on those crotchety bones."

In the end, of course, Robert took the bowl and growled his thanks. According to Chase, the old farmer might never regain his full pre-stroke coordination, but he could walk, and he was certainly feisty enough. Delaney, being an old farmer, too, liked Robert a lot.

"There she is!"

A young teenager, with the brightest swash of red and pink in her short hair Delaney had ever seen, squatted to greet Angel. The girl was one of Jill's students, he was given to understand, and she was a contrast in something—he wasn't sure what. Her party dress was pretty enough, in blues and greens with enough skirt to twirl. But some sort of black polish with sparkles adorned her fingernails, and she wore black boots only half laced up over blue knee-high stockings. She smiled at him shyly.

"They want a picture with Angel. Can I take her?"

"Of course, of course. I'll follow you."

He found a mini circus set up beside the barn, attended by a knot of relatives and friends. Delaney sidled up to his oldest son, Chase's father, who looked on in bemusement.

"He always has done things his own way." Chaz indicated Robert's enormous black-and-white Clydesdale mare, standing statue-still, her lead rope in the hands of a young girl in a wheelchair. "How can this be safe?"

"Thomlinson is right there." Delaney nodded at the veterinarian who'd walked Jill down the aisle. He couldn't have looked more like a proud daddy had he been Jill's own. "I get the feeling there aren't many animals in Jill's care that don't do exactly what she wants."

"He did convince a special girl to take him on, didn't he?" Chaz laughed, and put his arm around Delaney in a quick hug. "I'm proud of him, Pa."

"As well you should be."

A sudden groan rose from down the line of guests. "Oh, not the dress *on* the horse!" Jill's mother threw her hands over her eyes when her daughter, lace skirts and all, rose onto Gypsy's back with the help of Brody, David Pitts-Matherson, and Chase. Jill arranged herself as easily as if she rode sidesaddle every day, and stroked the horse's thick neck. The official photographer ordered people around until all at once the photo-of-the-day appeared in front of everyone's eyes. Jill gazed down, her eyes shining but focused on no one but Chase. He tilted his face upward, moony-eyed as a tamed wolf pup. The huge-eyed Clydesdale bent its crested neck around to look at them both. And Angel, sitting attentively at Gypsy's massive hooves, faced all three.

"Ah, the beauty and promise of youth." Gladdie Hanson and her sister Claudia touched Delaney on the shoulder and fell in, one to his right, the other between him and Chaz, as the wedding photographer clicked away. "So pretty," Gladdie continued. "If only we could freeze such moments and keep our lives permanently fresh and optimistic."

"Come now . . ." To everyone's surprise, Robert shuffled up and stood beside Claudia, who took his arm. "Where would be the adventure in that?"

A cheer went up, punctuated by one decisive bark from a very excited black-and-white dog. Delaney raised his eyes as Jill slid straight off Gypsy's back and in Chase's waiting arms.

About the Author

LIZBETH SELVIG lives in Minnesota with her best friend (aka her husband) and a hyperactive border collie. After working as a newspaper journalist and magazine editor, and raising an equine veterinarian daughter and a talented musician son, Lizbeth entered Romance Writers of America's Golden Heart® contest in 2010 and won the Single Title Contemporary category. That book, *The Rancher and the Rock Star*, became her debut novel with Avon Impulse. In her spare time, she loves to hike, quilt, read, horseback ride, and play with her four-legged grandchildren, of which there are nearly twenty, including a wallaby, an alpaca, a donkey, a pig, two sugar gliders, and many dogs, cats, and horses. She loves connecting with readers! Find her on Facebook, Twitter, and at www.lizbethselvig.com.

Visit www.AuthorTracker.com for exclusive information on your favorite HarperCollins authors.

Give in to your impulses . . .
Read on for a sneak peek at three brand-new
e-book original tales of romance
from Avon Books.
Available now wherever e-books are sold.

THE GOVERNESS CLUB: CLAIRE
By Ellie Macdonald

ASHES, ASHES, THEY ALL FALL DEAD
By Lena Diaz

THE GOVERNESS CLUB: BONNIE
By Ellie Macdonald

An Excerpt from

THE GOVERNESS CLUB: CLAIRE

by Ellie Macdonald

Claire Bannister just wants to be a good
teacher so that she and the other ladies of the
Governess Club can make enough money to
leave their jobs and start their own school in the
country. But when the new sinfully handsome
and utterly distracting tutor arrives, Claire
finds herself caught up in a whirlwind romance
that could change the course of her future.

What would a "London gent" want with her, Claire wondered as she quickened her pace. The only man she knew in the capital was Mr. Baxter, her late father's solicitor. Why would he come all the way here instead of corresponding through a letter as usual? Unless it was something more urgent than could be committed to paper. Perhaps it had something to do with Ridgestone—

At that thought, Claire lifted her skirts and raced to the parlor. Five years had passed since her father's death, since she'd had to leave her childhood home, but she had not given up her goal to one day return to Ridgestone.

The formal gardens of Aldgate Hall vanished, replaced by the memory of her own garden; the terrace doors no longer opened to the ballroom, but to a small, intimate library; the bright corridor darkened to a comforting glow; Claire could even smell her old home as she rushed to the door of the housekeeper's parlor. Pausing briefly to catch her breath and smooth her hair, she knocked and pushed the door open, head held high, barely able to contain her excitement.

Cup and saucer met with a loud rattle as a young man hurried to his feet. Mrs. Morrison's disapproving frown could not stop several large drops of tea from contaminating her white linen, nor could Mr. Fosters's harrumph. Claire's heart sank as she took in the man's youth, disheveled hair, and rumpled clothes; he was decidedly *not* Mr. Baxter. Perhaps a new associate? Her heart picked up slightly at that thought.

Claire dropped a shallow curtsey. "You wished to see me, Mrs. Morrison?"

The thin woman rose and drew in a breath that seemed to tighten her face even more with disapproval. She gestured to the stranger. "Yes. This is Mr. Jacob Knightly. Lord and Lady Aldgate have retained him as a tutor for the young masters."

Claire blinked. "A tutor? I was not informed they were seeking—"

"It is not your place to be informed," the butler, Mr. Fosters, cut in.

Claire immediately bowed her head and clasped her hands in front of her submissively. "My apologies. I overstepped." Her eyes slid shut, and she took a deep breath to dispel the disappointment. Ridgestone faded into the back of her mind once more.

Mrs. Morrison continued with the introduction. "Mr. Knightly, this is Miss Bannister, the governess."

Mr. Knightly bowed. "Miss Bannister, it is a pleasure to make your acquaintance."

Claire automatically curtseyed. "The feeling is mutual,

sir." As she straightened, she lifted her eyes to properly survey the new man. Likely not yet in his third decade, Mr. Knightly wore his brown hair long enough not to be following the current fashion. Scattered locks fell across his forehead, and the darkening of a beard softened an otherwise square-jawed face. He stood nearly a head taller than she did, and his loosely fitted jacket and modest cravat did nothing to conceal broad shoulders. Skimming her gaze down his body, she noticed a shirt starting to yellow with age and a plain brown waistcoat struggling to hide the fact that its owner was less than financially secure. Even his trousers were slightly too short, revealing too much of his worn leather boots. All in all, Mr. Jacob Knightly appeared to be the epitome of a young scholar reduced to becoming a tutor.

Except for his mouth. And his eyes. Not that Claire had much experience meeting with tutors, but even she could tell that the spectacles enhanced rather than detracted from the pale blueness of his eyes. The lenses seemed to emphasize their round shape, emphasize the appreciative gleam in them before Mr. Knightly had a chance to hide it. Even when he did, the corners of his full mouth remained turned up in a funny half-smile, all but oozing confidence and assurance—bordering on an arrogance one would not expect to find in a tutor.

Oh dear.

An Excerpt from

ASHES, ASHES, THEY ALL FALL DEAD

by Lena Diaz

Special Agent Tessa James is obsessed with finding the killer whose signature singsong line—"Ashes, ashes, they all fall dead"—feels all too familiar. When sexy, brilliant consultant Matt Buchanan is paired with Tessa to solve the mystery, they discover, inexplicably, that the clues point to Tessa herself. If she can't remember the forgotten years of her past, will she become the murderer's next target?

She raised a shaking hand to her brow and tried to focus on what he'd told her. "You've found a pattern where he kills a victim in a particular place but mails the letter for a different victim while he's there."

"That's what I'm telling you, yes. It's early yet, and we have a lot more to research—and other victims to find—but this is one hell of a coincidence, and I'm not much of a believer in coincidences. I think we're on to something."

Tears started in Tessa's eyes. She'd been convinced since last night that she'd most likely ruined her one chance to find the killer, and at the same time ruined her career. And suddenly everything had changed. In the span of a few minutes, Matt had given her back everything he'd taken from her when he'd destroyed the letter at the lab. Laughter bubbled up in her throat, and she knew she must be smiling like a fool, but she couldn't help it.

"You did it, Matt." Her voice came out as a choked whisper. She cleared her throat. "You did it. In little more than a day, you've done what we couldn't do in months, years. You've found the thread to unravel the killer's game. This is the breakthrough we've been looking for."

She didn't remember throwing herself at him, but suddenly she was in his arms, laughing and crying at the same time. She looped her arms around his neck and looked up into his wide-eyed gaze, then planted a kiss right on his lips.

She drew back and framed his face with her hands, giddy with happiness. "Thank you, Matt. Thank you, thank you, thank you. You've saved my career. And you've saved lives! Casey can't deny this is a real case anymore. He'll have to get involved, throw some resources at finding the killer. And we'll stop this bastard before he hurts anyone else. How does that feel? How does it feel to know you just saved someone?"

His arms tightened around her waist, and he pulled her against his chest. "It feels pretty damn good," he whispered. And then he kissed her.

Not the quick peck she'd just given him. A real kiss. A hot, wet, knock-every-rational- thought-out-of-her-mind kind of kiss. His mouth moved against hers in a sensual onslaught— nipping, tasting, teasing—before his tongue swept inside and consumed her with his heat.

Desire flooded through her, and she whimpered against him. She stroked his tongue with hers, and he groaned deep in his throat. He slid his hand down over the curve of her bottom and lifted her until she cradled his growing hardness against her belly. He held her so tightly she felt every beat of his heart against her breast. His breath was her breath, drawing her in, stoking the fire inside her into a growing inferno.

He gyrated his hips against hers in a sinful movement that spiked across her nerve endings, tightening her into an almost painful tangle of tension. Every movement of his hips, every slant of his lips, every thrust of his tongue stoked her higher and higher, coiling her nerves into one tight knot of desire, ready to explode.

Nothing had ever felt this good.

Nothing.

Ever.

The tiny voice inside her, the one she'd ruthlessly quashed as soon as his lips claimed hers, suddenly yelled a loud warning. *Stop this madness!*

Her eyes flew open. This was *Matt* making her feel this way, on the brink of a climax when all he'd done was kiss her. *Matt.* Good grief, what was she thinking? He swiveled his hips again, and she nearly died of pleasure.

No, no! This had to stop.

Convincing her traitorous body to respond to her mind's commands was the hardest thing she'd ever tried to do, because every cell, every nerve ending wanted to stay exactly where she was: pressed up against Matt's delicious, hard, warm body.

His twenty-four-year-old body to her thirty-year-old one.

This was insane, a recipe for disaster. She had to stop, now, before she pulled him down to the ground and demanded that he make love to her right this very minute.

She broke the kiss and shoved out of his arms.

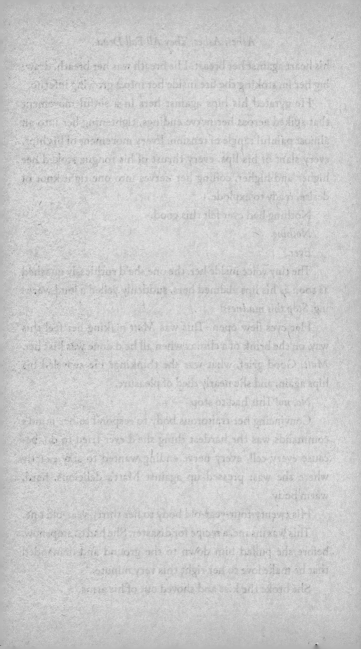

An Excerpt from

THE GOVERNESS CLUB: BONNIE

by Ellie Macdonald

The Governess Club series continues with
Miss Bonnie Hodges. She is desperately trying
to hold it together. Tragedy has struck, and she
is the sole person left to be strong for the two
little boys in her care. When the new guardian,
Sir Stephen Montgomery, arrives, she hopes that
things will get better. She wasn't expecting her new
employer to be the most frustrating, overbearing,
and . . . handsome man she's ever seen.

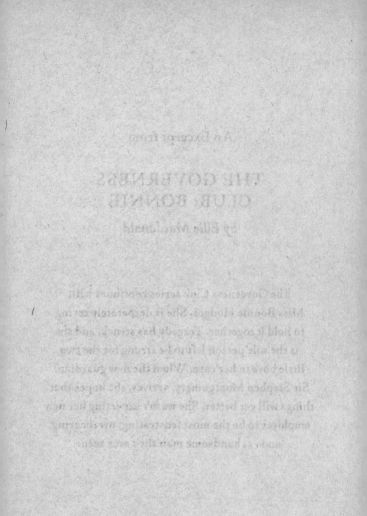

When he reached the water's edge, Stephen stopped. Staring at the wreckage that used to be the wooden bridge, he was acutely aware that he was looking at the site of his friends' death.

Images from the story Miss Hodges had told him flashed through his mind—the waving parents, the bridge shuddering before it collapsed, the falling planks and horses, the coach splintering, George's neck snapping, and Roslyn—God, Roslyn lying in that mangled coach, her blood pouring out of her body. How had she survived long enough for anyone to come and see her still breathing?

Nausea roiled in his stomach, and bile forced its way up his throat. Heaving, Stephen bent over a nearby bush and lost the contents of his stomach. Minutes later, he crouched down at the river's edge and splashed the cold water on his face.

From where he crouched, Stephen turned his gaze down

the river, away from the ruined bridge. He could make out an area ideal for swimming: a small stretch of sandy bank surrounded by a few large, flat rocks. Indeed, an excellent place for a governess to take her charges for a cooling swim on a hot summer day.

Stephen straightened and made his way along the bank to the swimming area. A well-worn path weaved through the bush, connecting the small beach to the hill beyond and Darrowgate. The bridge was seventy meters upstream; not only would the governess and the boys have had a good view of the collapse, the blood from the incident would have flowed right by them.

No wonder they barely spoke.

Tearing his gaze from the bridge, he focused on the water, trying to imagine the trio enjoying their swim, with no inkling or threat of danger. The boys in the water, laughing and splashing each other, showing off their swimming skills to their laughing governess.

Stephen looked at the closest flat rock, the thought of the laughing governess in his mind. She had said she preferred dangling her feet instead of swimming.

His mind's eye put Miss Hodges on the rock, much as she had been the previous night. The look on her face after seeing his own flour-covered face. Her smile had been so wide it had been difficult to see anything else about her. He knew her eyes and hair were certain colors, but he was damned if he could name them—the eyes were some light shade and the hair was brown, that he knew for certain.

And her laugh—it was the last thing he had expected from her. He was in a difficult situation—not quite master but regarded as such until Henry's majority. For a servant, even a governess, to laugh as she had was entirely unpredictable.

He shouldn't think too much about how that unexpected laughter had settled in his gut.

The image of Miss Hodges sitting on the rock rose again in his mind. The sun would have warmed the rock beneath her hands, and she would have looked down at the clear water. She would laugh at the boys' antics, he had no doubt, perhaps even kick water in their direction if they ventured too close. Her stockings would be folded into her shoes to keep them from blowing away in the breeze.

Good Lord, he could almost see it. The stockings protected in the nearby shoes, her naked feet dangling in the water, her skirts raised to keep them from getting wet, exposing her trim ankles. The clear water would do nothing to hide either her feet or her ankles, and Stephen found himself staring unabashedly at something that wasn't even there. He gazed at the empty water, imagining exactly what Miss Hodges's ankles would look like. They would be slim, they would be bonny, they would—

Thankfully, a passing cart made enough noise to break him out of this ridiculously schoolboy moment. Inhaling deeply through his nose, Stephen left the swimming area and made his way back for a closer look at the ruins.